Your favourite authors love to curl up with Cathy Bramley's feel-good fiction . . .

'Filled with warmth and laughter'
Carole Matthews

'Delightful!'
Katie Fforde

'A page turner of a story'
Milly Johnson

'Delightfully warm with plenty of twists and turns'
Trisha Ashley

'Warm, cosy and deliciously romantic'
Holly Martin

'A gorgeously romantic comfort read'
Rachael Lucas

'Magical, heart-felt and uplifting'
Carmel Harrington

'The perfect romantic tale'
Ali McNamara

'A wonderful warm hug of a book'
Alex Brown

'Merry, bright and sparkly'
People's Friend

Cathy Bramley is the *Sunday Times* Top Ten bestselling author of *A Patchwork Family*, *My Kind of Happy* and *The Lemon Tree Café*. Her other romantic comedies include *Ivy Lane*, *Appleby Farm*, *Wickham Hall*, *Conditional Love*, *The Plumberry School of Comfort Food* and *White Lies and Wishes*. She lives in a Nottinghamshire village with her family and a dog.

Cathy turned to writing after spending eighteen years running her own marketing agency. She has always been an avid reader, never without a book on the go, and now thinks she may have found her dream job!

Cathy loves to hear from her readers. You can get in touch via her website www.CathyBramley.co.uk, on Facebook @CathyBramleyAuthor or on Twitter @CathyBramley

Cathy Bramley

The Merry Christmas Project

ORION

An Orion paperback

First published in Great Britain in 2021 by Orion Fiction,
an imprint of The Orion Publishing Group Ltd,
Carmelite House, 50 Victoria Embankment,
London EC4Y 0DZ

An Hachette UK company

3 5 7 9 10 8 6 4

A CIP catalogue record for this book is
available from the British Library.

ISBN (Mass Market Paperback) 978 1 3987 0139 7
ISBN (eBook) 978 1 3987 0140 3

Typeset by Born Group
Printed and bound in Great Britain by Clays Ltd, Elcograf S.p.A.

MIX
Paper from
responsible sources
FSC® C104740
www.fsc.org

www.orionbooks.co.uk

For Milly Johnson
the best of women, the best of friends xx

Prologue

Merry

It was a glorious summer's day. Even high up in the Derbyshire Dales, the air was warm and sweet. The smell of ferns and flowers on the hillside and blackberries growing wild among the hedgerows was divine. Daniel and I were hiking for the first time, and I felt on top of the world.

With one last surge of effort, I reached the summit of Wysedale Peak only a second or two behind my much fitter boyfriend. Daniel was fit in all senses of the word. He was handsome, with pale blond hair, blue eyes and on his days off, like today, a smattering of golden stubble. He was lean and lithe too, thanks to his daily run. I admired his self-discipline. I tried to do a twenty-minute online workout in the mornings but invariably I ended up watching it instead, while getting dressed and hunting down a matching pair of trainers.

'Look at that view,' I said, as Daniel wrapped an arm around my waist. 'Aren't you glad I prised you out of bed this morning for an adventure?'

He grinned. 'I am. This is a great start to the Bank Holiday weekend. Who needs a lie-in anyway?'

'Not us, that's for sure.' I leaned against him, glad he had agreed to my spur-of-the-moment suggestion.

He had to get up at the crack of dawn every day in order to open Good Earth, his specialist greengrocer's. Today was a rare day off and he would have been completely within his rights to turn down my suggestion of setting off early for a picnic. But here he was.

We stood together, in a silence broken only by the occasional brush of wings from birds flying overhead. The scenery looked almost too beautiful to be real. The deep, deep blue of the wide sky, the lush green hills which seemed to stretch into infinity, intersected with ribbons of silver, streams heading downhill to join up with the wide river in the valley below.

Home. Me, Daniel, my new business . . . I sighed happily. Life didn't get much better than this.

It felt good to relax after such a hectic couple of weeks. A lot had happened, and my head was spinning with all the upheaval. Being here, out in the countryside, just him, me and miles and miles of green, was perfect.

'Quite a nice surprise, actually.' He took a swig from his water bottle and passed it to me. 'In the year we've been together, you've never once suggested going walking. I didn't have you down as a hiker.'

'Neither did I,' I said. The only time I'd ever done any hiking was during a very wet geography field trip in Wales, in kit borrowed from the school lost-property box. The boots had given me blisters after five minutes and my second-hand cagoule had a large rip in its hood, which I only discovered once the heavens had opened. It hadn't been an experience I'd wanted to repeat in a hurry.

I drank some water and handed the bottle back to Daniel. 'Some kids have outdoorsy families who do Sunday walks and camping holidays. I didn't have that sort of childhood, so I assumed it wasn't for me.'

Daniel smoothed the hair back from my face gently. 'I know it was hard for you, but don't let your childhood hold you back. You don't need permission, or to wait to be asked. There is nothing that is *not for you*. You're a gorgeous, intelligent woman in charge of her own life.'

He made comments like this from time to time. I knew he meant well, but he'd never really understand. My rocky childhood wasn't something I could just cast aside in adulthood; it was part of me. Daniel had shared a bedroom with his brother until he left home. I'd lost count of the number of rooms I'd had and who I'd shared with. And that was just one difference; there were a thousand others.

'I know,' I replied diplomatically. I took some sun cream out of my bag and dotted it onto my face. 'Besides, I had two options for today and I thought you'd prefer this one.'

'What was the other one?' He rubbed a blob of leftover sun cream into my cheek.

'A visit to an animal shelter. How would you feel about us getting a kitten?'

I scanned his face, hoping for a positive reception to the idea. I'd always wanted a pet and had never lived anywhere where animals were permitted until now.

'Oh, Merry.' Daniel's eyes shimmered with laughter. 'There's no way I'd trust you within five miles of an animal shelter.'

'Why not?' I asked, only half pretending to be insulted.

'Because you'd want to bring them all home. And instead of a kitten, you'd fall in love with a great big geriatric hound with halitosis and only three legs.'

'Possibly,' I admitted.

He had a point. Those adverts about dogs who'd been living in shelters for years because no one wanted to adopt them broke my heart. It was a bit too close to home for me. It crossed my mind to point out that he'd just said I didn't need permission to do stuff, but as it was his house, he had the final say.

'But just so you know,' I added, 'from that discussion, I'm taking away the fact that a kitten would be preferable to a dog.'

'I'm starving,' said Daniel, with a deft change of topic. 'Shall we sit down here and have our lunch?'

'Sure.' I dropped my rucksack to the ground and sat down. My legs were aching from all that climbing and I massaged my thighs and tilted my face to the sun while he unpacked the picnic.

'About getting a pet,' he said, taking out several plastic tubs, 'I'd rather not if you don't mind. I've just about got used to sharing my house with you, let alone anything else. I'm not a fan of mess, as you know.'

Was he implying that I was untidy, or that a dog would be messy? I wasn't exactly famed for my organisational skills. I glanced at him. 'If you've changed your mind—'

He cut off my protests by kissing the ticklish part of my neck below my ear. 'Not at all. You're a great housemate and you make the best . . .' he inspected a sandwich. 'Peanut butter and . . .?'

'Nutella,' I supplied with a gush of relief. Housemate wasn't the most romantic title I could think of, but at least I was great at it.

He laughed, shaking his head. 'You make the best peanut butter and Nutella sandwiches in the world.'

'Thank you.' I needed to hear that; it made me feel less like I was imposing on him.

4

He shared out the sandwiches, placing them neatly onto folded squares of kitchen paper and I poured us both tea from a flask.

Everything about Daniel was neat and tidy. I was grateful to him for making room in his house for me and I made a solemn vow to myself not to jeopardise the arrangement by leaving my stuff all over the place. Moving in together hadn't been one of those carefully planned scenarios where two grown-ups talk about taking their relationship to the next level. It had come about because a few weeks ago I'd left my job at Tractor World clutching a small redundancy payout and a vague plan to turn my hobby of candle-making into a business. I'd called it Merry and Bright and I had lots of ideas for it, but it would be a while before I made a profit.

'I'll throw all my energy into it,' I'd told Daniel. 'And if I can't make it pay in a year, I'll go back to having a nine-to-five job.'

'I love your determination,' he'd said, 'and I'm sure you'll be a great success, but in the meantime, why don't you move into my house to reduce your outgoings?'

That had been a month ago and now I was fully set up at Daniel's house and he had cleared out the garden shed for my candle-making. It was a risky move, setting up a business instead of looking for another job, but I wasn't scared of risks. My best friend Nell was in awe; she couldn't believe I'd decided to do something so major, so quickly. And in truth I'd have been in a bit of a pickle if Daniel hadn't been there to prop me up. But I had a feeling that starting Merry and Bright was exactly the move I needed.

'This is great,' said Daniel now, indicating the view and the picnic, 'but I'll have to do some work tonight when we get back. If I don't keep on top of it—'

'I know,' I supplied, 'you'll be playing catch-up all week.'

Along with keeping a tidy house, keeping on top of things was his perennial concern. Daniel had an ambitious streak and his plan was to open another store in the next town, and if that did well, another and another. My career ambitions were more modest: I didn't really have a plan other than making as many candles as I could and selling them, but I admired his forward-thinking.

I popped the last bit of crust into my mouth and jumped up to take a picture of the lovely vista below us with my phone. Unfortunately, my foot slipped on some loose stones and I twisted my ankle and fell backwards, landing with a thump on my bottom.

'OUCH. Shit. Ouch.' I bit my lip and tried not to cry.

'Merry Shaw, what am I going to do with you?' Daniel sprang to his feet to help me up.

'I didn't look,' I said, blowing out in short bursts, breathing away the pain like I'd seen in birth documentaries.

'Before you leapt?' he teased. 'Not like you.'

'If giving birth hurts more than this, I'm not sure I want to do it.'

'Give birth?' Daniel laughed nervously. 'What makes you say that? You're not . . . are you . . .?'

'No, of course not,' I said, wincing. 'It was just an observation.'

'That's all right then.' His shoulders relaxed. 'You had me going for a moment.'

The utter relief in his voice was unmistakable. But surely it wouldn't have been that much of a disaster? OK, it wasn't planned, but we were in a long-term relationship and in our thirties. We could easily accommodate a child into the life we were building for ourselves.

'So, for clarity,' I swallowed, fiddling with the turn-ups on my shorts, 'me being pregnant would be terrible news?'

6

'Seeing as you've just slipped on rocks up a mountain, twenty miles from the nearest hospital . . . if you were pregnant, I'd be worried about what was going on in there,' he said, pointing to my stomach.

My heart lifted. He was just being practical, as ever; of course he was.

I laughed softly. 'Phew, for a moment there I thought—'

'Although I have to be honest,' he said casually, 'it wouldn't be ideal, would it? You're trying to get a new business off the ground and I'm putting all my energy into the shop.'

'I guess not.' He was right, but I couldn't help feeling disappointed. 'I definitely need to focus on Merry and Bright.'

I sat back down gingerly, my ankle still aching, and Daniel joined me.

'Watch out, world,' he said, giving me a kiss. 'Merry is going to set you alight with her candles. Get it?'

'Very good.' I smiled weakly. It was on the tip of my tongue to say that from what I'd read and heard, there was never a right time to start a family and if we were to wait for a time when Daniel wasn't putting his energy into his greengrocer's, we both might have retired. Before I had chance to word it in a way that didn't provoke him, his phoned beeped loudly with a text message.

'I didn't think I'd get a signal this high up.' Daniel frowned as he whipped his phone out. 'It's from Tom.'

I pulled away from him while he read his younger brother's message and I picked up some crisps.

'Cheese and onion or beef?' I asked, holding out the choice to him. 'Or would you like some hummus and . . . Daniel?'

He was miles away, gazing out at the hills below us, the hand holding the phone still out in front of him. I felt a wave of fear.

'Daniel?' I said again. 'What's the matter? Everything OK?'

'Um, yeah.' He blinked a couple of times before briefly looking my way. He pressed the button on the side of his phone to lock the screen. 'Tom says they've recruited a new head teacher finally.'

The head teacher at Wetherley Primary School where Tom was the deputy had suddenly gone on long-term sick leave before the summer holidays and there'd been a scramble to recruit a replacement before the start of the new school year.

'Oh, good. Anyone we know?' I asked.

'Yes. Well, I do. You don't,' he laughed awkwardly and shoved the phone back in his pocket. 'It's a woman. Tasha Sandean.'

'How do you know her?' I said, crunching on a crisp.

He rubbed his fingers along his jaw. 'Friend from school, primary and secondary. She left Wetherley to go to university and never came back. Very bright girl. Top set for everything and brilliant at French because her parents were from Mauritius. They moved back there when they retired, I think. I haven't thought about her for years.'

He was certainly thinking of her now, I noticed, because he appeared to be blushing. Had she been a friend, or more than that?

'We can invite her round when she moves back; you can get to know her again,' I suggested, testing my theory. 'Reignite the old friendship.'

'Maybe.' He opened the beef crisps and chomped on a large handful. 'Funny story. When we were seventeen, we both got temporary Christmas jobs at a garden centre working in Santa's Grotto. I asked if I could kiss her under the mistletoe, but she dodged out of reach.'

8

'Aw, poor Daniel,' I teased, dotting his nose with my fingertip. 'Spurned and still sore about it.'

'It took a lot of courage, I'll have you know,' he said, grinning. 'It's not easy for boys; trying to work out whether girls like them or not.'

I raised my eyebrows. 'So you had a crush on her?'

He looked wistful for a moment.

'Everyone did.' He polished off the rest of his crisps and pinched one of mine. 'But we made a joke of it. She said if I wasn't married by the time I was forty, she'd kiss me then.'

'Like one of those marriage pacts to be each other's stand-by if you're still single by thirty or whatever; that's so funny!' I laughed, although something about the look in his eye niggled me. Then I remembered. 'Hey, you're forty this December.'

'I know.' He rummaged in the rucksack. 'Got any chocolate?'

'No, sorry,' I said vaguely, imagining him as a love-struck teenager mooning over a girl. 'Daniel?'

'Hmm?' he said, biting into an apple.

'If Tasha is going to be back in Wetherley this Christmas, maybe she'll want to kiss you under the mistletoe. If you're not married.'

I was only half teasing. I wasn't the jealous sort as a rule. But I didn't want some very bright girl, top set in everything, former crush of my boyfriend thinking she could just turn up with a sprig of mistletoe and expect him to pucker up for old times' sake.

He looked at me, amused. 'I'm sure she won't even remember it.'

'You remembered it,' I pointed out.

'*She* might be married,' said Daniel, laughing. 'Let's change the subject. It was just a silly story; I wouldn't have told you if I'd known you'd take it so seriously.'

'OK,' I said meekly.

But my mind wouldn't drop it, because an idea had just occurred to me. A spontaneous idea, the sort I specialised in. What if he *was* married by Christmas? To me. I couldn't imagine anything more romantic than a wedding in December. For as long as I could remember, all I'd wanted was for a proper family Christmas and if we were Mr and Mrs, well that would just be the icing on the Christmas cake.

If I proposed to him right now, it could actually happen. All it took was a question. Just one simple question. I felt the prickle of heat all over my body as the idea took shape and my insides began to tingle with adrenaline. Could I do it? This was the perfect setting, the perfect occasion and we loved each other. Admittedly it was a bit spur of the moment, but ever since we met, I'd been practising my married signature, just in case. And it would be so exciting and romantic!

You don't need to wait to be asked. Those had been Daniel's exact words just a few minutes ago. I hoped he meant it. Right. I blew out a sharp breath. I was going to do it.

'Daniel?' My pulse speeded up as I reached for his hand and dropped onto one knee.

'Yes, Merry.' He looked bemused. 'What are you up to now?'

'I love you with all my heart and I want to be with you for the rest of my life.' I swallowed, aware that my mouth was suddenly dry. 'So, will you marry me?'

The air around us was so still, the moment so heavy with tension that for a few seconds I forgot to breathe. I watched his eyes dart left and right as a succession of emotions crossed his face.

He gave a hollow laugh. 'It's not February twenty-ninth, is it?'

'No,' I said lightly, 'but you don't really believe that women only have one day in four years to propose and men get – whatever it is, do you?'

'One thousand two hundred and sixty-five,' Daniel supplied quietly. He was brilliant at mental arithmetic. 'And you're right. It isn't very fair.'

We held eye contact and I could read his thoughts as clearly as if they were tattooed across his forehead. The fact was that all those possible days had gone by when he could have asked me to marry him. But he hadn't.

The seconds ticked away and it was clear I'd said the wrong thing. As the size of my mistake grew bigger, my heartbeat grew faster. If I could have taken back my proposal I would have, but now it was out there like a big, embarrassed elephant flapping its ears in the breeze between us.

'Merry,' he murmured, reaching a hand to my cheek. 'I'm really flattered. Honoured to be asked.'

'Good, because I don't plan on ever doing it again; it's nerve-wracking,' I said shakily, ready to brush the whole fiasco under the carpet and rewrite it as a joke.

'Now you know how I felt under that mistletoe,' he said, attempting a joke of his own.

I gritted my teeth, wishing he hadn't brought her up again. 'Except you were a boy asking a girl for a sneaky kiss; I'm your girlfriend asking you to be my husband. It's not in the same league of commitment.'

'I suppose not,' he mumbled, looking down at his feet.

'So?' I attempted a casual smile. 'What do you say?'

'Look, Merry, I do really love you, but . . .' He drew in a breath and rubbed his hand through his hair distractedly.

'I'm sorry, I just don't want to be tied down at the moment. Not through marriage, or babies or even a kitten. In fact, now that you've brought it up, I'm fairly sure I never will. I really am sorry.'

'Oh.' My eyes burned with mortification. This was . . . earth shattering. Why had we never talked about this before? He didn't want anything that I wanted. Nothing. 'I had no idea that was how you felt.'

He looked uncomfortable. 'I suppose it's never come up.'

I looked at the stony ground through eyes blurry with tears. 'But I've mentioned kids before, I'm sure I have.' Although, now that I thought about it, he'd always changed the subject.

He reached for me, but I moved back quickly.

'What's wrong with me?' I said this out loud but it was as much to myself as to him. Regret started to seep into my bones. We'd been having such a nice day; trust me to do something impulsive and ruin it.

'Nothing. Nothing at all!' he insisted. 'You're amazing. This is all on me.'

I shook my head; there was no way I could accept that. A familiar feeling of rejection gnawed away inside me; I'd thought Daniel was the one I would be building a future with, putting down roots, making a home, a family . . .

I stood up, not sure what to do with myself. He got up too and took hold of my shoulders. 'I do love you though; you do believe me, don't you?'

I nodded, aware of the tickling sensation of fresh tears on my cheeks. I'd never doubted that he loved me. I thought we were meant for each other, that we wanted the same things. Until today.

'Good.' He kissed my forehead. 'This doesn't have to change anything.'

'Sure,' I murmured, swallowing down the lump in my throat.

But of course it did. Inevitably it changed everything.

Chapter 1

Merry

As I'd predicted, everything changed: from that moment on the hillside, our relationship had been a ticking time-bomb. Although my proposal had been on the spur of the moment, as soon as the idea popped into my head, I knew that what I craved was the *certainty* of us. I'd needed to believe that I'd found someone who wanted the same as me, who above all else wanted *me*. Despite Daniel's attempts to carry on as before, it was obvious to me that we couldn't, that at some point, we would have to go our separate ways to have the lives we wanted. As my hopes for the future fizzled out, so did our relationship and by the end of September, we were little more than housemates.

True to form, I hadn't planned the break-up; it just sort of came out all in a rush. One minute he was making a barbed observation about the number of cardboard boxes blocking the hall (I'd left it too late to take them to the post office) and the next, I was telling him of my decision to move out. I'd held my breath; this was his moment to say he'd had a change of heart and that he'd do anything not to lose me. But he hadn't tried to persuade me to stay.

It only took me two weeks to find somewhere else to live, which was why today, Nell's van was fully loaded with my belongings, and we were turning into World's End Lane, a long leafy road on the outskirts of Wetherley.

'The thing is,' I said, indicating to Nell that she should continue straight on, 'that if you're madly in love with someone and they propose, the only acceptable response is a big joyful *YES*. I don't want someone who loves me just enough to tolerate living with me. Although to be honest, I think he was having second thoughts about even that level of commitment. I want someone who can't imagine a future without me in it. And if I said please can we adopt this three-legged dog with halitosis, he wouldn't even think twice.'

'You've lost me.' Nell glanced sideways at me, frowning.

'Yes. I've lost Daniel too,' I said with a sigh, not bothering to relate the animal shelter conversation. 'Part of me worries that I might have thrown away the best relationship I'll ever have. But there's a little part deep inside me that says I've made the right decision and that's the bit I'm listening to.'

'Gut instinct is rarely wrong,' Nell pronounced, slowing down to peer at the cottages as we passed by. 'I listened to mine and ended up married to Olek.'

Her husband was a gentle giant who had moved to Derbyshire from Poland as a teenager with his parents. They'd been married for four years and as far as I could tell were still in the honeymoon period.

'I still love Daniel. But I want an Olek of my own. We're almost there.' I pointed to the very last house on the lane. 'You can go straight up onto the drive.'

Nell whistled as she pulled up in front of the very last house. 'This one?'

I nodded in confirmation.

'It's gorgeous, Merry!' she gasped. 'I love it!'

I smiled at my best friend, grateful to have her bound-less enthusiasm to propel me into this new chapter in my life, then I looked up at my new home: a small stone cottage with an ivy-covered porch and a wonky chimney, surrounded on three sides by trees.

'Me too,' I said, bravely.

I brushed away the thoughts of the life I'd left behind and forced a smile. Today was all about new starts; I was trying not to dwell on what might have been.

As if reading my mind, Nell reached for my hand and squeezed it. 'You're going to be happy here, I can feel it.'

'Come on,' I said, dismissing the prickle of tears in my eyes and pulling open the door of the van. 'Let me intro-duce you to Holly Cottage.'

We let ourselves in and I gave her the tour of my new abode. Nell didn't let me down, oohing and ahhing in all the right places. She admired the exposed oak beams, and the original flagstones in the hall, smooth in places where countless pairs of feet had worn grooves in them. Together we explored every nook and cranny, from the soot-stained stone fireplace in the sitting room, which promised cosy nights in front of the wood stove, to the deep window seat perfect for curling up on with a book. Upstairs the main bedroom under the eaves was pretty, with rose-sprigged curtains and a wooden dressing table, which we decided I could use for taking photographs of my candles. According to the lettings agent, the cottage was more than five hundred years old, hence there not being a single straight wall in the place. The house was on a slope too, so there were steps from the hall into the kitchen. I led Nell down them and she cast her eye over the pine dresser and the old-fashioned sink and dated kitchen cupboards.

'I know it's not exactly modern,' I said. 'But I like it all the more for its charm.'

'Absolutely,' Nell agreed. 'It's brimming with quirkiness and character. Suits you down to the ground. It'll be even better once we get your stuff in here.' She jingled her keys and together we went back out to the van to get started.

Half an hour later, all we had left to unload was the double bed. Holly Cottage was furnished, like all my previous rental homes had been, but I did have my own bed which I'd been storing in Daniel's spare room. We were still dissecting my break-up.

'He's been really good to me,' I told her, as we manoeuvred the mattress over the doorstep and up the stairs. 'Wouldn't accept any money for bills or anything so I'd have enough to see me through.'

'It's the least he could do,' Nell said, pushing the mattress up as I pulled from above, 'after the way he's behaved.'

'At least I found out before I'd got too comfortable living with him,' I said, panting with effort.

With a final tug, I managed to pull the mattress onto the tiny landing and rested it against the bannister.

She wiped a hand across her brow. 'Found out what, that he's an arsehole?'

I laughed despite myself. 'No, that a wife, kids, the whole shebang is not for him.'

'He doesn't have the brains he was born with. I mean who in their right mind would not want to marry you?'

'Exactly,' I said staunchly. 'He'll probably never get a better offer.'

'Unless,' she added with a glint in her eye, 'do you think deep down he might be gay, and he hasn't come to terms with it?'

'Nell! No!' I gasped, laughing despite myself. Between us we lifted the mattress onto the bed base and both collapsed onto it with relief. 'He might be scared of commitment, but he is definitely not gay.'

His brother Tom, who *was* gay, had come round for supper at the beginning of term, with his partner Chris, full of admiration for the new head teacher, Miss Sandean. What a breath of fresh air she was, and how popular she was with the parents and children etcetera, and Daniel had hung on his every word. It had been quite annoying, actually.

'Well, I wouldn't have let you go that easily, if I was him.'

'Ah, bless you,' I said. 'For that, I'll make you some coffee.'

'Finally,' Nell groaned, stretching her arms above her head. 'I'll just lie here while you find the kettle.'

'No, you don't,' I said, pulling her to her feet.

I tasked her with the easy job of hanging my clothes in the wardrobe and headed downstairs in search of refreshments. I found the box which Daniel had labelled 'kettle etc.' and unpacked it.

As much as he assured me that he was sad to see me go, I couldn't help noticing how much he had enjoyed clearing the surfaces of all my framed photographs, plants and the vast collection of scented candles I'd had all over the house. He had offered to help me today, but I'd declined. Instead, Nell had come round once Daniel had left for work and we'd done it between us. It was less awkward this way and I knew Nell would like to be involved.

I filled the kettle and switched it on to boil while gazing through the large window to an overgrown cottage garden and beyond that a thicket of trees.

So, this was it, I was officially single and living on my own again. Money was going to be tight for a while, but thankfully orders were coming in from my new website and Nell had started selling my candles on her market stall too. As long as I was careful, I should just about manage. The rent here was low, due to the fact it was only a short-term lease. Apparently this had put other potential tenants off, but it didn't bother me. Six months in Holly Cottage was a far happier prospect than committing to a lengthy stay somewhere I didn't like as much. And I'd have my own space to spread out and make as much mess as I wanted without Daniel tidying up after me.

'Coffee's ready!' I yelled up the stairs to Nell.

While I waited for her to come down, I found a packet of biscuits, then I pushed open the door into the garden and took our refreshments outside into the bright October sunshine.

The garden was a wilderness, but the autumn colours were glorious. The long grass was scattered with leaves in every shade of orange, red and brown. Rampant honeysuckle covered the old shed at the bottom of the garden and delicate cyclamen flowers bloomed in terracotta pots beside a wooden bench. The garden was surrounded by woodland which shielded it from the new housing development that I knew was beyond the trees. It probably wouldn't be long before the cottage had pristine new neighbours with en-suites and utility rooms and integral garages; I was lucky to have been able to rent it and enjoy the natural setting while it lasted. There were no neighbours at this end of the lane and all I could hear was the trickle of the stream which ran through the woods, the rustle of wind in the leaves and in the distance, a woodpecker hammering industriously at a tree. These sounds hadn't changed for hundreds of years, I thought, closing my eyes.

'Ooh, caffeine, come to Mama.' Nell's voice brought me back to the twenty-first century and I turned to see her step into the garden, following the scent of the coffee.

We headed to the bottom of the garden and sat down on the old bench.

'Thanks for helping today,' I said, handing her a mug. 'It would have taken ages without you.'

'What are best friends for?' she replied, nudging me affectionately. 'Besides, I couldn't wait to have a nose around.'

Nell and I had bonded on our first day at college aged sixteen and we had been each other's cheerleaders ever since. I'd been sitting at a table in the cafeteria on my own and, having eaten my homemade sandwich, I was slicing a banana when Nell, without asking, plonked her tray next to me and sat down.

I remember being totally in thrall; her wavy copper hair and freckles, her confidence that I'd want her to sit with me.

'Oh wow. Look at the way you've arranged that banana – so pretty.'

'Thanks.' I'd looked down at my sad banana pennies, spread along the inside of the banana peel to save using a plate.

'My mother would love you.' Nell squirted ketchup all over her chips and managed to get it down her T-shirt. 'Oh rats. You're a neat eater. Not like me.'

I laughed; I'd never met anyone who used *rats* as a swear word before. It was obvious that she was posh and rich. 'I'm not neat, I'm always getting in trouble for making a mess.'

She just smiled and pushed her tray towards me and offered me some of her pizza. 'Please help me out with some of this, or I'll be late back to the next class.'

'OK,' I'd said after a nanosecond of deliberation, 'but only if you share my banana.'

'Deal.'

After that we ate together every day. I brought something from home, and she bought enough food from the cafeteria for us to share. It was the best meal and the highlight of my day. The friendship wasn't all one way; I was a far better student than she was and regularly helped her out with her work. And I encouraged her to eat more healthily, which eventually led to her getting interested in nutrition. Our backgrounds couldn't have been more different: she was posh and privileged and had parents who smothered her and I . . . well, I didn't. But Nell didn't care, she loved me for me, and I loved her right back.

These days, she was still posh, but quite a bit poorer after marrying Olek, whom her parents disapproved of: Olek was a locksmith, divorced, with a thirteen-year-old son, Max, and he was ten years older than Nell. She'd compounded their disapproval by opening Nell's Nuts, a stall in Wetherley market selling dried fruit, nuts and seeds. It was a far cry from the life of luxury they'd envisaged for her, but Nell was much too in love to care what they thought.

Now, as Nell finished her coffee, I caught her taking in the state of the garden: the overgrown hedge and the swathe of thistles and brambles tangled into the border. 'I know it's a bit of a mess,' I said, 'but it's mine and that's what counts.'

'You're incredible.' Nell shook her head slowly. 'Being made redundant, setting up Merry and Bright, ending a relationship that wasn't working for you and then moving house. I'm proud of you.'

'Thank you. Although,' I gave her a secret smile, 'full disclosure: I wasn't made redundant. I volunteered for it.'

'What?' Nell's eyes widened. 'Why would you do that?'

'Because if I hadn't then one of my colleagues, Trisha, might have been selected and I couldn't let that happen to the poor woman.'

Tractor World had announced that redundancies were imminent, and Trisha was convinced she'd be chosen on the basis that she hadn't been there very long. She was supporting her husband who was ill and was saving for her daughter's wedding. I'd found her crying in the corridor and had taken a snap decision to volunteer in order to keep her job safe.

'You loon,' Nell laughed. 'You're too soft.'

I shrugged. 'Things happen for a reason. I never really had a passion for working there. Besides, it seemed like the perfect opportunity to try and turn making candles into a business. Because that is something I *do* have a passion for.'

'Just like that?' Nell marvelled. 'Amazing. It took me about four years to pluck up the courage to set up Nell's Nuts.'

Unlike me, Nell was the world's slowest decision-maker. Not bad, just slow.

The only time she had made a split-second decision was when her father told her he wouldn't support her marriage to Olek because he wasn't what he had had in mind for his only daughter. He forced her to choose between her boyfriend and her family. Good-natured Olek with his broad shoulders, shock of blond hair and total devotion to Nell won the day and planning began for the wedding the very next morning.

Relations had thawed a little since, largely because Olek, a family man, had encouraged Nell to keep trying with her snooty parents. Apparently her dad regularly boasted to his chums at the golf club that his daughter was a trader, which was true, except that she dealt in currants instead of currency.

'It was a risky move,' I admitted. 'Luckily it worked out. Unlike my marriage proposal. That was one risk too many. Daniel's right; I don't look before I leap.'

'You're spontaneous!' Nell protested. 'That's what makes being your friend such an adventure.'

'In that case . . .' I stood up. 'Shall we spontaneously go and tackle some of the boxes in my kitchen?'

She swiped the last biscuit and got to her feet with a groan. 'Yes, m'lady. After I've visited the smallest room.'

I showed Nell into the bathroom, which led off the kitchen.

'Won't it bother you,' she asked, 'having to go downstairs for a wee in the night?'

'Probably,' I admitted, shuddering at the thought of my bare feet on the cold flagstones. 'There you go, you see. I make rash decisions without considering the consequences.'

I got started on the boxes in the kitchen while she was in the bathroom. I filled the drawers in the dresser with cutlery and stacked crockery on shelves.

'But you keep keeping on,' Nell continued, drying her hands on her jeans. 'You pick yourself up and move on to the next challenge.'

I directed her towards the box of saucepans which needed unpacking and she got stuck in.

'But I don't want to keep moving,' I said glumly. 'When Daniel turned me down, he said it wasn't me, it was him. But what if it *is* me? I might keep keeping on, but I'm getting closer to forty and no closer to settling down.'

She eyed the row of mugs I'd already arranged on the dresser. 'You look pretty settled to me.'

'You know what I mean. No, I've been thinking that it's time for a fresh approach.' I leaned back against the

23

counter. 'Being spontaneous and taking risks is all well and good, but it isn't getting me to where I want to be. I don't want to go through the pain of another break-up like I've just had. If I want stability in my life, I'm going to have to be organised. No more rash moves. Make a plan and stick to it, that's my new motto. Look, I've even got myself a diary.'

I picked up the desk diary I'd bought at a knockdown price because we were already so far through the year and waved it at her. So far it only had one entry in it: *move into Holly Cottage*.

'This new motto.' She narrowed her eyes. 'This isn't about trying to get Daniel back?'

'No,' I said. 'But let's face it, being spur of the moment hasn't worked so far, has it?'

'Hmm. If you say so.' Nell didn't look convinced. 'Here, let me put a date entry in your diary.'

I perked up and handed it to her. 'Girls' night out?'

'Sort of.' She turned the pages forward ten days. 'It's the Christmas Project meeting to discuss what we are going to do to pay tribute to Benny Dunford.'

I hadn't known Benny well, but he had been Wetherley's most community-spirited citizen and his death in the summer had saddened everyone. He had been one of those people that brought others together, and it was lovely that he was being remembered. I'd helped out with community events in the past, but I didn't want to get involved with organising this one.

'Actually Nell, I wasn't planning on going,' I said. 'You know Christmas is always an odd time for me and this one . . . well, I'd really been looking forward to spending this one with Daniel. Like a proper family. So I was sort of hoping to forget all about Christmas this year.'

She pressed her lips into a line and folded her arms. 'You do know that *proper* families quite often eat and drink too much and end up falling out.'

'Well, even so, I don't fancy sitting through a long boring meeting while someone ticks items off a never-ending agenda, so I think I'll give it a miss.'

Nell smirked. 'Daniel said you'd say no.'

I stared at her. 'When did he say that?'

'He popped over to the stall to buy some cashews. He's joined the committee. So has the school's new head teacher.'

I straightened up instantly. 'Tasha Sandean?'

Nell nodded. 'Apparently she's really shaking things up at the school. She sounds like someone we ought to meet.'

'Actually, Daniel knows her.' I told Nell about Tasha and the promise to kiss him under the mistletoe if he was still single at forty.

'Wow.' Nell's eyes widened. 'That's it then. I'm definitely going and so must you. Aren't you curious to see what she looks like?'

'Not really,' I said airily. 'But I suppose now that I run a local business, I should get more involved – it might help me develop some new contacts.'

Nell tried to hide her smirk. 'Absolutely nothing to do with Daniel or Tasha going along and you being nosy as heck.'

'Nothing at all. I've always liked a project.' I handed her a cardboard box full of kitchen utensils. 'Now, are you going to help me unpack these wooden spoons, or have you done enough stirring for one day?'

Chapter 2

Cole

Behind the wheel of his van, Cole's body was wound like a spring, his arms tense, jaw taut. Seven minutes until the video call would come through. Seven minutes to get home and be in front of his iPad to take it. This call was too important to risk the dodgy signal in the Portakabin on the Wetherley building site. It would be a lovely place to live eventually, surrounded by trees, but right now it was an internet black spot.

He'd arranged his whole afternoon around this, told Josh, his site foreman, that whatever happened, he'd be leaving at three today. He'd set off in plenty of time, or so he'd thought, but his half-hour journey had been fraught with diversions and hold-ups and now he was cutting it dangerously fine. The fear he'd mess this up was real and he was beginning to sweat.

'Change, change, change,' he chanted under his breath as he approached yet another set of traffic lights. But they remained resolutely on red, forcing him to brake.

As soon as the way was clear, Cole put his foot on the accelerator and picked up his speed. A quick glance at the clock told him he could still make it. Within a couple of minutes he'd turned into Rectory Lane. Slowing down to navigate the speed bumps made him grit his teeth, but it had to be done; families lived in the luxury detached houses either side of him and the traffic calming was there for a reason. Finally, he pulled into the driveway of number sixteen, turned off the engine and yanked on the handbrake.

The next second he was out of the van and racing up the metal staircase which led to the self-contained annexe above the garage. His phone flashed with a new text message from Lydia. He didn't have to open the message from his ex-wife to know what it said. *Don't forget. Be there when Harley calls. He's dying to talk to you.* He couldn't blame her for checking up on him; he had form for letting them down in the past. But he'd learned his lesson the hard way and now he was trying to do better, and he hadn't forgotten – how could he? Today's date would be imprinted on his memory for ever. It was the day he'd become a father.

He fumbled with his door key, pushed his way inside, just as the iPad on the coffee table began to ring. He launched himself onto the sofa and touched the screen to accept the WhatsApp video call and his two most precious things appeared in front of him.

'Hello, Dad!' they yelled in unison.

Cole grinned, his breath ragged after rushing. 'Hey, good morning, you two, and Harley, happy birthday, son.'

'Thanks, Dad.'

Cole tried to ignore the prickling sensation in his eyes. His beautiful boy, twelve today and growing up fast. Squashed beside him was eight-year-old Freya, his darling girl. And currently four and a half thousand miles away from him.

He remembered the night he'd dropped the kids back off at Lydia's and she'd explained how she'd been headhunted out of the blue for her dream job and he'd nodded along, pleased for her, all the time wondering what the catch was, the reason why her body language was taut and jumpy, her eyes looking everywhere but at him. And then out it came: the job was in Whistler, the ski resort in Canada, a year-long contract overseeing the seasonnaires, the temporary staff recruited each winter to work in the hotels.

She'd listed all the reasons why it was a good move, not just for her, but for the kids too. She'd said her living expenses would be covered, there were excellent schools for the kids and a family ski pass giving them access to world-class slopes for an entire season. She'd acknowledged that it was a lot to ask and a lot to take in, and that she'd turn it down if he was really opposed to it, but that she'd truly felt that Harley and Freya would love the experience. He'd listened earnestly, promised to think it over properly and asked if she'd let him sleep on it. Then he went home and cried like his heart would break.

He looked at them via the screen now. They both had his colouring: dark red hair and brown eyes. Freya had Lydia's fine glossy waves, but Harley's was thick and straight like all the Robinson men. Cole swallowed the lump in his throat; seeing their faces was the highlight of his day, but not being able to hold his children was torture.

When they first left, he couldn't imagine ever being able to sleep soundly again, knowing they were on the other side of the world, out of reach, out of touch and that if anything bad happened, it would take him a day to get to them. Two months on, he was learning to live with it, but he'd never fully relaxed since then.

'Have you had anything special for breakfast?' he asked, loading his voice with enthusiasm.

Harley nodded. 'Pancakes with maple syrup and bacon.'

'I had jam on mine.'

Cole grabbed his stomach and groaned. 'So jealous, you lucky things. I want some too.'

His kids laughed and he laughed along with them, his heart bursting with love.

Cole always put a positive spin on their separation, telling them how amazing it all sounded, how lucky they were to be living where they were. But on some days maintaining the façade was agony. Scheduled video calls were great, but he missed pretending to tackle Harley as an excuse to hug him, he missed driving him to football practice which was when Harley would confide in him about what was going on in his life. He missed Freya running into his arms so he could swoop her up, hold her tight and smell her strawberry shampoo, he missed playing teddy bears' picnic with her and though he never thought he'd say it, he even missed being forced to watch *Moana* on Saturdays.

'Can I open my presents now?' Harley held up the big airmail box of presents that Cole had sent weeks in advance to make sure they arrived on time.

'Of course.' Cole grinned as Freya had to sit on her hands to stop herself from 'helping' while Harley ripped into the box.

'Harley,' Freya wheedled, 'please may I open one?'

Her brother ruffled her hair and sighed. 'I suppose so.'

'There's one with your name on, sweetheart,' Cole told her. 'The wrapping paper has rainbows on it. Happy unbirthday.'

Harley held it out to her, and she gasped with joy.

Five minutes later the box had been emptied and Harley's bed was covered in discarded wrapping paper.

'Thanks for the headphones and the trainers, Dad,' said Harley, already fitting the buds in his ears. 'And I'll call Granddad and Auntie Hester later to thank them.'

'Good lad.' Cole was proud of his eldest; he was a good kid, smart and sociable, and according to Lydia, he was thriving in the outdoor life of the Canadian ski resort. He had a sudden flashback to the day Harley was born. He'd held his firstborn in his arms and made him a promise: *I'll always be there for you, always.* Yet somehow, his boy was growing up on the other side of the world. If ever Cole had needed a reminder that he'd failed at fatherhood, this was it.

Freya held up her new bear to the screen. 'I'm calling her Daisy. Kiss her, Daddy.'

Cole blew a kiss to the screen. 'Hi Daisy, pleased to meet you.'

The significance of the name wasn't lost on him. Daisy was the name of the best friend Freya had left behind when Lydia relocated to Canada, taking his kids with her. Two months was a long time in a child's life to be away from a good friend. Maybe this was Freya's way of telling him that she did miss home after all.

'Say goodbye to Dad now, kids,' he heard Lydia say in the background, 'the school bus will be here soon.'

Cole felt his stomach sink; in a few seconds they'd be gone again. 'Have a great birthday, Harley, send me some photos later so I can see what you get up to. Bye bye, Freya, have a good day. I love you both.'

After the children had said their goodbyes, Cole got off the sofa, fetched a can of Coke from the fridge and took a long cool drink before heading to the shower, to wash off the grime which came with the territory of building houses for a living.

They were great kids, he thought, stripping off and shoving his clothes in the laundry basket, Freya asking politely to open a present and Harley kindly saying yes.

Even though he missed them like crazy, he had to admit that Lydia was doing a great job with them.

As the steam from the hot water engulfed him, he cast his mind back to the last time he'd seen them in the flesh, the day they'd left the country. Lydia had said they could get a taxi to Manchester Airport for their Vancouver flight, but Cole had wanted to eke out every last second with them, soaking them up, storing up their quirks and habits and mannerisms to tide him over until he saw them again. So he'd driven them there and helped Lydia check in their vast pile of luggage. As they'd made their way across the concourse towards the departures lounge, he and Lydia following closely behind the kids, he'd looked at the airline tags fastened to his children's backpacks and had felt the knot of dread in his stomach grow bigger and bigger. He'd known for weeks that his kids would be leaving him that day, but part of him had been in denial. There was no getting away from it now though.

He'd willed himself to keep it together as he said goodbye to them. Freya had had to be peeled off him and even Harley had let his guard down for a moment and permitted his dad to kiss him. And then it was Lydia's turn.

'Thanks,' Lydia had said, kissing his cheek lightly.

He shrugged. 'No worries, I was glad to give you a lift.'

'I mean for letting us go,' she clarified. 'For letting me take this job. For making it easy for me. Lots of ex-husbands would have kicked up a fuss. So thanks.'

'Just promise me they'll keep in touch,' he said gruffly. 'I'm going to miss them.'

'I promise.' Lydia scrabbled in her bag. 'Here's my work email. Just in case.'

She handed him a business card. His eyes fell on her name: Lydia Broom, Head of Recruitment, Premier Ski

Resorts, Whistler. She'd reverted to her maiden name, he realised with a stab of sadness.

'I thought it was time,' she said, a slight flush to her cheeks. 'A new job, new start.'

He tapped the card on his fingertips. 'Just a year, right?'

'The contract is just for a year, yes. And then we'll come home.'

He nodded, hoping that his kids had a great time but not so great that they never wanted to come back to England. 'I'm proud of you,' he'd said, kissing her cheek. 'You deserve this.'

Lydia had worked in human resources for a hotel chain before having Harley. She'd gone back part-time afterwards, until Freya had come along. But juggling childcare and a demanding job alongside Cole's long working hours had proved unsustainable and Lydia had put her own aspirations on hold. Since their divorce, she'd been looking to resume her career and he had, of course, supported her fully. What he couldn't have predicted was that her job would take his kids so far away from him.

'Thank you,' she said, her eyes sparkling with tears. 'You're a good man.'

She'd put her arms around their children and they walked away from him and through to departures. He'd watched until they'd disappeared from view, and then with a heavy heart had set off back to the car park.

A good man, Lydia had said – but not good enough to be her husband anymore, Cole thought.

Ten minutes later, he'd pulled on a T-shirt and joggers and was rubbing his hair dry with a towel. There was a rhythmic thud coming from downstairs, which meant that his brother-in-law Paul was putting a client through their paces. Paul had been an accountant when he had first met Hester, Cole's sister, but recently retrained as a personal trainer and motivational coach and now ran Smart Fitness Solutions from the double garage which he'd converted into a gym. The room above had been kitted out as a self-contained studio apartment at the same time. It was open plan with a double bed at one end, a sofa facing the TV in the middle and a kitchen sink plus a couple of cupboards and a fridge near the door. Cole had a kettle, microwave and coffee machine and for any serious cooking he went over to the main house.

The annexe was small for his bulky six-foot frame, but with the Wetherley building site, plus the high street renovation project he'd taken on, he didn't usually spend much time here.

After Lydia and the children had gone to Canada, Hester and Paul had suggested he move in with them. Up until then he'd been renting a three-bedroomed house near Lydia so he could have the children over to stay, but the rent had been high and he was paying for rooms he no longer needed. Living with his sister and brother-in-law was the perfect compromise: affordable living accommodation at a time when all his capital was tied up, and company when he needed it.

It was only a temporary arrangement; by the time the kids came back to the UK he planned to be settled in a decent house. So far it was working out well. He looked out of the window down at the drive; his sister's little two-seater Mercedes had appeared, indicating she was back from work. He thought about going over for a chat, to tell her that Harley had liked his present but then remembered all the work he'd brought home with him. For the next couple of hours, he decided, he'd catch up with some paperwork.

Cole pressed send on his final email and glanced at the time: five o'clock. The last hour or so had flown by. Admin was a necessary evil; he much preferred working on-site, being hands-on, but this build was the biggest he'd ever taken on and the only way to keep the project on schedule was to ensure Josh, as site foreman, had the manpower and the materials he needed when he needed them. He stretched his arms over his head to unlock the tightness in his shoulders and looked out of the front window. The light had faded from the day and the sky had turned dusky grey. His stomach rumbled but it was too early to start cooking dinner; Paul didn't usually finish with his last client until eight and the three of them had fallen into a habit of eating together. Since living on his own he'd discovered that he quite liked cooking, which was just as well, because despite having a kitchen that resembled the flight desk of a spaceship, Hester didn't enjoy cooking and Paul would happily exist on protein smoothies. To keep the hunger pangs at bay, he checked the cupboards for snacks and found some crisps and the end of a loaf.

The two things together made him think of Freya and crisp sandwiches; that was what she liked to 'cook' when she was at his house. The thought made him want to ring her up and ask her whether she'd managed to find her favourite prawn cocktail flavour in Canada, but she'd be at school now.

He'd just shoved some crisps in his mouth when he heard the sound of footsteps running up the stairs. There was a light tap on the door before Hester let herself in.

In jeans and a shirt tied at the midriff she looked much younger than her thirty-two years. She still had freckles across her cheeks, a tiny gap between her two front teeth and the haphazard strawberry blonde hair, now piled up messily on her head, that she'd had as a little girl. In those days his little sister had been the bane of his life, gatecrashing his room when he had friends over and following him everywhere like his shadow. Now he couldn't imagine life without her.

'How's my favourite lodger?' she asked, giving him a hug. 'Have you spoken to Harley? Ooh, give me a crisp.'

'Help yourself,' Cole said dryly, after she had already taken a handful. He buttered some bread and she helped herself to a slice of that too. 'I spoke to both kids before they went off to school. Harley seemed to be enjoying his first birthday away from his friends and family. He says thanks for the hoodie, by the way.'

He scattered the last few crisps onto the bread, squashed another slice on top of it and bit into his sandwich without bothering to cut it up.

'And how are you feeling?' Hester asked.

He held her gaze and sighed.

She took a seat on the sofa and patted the cushion next to her. 'Hey. Talk to me.'

Cole lowered himself beside her and set his plate on the table in front of them. Most of the time he was fine: positive, optimistic and determined to make the best of his life. But just occasionally the full force of his situation caught up with him. It was just so far from where he'd thought he be.

'Hey,' she nudged him. 'Talk to me.'

He let out a sigh. 'I had it all: the car, the house, a beautiful wife, two gorgeous kids. Now I'm divorced, living above my sister's garage and I have to wish my son happy birthday through a screen. What an idiot.'

'You haven't lost your kids,' she protested. 'OK, you're not married anymore, and I know you loved Lydia, but come on, don't catastrophise, you'll survive.'

'Sorry, you're right.' He gave her a lopsided grin.

He loved this woman, she was irrepressible. She'd struggled with school and had left without many qualifications, but she'd been determined to work in television. After applying unsuccessfully dozens of times, she'd offered her services free of charge, which had eventually paid off. She started as a researcher and now presented her own show on a shopping channel.

'No, I'm sorry,' she said, looking humble. 'I told you to talk and then shut you down.'

'That's OK,' he nudged her arm. 'I don't bother talking about it much because it's such a cliché: I put my business first. I thought working hard to provide for the family was what I was supposed to do. But I neglected them, I see that now.'

'I'm a workaholic too,' Hester admitted. 'I wonder how much of that is how we were brought up. Dad thought any time not spent working was a waste.'

'Mum wasn't much better,' Cole reminisced fondly. 'If she wasn't at work, she was at the allotment, and I can't ever remember her sitting down without her hands being busy: knitting, darning, shelling peas. Dear old Mum.'

'I miss her too.' Hester gave him a sad smile.

She'd had a series of strokes just after their dad had retired, ending with a fatal one at the beginning of the previous year. Their father had since sold the family home and moved into a retirement complex in Wetherley.

'But I am to blame,' he insisted. 'I didn't see the signs; I didn't listen to Lydia when she told me she was fed up living like a single parent, I said it wouldn't be for much longer. I got that bit right: she left me and took the kids with her.'

Cole had begged her to give him another chance, but she'd refused. She loved him, she told him, but she wasn't in love with him anymore; she wanted to pursue her career again, not play second fiddle to a man. Six months later she'd filed for divorce and he hadn't stood in her way; it pained him to see it, but she'd blossomed without him. As far as he knew, she hadn't dated anyone else yet: she seemed genuinely happy to be single again.

The irony wasn't lost on him that he'd seen more of the children since Lydia left him than when they were all living under the same roof.

'All marriages are different, some stay the course and some have a limited life. Maybe yours was always destined to be your first marriage and your forever partner is out there somewhere waiting for you. Besides, it takes two to make it work,' said Hester loyally.

'Maybe,' said Cole, not wanting to lay the blame at Lydia's feet. 'But as far as a partner is concerned, I'll take a rain check. There's just no room in my schedule for another woman right now.'

'Then your schedule needs looking at,' she said with a grin as she got to her feet. 'I've had all my single girlfriends asking about you since you moved in – don't break their hearts.'

He shook his head, laughing, not believing that for a moment.

'I thought we could get a Chinese takeaway tonight,' she said, heading to the door. 'If you fancy it?'

'Or how about I cook for us, as a thank you for putting up with me? I can cook tacos, Harley's favourite.' He gave his sister a half smile. He'd love to be cooking an actual birthday dinner for his son, but this would be the next best thing.

Hester looked at him, understanding. She crossed the room and buried her head in Cole's chest, her eyes shiny with tears. 'That's a lovely idea, we can send him pictures.'

'What if the kids forget me?' Cole said.

'They won't! They adore you,' Hester said firmly. 'Just make yourself available twenty-four-seven. It's a digital world now, Cole, and kids are better at that than anyone. You can always send them videos, so they see you when they wake up. Read Freya a story at bedtime. Send them photos through the day so they know you're thinking of them. And what's to stop you jumping on a plane and visiting them whenever you like?'

'You're right,' he nodded, calculating that Freya's bedtime would be during the early hours of the morning in the UK, but he could manage it once a week, maybe? 'But if I can get the new houses built and sold, I'll be one step closer to having a house for myself, and a home for the kids to come back to. That's more important than anything to me right now. A family home.'

Chapter 3

Merry

Holly Cottage was beginning to feel like home. All my belongings were unpacked and the kitchen had become the headquarters of my Merry and Bright empire. Days had developed a bit of a routine: first a cup of tea at the kitchen table while scrolling through emails and orders on my phone, followed by a bath, breakfast and then down to business.

I had settled on a product range of three different scents: lemon, lime and rosemary; raspberry and black pepper; and peony and sandalwood, and I was producing them in two sizes of glass jars. I'd got proper logoed labels and I'd sorted out packaging. Daniel had helped me to set up an Etsy shop before I'd moved out and I was selling them through that and via Nell's market stall. I had an Instagram page too and orders from there were taking off. Production was slow; I was still learning how to scale up from being a hobbyist to a fully-fledged business, but it was immensely satisfying. And being busy kept me from dwelling on my newly-single status.

By mid-afternoon, I was so absorbed in my work, and singing along to the radio to fill the emptiness of the cottage, that it took me a while to hear the doorbell. I turned off the radio, pulled the pan of melting wax off the hob and hopped up the steps and along the hall to open the door.

A tall, thin woman in a long patchwork coat beamed at me as her small toffee-coloured dog jumped up with excitement. It was Astrid, my old art teacher, who over the years had become my mentor, surrogate auntie and one of my most favourite people all rolled into one. In fact, it was because of her that I lived in Wetherley. After she retired from the school in Bakewell where we'd met, she'd moved into a block of retirement flats near the centre of town. And when the job at Tractor World had come up, I'd decided it was too good an opportunity to miss, so I'd moved from Bakewell to Wetherley too. Apart from Nell, she was the nearest thing I had to family and we both enjoyed being close to each other.

'Hello!' I cried, delighted to see her. 'What a lovely surprise!'

'Hallo, *mein Schatz*! I thought it was time I checked up on you again. May we come in?'

She'd been to visit me on my first weekend at the cottage and once I'd shown her around, she'd comforted me while I'd shed a few tears of sadness over my break-up. It had been my decision to move out of Daniel's house, but it was still painful to accept that we were over.

Before I could respond, the dog, Otto, bolted past me and started to explore and we both laughed at his cheekiness.

'Of course you may.' I kissed her on both cheeks. The German way, she'd insisted, once we'd reframed our relationship as friends and not teacher and pupil anymore. Her skin was cold but soft against mine. She didn't own a scrap of make-up, but kept her skin immaculate with her own blend of argan and rose oil. It was the little bottle of that she'd once given to me that had sparked my interest in essential oils.

'*Wunderschöne Kerzen*,' said Astrid, inhaling the scent of the newly poured batch of candles as I led her through to the kitchen. 'The house smells wonderful now. It's like walking into a spa hotel.'

Astrid spoke excellent English but had retained her German accent. Ever the teacher, she had a habit of dropping German words into conversation in a thinly disguised attempt to teach me her mother tongue. It worked, although my vocabulary consisted mostly of food and endearments with a few swear words thrown in. *Kerzen*, I remembered was the word for candles.

'It's definitely an improvement on the musty unlived-in smell the cottage had when I first arrived,' I agreed.

Astrid made us a pot of peppermint tea while I lined up the candles which had been recently poured on the kitchen windowsill to cool. Otto appeared again and sniffed at Astrid's bag hopefully. She produced a chew stick and once he'd sat down obediently, she let him have it and he retreated under the table to eat it. He was an adorable little thing, a hybrid of two breeds which I could never remember, but essentially he looked like a small teddy bear.

'They look very professional too,' Astrid said, handing me a mug.

'Thanks.' I blew on the tea before sipping it. 'I'm really happy with these. Perfectly even and no sinkholes.'

'*Sehr gut*,' she said, shrugging off her coat to reveal a long blue velvet dress with multicoloured beads sewn around the neckline. 'I knew you'd end up with a creative career eventually. I spotted your talent when you were only twelve years old.'

'You were the only one who did,' I said, filling a bowl with water for Otto and setting it down by the door. 'And I'll be forever grateful to you for that.'

'My dear girl.' She touched my arm and her eyes shone with pride. 'It has been my honour to see you grow and thrive.'

Astrid Beckmann had been my favourite teacher in secondary school by a country mile. I'd have drowned completely in the education system if she hadn't been there to throw me a lifeline.

In truth I had been an enthusiastic rather than an exceptional art student, but Miss Beckmann, as I'd known her as then, would sail around the classroom, all kaftans and bangles, pointing out the positive in everyone's creative offerings and we all loved her. Being encouraged had been a revelation. I revelled in her praise like a cat basking in sunlight.

One year, when I was about fourteen, she had set up an art club after school. I'd been delighted as it meant there would now be another evening when I could stay later rather than go straight home. I'd been the only student to turn up to that first class and my disappointment knew no bounds. I was convinced that Miss Beckmann would cancel the club due to lack of interest. But she'd declared herself thrilled that I'd joined her club and for one hour for the rest of that term, I had her and the art room to myself. Over the next weeks, while my hands were busy with chalk, watercolours or clay, I began to open up to her in a way I hadn't been able to with an adult other than my mum. And Miss Beckmann listened and encouraged and cared. She became something of a guardian angel to me and, crucially, an adult who I could trust. It was my favourite hour of the week.

'Thank you,' I said, giving her a brief hug. Otto gave a yap and we looked down to see him at our feet and laughed. 'He's jealous,' I said.

'Here, sit down for a moment,' she said, getting a plastic tub from her bag. 'Have a cookie and talk to me. How is everything?'

We both sat at the table and I took one of her freshly baked cookies.

'Well, I took an order for candles for a fortieth wedding anniversary today, and this afternoon's batch are for Nell's stall. Running my own business is wonderful,' I said, biting into my cookie. It was buttery and crumbly and studded with cranberries. 'This is delicious. Sales are beginning to drip through; I don't really know how to run a business but I'm loving every minute of it.'

Astrid cradled her mug and nodded. 'I remember reading something Oprah Winfrey said once about knowing you were on the road to success if you'd still do your job even if you weren't being paid for it.'

'In that case Merry and Bright is definitely on the right path. I would do it for free, but I hope I don't have to,' I admitted. 'The rent on this cottage is very reasonable, but I don't think they'd appreciate being paid in candles.'

Otto hoovered up a crumb that I'd dropped and then settled under the table by our feet. I reached down to run my fingers over his soft fur.

'And you are making yourself at home here, I notice?' Astrid cast an amused eye over the kitchen surfaces. What little she could see of them.

I cringed; that was her way of pointing out how messy I was. I used to get in trouble in her art class for the same thing.

'I know, I know. But at least I'm not bothering anyone,' I said. 'There's nobody to raise an eyebrow at the spilled

43

wax. And there's no need to tidy away my paraphernalia at mealtimes either. I'm quite happy to squeeze on the end of the table to avoid moving everything.'

She nodded. 'There are advantages to living alone, yes.'

Although she had never married, Astrid had had a partner for many years. But after he died in a car accident, she had never met anyone else and seemed perfectly happy to be solo. I was gradually getting used to there being no one to talk to, but I didn't think I'd want to live like this for ever.

'I suppose there are,' I said, forcing a smile.

'And Daniel?' Astrid asked. 'Have you seen him?'

I'd never really known whether she liked him or not. She was pleasant to him when their paths crossed, but slightly reserved in his presence.

I shook my head. 'I miss him, Astrid.'

That was an understatement. I missed him acutely. The feel of his manly face against mine. The way we used to interlace our fingers and his thumb would stroke the back of my hand. I missed the way he made the bed in the morning as if he was preparing for a military inspection, my old T-shirt folded under my pillow neatly for me, his pyjamas trousers with their ironed-in creases. Catching up on our respective days over dinner which we'd taken in turns to cook. Whenever I thought about what I'd lost, I ached with sadness deep inside me.

I'd gone round and round in circles thinking about the breakdown of our relationship. Being on my own had given me too much time to dwell on it. Maybe I should have stayed with him and accepted that marriage wasn't the be-all and end-all, but in my heart of hearts, the yearning for a family of my own was something that I knew would never go away. Daniel had seemed so adamant; I believed him when he said he wouldn't change his mind.

'Of course, you do, *mein Liebling*.' Astrid smiled ruefully. 'You're not having second thoughts about moving out, are you?'

I heaved a big sigh.

'I know things have worked out for the best, but I haven't stopped loving him. He wants to stay friends and sends me texts, letting me know what he's up to and asking how I am. It's really sweet, but I can't think of him as just a friend yet; he's the man I'd thought I'd grow old with.'

'He will be feeling guilty, I imagine,' Astrid declared. 'You gave up your flat to move in with him. You have moved home twice this year. He knows that it is his fault that you are apart.'

I decided to change the subject. We were two people who wanted different things. No one was to blame.

'I might see him later at the community meeting for Benny Dunford. If I go.'

A shiver of apprehension ran down my back. The meeting to discuss the Christmas Project was only hours away and the closer it got, the less I was sure that I was going. Was I ready to see Daniel again? How would we greet each other: kisses on the cheek, hugs, or a polite nod? And Nell had said that Daniel's old crush, the new head teacher would be there; that was a whole different set of butterflies in the stomach . . .

Astrid gave me a stern look. 'I saw Nell at the market and she thought you might have second thoughts when it came to it. I told her that she was wrong, that the Merry Shaw I know had more grit than that.'

I hid my smile behind my mug; she had always known how to get the best out of me.

'I suppose I did promise Nell.' I swirled the last inch of tea around the bottom. 'I just hope I don't get all emotional when I see him.'

'You will be fine.' Astrid put her mug down and stood up. 'You will walk in there, head high and looking as radiant as ever. He will be the one feeling emotional, I promise. Have another cookie. It'll give you some energy.'

'Why don't you come too,' I suggested hopefully. 'Safety in numbers, etcetera.'

'*Meine Gute,*' Astrid tutted, putting on her coat. 'OK, time for tough love. Stop making excuses. It's a meeting to support the community. You are part of the community. The town needs young creative minds like you.' She kissed my cheeks and clicked her fingers to summon Otto. 'See you later. *Bis bald.*'

'All right, all right,' I grumbled to myself as she saw herself out. 'I'll go.'

A couple of hours later, I glanced at the kitchen clock and yelped. I'd been so absorbed in my work that I hadn't kept track of the time. It was six o'clock already; the meeting started at seven. I untied my apron and bolted upstairs to get ready. I'd planned on washing my hair and making an effort before seeing Daniel again. Now I didn't even have time for a shower.

I changed into a clean jumper and jeans, dragged a brush through my hair, sprayed on some perfume and tried to ignore my rumbling stomach. All I'd had to eat since breakfast was Astrid's cookies. Too bad, there was no time for dinner now. I quickly added a new layer of mascara on top of the old, tucked a pen, my new diary and a banana for emergency energy into my bag and dashed to the door. Was radiant the same as hot and flustered, I wondered, remembering what Astrid had said.

My mobile rang as I was locking the door.

'Hello!' I answered, tucking the phone under my ear.

It was Nell. 'Just checking you hadn't forgotten about tonight.'

'Of course not,' I said, pretending to be insulted. 'I'm a very organised person, I'll have you know.'

'Oh yes,' she replied with a snigger. 'That had slipped my mind for a moment.'

'Anyway, it would be difficult to forget about the community meeting when you've sent me endless texts and reminders about it and sent Astrid to check up on me.'

'So, you're definitely coming?'

'Definitely,' I confirmed, stowing my house keys in my bag. 'If you get there first, save me a seat. I'm on my way.'

Chapter 4

Cole

Cole was almost done for the day. His mug was washed and ready for tomorrow and his laptop was just doing a round of updates before it closed down. All that was left to do was clean the floor. He whistled to himself as he swept up the clumps of clay soil from the site cabin floor and dropped them into the bin. It was one of his rituals: leave his work space clean and tidy to come back to in the morning. There was a thud of boots on the steps up to the cabin and Josh's weather-beaten face appeared at the door.

'That's us finished for the day, boss,' Josh said. 'Unless you wanted to go over the plan for tomorrow?'

At six feet tall, it was rare for Cole to feel small beside someone, but Josh towered over him. In truth, Cole could have managed the site without the younger man, but Josh had been desperate for work after he and his girlfriend, Vicky, had discovered she was expecting. And even though he was now a new father to baby Alice and not getting very much sleep, Josh was a hard worker and Cole had never had reason to regret his decision.

Cole shook his head. 'No, you get off home. In fact, I'll come with you and we can lock up.'

48

He shoved his laptop into a battered case and clicked the electric heater off with his foot, while simultaneously threading his arms into his neon yellow jacket.

Josh descended the steps while Cole locked the door. The air smelled of autumn: damp earth and woodsmoke.

'Looking good,' Cole said, inclining his head towards plot five which the men had been working on today.

'Hmm.' Josh frowned, which Cole knew was his way of acknowledging the compliment. 'We managed to get a decent day in once the rain had stopped.'

Rain never stopped play on a building site, but it did slow it down and at this time of year, every day of fine weather was a bonus. They walked across the churned-up ground towards the metal fence that surrounded the site.

'Concrete is booked for next Friday,' Cole told him. 'Will we be ready?'

Cole loved this part of a build; the concrete arrived by tanker and was poured into the footings from a vast hose. It was such a quick and satisfying transformation; one minute you were looking at a series of muddy trenches, and then the next, the footprint of a building appeared before your very eyes.

'We will,' said Josh confidently. 'I'll make sure we are.'

They reached the perimeter fence and Cole wrenched open two of the metal fence panels to let them out.

'Good man,' Cole nodded his approval. 'See you tomorrow.'

'Yeah. See you, boss.'

Josh got into his van and drove away while Cole secured the two fence panels with a padlock. Although the light was dim, Cole could still make out the eight sets of footings and could already imagine how it was going to look when it was finished.

Eight houses.

A mix of pride and nerves flared in his chest. Orchard Gardens was his biggest-ever project. He'd taken a massive gamble when he bought the land and he needed it to go well. His future was riding on it. The plot was on the edge of the new Wetherley housing estate, which had been developing steadily over the last decade. It was proving popular with people who wanted the benefits of a modern house in a semi-rural setting, but still within easy reach of the town.

Cole had tightly planned and budgeted his small development with a modest buffer for contingency. But that budget would only work out if he managed to sell seven of the properties; the money from the deposits was needed to keep paying his suppliers. He knew from experience how lack of cash flow could snuff out even the most promising business. If the build went well and he sold the seven houses at a decent price, he should be in a position to keep the last one for himself. Then he'd be able to put down roots again for when the kids returned from Canada.

So far, he'd taken deposits on two of the properties, which was good, but he wasn't going to celebrate just yet. He'd have to keep on top of everything to ensure the project stayed on track; there was no room for any major hiccups between now and completion next spring.

Lydia had claimed that the main reason their marriage had broken down was because he was a workaholic, but ironically, throwing himself into this build had been his saviour. Keeping himself mentally and physically busy had filled the void that the loss of family life had created.

Cole swapped his site boots for a pair of trainers, stowed his neon coat and hard hat in the back of his van and set off towards Wetherley. Later on, he was going to the

Benny Dunford meeting, but before that, he was calling in on his dad. Family should be cherished before it was too late; he knew that now, he'd learned it the hard way.

Cole pressed the buzzer for his dad's flat and waited for him to answer. The Rosebridge retirement complex was a pleasant modern building tucked behind the church just off the market square in Wetherley. He and Hester had been shocked when, only weeks after their mum's funeral, Fred had announced that he was selling the big family home they'd grown up in with its large garden, double garage and vegetable plot and swapping it for a two-bedroomed apartment. But they'd gone along with it, desperate to do anything to make their dad smile again.

Fred hadn't just downsized his home, he'd downsized his whole life. When he lost his wife, it was as if someone had flipped a switch inside him. He'd changed almost overnight. He'd always been a doer, a DIYer with multiple projects on the go. But after Val had gone, he lost interest in doing anything that he'd once enjoyed.

To begin with, Cole thought his dad might be suffering from depression. Hester wondered if it was just a temporary thing, his way of dealing with grief. But Fred was adamant he was fine.

'I've worked hard all my adult life and now I'm stopping,' he'd told his two children. 'If I stay in this big house, I'll be rattling round and it'll be a constant round of jobs. Your mum and I never got to slow down and enjoy our retirement together. So now it's up to me to go it alone.'

'What will you do all day?' Hester had asked.

'Read all the books I've never read, watch all the films everyone else can quote verbatim,' Fred had replied calmly. 'Get up late, go to bed late . . . whatever I want.'

Cole was unconvinced. 'You'll get bored, Dad.'

Fred had shrugged. 'I'll worry about that when it happens.'

He'd sold up and given both his kids a lump sum of money. 'You might as well have your inheritance now, otherwise it'll only end up in the taxman's pocket', he'd said. A year on, Cole had to admit, his dad did seem more relaxed than he'd ever been.

'Hello?' His dad's voice came over the intercom, sounding suspicious even though Cole had spoken to him on the phone only five minutes ago, to let him know he was en route.

'Trick or treat,' said Cole in a deliberately gruff voice.

'You daft sod,' Fred chuckled. 'Come on up, Son.'

'Any chance of a cuppa, Dad?' he asked when the two of them had exchanged hugs disguised as manly slaps on the back.

'Thought you'd never ask,' said Fred, shuffling in his slippers back to his armchair. He'd shrunk in the last year, and his shoulders were a little more stooped each time Cole visited. He'd still got his thick thatch of white hair though, not to mention his sense of humour. 'Just a drop of milk in mine please, no sugar.'

Cole grinned. 'Yes, I remember.'

It was only six o'clock but the smell of cooking already hung in the air. His mum used to have a meal on the table at half past five without fail and his dad had kept rigidly to her timetable after her death. It was quite sweet really. He even bought exactly the same food that she'd brought home in the weekly shop.

Cole took the kettle to the kitchen tap to fill it up. In the sink was a single used plate and a knife and fork. The sight of it made his throat tighten. Fred and Val had worshipped each other; it was sad to think that Dad would spend the rest of his years alone. Like father like son at the moment, he thought glumly.

He took the tea through to the living room. 'Had a good day?'

'I have.' Fred closed the book he was reading and picked up his phone. 'I woke up to a drawing from Freya. I'll show you.'

He swiped at his phone and then pointed the remote at the TV. Freya appeared on the TV screen, holding up a drawing of a witch, a pumpkin and a black cat and the words 'Happy Halloween' at the top of the page.

'That's great,' Cole said huskily.

'Talented kid,' said Fred.

Cole nodded. She always asked for new paints and colouring pens for every Christmas and birthday. She'd kept all her art supplies neatly in a special box he'd made her. He wondered if she'd got a new box now and whether she still had the set of coloured pens with unicorns on them that he'd bought for her.

Fred swiped at the screen again and the picture changed to a photograph of a bird on his balcony.

'How did you get the photos on the TV?' Cole was impressed. He'd tried watching TV in Hester's living room recently and had been bamboozled by the three remote controls and had ended up watching the shopping programme it had been tuned to because he couldn't work out how to change the channel.

'Screen mirroring,' said Fred proudly. 'You just press a button and hey presto.'

'Amazing,' said Cole, slightly envious of his dad's skills.

To give Fred credit, he'd certainly mastered the digital world; he was comfortable using a laptop and phone to keep in touch with his grandchildren, doing his shopping, his banking and even communicating with his doctor.

'And Harley sent me a Facebook friend request,' Fred continued. 'So now I can watch all the silly prank videos he likes to share.'

Cole sipped his tea and smiled. He was glad they were making an effort to keep in touch with him. Lydia's dad wasn't on the scene and her mum had passed away the year before they got married. Granddad Fred was their only remaining grandparent.

On the dresser behind Fred's armchair, Cole noticed that the electric screwdriver had been plugged in to charge up. He nodded to it. 'What are you up to?'

'Ah, well, I'm glad you asked.' Fred slurped his tea. 'You saw that photo of the bird on my balcony? I took it last week. It was a beauty, gold-green feathers. I'd never seen one before. Took me ages to work out what it was. I had to pop to the bookshop and buy a book on garden birds before I could identify it.'

'What was it?'

'A greenfinch!' Fred said proudly. 'They like eating sunflower seeds so I put some out on the balcony railings and more birds came back the next day. In one day I spotted the greenfinch again, a coal tit, a robin and something else which might have been a dunnock. It was fascinating, watching them. So I bought a bird table, a self-assembly job. It's out there on the balcony in a box ready to be assembled.' He narrowed his eyes at Cole. 'What are you looking so pleased with yourself about?'

'I'm trying not to say I told you so.' Cole rubbed a hand across his stubbly chin to hide his smirk. 'But I knew you'd get bored of reading and watching TV eventually.'

'You did,' Fred acknowledged. 'But I just had to get there in my own time. And I'm not bored exactly; just, you know, ready to get interested in things again.'

Cole didn't want to make a fuss but this was music to his ears. Hester was going to be pleased too. Mum had always fed the birds and had been able to reel off all their names; it would be a nice hobby for Dad and might even encourage him to get out more. He finished his tea and set his mug down. 'Come on, let's build it now. It'll be easier with two pairs of hands.'

His dad brightened. 'Would you? That is kind of you. I'll get the instruction leaflet for you. And there's another screwdriver knocking about somewhere in case the electric one isn't ready.'

Cole got up from the sofa and inspected it: ten per cent charged. It couldn't have been on for very long.

'When did you plug it in?'

Fred puffed his cheeks out and scratched his head. 'Let me think.'

Cole let out a hoot of laughter. 'You plugged it in after I called to say I was on my way, didn't you?'

'Any more tea in that pot?' said Fred blithely, heading into the kitchen.

Cole shook his head fondly. 'Cheeky sod. I'll do you a deal. Knock me up some scrambled eggs on toast and I'll build the bird table for you.'

Fred tutted. 'You drive a hard bargain, but it's a deal.'

In the time it took Fred to prepare the food, Cole had built a small wooden table covered with a roof like an open-sided house. All he had to do now was to fix it to the wooden support post and clip on the rubber feet.

'Grub's up,' Fred said.

Cole put the screwdriver back on charge while he ate his food sat on the sofa.

'So, I've updated you on my day. How are you?' Fred asked, offering him salt and ground black pepper.

'Fine.' Cole added pepper to his eggs and sneezed as it got up his nose. 'Absolutely fine. The build at Orchard Gardens is on track. Plenty of interest. We're pouring concrete soon, all being well.'

Fred raised an eyebrow. 'I didn't ask about work. I asked how you are.'

He looked back at his dad. 'What do you mean? I'm fine.'

'You and Lydia split up almost three years ago,' Fred said gently. 'Don't you miss having someone to share your life with?'

'No. I miss the kids,' Cole mumbled through a mouthful of toast. 'They're on my mind all day, every day, but as far as meeting another woman goes, no. I'm using the time they're away to crack on with the build. A relationship would only complicate things.'

Fred sighed. 'You're a good lad, I just want to see you happy, that's all.'

'As a wise man once said to me, I'll get there in my own time.' He flashed his dad a grin.

'Touché,' Fred chuckled. 'And talking about time, weren't you supposed to be at that community meeting? It started half an hour ago.'

Cole checked his watch and groaned. 'Damn. It's probably not worth going now.'

'He was a good man, Benny Dunford. You should go,' said Fred.

'In that case, why don't you come with me?' Cole said, threading his arms into his jacket and patting his pockets to make sure he still had his keys on him. 'It's about time you started to get to know your new neighbourhood.'

'Can't, can I?' said Fred slyly, looking at the bird table. 'Someone's got to finish the job properly.'

'Very funny.' He gave his dad a quick hug. 'I'd better run. See if I can sneak in at the back without anyone noticing.'

Although as he was a six-foot-tall redhead wearing a neon yellow coat, that might be easier said than done.

Chapter 5

Merry

The town clock was already striking seven as I headed to the meeting. I loved this part of Wetherley, it was such a pretty place; most of the buildings had scarcely changed in centuries and the market square still had cobbled streets. Now that the market stalls had been packed away for the day, the shops were closed and the hum of traffic had faded, it was easy to imagine how it would have looked in the age of horses and carriages, promenading ladies in long dresses, and handsomely attired men in their top hats and tailcoats.

My destination was the Buttermarket, a solid stone single-storey building tucked into the edge of the market square. Its origins dated back to the sixteenth century, when it would have been open to the elements and farmers' wives would have gathered to sell their dairy produce. Over the years it had been modernised and now had windows, walls and neon strip lighting. Despite its rather unsympathetic renovations, it was a great place for community meetings and I'd attended many a fund-raising event since I'd been living in Wetherley.

I pushed open the heavy wooden door and made it inside just as a man at the front table was clearing his throat and tapping papers on the desk in readiness to start. Next to him, head bowed, was Pam Dunford, Benny's widow.

Benny Dunford had been the manager of Wetherley's only bank. The bank had closed its doors some years ago, certainly before I'd even moved here. Benny had retired when the bank closed, but he'd remained the town's unofficial banking advisor until he died during the summer. Both Nell and Olek had picked his brains about monetary matters and Daniel had asked him to look over the business plan for his greengrocer's too. Every town needed someone like Benny. Someone to rally the troops, guilt-trip people into helping out for the good of the community, cajole people into selling raffle tickets and if you were a business, he was very persuasive when it came to buying advertising space in the town magazine, edited, of course, by Benny himself. He'd been a great organiser too, of everything from Easter egg hunts to trips to the seaside for the older folk. His passing had left a huge hole in the town. And tonight's meeting would make sure that although he was gone, he wouldn't be forgotten. Because more than anything else, Benny had loved Christmas.

The room was set out theatre style: five rows of chairs with a central aisle, facing the front table. There were about twenty people here, half of whom I recognised, including Nell who waved me over. But no sign of Daniel, which made my stomach twist; though whether in disappointment or relief, I couldn't be sure.

'I must be hallucinating!' Nell smirked, pulling me down into the empty chair beside her. 'You actually made it.'

'You underestimate my community spirit,' I said primly.

'My heartfelt apologies.' She pulled a plastic tub out of her bag. 'Have a nut.'

Pam tapped her pen on the side of her thermos flask and conversation promptly fizzled out. She stood up, a handkerchief balled in her fist. My heart went out to her.

'Poor Pam,' I whispered. 'She looks utterly lost.'

'Heartbreaking,' Nell agreed. 'She and Benny were inseparable. Imagine losing the love of your life just like that.'

But how lucky to have found someone to journey through life with in the first place, I thought wistfully.

'Hello everyone,' Pam began, sounding a bit wobbly. 'Thank you for coming. Benny would have been so proud that his friends had turned up to hear what Jim and I have to say—' Her voice cracked then and the man beside her coaxed her back to her seat and cleared his throat.

'Evening all. I'm Jim Dunford, Benny's brother,' Jim began and then immediately stopped as the door opened and Daniel appeared. My heart speeded up at the sight of him. Right behind him was a smartly dressed woman with dark hair.

'Wowsers.' Nell helped herself to the nuts. 'That's got to be the new head teacher.'

All heads turned and a buzz of curiosity ran around the room.

'It is,' I said, without tearing my eyes away from the pair of them. 'Tasha Sandean, I googled her.'

Although the grainy photograph I'd found of her on the Wetherley school website didn't do her justice. She was quite simply stunning. She was wearing a lightweight coat and heels. A cloud of dark curls skimmed her shoulders. She was city chic, a bird of paradise among a flock of garden sparrows.

'Did you? Why?' Nell sounded bemused.

'Oh, you know.' I waved a hand dismissively. 'Curious.'

Curious to see the woman Daniel had admitted to having a schoolboy crush on right before he crushed my dreams.

Tasha smiled as if she she'd been looking forward to this moment her entire life. 'Hello everyone, so sorry we're late. Please don't let us interrupt!'

Daniel, who had closed the door as quietly as he could, stood behind her, his hand hovering around the small of her back. He looked great: jeans, boots, and the cable-knit jumper that I'd bought him last December for his birthday.

'I love a red lip,' Nell breathed in awe. 'She's very glamorous.'

'Hmm.'

My lacklustre response drew Nell's attention. 'You OK?'

I blinked rapidly. 'Seeing him is harder than I thought.'

She squeezed my hand and I was grateful for her support.

'Let's get on with it, then,' I grumbled as Jim Dunford shook hands with the latecomers.

Daniel and Tasha took seats in the row in front of us. Daniel made whispered introductions and Tasha smiled warmly at us as she sat down.

Jim cleared his throat again.

'As you know, my brother Benny passed away in August. For many years, he was the manager of the bank just across the square from where we are now. Benny loved this town and he loved Christmas too and it was he who first negotiated with the local council to supply Wetherley with an annual Christmas tree, on the condition, as you all know, that the bank supplied the power to light it up for the season. Of course, the old bank has new owners now, but I'm sure the tradition will continue for many years to come . . .'

Jim appeared to be delivering a eulogy and I found myself tuning out and focusing on the body language of the two people in front of me. I'd been wondering whether Daniel had been in touch with her since she'd moved back to Wetherley and now I knew. I couldn't take my eyes off him. Or her. At one point the doors opened and a man in a bright yellow coat arrived, but I didn't even turn around for long enough to see if it was anyone I recognised. I was watching Daniel and Tasha for signs of . . . well, I wasn't sure what, but at any rate, there weren't any.

'And now we come to the reason you're all here: this Christmas,' Jim said, raising his voice and dragging my attention back to the meeting. 'Pam, would you like to carry on?'

Pam got to her feet. 'Benny always had a project on the go, but none as important to him as his Christmas Project, which he started planning straight after Bonfire Night. Turning on the Christmas tree lights in the square was something he looked forward to immensely. Flicking that switch at the beginning of December, seeing everywhere light up, the tree taking centre stage . . . It was a special moment for him, particularly as he'd had to work hard to get Wetherley a tree in the first place.'

'It was special for us too,' piped up a man with a shiny bald head and wispy grey beard, the end of which reached his pot belly. 'If he hadn't been there to organise us, none of it would have been possible.'

'Hear, hear!' a couple of others chimed in.

'And then of course, his *pièce de résistance*,' Pam continued. 'Christmas Eve.'

'Ah, Christmas carols around the tree,' said a woman wistfully. I recognised her from the market: Audrey's Vintage China. I'd bought a couple of teacups from her once with the idea of making candles in them. 'Gathering together to celebrate, before we all dash off to our own homes, is always such a lovely moment. It's my favourite part of Christmas.'

'Thank you, Audrey.' Pam blew her nose. 'It was Benny's too, and he would want the Christmas spirit to carry on in Wetherley for generations to come. Which is why he left a sum of money in his will to be put towards this year's celebrations.'

There were gasps from around the room. One person started clapping and everyone else followed suit.

'That is just like Benny,' Nell said, looking quite moved. 'He was so generous.'

Jim stood and raised a hand and the applause died down. 'It's time for the Dunfords to step back and let new faces take over. So, Pam and I are suggesting that you get your heads together and come up with some ideas to make this Christmas the best Wetherley has ever seen.'

'Absolutely!' cried a voice at the back. 'Any volunteers?'

There was a moment of silence before Tasha raised a hand and got to her feet.

'I'm new here, and I would hate to tread on anyone's toes,' she said, addressing the room. 'But I'd be happy to manage Wetherley's Christmas celebrations. The children at my school would love to be involved. And I'm sure I could even rope in the PTA. Also,' her liquid brown eyes narrowed in thought, 'the school will be presenting a nativity play for the parents – perhaps we could repeat the performance *al fresco*?'

'No!' I blurted out.

Tasha bit her bottom lip. 'Oops, my apologies, have I spoken out of turn?'

Daniel turned to stare at me in amusement and I felt the heat rise to my face.

'No, no,' I added hurriedly. 'I mean, that would be nice, of course, and very generous of you. But I'm sure you already have enough to do in your new job. And everyone knows schools are busy places in the run-up to the end of term.'

Tasha opened her mouth to reply but was interrupted.

'Good point,' said the man with the beard who'd spoken earlier. 'Anyway, why should the kids have all the fun? I've got a few tricks up my sleeve.' He rubbed his hands together gleefully. 'Leave it with me.'

'I dread to think,' Nell sniggered. 'That's Nigel from the hardware store. Remember last year he had an inflatable Santa doing a moonie on the roof?'

I nodded absentmindedly, my face still burning from my outburst. What had I been thinking?

'There you go, Pam,' said Jim, beaming at his sister-in-law. 'Three offers of help just like that. I knew you needn't have been worried.'

Three? Tasha, Nigel and . . . My eyes widened.

'He doesn't mean me, surely?' I muttered. 'I'm not doing it.'

Nell snorted under her breath. 'Serves you right.'

'Thank you everyone, it's a weight off our minds,' Pam said. 'It's important to me that we do Benny proud with his bequest.'

She leaned across to whisper in Jim's ear and I looked at Nell and groaned.

'I'm going to have to say something,' I hissed. 'The last thing I want to do is organise a town-wide event.'

'Fine,' Nell shrugged. 'Let Tasha win. I'm sure she can handle it.'

I scowled, weighing up how I felt about her swanning into my town and bossing the committee around for the next two months, versus actually stepping up to the plate myself.

Daniel turned around and looked at me, his pale blue eyes meeting mine.

'Good for you,' he said with a smile, 'you'll be brilliant at this.'

'Thanks,' I mumbled, ignoring Nell who I could sense was on the verge of laughter. 'Just doing my bit.'

'Pam has just had a very good idea,' said Jim, commanding everyone's attention again. 'Why don't each of our three volunteers come back in two weeks for a special Christmas Project meeting and present their ideas? We'll all vote, and the most popular scheme will go ahead, run by its creator, of course.'

'Fair enough,' said Nigel, stroking his beard. 'I can live with that.'

Tasha leaned right over to Daniel, smiling broadly, and whispered into his ear just loud enough for me to hear, 'This is so exciting, I love this sort of thing and I've got a few ideas already.'

Daniel smiled back, looking completely enchanted by her and I felt my heart sink. I opened my diary and pencilled in the next committee meeting, sixteen days from now.

All of a sudden I'd never wanted to win anything so badly in my entire life.

Chapter 6

Cole

Cole rolled his shoulders back and eased his head from side to side; he was stiff from sitting in the same position. He had been on site since nine and it was now almost noon. Saturday mornings were a good time to get things done without interruption and it meant that Mondays could get off to a good clean start. But this morning hadn't just been about paperwork; he'd had a viewing.

A rush of elation went through him and he forced himself not to get too excited. It was early days and it might fall through. But if it didn't – he allowed himself a smile – he might have sold not one but two of the houses.

An hour ago, he'd shown two sisters around the site. They were very close, they explained, and wanted to buy houses next door to each other so that their children could all grow up together and they'd have a readymade social life on their doorstep. Cole couldn't believe his luck, especially as they'd seemed keen on the two corner plots, which had the biggest gardens and therefore the biggest price tag to match.

They'd stayed for a long time and had gone for a walk around the area before leaving. The viewing couldn't have been more positive and he was keeping his fingers crossed that they'd make an offer. If the sisters went ahead, that would mean half of the build was sold, which would be a big weight off his mind. The sisters' main concern was whether the houses would be ready to move into on time, which according to Cole's schedule would be early March. They had properties to sell, they said, and one of them already had an interested buyer who wouldn't agree to any delays. Cole had talked through the timeframe with them to reassure them and they'd gone away to think about it and said they'd be in touch. It was just about possible if everything went to plan. But he'd have to keep on top of everything; he couldn't afford any major hiccups between now and completion next spring.

An hour on and he had worked through the entire month's delivery notes and receipts. He gathered all the various bits of paper into a pile and stuffed them in an envelope ready for dropping off at his accountant.

A good morning's work that. He got to his feet, pleased with himself, and put his coat on.

He opened the door to the site cabin and a whoosh of cold air rushed in. Just what he needed, he thought, stepping outside – something to wake him up.

There'd been a heavy frost last night and the ground was hard under his feet. He kicked through the leaves as he walked around the site, keeping his eye on the ground for any dropped screws and bits of wire. His team were a methodical bunch, but there were inevitably bits and pieces dropped and forgotten. He put his findings in his pockets and started to collect up anything that would burn. There were several old pallets and unwanted bits of wood and he stacked them up to make a fire. He was tempted to set light to it now, but he'd leave it; the men loved to have a fire in the mornings to chase the cold out of their bones.

There were some huge trees on the perimeter of the site which would form a leafy backdrop to the houses when they were finished: mature oak and horse chestnut trees which must have been planted at least a century ago. The sisters had commented on how nice it would be for their kids to build dens in the woods. He picked up a shiny conker and automatically put it in his pocket to save it for Freya. Then he remembered. It would have gone dull with age by the time he saw her again. He shook away the thought, took his phone out and took a photo of it instead. He pressed send and hoped it didn't wake her up.

Once he'd run out of jobs, he walked back towards the van and cast his eye over the area of scrubland at the front edge of the site, just beyond the gates. It was a bit of an eyesore at the moment, a tangle of self-seeded trees, blackthorn mostly. He had planning permission to clear this section to make way for the landscaping: driveways and verges; the finishing-off bits that would help turn Orchard Gardens from a muddy site into an attractive development. He made a mental note to check when the contractor was booked in for and started to close up the site for the day.

As he was digging in his pocket for the key to the padlock, a car horn tooted, and he looked over his shoulder to see Josh's pick-up truck arriving.

He waved at him. 'What are you doing here?'

Josh jumped down from the cab and grinned. 'I was going to ask you the same question.'

'A viewing that went well and sorting out paperwork,' Cole replied. 'Got to keep the taxman happy. So what's your excuse?'

Josh grinned. 'Vicky and the baby are having a nap, so I thought I'd come and check over the site. Now it gets dark earlier, I don't always have chance to make sure we're leaving it tidy at night.'

'Beat you to it,' said Cole, digging in his pocket and producing half a dozen screws and two pieces of steel wire.

'In that case, I'll just round up the waste wood.'

'Already done and in the incinerator.'

'Oh.' Josh looked past him through the fence. 'I'm sure there's something I can do.'

Cole put a hand on his shoulder. 'Mate, we're not behind schedule. It's Saturday. Go home and put the kettle on ready for when Vicky wakes up.'

Josh shook his head and laughed which turned into a yawn. 'One day, just one day, I'd love to be one step ahead of you!'

'So now you have no excuse not to go back and spend some time with Alice – enjoy the baby years.'

'Yeah, I suppose,' Josh conceded. 'It's just that this job means the world to me. Well, me and Vix and Alice now. I want to prove myself and put in the hours.'

'I appreciate that,' Cole replied, steering Josh back to his car. 'And I expect hard work from my team, Monday to Friday. But the weekends are your own. I'm here on a Saturday because I ballsed that up – I put work above my family and look where it got me.'

'Point taken.' Josh gave him a sympathetic smile. 'I know how lucky I am. Even if Alice did get us up at five o'clock this morning. If I'm honest with you, sometimes I feel like coming to work is easier than staying at home with her.'

'I remember the broken nights well,' Cole grinned. 'But the thing is, this time next year, these homes will be built, people will be living in them and we'll have left the site.

Whether you came in today and put in another few hours in won't have made any difference. But it matters now to Vicky and to Alice, and if you play your cards right, they'll be with you for ever.'

Josh tossed his keys from one hand to the other. 'You're right, boss. Thanks for the advice. I'll see you Monday.'

Cole pulled some notes out of his wallet and handed them to the younger man. 'Get a takeaway tonight, so neither of you has to cook, have a glass of wine on me. Talk to each other, listen to each other and tell Vicky what you just told me: that you know how hard it is to stay at home with a newborn. She'll appreciate it.'

Josh tried to protest, but Cole insisted. He watched him drive off and thought about what Josh had said, about it being easier to come to work than stay at home with the baby.

Funny how we don't realise how lucky we are, he thought. He'd give anything to have someone to rush home for. There was no one waiting for him to clock off and spend the afternoon with, no one to pour a glass of wine for and cuddle with while they watched a bit of Saturday night TV together. It was the simple things like that he missed. It hit him suddenly that he was lonely. And it wasn't just because he couldn't see his kids, he realised. He'd told his dad the other day that he didn't miss sharing his life with anyone.

But now he wasn't sure if that was true.

Chapter 7

Merry

Behind the counter of Nell's Nuts stall, in Wetherley's market square, the cold was beginning to seep through my bones. I'd been here for hours and hardly moved from the spot. I knotted my scarf around my neck a little tighter and stamped my feet.

'I am freezing,' I said, trapping my hands under my armpits. 'How do you do it?'

'Thermal long johns, big pants and at least two pairs of socks,' said Nell, chucking me a pair of fingerless gloves with her good hand. She kept the other one, which was wrapped in a thick crêpe bandage, pressed to her chest. 'Although going to the loo can be a bit of an ordeal. Today isn't that cold; you want to try standing out here in February when the wind is so sharp it makes your eyes water.'

'I'll pass if it's all the same to you,' I said, pulling on the gloves. 'Making candles is a much warmer way of making a living.'

'Well, I do appreciate your help,' she said. 'I *could* have managed but I'm glad I didn't have to.'

She had had an accident last night while filleting a sea bass. The knife had slipped and cut her forefinger right

71

over a joint. She had been adamant that she didn't need stitches, so Olek had cleaned it up and put a bandage on it. I'd volunteered to help her out on the stall as Saturday was Wetherley market's busiest day of the week.

'Anytime,' I said, 'besides, it'll do me good to get out of the cottage for the day and talk to someone other than myself. Ooh, customer.'

I straightened and smiled as a man approached the stall.

'One of my regulars, I'll serve him.' Nell beamed at the man. 'Hello! What can I get you today?'

It was the beginning of November, so technically we were still in autumn, but there was definitely a wintry chill to the air. There was no getting away from it: Christmas would be here before I knew it.

That thought led me to my ideas for the Christmas Project. Or to be more accurate, the absence of any decent ones. I gave an involuntary shudder, hoping that I hadn't bitten off more than I could chew. So far, in the days since the meeting, I'd opened a new file on my laptop, jotted down some random thoughts in a notebook and created a mood board on Pinterest, but nothing concrete had really come to me; I was certainly a long way from presenting something that the committee would *ooh* and *ahh* over.

Now that I'd inadvertently found myself in the spotlight, pride had kicked in and I wanted to shine, or at the very least not fall flat on my face. Nigel and Tasha had said in the meeting that they already had ideas. I didn't mind too much if my scheme wasn't chosen for Benny Dunford's tribute; in all honesty I'd rather be using my time to focus growing Merry and Bright, but I needed to acquit myself admirably at the very least. My idea needed to dazzle.

Hopefully spending a few hours here would help my creative juices to flow. The market square was always at the heart of Wetherley's Christmas celebrations. The giant Christmas tree provided the main focal point, erected at the edge of the square, opposite the old bank. But the whole town made an effort, all the shops decorated their windows and coloured lights criss-crossed all the main shopping streets.

On Christmas Eve, once all the market traders had cleared away their stalls, carollers would gather around the tree. Local people would join in and according to Nell, a lovely time was had by all. In previous years, I'd volunteered to work on Christmas Eve, to let my colleagues with family commitments have the time off instead. But this year, for the first time, it looked like I'd be spending the evening here. I could think of worse places, I mused, gazing around and imagining how pretty everywhere was going to look, festooned with twinkling lights . . .

'Oof.' Nell struggled to lift a bulging carrier bag onto the counter one-handed, and I dragged myself from my thoughts. I was supposed to be doing all the heavy work for her.

'Whoops. Sorry,' I said, wrestling the bag off her. 'Let me do that.'

'Thanks, Merry. There you are, lovey, that'll be five pounds fifty, please,' said Nell, allowing me to pass the bag to the customer. The man counted out the exact money and placed it in her palm.

'And here's a free sample of Nell's new wasabi peas for you to try,' I said, handing him a small paper bag.

'Cheers, ladies,' he said, pocketing the freebie. 'Just the job to spice up my Saturday night, eh?'

After he'd gone, Nell thrust both hands into her pockets and instantly cried out in pain. 'Ouch!'

This was about the tenth time she'd forgotten about her bad hand and hurt herself.

'Not again!' I said, wincing at the look of agony on her face.

'Just sit down over there out of the way,' I said firmly, nodding to the stools behind us. 'I can serve the next customers.'

'But I know what my regulars like and you're too stingy,' she moaned until noticing my stern expression. 'OK, fine.'

She sat down underneath the shelves containing my candles and a sign that I'd bought her for her birthday a few years ago which read: *You don't have to be nuts to work here, but it helps.*

'I'm thinking of your profits,' I retorted. 'Left to you, you'd give them double and charge them half.'

'But that's what makes small businesses special: service with a smile and a little something extra for their loyalty,' Nell replied. 'I know I'm a soft touch, but I can't help it.'

'You're perfect just as you are,' I said. 'Nutty, but nice.'

Other stallholders yelled out their offers at the top of their voices, competing with each other for the best bargains. But it occurred to me that Nell's welcoming smile and natural warmth spoke far louder than their brash announcements.

For the next few minutes, she stayed put, watching me like a hawk as I scooped up hazelnuts and almonds, chocolate-covered raisins and dried dates, figs and apricots for a steady stream of customers.

'Time for a break, I think,' I said to her during a lull in business.

Astrid had dropped off a flask of hot chocolate and some of her homemade *pfefferkuchen* biscuits on her way to take Otto for his big weekend walk and I poured us both a cup each and joined her on the other stool.

'This tastes of Christmas,' I said, inhaling the cinnamon-scented steam. 'Curled up on the sofa under a blanket, the rosy glow from the lights on the tree and the flames of the log burner. Heaven.'

Of course, ideally there would be someone I loved with me under that blanket, but it didn't look like that would be happening this year unless Daniel had a complete change of heart. I suppressed a sigh. For a woman who'd always wanted to settle down with a partner and a houseful of children, I'd been categorically unsuccessful. Still, I thought, setting my shoulders back purposefully, maybe my new strategy of being organised would help. My spur-of-the-moment approach certainly hadn't worked so far.

Nell sighed blissfully. 'That sounds very romantic. My Christmas will be wall to wall relatives with an array of digestion issues from eating too much chestnut stuffing, or overindulging on the Baileys.'

'I doubt mine will be romantic either,' I said ruefully. 'This was supposed to be mine and Daniel's first Christmas together.'

She pulled a sympathetic face. 'I know. But we can still have a great time. I'm not having you being on your own.'

I'd envisaged us going for a moonlit walk on Christmas Eve, looking at all the Christmas lights, wishing everyone we met a Happy Christmas and then waking up together, toasting Christmas Day with kisses and champagne before driving over to his parents' house to join the rest of the family for dinner. My first proper family Christmas in decades.

'You're a good friend,' I said softly. 'And whatever happens, I certainly think Holly Cottage will be lovely and cosy at Christmas. I woke up the other day to find that a load of logs had been delivered for me. A gift from the landlord, according to the lettings agency.'

'Who is the landlord?' she asked.

I shrugged. 'Not sure exactly. I did ask but it's owned by a trust fund.'

'Ooh.' Nell eyes sparkled. 'Perhaps it's a mysterious eligible millionaire?'

'More likely a savvy saver,' I said, shaking my head at her. 'Don't you avoid paying inheritance tax if you put your assets in a trust fund?'

'A man with large assets?' She nudged me. 'That'll do.'

I left her fantasising on my behalf while I served a woman with twin boys who each had one pound to spend. While her sons were deciding between yogurt- or chocolate-covered raisins, the woman noticed my range of candles on the back shelf and bought three for Christmas presents and one for herself.

Christmas shopping in November – how sensible. That was what I should be doing, now I'd vowed to be organised, I thought, and made a mental note to start a gift list sooner rather than my usual later.

After the family of three had gone, the boys bickering about who'd got the most chocolate, I sat back down with a sigh. I had good intentions to be more proactive and less reactive, but I never seemed to get on top of my to-do list. More things appeared on it before I'd managed to cross any off. And now that I'd somehow managed to get embroiled in this community thing, I had even more to do.

'How's your pitch coming along for the Christmas Project?' Nell asked, as if reading my mind.

'Let's just say that my ideas are still in the infancy stage.' I pulled a face. 'I want a really good theme to pull the whole thing together, but I can't think of one.'

She helped herself to another of Astrid's biscuits. 'Perhaps try *not* thinking about it, that always works for me.'

'I haven't got time to *not* think about it. I bet Tasha Sandean has already created a Powerpoint presentation complete with soundtrack and animation,' I said huffily.

Nell opened her mouth as if about to say something and then snapped it shut again.

'Nell?' I demanded. 'What have you heard?'

'OK,' she said, relenting. 'This might be nothing, but Sally, the school secretary, bought some peanuts yesterday, she puts them in the garden for the squirrels, which I think is crazy. If I know anything about squirrels, it's that—'

'About Tasha?' I reminded her.

'Oh yes. Well, Sally said she heard Tasha on the phone talking to someone about hiring reindeer.'

I blinked at her. 'Real ones?'

Nell nodded. 'But she could have been enquiring on behalf of the school. For the Christmas party or something. Either way, a bit ambitious, I thought.'

I could see it now: fake snow, a Santa's grotto, elves, reindeer . . . it was brilliant.

'Right, that's me well and truly trumped,' I said, groaning. 'I'd vote for that myself.'

'Hey.' She patted my shoulder gingerly with her bad hand. 'Your ideas will be even better, I have every faith. But are you sure you won't fall behind with your candles because of this?'

'Sure,' I confirmed. 'In fact, I'm actually on top of all my orders.'

Nell looked impressed. 'Who even are you?'

I laughed. 'I keep telling you, I'm a changed woman. On track, on target. The days of flying by the seat of my pants are a thing of the past. Well, mostly,' I added, recalling that I'd run out of wicks and that an Etsy order had come in on Friday and I still hadn't fulfilled it.

Nell sighed. 'Shame. I really liked that Merry. Remember when you found those flights to Paris for fifteen pounds and we just went?'

I nodded. 'How can I forget? We were twenty-two, single and had no one to please but ourselves. Six hours later we were dunking croissants in *vin chaud* and drawling *ooh-la-la* suggestively at every handsome French boy that passed.'

'Oh well,' she said, topping up my hot chocolate, 'this is almost as good. Ooh, look and there's even a handsome man coming this way too.'

She nudged me with her elbow as a tall broad man approached the stall. Not that he was easy to miss – he was wearing a hi-vis jacket in neon yellow. His hair was hidden by a woolly hat, but as he walked by, he glanced at us briefly and I caught a glimpse of deep brown eyes and a hint of copper-coloured stubble.

'*Ooh la la*,' I murmured, making Nell snort with laughter. 'Shame he didn't want a date.'

'I mean it, you know, I'd never have gone to France on a whim if it hadn't been for you, telling me to just go for it,' she said. 'I've always loved how decisive you are.'

'Oh yeah,' I agreed drily. 'I can make decisions quick enough, but unfortunately they're not always the right ones. Anyway, we're respectable businesswomen these days, we can't just drop everything and flirt with hot-looking boys—'

'Why not? It sounds fun,' said a low voice.

Nell and I looked up to see a customer leaning nonchalantly on the counter. My breath caught in my throat; it was the man in the yellow jacket we'd just been gawping at. His eyes, even lovelier close up, were shining with amusement.

'I'm so sorry. We were talking about having dates,' I said hurriedly, tugging at my scarf to loosen it. The hot chocolate had made me feel very warm all of a sudden.

'With hot-looking boys, yeah, I heard,' he said with a laugh in his voice.

'Those were the days,' said Nell.

'I mean adventures,' I corrected. 'Having adventures, not dates.'

He raised his eyebrows. 'Even better.'

I found myself smiling back. He really was rather handsome; he had a nice smile and lovely white teeth.

'Although if you did want a date, I'm sure my friend will be only too pleased to oblige,' said Nell, taking my cup from me. 'Go on, oblige please.'

'Of course, sir,' I said, getting to my feet and ignoring her pun. 'We have Medjool dates and er, these other smaller ones.'

'Sukkhari,' Nell supplied for me.

'Exactly,' I said. 'It had been on the tip of my tongue. Plus, of course, we have a wide variety of . . . other stuff.'

I picked up the scoop and waved it vaguely over the dried fruit display. It was most peculiar, I'd been serving customers all day and knew what I was doing, and there wasn't one of Nell's innuendos about nuts I hadn't heard before but for some reason all the names of things had gone out of my head. Behind me I could hear Nell sniggering under her breath.

'That's very helpful, thank you,' the man said, pretending to nod earnestly. 'I'll take some sunflower seeds and pumpkin seeds please, a scoop of each. My sister sprinkles them on salads. For some weird reason.'

I tipped some of each into bags and set them on the counter.

'That looks nasty,' he said, indicating Nell's hand and then looking back at me. 'Did that happen during one of your adventures?'

'Er . . .' I blinked. He had such an intense gaze, as if he was giving me one hundred per cent of his attention. As if anything could happen around us and he wouldn't even notice. It was a few seconds before I realised I hadn't given him an answer.

'Yes,' Nell piped up. 'You should see the other guy.'

'Actually, she was wounded during a fight with a fish,' I corrected.

'Really?' He looked amused.

'I won,' Nell punched the air with her good hand. 'The fish got battered. Do you get it? Battered?'

'And when the chips were down, I stepped in to help on the stall,' I nudged Nell. 'Chips!'

We both laughed and the man stared at us, bemused.

'Ahem, anyway,' I said. 'Can I get you anything else?'

'Some almonds please, the flaked ones.'

'For your sister again?' Nell asked. 'Or someone else?'

I shot her an amused look; she was so transparent. She might as well have come out and asked him if he was married.

'No, these are for my dad, he has them on his porridge.'

'Very healthy,' I said.

He grinned. 'It would be if he didn't add a lake of honey and cream on top of it.'

'Now that is my sort of breakfast,' I said, putting the almonds next to his other purchases.

'Apologies for my friend,' said Nell butting in, 'it's very presumptuous of her to give her breakfast orders to men she's never met before.'

'Apologies for *my* friend,' I added, 'who thinks that every conversation with a stranger must be a prelude to a full-blown romance.'

'You two ladies are quite a double act,' he said, retrieving his wallet from an inside pocket of his coat. 'And actually, we might not have met, but I think I saw you both at the meeting about the Christmas tribute for Mr Dunford recently.'

Nell narrowed her eyes as if trying to place him. 'I don't remember seeing you there.'

A sudden image flashed into my head of a man in a yellow coat sneaking in.

'I do!' I said. 'You arrived a bit later and sat at the back.'

'Guilty,' he said sheepishly. 'I got held up at my dad's.'

'So you're local?' Nell looked surprised. 'I haven't seen you at the market before.'

He shook his head. 'I live in Bakewell at the moment. My dad lives in town though. I'm trying to encourage him to get out and about a bit more. He's become a bit of a recluse since my mum passed away. I thought if I came to the meeting, he'd come with me because he knew Mr Dunford. But it didn't work.' He gave a small sigh. 'Parents, eh?'

I smiled in response. 'Sorry about your mum.'

He scratched his forehead self-consciously. 'No, I'm sorry. Giving my life story to strangers instead of paying and getting out of your way.'

'Not at all,' said Nell. 'And we're no longer strangers. I'm Nell, obviously; this is Merry, and you are?'

'Cole,' he said with a grin. 'Pleased to meet you both. Now at the risk of holding you up even longer, I do actually want something for myself because I'm trying to eat less chocolate and I thought nuts would be a healthy alternative.'

'That sounds very virtuous,' I said, 'although Nell is the expert, being Wetherley's queen of nuts.'

Nell inclined her head graciously, accepting my compliment. 'You can't go wrong with an almond. It's your classic all-rounder . . .'

I took a step back – this was her specialist subject. While Cole listened to her spiel I studied him surreptitiously. Late thirties, rugged and tanned as if he spent a lot of time outside.

'Eat two or three Brazil nuts and you've got a whole day's worth of your selenium requirements,' she continued.

'Thank goodness I stopped by, I wasn't aware I even needed selenium – I must be dangerously low,' Cole said, deadpan. He caught my eye and we shared a conspiratorial smile.

'You'll thank me one day. Now, if you like chocolate, I'll give you a tip.' Nell leaned over the counter towards him as if she was about to impart a state secret. 'If you stuff a Medjool date with some peanut butter and dip the end in some very dark chocolate, you'll have a healthy version of a Snickers bar.'

'Good tip,' he said, tapping his nose. 'I think I'll go for the Brazils. Two hundred grams please. That should sort out my raging selenium deficiency.'

I got to the nut scoop before Nell.

'Good choice. These are my favourite kind of nut,' I said, popping some into a paper bag for him. 'Especially when they're covered in chocolate. Mind you, cover it in chocolate and I'll eat anything.'

'Really?' He raised a dark eyebrow.

Beside me I could tell Nell was doing her best not to laugh.

Cole patted his stomach. 'I'm trying to cut back. I've been living on junk food for too long.'

'You look OK to me,' I said automatically.

'Only OK?' His lips twitched in amusement as he pulled himself up tall. 'That settles it: I'm on a new mission to shape up. Next time you see me I'll be aiming for *good* at the very least.'

'Well . . .' I felt tongue-tied all of a sudden, wondering when that might be. 'It's always good to have a goal in life.'

'Thanks.' He chewed his lip as if holding in a smile. 'I'll bear that in mind.'

'Don't take any notice of my friend,' Nell said smoothly. 'She's newly single and has forgotten how to talk to the opposite sex.'

'Nell!' I gasped. 'Cole's not *the opposite sex*, he's a customer.'

He burst out laughing. 'Thank you for that. And now that you've just relieved me of my very last shred of self-esteem, I'll take my nuts and go.' He squeezed his eyes shut for a second. 'I can't believe I just said that.'

'Oh yes, hold onto those,' I said, smirking back at him. *Oh God.* I turned away from the counter, unable to believe how it was even possible to say so many embarrassing things in the space of two minutes.

Nell, still struggling to stop herself laughing, took his money and I was about to hand him his free sample of wasabi peas when a disturbance three stalls down drew my attention. There was a flurry of movement and a crash of something being knocked over, followed by shouts of 'Oi' and 'Watch out!' and an all too familiar yappy bark.

'*Scheisse!*' yelled a voice. 'Catch that dog!'

There was only one person in Wetherley who swore in German: Astrid. I dashed out from behind the stall just in time to see Otto bounding towards us.

'Otto, stop!' I cried, trying to grab his lead. But it was too late – Otto had already left the ground and was flying through the air towards Cole.

'Whoah!' Cole staggered backwards and miraculously caught the dog mid-air. He held him at arms' length and laughed. 'Well, hello little fella.'

Otto wriggled and licked his face.

'Sorry about that, it's my friend's dog!' I gasped, finally getting hold of the end of Otto's lead.

'It's OK, at least I won't need a wash later,' he said, putting the dog down and wiping the slobber from his cheek.

Otto looked up at us like butter wouldn't melt, his tail sweeping the floor vigorously.

'I'm so sorry!' Astrid arrived at the stall, breathless. 'One minute he was trotting along, then he must have spotted you, Merry, and darted off so fast that he jolted the lead from my hand.'

'Don't worry,' I said, handing the lead back to her. 'He only doled out a canine kiss.'

'Yes, no harm done and at least I've made an impression on someone today,' Cole teased, directing his smile at me. He stuffed his purchases into his coat pocket and bent down to ruffle Otto's ears. 'Nice to meet you, Otto. Goodbye, ladies. It's been . . . quite an experience.'

'Likewise,' I said, holding his gaze.

'Come again soon,' Nell added.

Astrid gave a low whistle as he strode off through the market. 'Who was that?'

'Cole,' said Nell, with a shrug. 'From Bakewell.'

'Well, Otto certainly took a shine to him,' said Astrid.

He wasn't the only one, I thought, still keeping an eye on Cole's movements. 'Hey, look, he's letting himself into the bank.'

We watched as Cole put a key into the lock and then, shoving the door with his shoulder, pushed his way in.

'Maybe he's the owner,' said Nell.

The building had been empty since the bank closed and apparently had changed hands a couple of times over the years. For the last twelve months, the lovely old façade had been hidden behind scaffolding. Daniel, whose shop was next door but one, had heard a rumour that it was to be converted into a residential property, but apart from various workmen appearing, no one had never seen anyone who looked like they might be in charge.

'Hopefully that scaffolding will be coming down soon,' Astrid frowned. 'I can see it from the window of my flat. It spoils the beauty of the square.'

'Go over and ask him, Merry!' Nell urged. 'Find out what his plans are.'

I chewed my lip; it was tempting. He was the first man to have caught my eye since Daniel.

'No,' I decided, suddenly feeling a flutter of nerves. 'Not today. When I know more about the Christmas plans, I'll go over then and try to persuade him to join in. And maybe his dad too.'

Nell gave a shiver of pleasure. 'I can't wait for Christmas. Only another month until the big tree goes up. Christmas trees are magical.'

'Oh *ja*,' Astrid agreed, her eyes sparkling. 'Choosing our tree was always such fun. It marked the start of Christmas in my family. We would go to the forest in Bavaria and pick out the best one. My brother wanted the tallest one, but I always looked for a perfect shape.'

'Ours was always fake,' said Nell, pulling a face. 'Hugely expensive, but fake. Mum didn't want the mess of needles falling on her Persian carpets. I still loved it, especially because I always got to put the angel on the top every year.'

'My family used to decorate ours with candles on Christmas Eve. The smell filled the house and the light was so beautiful.' Astrid began to sing a couple of lines of 'O Tannenbaum', and Nell joined in in English.

I smiled, enjoying their stories. Mum and I had never had much money for decorations, but she had always made sure we had a tree, however tiny, and that I had something to open on Christmas morning. We'd have breakfast in the bed we shared and watch a Christmas film while I opened my present. They'd been the best Christmases. There were family traditions at the foster homes I'd been in but none as special as those early years. I did have some fond memories of decorating the Christmas tree at the one children's home I'd spent the most time at. The staff had always done their best to make Christmas special, particularly for the children who wouldn't be seeing their relatives over the festive period. Children like me. The tree had always been the centre of all the Christmas activities. Most people had trees of some description, didn't they? It was a sort of universal symbol of Christmas, something which united us all.

I felt an arm through mine and I dragged myself from my thoughts.

'You look preoccupied,' said Nell, full of concern. 'Have we upset you talking about Christmas and family stuff?'

'No, I'm fine,' I promised, smiling at her. Something had just struck me about Christmas trees; I was pretty sure I'd just had my big breakthrough for the Christmas Project.

Astrid narrowed her eyes. 'I recognise that look. She's had the same expression since she was a girl. It means she is thinking.'

'Correct,' I smiled, pleased that she could still read me so easily. 'And I've just had a lightbulb moment, or should I say a fairy-light moment.' I turned to Nell. 'Will you be able to manage if I get off home now?'

'Sure.' She kissed my cheek. 'You've been brilliant.'

'You're welcome,' I said, scooping up my handbag. 'I've loved every moment.'

Nell caught me glancing over towards the bank and smirked. 'Some moments more than others.'

I refused to take the bait and gave Astrid a quick hug goodbye. There was no time to lose; I needed to get home and write my idea down while it was still fresh in my mind.

Chapter 8

Cole

A pile of post had built up behind the front door to the old bank. Cole had to force the door to get in. It was all junk mail. Anything important went straight to his accountant's address. Until he was settled into a home of his own, his accountant had agreed to help him out. For a man who was a true homebird by nature, he'd felt like a nomad for the past three years.

He stacked up the letters and leaflets and takeaway menus into a neat pile to take out with him when he left and then wandered around the ground floor. The air was cold and smelled of damp and dust, and Cole was grateful that he'd kept his site coat on.

Cole was generally a man to stick to a plan and buying an old bank which had been abandoned midway through renovation had not been in it. There were risks involved, namely taking on more than he could handle, especially as Orchard Gardens was taking up so much of his time and money.

But at the beginning of the year, Fred had suggested he come and take a look at it. He'd heard from Benny Dunford who'd heard on the grapevine that the company that owned it was having financial problems and needed to get rid of it as soon as possible. Cole was already stretched and had resisted at first, until Fred persuaded him to look at the figures. He'd seen the potential immediately, both in terms of what the property could look like after renovation and the profit it might make. In short it had been too tempting to walk away.

To his surprise, Hester and Paul asked if they could invest in it with him as silent partners. They'd been looking at options since Fred had given them a lump sum from the sale of the family home and wanted to do something different with their money. This way, they explained, they could share the risk with Cole and, if his predictions were right, share the profit too.

'On the understanding we don't have to be hands-on,' Paul had clarified. 'We don't want to tread on your toes.'

Hester had slipped an arm around her husband's waist. 'Absolutely. And besides, you two are both too stubborn to work together.'

'You mean decisive.' Cole and Paul's voices collided and the three of them laughed.

'You see,' said Paul with a grin. 'We're already think along the same lines.'

'So is it a deal?' Hester had asked.

'It's a deal,' Cole had said, touched that they trusted him with their money.

They'd quickly set up a separate business called R&S Developments and within a remarkably short time, the sale had gone through and the deeds transferred. Since then, Cole had unravelled a plethora of time-consuming issues. Previously, work had been carried out without the correct permission. And since it was a listed building, the work had had to be undone, new permission applied for and lots of reassurances given to the powers that be, that from now on, all remedial work would be exemplary.

It had been relatively smooth since then; just a couple of jobs to be done on the roof and then the scaffolding could come down. Once that was out of the way and the building was completely watertight, Cole would get cracking on the interior. His stomach lurched; he was working flat out at Orchard Gardens and he needed to make sure he didn't neglect this project as a result. There was no way he could live with himself if he let Paul and Hester down.

It was probably just as well he didn't have anyone waiting at home for him, he thought, returning to his earlier conversation with Josh. At least this way he could spend the rest of the weekend here; he made a decision to do that, getting the schedule of works up to date to make sure he stayed on top of things.

Downstairs wasn't too bad. Despite being used as a bank for goodness knows how many years, structurally it had remained largely untouched and it had some lovely Tudor features, which the council was at great pains to preserve. Dark oak beams ran across the width of the ceiling, which he reckoned Josh's head would probably only just about skim under unscathed; the thick oak floorboards were pitted, uneven and creaky, but obviously original, so they'd be staying. Downstairs had been partitioned into two main sections: the front, where he now stood, would have been where the bank's customers would have come in to do their banking, a counter service perhaps, a welcome desk, a place to fill in forms, etcetera. The stud walls had been ripped down, but apart from that nothing had been done.

Deep mullioned windows looked out onto the market. He looked through the dirty glass now, wiping it clean with the sleeve of his coat. From here he could just make out the two women on the nut stall. A smile hovered at his lips; he'd enjoyed the conversation with them, they were clearly good friends who had fun together.

What was it the blonde one had said: *he's not the opposite sex, he's a customer*! He laughed to himself again and pulled the free sample bag out of his pocket, trying to remember what it was. He opened the bag and sniffed. Still no idea. They looked like baked peas. He'd never had a baked pea before, but he took a handful and tipped them straight into his mouth anyway.

He'd crunched them a couple of times before the flavour hit the back of his nose.

JEEZ. What the hell was that? He spat the chewed-up pieces out into his hand but the damage had been done. His mouth was on fire and his nose was burning. Why hadn't he brought a drink with him? He bolted up the stairs to the toilet, which bizarrely had a Yale lock on the outside. Keeping his foot wedged in the door to avoid getting locked in, he turned on the tap over the hand basin and scooped water into his mouth. Ugh. He wouldn't be trying those again. No wonder they were free, they were horrific. At least his sinuses would be clear for the next decade.

He blinked away tears from his watering eyes and sniffed. There was no tissue to blow his nose or wipe his eyes. There was a mirror though and he caught sight of himself and laughed. He looked exactly like someone who'd had a red-hot poker stuck up his nose. What an idiot.

He walked out of the bathroom and into the front part of the building. This must have been a meeting room in the past. The walls were wood-panelled and the ceilings ornately plastered. Curved windows overlooked the street below. His eyes strayed automatically to Nell's Nuts again.

The one with the bandaged hand was still there but the blonde one had gone. He felt disappointed for some reason and turned his back on the window.

The proportions of the room were great. It would be a stunning living room; it wouldn't take much to tart up the wooden floorboards, add some decent lighting, flat-screen TV on the wall and a couple of distressed leather sofas, perhaps a recliner for watching films? It would be a cracking room. The plan was to keep the building as an investment and rent it out. If he hadn't had the children to consider, he might even have wanted to live here himself. He headed back out into the corridor and into the space which would become the large kitchen diner. When he came back tomorrow he'd measure up for a new kitchen. He'd get a company to come in and do it: plumbing, electrics, appliances, the works. Modern or traditional? Either would probably work . . . His train of thought was interrupted by his phone buzzing.

It was Harley FaceTiming him.

'Hey!' Cole grinned at his boy, still in his pyjamas, thick red hair sticking up in tufts. 'How are you?'

'Good thanks, but erm, Dad?' Harley's brow furrowed and he brought the screen closer to his face. 'Are you crying?'

Cole laughed and pulled the bag of peas out of his pocket. 'Just been pranked, I think. I've been given a free sample of Devil's food. Imagine swallowing strong mustard and horseradish and multiply it by ten. My eyes were watering like mad and I think I've destroyed the lining of my nose.'

'Oh Dad, you plonker, they're wasabi peas!' Harley crowed, clearly enjoying his dad's misfortune. 'They have them here at the sushi place we go to. It's all right if you just have a tiny bit.'

Cole smiled ruefully; every part of that sentence empha-sised the distance between them. Harley was doing things, going places, eating at Japanese restaurants, for heaven's sake, and his dad wasn't part of it.

'You've learned some stuff since you've been in Canada!' he said lightly. 'Where's the boy who ordered chicken nuggets and chips wherever we went?'

'Da-ad,' Harley said with a groan. 'That was when I was just a kid. I eat most things now. I even had a green smoothie yesterday.'

'You're right, you are growing up, you're a braver man than me,' he replied, pulling a funny face. 'What's wrong with orange squash?'

Harley rolled his eyes. He was still in bed and wearing an old Foo Fighters T-shirt.

'Hey, is that my T-shirt?'

Harley gave a snort of laughter and pulled the covers up to hide it. 'Might be.'

Cole grinned. 'I wondered where that had gone.'

'I just . . .' Harley's voice was gruff. 'I wanted something of yours to bring with me. Do you mind?'

This was the closest his son had come to admitting that he missed him, and the words were like balm to Cole's ragged heart. 'Not at all. It suits you.'

He exhaled slowly, allowing his features to rearrange themselves into something less melancholy. The way his children had adapted to new circumstances amazed him. According to WhatsApp messages from Lydia, they'd made friends, settled into school and were loving life in Whistler. Cole was glad about all of that, but he was even more glad that he hadn't been forgotten.

'Anyway,' he cleared his throat, aware that his eyes were beginning to sting again and this time not from wasabi. 'It's Saturday, what have you got planned for the day?'

'That's why I called.' Harley's eyes gleamed. 'I'll show you.'

He shifted across to pull on a cord at the side of the window. As the blind lifted all that Cole could see was a bright white light.

'Is that snow?' Cole asked.

'Yup. Look.' Harley got out of bed and held up the phone.

'I'm meeting my friends and we're going snowboarding. I wish . . .' Harley faltered and his cheeks went pink. 'I wish you were here.'

'Yeah, me too, mate,' he replied softly.

'Snow! It's snowing! Harley, have you looked outside!' Freya squealed in the background.

Harley pulled a face at Cole. 'Duh, I know,' he said to his sister. 'I'm talking to Dad.'

'DAD!' she squealed.

A blur of pink flashed in front of the screen as his daughter divebombed onto Harley's bed.

'OW! That was my leg!' Harley howled. 'Get off.'

Undaunted by her brother's less than effusive welcome, Freya pushed her face into view.

'Daddy, the mountains are all covered in snow and Mummy says she's taking me and River sledging later.'

His heart melted; bloody hell, that little face peeping out of the hood of her unicorn onesie. He wished he could reach out and hug her, hug both of them. 'That sounds amazing, darling.'

'River is her boyfriend!' Harley yelled over the top of her head. 'Kissy kissy.'

'So immature,' said Freya, primly.

'You need to get out my room now, frog-face.' Harley pushed his sister off his bed.

'Harley,' Cole warned.

'Just one more amazing thing, Dad,' she forced herself back in front of the camera. 'We're going to this brilliant place for Christmas and there's a hot tub outside where you can look up at the stars and there's a ski lift right at the end of the garden and a barbecue hut with fairy lights.'

'For Christmas?' Cole froze. Lydia and the kids were supposed to be flying back to the UK. Perhaps Freya was getting muddled? 'Are you sure?'

'Um . . .' Freya chewed her lip.

'Freya Robinson!' Lydia barked from somewhere in the apartment. 'What did we say just five minutes ago?'

'Uh oh,' Harley muttered. 'You're in massive trouble now.'

The little girl shrank back from the screen, her eyes wide. 'Sorry.'

'Harley, tell me,' Cole said, trying to keep the urgency from his voice. 'What brilliant place?'

'Give me the phone,' said Lydia. 'One second, Cole.'

Then all Cole could see was a whirl of shapes while presumably, Lydia took Harley's phone and moved into another room. He swore under his breath. He'd booked two weeks off work over the Christmas period so he'd be able to spend every minute with the kids.

'Sorry about that,' said Lydia, tucking a strand of her hair behind her ear. She was wearing a pale blue top which suited her fair colouring and her hair was piled up loosely in a bun. She was make-up free and looked no different from when he'd first met her fifteen years ago.

'So when were you planning on telling me?' Cole demanded.

'I was going to speak to you about it, today actually,' she said calmly. 'But obviously Freya is too excited to wait as I asked her to.'

'I thought you were flying back for Christmas?'

She rubbed her slender neck. 'I never actually promised.'

'You implied!' he spluttered. 'Lydia, this is not OK. You have no idea how awful it is getting into bed at night, knowing that your kids are out of reach, knowing that it'll be weeks before you see them.'

'You've been great all through this,' Lydia said. 'I do know that. And you're entitled to be disappointed. This is all my fault, but when I put in for some annual leave over Christmas, I was denied the full amount. I've literally only got four days off and that's over Christmas itself. And then this mini-break came up and with flights back to the UK in December being so expensive, it makes sense to stay here.'

'I'll pay for the flights,' he said, kicking himself that he hadn't thought of that before. 'Just come for a few days.'

She cast her eyes down; he knew then that it wasn't about the money. She'd made her mind up. He could stand his ground, demand that he be allowed access to Freya and Harley over Christmas as he had in previous years. He sighed inwardly; he'd worked so hard to maintain a good relationship with Lydia. Was this worth arguing over when they were so far away from each other?

'Cole,' she said quietly, 'this will be our only Christmas in Canada and the kids are excited about it.'

'I see,' he said, swallowing his disappointment. 'So tell me about it then.'

'It's my boss who organised it.' She glanced warily at him, as if not sure of his reaction. 'There'll be another couple of staff and their kids, all people from outside the area like us. He's rented a big house and offered us one of the rooms. Freya and Harley have already made friends with Steve's kids.'

'Steve?' he asked casually.

'My boss, and if you were wondering, there's nothing going on between us.'

'I guess I could fly to you?' he suggested. 'I haven't got any other plans.'

'I'm sorry but that wouldn't work,' said Lydia firmly. She looked away and then back at him. 'The offer is for me and the kids, one room. I couldn't . . . I wouldn't . . .'

'I'm gutted not to be seeing them,' Cole admitted. 'I used to love our Christmases together, the four of us.'

Being woken up early by two excited children, creeping downstairs to see if Santa had been . . . special times. Noisy, messy, a house full of warmth and laughter and love. None of the presents under the tree could compete with being at home for Christmas, he'd had everything he could wish for.

They looked at each other for a long moment and he wondered if she was remembering the same thing.

'Cole,' Lydia softened her tone. 'Let's not fight about this. The kids have some time off school in February. Why don't you fly over then? I'll get you a family room in the hotel and they can stay with you. They'd love that and I know you'll love it too.'

'Let me speak to them,' he said, not quite willing to give in yet. 'Let me ask them if they'd prefer to come home for Christmas and see me and Granddad and Auntie Hester and Uncle Paul.'

Lydia looked at him for a long moment and gave him a sad smile. 'Oh, Cole.'

He knew he couldn't do that to them. He wouldn't make them choose. A luxury mountain lodge in the snow versus listening to Granddad Fred snore all the way through whatever film they ended up watching after Christmas lunch.

No, he'd be the bigger person here. There'd be years of British Christmases for his kids, but only one Canadian one.

'OK, fine,' said Cole, 'February it is, but please can we firm up the dates this week, so I know it's definitely happening?'

'MUM!' Harley yelled from behind a closed door. 'I need my phone back.'

'Sure. Thanks, Cole.' Lydia sighed and smiled at him. 'I'd better go. Let's speak soon.'

After she ended the call, he shoved his phone back in his pocket and let out a long tense breath. Well, that had put the dampener on his weekend. He'd been so looking forward to getting his kids back at Christmas. Christmas was all about doing stuff for them and with them. It was going to be pretty dire spending it alone. No tracking Santa's journey across the globe with Freya, no watching them opening their presents; Christmas afternoon wouldn't be spent poring over instruction manuals and hunting for the correct batteries, or watching cheesy films . . .

He headed back downstairs and prepared to lock up and leave. He'd just have to keep busy over the festive season, he thought, and maybe then he wouldn't notice just how miserable he was.

Yes, that was a plan. This year, Christmas was cancelled.

Chapter 9

Merry

'You've gone pale,' said Nell.

'That's because I'm terrified,' I muttered, running a hand through my hair. 'What was I thinking? I'm rubbish at public speaking.'

It was the night of the follow-up community meeting and we were in the Buttermarket wating for Nigel to arrive. I'd spent a lot of time working on my idea over the last week, modifying it and adding details to it and, for someone who hadn't wanted to get involved, I was quite pleased with what I'd come up with.

Despite my preparations, I was a bag of nerves. Outside the wind howled and rain lashed against the windows. I hoped that the awful weather would mean that fewer people would turn up for the meeting. The smaller the audience the better as far as I was concerned. So far there were about ten of us, including Tasha and Daniel sitting together in the front row on the other side of the room from Nell and me.

I watched them chatting easily to each other. Tasha put her hand over her mouth and laughed. I wondered what Daniel had said. Perhaps he'd just told her that he was forty in December and reminded her about that kiss under the mistletoe. I did a mental check to make sure mistletoe didn't feature anywhere in my idea. It didn't.

'I can feel your leg trembling.' Nell delved into her bag and produced a biscuit. 'Eat this for energy.'

I bit into it, hoping it wouldn't make me feel even more sick. 'Distract me,' I said. 'Talk to me about something nice.'

'Ooh,' her eyes sparkled. 'I know just the thing. Max is coming for the whole of Christmas!'

Nell adored her stepson and I knew this was a big thing for her. She and Olek normally only got to see him for one day and night. She told me that she was planning Christmas Eve movies in matching Christmas pyjamas and she was going to do stockings for both Max and Olek even though Olek was forty-five and Max was thirteen. Olek's parents, whom she loved dearly, would be there too. The house would be full to bursting with people and Christmas bonhomie.

'And you're welcome too, obviously.'

'Thanks,' I mumbled, shifting my legs to the side to let more people into our row.

'That's what I like to see,' Nell said drily. 'Plenty of enthu-siasm. Stop turning round, it'll only make you clammy.'

'I'm looking to see if Cole is here,' I explained. 'The one from the market. But he's not.'

Nell smirked. 'Ha! I knew you fancied him. This is very good news. You have my blessing in that department – he was very cute.'

I gave her a stern look. 'I want to ask him when the scaffolding is coming down, that's all.'

I wasn't ready to start dating again, it wouldn't be fair on any new man; I wasn't totally sure I'd got over Daniel yet.

As if I'd conjured him up, my phone buzzed with a text message from the man himself.

Good luck tonight, I know you'll be brilliant.

Warmth flooded through me, that was so sweet of him.

'Look.' I showed Nell the screen. 'He still cares.'

'Of course he cares,' she said briskly. 'He's being supportive, that's what friends do.'

I nodded and said nothing, but what if it was more than that? Maybe he was having second thoughts? If he was, well . . . I felt a leap of joy. I missed being part of a couple; I loved Holly Cottage, but I'd love it even more if I had someone to share it with. Was there still a chance for us? My eyes sought him out across the room and found him looking straight at me. He was wearing the blue jumper I'd bought him for his birthday under his down jacket. I'd always liked him in that jumper. We both smiled as I mouthed my thanks and he gave me a thumbs up in return. I wasn't imagining it, there was definitely something still there between us.

The door banged open at that moment and a man appeared in a rain mac with his hood pulled up, a long bedraggled beard poking out.

'Sorry I'm late, everyone.' Nigel shook the raindrops off his coat and then spotting the refreshments, tiptoed towards them like a villain in a pantomime and poured himself a drink.

'Let's start,' said Jim, calling us all to order. 'Just to recap for any newcomers, Benny set aside some money in his will to help celebrate Christmas in Wetherley this year. So without further ado, I'd like to invite Merry Shaw to present her ideas for the project.'

Pam started to clap, everyone else followed suit and all eyes were on me. My heart began to thud; I'd assumed there'd be more of a preamble than that but suddenly I was in the spotlight.

'Go on.' Nell nudged my arm. 'That's you. Good luck!'

I stood and walked to the front of the room. At least going first meant that I could relax and listen to the other two without panicking that mine would be the worst.

Pam gave me a twinkly smile. 'The floor is yours, love.'

'Good evening everyone. For those of you who don't know me, I'm Merry Shaw, local business owner of the Merry and Bright candle company.'

Out of the corner of my eye I saw Nell beaming proudly.

'I've never done anything like this before, so I wasn't sure whether to bring anything to show you. But I haven't, so . . . you'll have to use your imaginations.' I was shaking. Hopefully no one would be able to tell from where they were sitting.

'I started my planning with Benny. If he could choose his own tribute, what would it be? We know that getting the community together was very important to him, so I think he'd like something that would reach out to every resident of Wetherley.'

Somebody started a round of applause, which was encouraging, even though no one else joined in and it quickly fizzled out.

'And then of course, there's the annual Christmas tree in the market square, which is a very special part of Benny's legacy to Wetherley.'

'Hear, hear,' said a lady in a purple bobble hat. 'My kiddies still come back to see the tree and they're in their twenties now.'

'Every family, every person, every single part of the community celebrates Christmas in their own way. Not every culture celebrates with a Christmas tree but many of us do. We all have our little traditions passed down through the years; from what sort of tree we prefer, be it tall and skinny, or short and plump, when we put it up and what we decorate it with.'

To the side of me, Jim coughed and tapped his watch. I nodded, understanding that I needed to speed it up.

'I propose that we completely fill Wetherley market square with Christmas trees. From rough calculations I think we can squeeze fifty trees in. My plan is that we'll invite community groups to put their name down for a tree and decorate it however they wish. From the Women's Institute to the children's playgroups, to the Rosebridge retirement complex to the yoga club, everyone is welcome to a tree. It will be a celebration of our town, of all the cultures and traditions and personalities that make Wetherley so special. The market square will not only be brimming with Christmas spirit, but community spirit too and I think Benny would love that. The climax of the festivities will be on Christmas Eve, as we all gather to mingle, view each other's trees and we, the committee, will provide mulled wine and traditional Christmas snacks. Thank you.'

The applause was so enthusiastic that I just stood there, frozen like the proverbial rabbit.

'Goodness!' I swallowed. 'Thank you. Again.'

I raised my hand in a little wave and was about to sit back down when Jim spoke up.

'Thank you, Merry. Hold on there a minute, while we take questions from the floor.'

I swallowed. This was potentially even more nerve-wracking.

'What if more than fifty people or groups want a tree?' asked Nigel, who while I was speaking had been perched on the edge of his seat, listening to every word.

'We'll have a list for people to sign up by the first of December. Which is of course also the day that the town's Christmas lights are switched on. If there are only a touch over fifty, I'm sure we can squeeze them in. Failing that we draw straws.'

He nodded. 'Fair enough. Good plan.'

'Thank you, Nigel, I appreciate that.' That was rather generous of him considering in theory we were in competition. Perhaps like me he didn't want to win either. Although I had to admit, seeing all the smiles on people's faces was giving me a real boost.

The young woman who owned the hairdressers in the main street put up her hand. 'Can businesses like my salon have a tree?'

'I don't see why not,' I said with a shrug. 'But we'd want to ensure there were still enough trees for the community, so maybe we say no more than ten trees for businesses. First come first served?'

'Good idea,' called out the landlady of the Bristly Badger pub. 'And you can put us down for supplying hot mulled wine on the night. No charge.'

'That would be great!' I'd been wondering about the logistics of that, not to mention the cost.

'Excellent.' Jim stood up. 'If there's no more questions, we can . . . Oh, I see a hand up.'

It was Tasha; my heart sank. I hoped she hadn't spotted something glaringly obviously wrong with my idea.

'It's a very sweet idea. But on the subject of cost,' she said, with a wince. 'Fifty Christmas trees, maybe more, will be very expensive. Can we afford it?'

I felt a prickle of annoyance at being challenged by her, but luckily I had a good answer.

'I've arranged a cut-price deal with a Christmas-tree farm and I got their number from Wetherley's normal Christmas-tree seller. If we place a bulk order by the first of December, the farmer will deliver for free and collect again afterwards so that the trees can be recycled. The cost falls within the amount kindly bequeathed to us by Benny. But, if this was something we wanted to consider doing again, then we could always start a fund-raiser for it.'

Tasha gave a satisfied nod. I half expected her to say 'no further questions, your honour'.

'Thank you, a very thorough answer,' she said, sitting down.

Next to her, Daniel looked impressed. I scurried back to my seat feeling quite pleased with myself. Nell started clapping really, really loudly until everyone else was forced to join in.

'Thank you, Merry,' said Jim briskly. 'Next can I invite Tasha Sandean to present to us.'

Tasha strode to the front, tapping her folder against her other hand. She was immaculately dressed again, tonight in a caramel-coloured wool coat and high-heeled boots. I had to admit it, she did command the room well.

'I believe that children are at the heart of Christmas,' Tasha said. 'And at the heart of the community. And we know community was at the heart of Mr Dunford.'

'She copied that off you,' Nell murmured. 'She doesn't know him from Adam.'

I shushed her, not really minding what happened next. I was just glad to have got my bit over with. Tasha could take over from here as far as I was concerned. I sat back and waited to be wowed by her ideas.

'Santa's grotto might not be a new idea, but to my knowledge it hasn't been done in Wetherley for a while and it is a firm favourite with families. We can run daily sessions in the week running up to Christmas Eve, and due to Benny's kind bequest, gifts for the children will be completely free, ensuring that no child need miss out because parents and carers are on a low income.'

I had a sudden flashback to one Christmas when my mum had taken me to a shopping mall. A snowy lodge had been built in front of McDonalds and there was a long queue of overexcited children waiting to see Santa. I asked Mum if we could join the line but she'd said we didn't have time. I was too young to understand that an audience with Santa cost money that she didn't have. But after dinner that night, she'd helped me to write my first letter to Santa and the next morning we posted it in the red letter box on the corner of the street. I'll never forget the day I got a reply from the North Pole. I'd been so excited I hadn't been able to sleep for days and it had been far more magical than a rushed conversation with a sweaty Santa wearing a nylon wig and beard.

I felt my eyes prickle with tears at the memory of a young mum doing her best for her daughter.

'That is a nice idea,' I murmured.

'Only if you've got kids,' Nell pointed out. 'What about the elderly? Yours was much more inclusive.'

'On Christmas Eve itself, I suggest that we sing carols as usual,' said Tasha.

I frowned. 'Damn, I forgot about the tradition of carol singing, that'll count against me.'

'I thought you didn't want to win.' Nell raised a quizzical eyebrow.

'Yes, well,' I said sheepishly. 'Turns out I don't want to lose either.'

'This year led by the Wetherley Primary School Choir,' Tasha continued. 'Dressed in Victorian clothing, carrying lanterns to give an extra traditional feel to the event. And that concludes my proposal. It is simple, but I believe the best ideas often are, and if executed well, like Benny himself would have done, it will be a triumph. Thank you. Any questions?'

Nell's hand shot up. 'Will Santa's grotto have any real reindeer?'

Tasha blinked uncertainly before she rallied. 'I did look into it, but the rules and regulations were quite prohibitive. So no, I'm afraid.'

There were a few mutters of disappointment around the room.

'I hope you haven't just landed the school secretary into a pile of bother,' I whispered.

Nell shrugged. 'I could have just asked her the question innocently, nothing to do with loose-lipped Sally at all.'

The pub landlady put her hand up. 'What if you haven't got kids? Like me. What's in it for us?'

Tasha smiled. 'We were all children once; this scheme gives us a chance to see Christmas through a child's eyes, remember how we felt, rekindle the Christmas magic.'

'Hmm,' the pub landlady grunted.

There appeared to be no more questions, so I started off a round of applause and everyone else joined in as Tasha took her seat. Daniel was clapping but if I had to put money on it, I'd say he clapped harder for me. I looked at my watch and suppressed a yawn. Could I sneak out, I wondered?

'You can't go yet,' Nell whispered, reading my mind. 'We've got to listen to Nigel and then vote.'

'I suppose you're right,' I said with a sigh.

'Last but certainly not least, Nigel Taylor, let's hear your proposal please.' Jim waved an arm to the spot vacated by Tasha.

Nigel came up to the front of room. He stood feet wide apart and rubbed his hands together.

'Thanks, Jim. First of all, apologies for my late arrival. My little Nipper got scared when some inconsiderate shit-fer-brains neighbours, who shall remain nameless, let off a load of firecrackers. It took me and my wife two hours to find him. He was shivering with fear and at some point he had taken a dive in some fox poo.'

'Poor kid,' I whispered.

Nell stifled a giggle. 'Nipper is his Jack Russell. Fox poo was probably an improvement. I didn't think dogs could have BO until I met Nipper. And I say that as a huge lover of dogs.'

'Anyway, all's well that ends well,' Nigel concluded. 'Now. On to my idea for Benny's tribute. I've taken my inspiration from Brooklyn in New York and added my own special twist.' He beamed proudly. 'Imagine if people came from far and wide just to see the decorations in Wetherley Square, just like they do in Dyker Heights in Brooklyn. We'd be a local a tourist attraction.'

Nigel had me at *tourist attraction*. How cool would that be if Benny's Christmas decorations were so popular that visitors came to Wetherley especially to see them. Imagine the effect on trade. It was a brilliant idea.

Nell leaned into me. 'Ugh. If he says he wants to fill the market square with inflatable Santas, kill me now.'

I shushed her and tuned back in to Nigel.

'So, my big idea is . . .' he paused for dramatic effect. 'Inflatables.'

He didn't have much more to say after that, other than to describe how 'brill' Wetherley would look if the market square was full of large air-filled Christmassy Santas, reindeer, trees and snowmen.

'Now what?' I said to Nell, watching as Pam and Jim exchanged hurried whispers and head shakes.

'We vote, I guess,' she replied.

My stomach did a loop-the-loop. 'You will choose mine, won't you, so I get at least one vote?'

'Not sure,' Nell teased. 'Let's think, do I want a forest of Christmas trees or an eight-foot Santa baring his arse?'

'OK,' said Jim clapping his hands together. 'Let's vote.'

Chapter 10

Merry

'Well, folks . . .' Pam tapped her pen on a sheet of paper two minutes later. 'Looks like we have a clear winner. Congratulations, Merry, you will be in charge of organising this year's Christmas celebrations!'

'Me?' I spluttered. 'Shit the bed.'

'Woohoo!' Nell cried, leading the applause.

'Um, wow. Thanks everyone!' I gave a weird two-handed wave. 'I think.'

'Well done.' Nell gave me a hug. 'I'm really proud of you. Does this mean we'll be renaming it the Merry Christmas Project?'

'It looks like it.' I stared at her as the reality of what had just happened started to sink in. 'Christmas for me this year was going to be a non-event. How on earth have I ended up organising Wetherley's *main* event?'

Nell shrugged. 'I don't know, Grinch, but you're wanted.'

Pam was beckoning me up to the front. 'Up you come, love. You'll need to set the date for the next meeting.'

I dashed to the front and addressed the crowd again. 'I'm flattered, really flattered. And I think that there are elements of Tasha's and Nigel's schemes that will work with mine, so really we're all winners.'

'And don't forget you'll have to find someone to switch the Christmas lights on this year,' Jim reminded me.

I groaned inwardly; this was the gift that kept on giving. 'Of course,' I found myself saying, 'if anyone has any suggestions, let me know.'

Somehow I managed to come up with a date for a follow-up meeting and secured the help of several others to get Benny's tribute onto the next stage before dropping back into my seat, feeling shell-shocked. Pam called the meeting to a close and soon people were pulling on coats and wrapping scarves around necks and saying their goodbyes.

'I need a drink,' I said as Nell pulled me to my feet. 'And don't suggest mulled wine, or I won't be responsible for my actions.'

'OK,' said Nell meekly. 'How about eggnog?'

I had my hands around Nell's neck pretending to throttle her when I heard my name being called.

I whirled round to come face to face with Daniel.

'Hey.' His eyes crinkled with warmth. 'I'm not interrupting anything, am I?'

'Just trying to convince Scrooge here that Christmas is not all bad,' said Nell.

Daniel blushed. He knew, because I'd mentioned it about three thousand times, that I'd been looking forward to Christmas this year because I'd be spending it with him.

'You put on a good show of being up for it,' he said. 'You did really well tonight.'

'Thanks,' I said, outwardly calm. Inwardly, my resident butterflies were high-fiving each other left, right and centre.

'Got to go. See you soon, O Queen of Christmas.' Nell gave me a swift kiss, adding in a whisper, 'Play it cool, I beg you.'

'I'll be as cool as Frosty the snowman,' I whispered back, pulling her in for a hug.

'Listen,' Daniel said, when Nell had gone. 'I was thinking, could we get together one day soon for a chat over a coffee?'

He shifted from foot to foot, looking as nervous as I felt.

'OK,' I replied, trying to act nonchalantly when it was all I could do not throw my arms around his neck and kiss him.

'Not now,' he said looking over my shoulder, 'I've got to shoot off, but one day soon?'

'Why not visit me at Holly Cottage?' I suggested. He hadn't seen it yet and it would be a good opportunity to show him how my kitchen-table business was flourishing.

He nodded. 'I'd like that.'

We held eye contact and I could feel the heat in my face. There was a piece of fluff on the front of his jacket. As I reached up to brush it away, I heard him take in a breath.

'Merry, I—'

'Hey, congratulations!' Tasha appeared at Daniel's side and startled us both. He took a step back to bring her into the conversation. 'I think it's a lovely idea. Especially with the old-fashioned lamp posts around the market square; it'll look like Narnia.'

'Oh. Thank you,' I said, taken aback. That was very magnanimous of her. 'I thought yours was very good too.'

'I think I blew it by focusing on the kids.' She pulled a comical face, making me smile. 'Occupational hazard.' Then she pressed a hand to her forehead. 'Oh no! What a wally. Me and my big mouth, I've already mentioned it to Mrs Flowers, who's in charge of the choir. It wouldn't surprise me if she's already told the kids, who'll have told their parents. They'll be so disappointed and my name will be mud.'

'I don't know,' said Daniel. 'Maybe if you're expecting parents to produce Victorian outfits, they might be grateful it's not happening.'

She shook her head. 'We've got costumes left over from a production of *Oliver*. I'd worked it all out.'

'Don't worry, I'm sure we can accommodate the school choir,' I said, secretly quite enjoying wielding my newfound power. 'I'll add it to the agenda for the next meeting.'

I slid my eyes to Daniel to make sure he'd registered how organised I was these days and was rewarded with a warm smile.

'Really? You're a lifesaver,' Tasha sighed with relief. 'You wouldn't believe the politics involved in making sure everyone's little darling gets the part they deserve in our various Christmas performances. I mean, bless them, they're all gorgeous but I'm sure if I had children, which I don't plan to, I wouldn't blithely assume I'd spawned the next Chris Hemsworth or Jennifer Lawrence.'

Daniel laughed. 'I do believe it! I remember Mum trying to persuade Tom's form teacher that he should be allowed to be Angel Gabriel and it was sexist to always give the part to girls.'

'Happens all the time,' said Tasha.

I smiled along with the conversation, but all I could focus on was the fact that Tasha had said she didn't want children.

'Right, Merry,' she turned her attention back to me, 'as a thank you, I insist that you come to our Christmas Fair at school on December the eighth.'

'Thanks but I don't think so,' I said quickly. I'd had a bad experience as a child at a school Christmas event and had no wish to revisit it.

'But you must,' Tasha insisted. 'We're inviting lots of small businesses to sell their goods. I'll make sure you get a stall. I haven't seen your candles but I'm sure they'd be very popular as gifts for Christmas. Am I right?'

'Yes,' I admitted reluctantly. 'But—'

'Great!' Tasha looked very pleased with herself. 'Daniel will be there too, won't you?'

He nodded. 'Wouldn't miss it for the world. I'm running the raffle.'

'Two Robinson brothers, what a treat,' Tasha teased. 'And Merry's candles too. You'll love it. It's the perfect start to the Christmas season.'

I took a deep breath as the memory popped into my head, as clear as if it had been yesterday. I must have been around seven. At school the reading corner had been decorated with signs saying 'North Pole This Way'. Inside, on an armchair covered with a red blanket, sat Santa. We all took turns to sit on his knee and receive a present from his sack . . . No sooner had I clambered onto his lap, than there was a power cut and we were plunged into darkness. Santa cuddled me perfectly kindly and told me not to panic. However, there hadn't been many men in my young life and his grip took me by surprise so much so that I wet myself. Luckily he saw the funny side and made sure I still got my present, but I was mortified and I would never sit on Santa's lap again.

'Daniel, what's the name of the lady who offered to make mulled wine?' Tasha smiled at him sweetly, completely changing the subject.

'Sadie,' he supplied. 'From the Bristly Badger.'

'Excuse me one second, I need to have a quick word with her,' she said, and then called her name across the room: 'Sadie!'

★

It was another fifteen minutes before I left the Buttermarket. I'd stayed behind with Pam and Jim to clear up the refreshments and tidy the chairs away. And then just as I was ready to go, Pam told me that she and Jim were going away for three weeks to Lanzarote to scatter Benny's ashes on his favourite beach. Finally, I wished them good night and left them to lock up. I stepped outside into the darkness and crossed the market square. The night air was chilly after the fug of the room, so I tugged the zip of my coat right up to my chin and tucked my hands in my pockets. I'd parked in a side street near Astrid's flat which wasn't too far away, but I walked quickly to keep myself warm.

A light was on in Good Earth, Daniel's greengrocer's. I frowned; that was odd. When he'd left the meeting a while ago, he'd said he was heading home, and he never normally left lights on in the shop overnight. A sudden movement caught my eye and my skin prickled; someone was inside. Was there a burglary in progress? I reached into my handbag for my phone, ready to call for help and crossed over to the other side of the pavement to get a closer look.

I stopped suddenly in disbelief, my heart racing. I wasn't looking at one person, I was looking at two. A man and a woman totally entwined in each other, kissing passionately. The woman in a caramel wool coat, her long dark hair a stark contrast to his pale blond head. His hands cupping her face, his body pressing against hers, her arms wrapped around his neck.

The mistletoe might have been missing, but Daniel had finally got his kiss from Tasha.

My throat burned with the effort of trying not to cry. I squeezed my eyes shut, desperate not to be seen, even more desperate not to watch their intimate moment. Too late for that, I thought miserably; the image of them kissing would be burned into my memory for ever. I turned away, stumbling over the cobbles; I just wanted to get home and cry my tears in private.

Now I knew why he wanted to see me. Not to tell me he still had feelings for me, but to confirm he definitely didn't.

So that was it. Over. There was no point in my holding onto the notion of us getting back together. Daniel had officially moved on. And it was about time I did too.

Chapter 11

Cole

Cole was woken up by a terrible noise. His first thought was that it had to be a woodpecker. His dad would know, he thought with wry amusement, seeing as he was now into birdwatching. If it was a woodpecker, it was a bloody loud one; it sounded like it was perched on his head, with its beak rat-a-tat-tatting into Cole's brain. He attempted to open his eyes and lift his head off the pillow but gave up. It was all coming back to him now; he'd drunk copious amounts of red wine with Hester last night.

Oh crap, so not a woodpecker then, a hangover. He opened his eyes again, grateful for the blackout blinds at the annexe windows and forced himself to sit up. That bloody noise was still going, rattling his brain. It served him right. He'd been drinking far too much recently; he was normally a one or two pints on a Friday and Saturday man. This was not good, he really needed to get a grip.

With sudden comprehension, he reached for his phone beside his bed, turned off the alarm and the noise stopped.. Now all he could hear was the wind battering the roof and whipping up the fallen leaves.

It had been one hell of a stormy night. The fence between Hester's house and the next-door neighbour had blown down and cartwheeled down the garden. The elderly lady who lived there had been quite anxious about it, so he and Paul had gone out in the wind and rain with only a head torch and the security light to guide them to retrieve the damaged pieces of wood. Wrestling against the wind to carry the panels and store them safely along the side of the house had exhausted both of them. Paul had gone up for a bath and when Cole had tried to say goodnight, Hester had forced him to sit with her in the living room.

'You can't sulk over there for ever,' she had said, sounding so much like their mum that he felt a lump form in his throat.

'Maybe not for ever,' he'd replied. 'But right now, I'm terrible company. I'm doing you a favour.'

Cole had been feeling low since Lydia had dropped her bombshell about not spending Christmas in the UK, and rather than inflict his bad mood on Hester and Paul, he'd kept himself to himself.

'Sorry,' Hester had said, not looking in the least bit apologetic. 'But you can't go back to your hermit's hole until I've shown you the Christmas present I've got for Dad.'

He didn't resist too forcefully; he was cold after being outside and their living room was cosy and warm. Three soft leather sofas were arranged in a U-shape in front of a roaring fire, which wasn't real but you'd never guess at first glance, and above the fire was a huge TV.

'It's for research,' Hester had told him when he'd commented on the size of it. 'I have to know what's happening across all our competitors' shopping programmes.' She'd grinned at him. 'I know, I get paid to watch TV, it's a tough life.'

He sometimes forgot his sister was a minor celebrity. She wasn't household-name famous, but she was on TV four times a week and consequently had a lot of fans and was sometimes recognised when she was out in public. It always tickled him when he was with her when it happened because she pretended to be embarrassed, but secretly loved every second of it.

'Go on then, where's this present?' Cole said, making himself comfortable on the sofa. 'And can it be from me too? I hate Christmas shopping.'

'No it can't,' she replied firmly. She picked up the TV remote and pointed it at him. 'You need to get your own gifts, but I'll come shopping with you.'

'I'm holding you to that,' he said. 'I've got to get stuff for the kids now and make sure I send it off before the cut-off date. At the very least I want them to have presents from me to open on Christmas Day, even if I'm not there in person.'

'Deal,' she said, adding tongue-in-cheek, 'and maybe it'll help you get into the Christmas spirit.'

'I've told you,' he said, nudging her with his socked foot. 'I'm cancelling Christmas this year. I'm fitting a new kitchen at the old bank from Christmas Eve until New Year's Day. The sooner the festive season is over, the better.'

'Oh Cole,' she said with a sigh. 'I hate to see you like this. I wish there was something I could do.'

'Sorry, I'm being a Grinch, I just . . .' He paused and shrugged.

'I get it,' she said kindly and then smiled as the screen lit up. 'This will cheer you up, look.'

Cole watched as a little girl on a bike appeared, head to toe in a green camouflage outfit, two red plaits hanging from underneath her bicycle helmet. Her face creased with concentration as she pedalled furiously. Their dad, Fred, was jogging alongside her with his hand on the back of the seat, steadying the little bike.

'Mummy, look, I'm doing it!' she cried as she wobbled past their mum who must have been holding the camera.

'Well done, darling!' Mum cheered.

In the background Cole cycled by with his arms folded casually, a big smirk on his face. Seconds later there was a crash and a howl of pain.

Hester grinned at him and pressed pause. 'Remember that?'

Cole hooted with laughter. 'Very clearly. I was so busy showing off, I hit a tree stump straight after I went past Mum. I've still got the scar to prove it.'

'Served you right for stealing my moment in the spotlight,' Hester said with a snort.

'And now look at you,' Cole said proudly. 'A star of silver screen and always in the spotlight. Dad is going to love this film, you old bag, I'm going to have to go big to top this present.'

'Yes you are,' she said triumphantly. 'I got one of the guys at work to help me edit it all together. There are hours of footage. We could make an entire box set out of them, but I've just stuck to our growing-up years for now. Want to see more?'

He nodded and she pressed play again.

The film showed him happy memory after happy memory: birthdays, camping holidays in Wales, a plethora of ill-judged teenage haircuts (Cole) and outfits (Hester). Then the first Christmas video popped up and Cole felt his heart begin to ache.

The Robinson family Christmases hadn't been particularly lavish, just a happy family enjoying the day, but the house had been full of love and laughter and togetherness.

All the things that this Christmas was going to lack. It had been at this point that Cole had opened the wine.

A decision that this morning, as he got out of bed, one hand pressed to his temple, he was now regretting. His mouth felt furry and his brain felt too big for his head. He stumbled into the bathroom, avoiding the mirror and after he'd been to the loo, dragged himself towards the coffee machine. He blinked twice at the time on the microwave. That couldn't be right? It was after seven. He was normally at work by now. He grabbed his phone. Shit. How the hell had he slept through his alarm for a whole hour?

Coffee, extra strong, was required before he could even think about having a shower. He turned on the machine and then winced – why did making coffee have to be so loud? He clapped his hands over his ears to drown out the noise and almost missed his phone ringing.

He picked up and answered the call. It was Josh.

'Everything OK, boss?' His foreman was obviously outdoors; the noise of the wind made his voice sound distorted.

'Um.' Cole's mouth felt even worse when he started to talk. He attempted a laugh. 'I overslept, which never happens.'

'You must have needed it, as my mum always says.'

'Yeah, mine did too.' He tucked the phone under his chin and stretched both arms up. 'I'll grab a quick shower and I'll be with you as soon as I can. Thanks for checking on me, I appreciate it.'

He realised as he said it there were very few who'd wonder where he was. Paul and Hester would be getting on with their own working days; he didn't usually see them until the evening. He hoped his sister felt better than he did. She was filming in Manchester later today.

'Actually,' Josh cut in as Cole was about to end the call. 'I was calling to let you know that it's a bit of a mess down here. The storm created quite a lot of damage.'

'You're joking?' Cole strode to the window and pulled up the blinds. The wind was still strong and it had clearly been raining heavily in the night. 'What sort of damage?'

He walked back to get his coffee and gulped it down, grateful for the hit of caffeine.

'I wish I was, but I'm afraid we're flooded. I don't think we'll be getting any work done on site today.'

'What? According to the surveys I paid for, there's never been any problem from the river.' Cole swore under his breath. He didn't need this. Not when the build schedule was already ambitious. The two sisters were due back any day, this time bringing their husbands. He couldn't afford for them to lose interest because of delays.

Josh sucked in air. 'Looks like those trees that got cleared yesterday have caused it.'

Cole frowned. If he hadn't had a headache before, he certainly had now. 'I told the contractor to get rid of it all.'

'They did.' There was a pause. 'It looks like they dumped all the debris in the river.'

Cole massaged his forehead. 'The bloody idiots. What were they thinking? It's so irresponsible, not to mention illegal.'

'I rang them straight away and left a voicemail. No reply as yet.'

'Thanks, Josh.' He dropped down onto the sofa heavily. 'How far does the flooding go?'

'Difficult to tell from on site, I'm just going to take a walk down through the woods now. But I would think that the water will have reached the houses on World's End Lane.'

'Bloody hell.' Just when he thought this build was going smoothly. Cole closed his eyes. Not only was this going to slow down the build, but if houses towards town were flooded, he might end up having to sort out compensation, or rather that dickhead contractor would. 'OK. Take plenty of photos, please, Josh, and see how bad the damage is. If anyone asks, treat it like you would a car accident: don't admit fault. Not yet. We need to establish whether the flooding really was caused by the trees being dumped in the river or whether it would have flooded anyway.'

'OK, will do.'

'Oh and Josh,' Cole put in quickly as his site foreman was about to ring off. 'Let me know if Holly Cottage is affected? That's the one nearest the river at the far end of the lane.'

'Sure, I'll check there first.'

'Shit,' Cole muttered again.

'Sorry about this, boss.'

'There's no need for you to apologise,' Cole assured him grimly. 'But I'll be having strong words with that cowboy contractor.'

Josh rang off and Cole nipped into the bathroom for a shower. He was pulling on his fleece and jeans when Josh called him back.

'Well?' Cole asked. 'What's the story?'

'Holly Cottage has definitely been flooded,' said Josh. 'I could see it through the trees. Shall I go round?'

Cole groaned. The property was his, or rather the one he'd bought and put in trust for Harley and Freya. A single woman had taken over the tenancy recently, which meant not only was he responsible for flooding his own property, but he might even have to evacuate his new tenant too.

'No thanks,' Cole growled. 'Leave it with me – I'll call in myself.'

He'd have to have another coffee first; in fact, he'd make it a double. It was going to be that sort of day.

Chapter 12

Merry

I was already awake when my phone buzzed with a text message. I ignored it, not quite wanting my day to start just yet. Besides, my head hurt when I moved. I was lying in bed, snug under the duvet, listening to the wind rattling the old window frames and thinking about Daniel. He'd texted me last weekend, reminding me that he wanted to come and see Holly Cottage and we'd fixed on today.

He and Tasha had been occupying my mind a lot since last week's community meeting. Tasha had been back in Wetherley since September. Had Daniel already been seeing her before I moved out in October? They were clearly an item now, so when did it start? Or had I, with the most awful timing, witnessed their first kiss? Or was it actually *good* timing, because now I knew with absolute certainty that there was no going back for us. A week on and I was still mulling it over.

The weird thing was that after the initial shock of seeing them in each other's arms, completely oblivious to the world outside of Daniel's shop window, and the devastation which followed for the next forty-eight hours,

125

I'd come to terms with it and I was actually OK. I felt a sort of calm, a release. I was no longer clinging to the hope that if Daniel saw me in a different light – Merry the organised businesswoman, mastermind of Wetherley's Christmas Project, the days of making reckless decisions behind me – he might realise I was the woman for him after all. Now I was free to simply accept that he was a friend and not keep analysing his every look and word for signs that he was still in love with me.

Of course, Daniel's love life hadn't been the only thing keeping my mind spinning since last week. There was also the fact that given all the many fans of the festive season who lived in Wetherley, it had fallen to me to deliver the christmassiest Christmas Eve ever in honour of Benny Dunford. And find someone with clout to switch on Wetherley's Christmas lights in just over two weeks from now.

My stomach twisted with nerves. I should probably have already done something about it by now, but I'd had a flurry of orders for candles and I was working flat out to keep up with demand. Which was a good problem to have, Nell had pointed out last night as we'd propped up the bar at the Bristly Badger and somehow managed to drink them dry of mulled wine. It had been her idea to go out – declaring that my scheme for the Christmas Project was voted the winner by the rest of the group and that every win, no matter how small, should be celebrated. Thankfully, they'd only made two bottles worth, otherwise the pounding in my head would have been even worse than it was right now.

My need for coffee was competing with my reluctance to leave the warmth of my bed so I sat up gingerly and winced as a sharp pain shot through me. I reached for my phone to read the message. It was from Nell.

Hope you're feeling better than me. My tongue feels like one of my mother's Afghan rugs. I keep trying to get up, but my head feels too heavy.

I laughed and tapped a reply.

Never, never again. I'm putting the blame for my hangover firmly at your door. I knew there was a reason I don't drink mulled wine. It is evil.

Haha, sorry. At least I've got the day off. The market is closed obviously, no one wants soggy nuts. Olek made me a massive coffee and I'm staying in bed for at least another hour.

Bliss. I felt a pang of longing for coffee and an even larger pang for someone who knew just how I liked it. Hold on, the market was closed? My brow furrowed, I was still in pre-caffeine mode and my brain was lagging behind. I typed a message back:

No market? Why?

Nell sent a row of laughing emojis followed by:

Er . . . the storm???

I rubbed my eyes and got out of bed, pulling on my dressing gown on the way to the window.

'Bloody hell!' I gasped once I'd opened the curtains.

My bedroom was at the front of the house and had a view down the whole of World's End Lane to the houses at the other end of it. The lane was covered with tree debris: twigs, leaves and small branches. My end had borne the brunt if it. The road had turned into a shallow lake; the car was sitting in several inches of water, the dustbin had overturned and bags of rubbish were strewn across the drive, some floating in the road. Directly below me, two terracotta pots had blown over and smashed.

> It's like a war zone out there. I can't believe I slept through it.

> I can. Don't you remember singing White Christmas to Olek last night when he picked us up and repeating the merry and bright line over and over?

I sniggered to myself; it was starting to come back to me now. Poor Olek. I sent her a line of embarrassed face emojis.

> Nah, he loved it. He said it was worth it to see you get into the Christmas spirit. Right. I was just checking your cottage hadn't been blown away Wizard-of Oz style which it hasn't. So now I'm going to go back to sleep. You should do the same.

> I can't. Daniel's coming over first thing.

> OMG I forgot! Good luck, I love you, don't do anything rash!! PS. You've probably got a purple tongue.

> Love you too. Call you later xx

I put my phone down and I checked my tongue in the mirror, straight away wishing I hadn't; not only was my tongue the colour of mulled wine but so were my lips.

'Gross,' I muttered and took my fuzzy head, sour breath and stained mouth downstairs to put the kettle on.

I was almost on the last step before I realised that something wasn't quite right. The smell was off. I could normally smell yesterday's candles, but today the air smelled dank. I put my bare foot on the rug and recoiled; the floor was sopping wet. I looked up automatically, checking the ceiling for a leak, but there was nothing there.

As I squelched down the hallway and opened the door into the kitchen, my heart plummeted.

The kitchen floor was underwater. Only a couple of inches now but the water level had been higher at some point because the cardboard boxes . . .

'Oh no, the boxes!' I groaned.

I'd had a huge delivery of stock yesterday: the labels, the ribbons, wicks, and the pretty little boxes I pack each candle in. I'd bulk-bought enough to see me through to January and it would all be ruined. I could have kicked myself for not moving everything to the spare bedroom yesterday, but I'd run out of time and was too tipsy to do anything about it when I got in last night. I paddled over to the boxes and tried to lift one onto the kitchen table, but it disintegrated in my hands and all my lovely Merry and Bright packaging fell into the dirty water. The cold water, I realised belatedly, as I started to shiver. The house was freezing. Had the heating gone off? And the electrics? DIY was not my strong point; I knew how to change a fuse, but beyond that I called in the experts every time.

This was all I needed. I pressed my hands to my face, not knowing where to start.

Phone the landlord? Rescue my stuff? I paddled across the tiled floor and picked up the kettle. Everything could wait for a few minutes. I had an urgent need for strong coffee. Was it too early to add a dash of brandy . . .?

Before I'd even had chance to turn on the kitchen tap, there was a heavy, insistent knock at the front door. I splashed back along the hall, cursing myself for not having put my wellies on and yanked it open.

A man dressed head to toe in sensible waterproofs was moving some of the pieces of terracotta pot from the porch and stacking them to one side. It looked like he'd already righted the dustbin and collected some of the rubbish. He turned, his face lined with concern. It was Daniel. I'd never been so pleased to see a friendly face in my life.

'I know I'm early,' he said. 'But I heard about the flooding and wanted to check on you. Are you OK?'

Now that he mentioned it, I wasn't OK. The tears, which had been waiting for their opportunity to strike, sprang out of my eyes.

'No,' I sniffed. 'The house is flooded, or at least the kitchen and the hall are. Not sure about the living room yet.'

'Oh, mate, I'm sorry.' He gave me a sympathetic smile. 'Shall I come in?'

Mate. I tried to ignore all the implications of that word and focused on the fact that I was no longer having to deal with the day from hell on my own.

'Yes please,' I mumbled, wiping my tears on the sleeve of my dressing gown.

It was very gloomy outside and I realised the house was still in darkness. I reached around to switch the hall light on, but the Daniel lunged forward and caught hold of the edge of my dressing gown.

'Don't touch the electrics,' he yelled. 'In case they blow up.'

'Arggh!' I flinched and snatched my hand back from the light switch.

'Sorry about that,' he said, releasing me. 'But we need to switch the electrics off completely in case of water ingress.'

'*I'm* sorry for being pathetic and crying,' I said, attempting a smile. 'But I've woken up with a . . . headache. I desperately need a coffee and I think all my new delivery of stock is ruined. And I'm really cold and wet.'

Daniel gave me a hug. 'OK, first things first. Why don't you go and get dressed and warm yourself up while I investigate?'

I nodded mutely, grateful for his help, even if I was only his *mate* and then went upstairs, leaving him to look for the fuse box.

Five minutes later I was back down, having dressed in several layers of warm clothes, thick socks and boots. I'd also spoken to a woman from the lettings agency, who had been lovely and promised to send someone round to assess the damage within the next couple of hours and in the meantime not to touch anything. She'd run me through some possible scenarios such as moving me to a hotel for the night or possibly finding me alternative accommodation, but had assured me that whatever happened, the landlord of the property would make certain I was looked after.

At least my hangover seemed to have vanished; it had probably slunk off because I wasn't giving it enough attention. I had far more important things to be getting on with than wallowing around with a sore head.

I found Daniel in the kitchen sweeping water out through the back door.

'I've alerted the lettings agency. So help is on its way,' I said.

'You're in luck,' he said, moving the sodden boxes onto the kitchen table. 'The flood didn't reach the living room. So at least that room is dry.'

'Not sure lucky is the word I'd use at the moment.'

'No, maybe not,' he agreed with a sympathetic smile. Although I was lucky that he'd turned up when he did. Daniel was sensible, practical and kind and his company was just what I needed. I smiled at him, realising that somewhere along the line, my feelings towards him had changed. My head had known for a while that he wasn't mine anymore, but my heart had had difficulty accepting it. And now it had.

The truth was that I still loved him, but as a good friend or a big brother; *yes*, a brother, I liked that. I turned away from his gaze, my heart swelling with these new feelings. I steeled myself not to cry again and looked out through the window at the back garden. Already the surface water was starting to drain away.

'The rain must have been of biblical proportions to flood the house,' I said, trying to keep my voice casual.

Daniel joined me at the window and strained to look down to the end of the garden. 'Actually, I've just had a phone call from the shop; there's a rumour that the builders at the edge of the new estate caused it by dumping rubbish in the river.'

'What?' I gasped in outrage. 'If that's the case they can come and sort this mess out and pay for replacement stock.'

He nodded. 'But in the meantime, it's worth letting your insurance company know too.'

'My insurance company?' I blinked at him.

That hadn't even crossed my mind, although now I came to think about it, I wasn't entirely sure I'd got round to paying for a policy. So much for the new, organised Merry.

'Your home contents insurance?' he prompted.

'Um.' I remembered starting to fill in an online questionnaire to get a quote, but I got interrupted and then never got around to it again. 'Of course. Absolutely. Yes, good idea.'

Daniel, who knew me too well, gave me a resigned look. 'OK. I've turned the electrics off for now. I suggest I light a fire in the living room, boil water for a hot drink and then clear as much debris as we can.'

'If you don't mind, while you do that,' I said, slipping my arms into my coat, 'I'm going to see if I can see anything through the fence at the bottom of the garden.'

The wind whipped my hair around my face and I pulled my hood up and zipped my coat up tight. The rain had stopped now and the cloud was thinning above, but the air was heavy and damp. The lawn was completely waterlogged. I squelched my way to the bottom boundary, pushed my way past the overgrown shrubs behind the shed and peered through the bare branches of the trees. Running left to right through the trees and in parallel with the bottom of my garden was the river. It wasn't a major waterway; this stretch was normally only three or four metres wide but right now, it had burst its banks and water pooled either side for quite a distance.

It didn't take a genius to work out the cause of the flood; a little way downstream, a pile of logs and branches had clumped together and formed a dam. I'd noticed yesterday that I had a better view through the woods; the two things were obviously linked. I could even still see the ridges of mud and tyre tracks left by big machines.

What sort of idiot would dump logs in a river? Especially during the last twenty-four hours when the bad weather had been forecast. It might even be illegal.

On the other side of the woodland, I could see the building site. I didn't envy them working outside in all this mud today.

The despair I'd felt earlier was beginning to morph into anger. My cottage, my lovely quirky cottage that had been my home for only a month had turned into a paddling pool. This wasn't acceptable, I thought crossly. This was my home, I had a business to run, a very busy business at the moment. Those builders were clearly responsible, and I had every intention of making them put things right.

I stomped back inside feeling fired up and ready for a fight.

'That rumour is right – it is the builders' fault!' I fumed, finding Daniel on his knees in the living room fanning the flames of a fire. 'They've made a right mess of the river as well as my cottage. I'm going round there now and kicking up a stink. They can bloody well clear up the mess they've created.'

He shut the door to the little stove and got to his feet, taking hold of my shoulders. 'Whoa, let's not be hasty and start arguments. You've already got the ball rolling with the lettings agency – let them do the fighting for you. Let's focus on you and what you need right this minute.'

'OK.' I let out a deep sigh and nodded. 'You're right. Thanks.'

'I haven't really done anything,' he said with a shrug.

'Just being here is helping,' I assured him, dropping down into the armchair. 'I don't usually mind being alone, but sometimes . . .'

My voice faltered and he looked down at his feet uneasily.

'So,' I said swiftly, not wanting to make him feel guilty about me being single, 'what do you think of the cottage?'

He pasted on a smile as he looked round him. 'It's very er, it's very er . . .'

'Soggy?' I supplied and we both laughed.

I pressed my hands to my face and groaned. 'I was looking forward to showing off my little house and now look at it. What a disaster.'

'It's not your fault.' He cleared his throat and sat down on the sofa. 'Look, now that I'm here, I wanted to have a chat with you about something.'

He started jiggling his legs, a classic sign that he was nervous. He was building up to tell me about Tasha, I could tell. Suddenly I wanted it all out in the open so we could move on and be natural with each other again.

'I know about you and Tasha,' I blurted out.

His eyes widened. 'What . . . how? No one else knows, I'm sure. I wanted to tell you myself.'

'It's fine,' I said calmly. 'Honestly. I saw you together after the committee meeting last week in the shop. No one else knows.' Except Nell and Olek. Oh, and Astrid, I thought.

'Did you?' He blushed and raked his hand through his blond hair. 'Oh hell. I'm sorry. Tasha asked to see inside the shop and then, well.' He broke off, looking mortified.

'You got passionate among the parsnips?' I finished for him.

He gave me a serious look. 'I've been working up to telling you this for days and all you can do is make a joke.'

'It's a coping mechanism,' I said, still teasing. 'Inside I'm crying. You never so much as kissed me behind the curly kale.'

'Merry!' he groaned.

'Sorry,' I said, holding my hands up. 'I'll stop, and I'm happy for you both.'

He got up and sloshed the hot water into mugs and handed me a coffee, barely lukewarm. The granules hadn't even dissolved. I gulped it down gratefully nonetheless.

'Really?' he said warily.

I nodded, acknowledging to myself as much as him that it was true. 'You waited long enough for that kiss.'

'It's very new,' he said, looking at me earnestly to make sure I believed him. 'Last week in the shop, that was the first time we'd . . . you know.'

This was his way of telling me that there'd been nothing between them while he and I were still living in the same house. I smiled, appreciating his honesty.

'Can I ask you something?' I said once my mug was empty. 'You know how important children are to me. Yet you never told me that you didn't want to be a father. Why?'

He stared down at the floor. 'I thought not wanting kids was something I'd grow out of, I thought maybe loving you would be enough to make me want what you wanted.'

'You're thirty-nine! I think you'd have grown out of something like that by now.'

He pressed a hand to his forehead. 'You're right. I know that now. I let you down. I'm so sorry for the way it turned out between us. But I honestly think you and I—'

'Please.' I held up a hand to stop him. 'I've said I'm happy for you, and I meant it, but spare me the details about why I'm not the one. Just because I'm not right for you doesn't mean there's anything wrong with me.'

'Of course not.' He looked horrified. 'Merry, you're amazing, you blow me away with your energy and enthusiasm for life. I'm sorry if I ever made you feel differently.'

A wave of relief washed over me. All this time I'd been blaming myself for our break-up, but no one was to blame. It simply wasn't to be.

'Oh, well in that case,' I said flippantly, 'I forgive you.'

He met my eyes, his gaze sincere. 'I don't blame you if you don't want to, but I really do want us to be friends.'

'Me too.'

As if by mutual agreement, we both stood and hugged each other. He glanced over my shoulder out of the window.

'Looks like whoever your lettings agency sent has arrived already.'

'My knight in shining armour!' I said, turning to look, as a tall broad man got out of a pick-up truck parked behind my car.

The man spotted us looking at him and raised a hand.

'I had to park my car further down the road where the flooding wasn't so bad,' said Daniel enviously, eyeing up the sturdy vehicle.

'Listen,' I said, stepping away from Daniel, 'now that the cavalry has arrived, I'll be fine. I'll let you get on with your day.'

'Well, if you're sure,' he said gratefully. 'I am very busy.'

'I'll show you out.' I suppressed a smile; Daniel was always very busy.

The man knocked at the door as I was opening it. I acknowledged the visitor with a brief smile and stood back to let Daniel out.

'I'll call you later,' said Daniel. He nodded to the other man and strode past him.

'Am I glad to see you,' I said, turning my attention to the stranger.

Except he wasn't a stranger, I realised; we'd met before.

Chapter 13

Merry

'That's a promising start,' my visitor said warily, as if he wasn't sure whether I was joking or not.

He wore a black padded jacket, jeans and heavy duty boots, and with his charcoal grey woolly hat pulled down low over his ears, I couldn't see much of his face. But it was enough. The russet hair and melty brown eyes gave it away. It was Cole. The man from the market, the one I'd made silly jokes about dates and nuts with. The nice one.

'Which is more than can be said for my day,' I replied, suddenly aware of the state I must look.

The last time I'd looked in the mirror, my lips and tongue had been purple and last night's eye make-up had been doing a great job of highlighting the bags under my eyes. A small, vain part of me wished he hadn't seen me looking like I was auditioning for a part in Zombie Apocalypse – The Revenge. Another small part was pleased that this hadn't even crossed my mind while Daniel was here.

'You've had some flooding, I understand?' Cole looking past me and down the hallway.

'Do you think?' I said, splashing my boots up and down on the rug.

'Sorry.' He gave me a sheepish smile. 'It was a daft thing to say, given the swimming pool behind you.'

'No, I'm sorry,' I said, taking a step back into the gloom of the hall. 'I'm like a bear with a sore head this morning.'

He hadn't recognised me, which either meant I was unrecognisable from the day he met me, or he'd forgotten me as soon as he'd left the market.

'Same here.' He pulled his hat off and raked a hand through his hair. He had very shiny hair and lots of it. There was a small tuft at the back of his crown which was now sticking up. If I hadn't been in such a bad mood I'd be tempted to reach up and flatten it down for him. I bet his mum had had to do that every morning before school when he was a little boy. 'I had too much red wine last night. So, my bad head is self-inflicted. Being flooded is a much more valid reason to be grumpy.'

'I'm not bothered if you're grumpy,' I said, 'I'm just glad you came so quickly.'

He shrugged. 'No problem. Listen, I've got a flask of coffee in the van, how about I fetch it and then we can share it while I look at the damage?'

'That's the best offer I've had all day,' I said with a sigh. 'I've only had one barely warm drink so far.'

'Be right back.' He smiled and little lines feathered around his eyes.

By the time I'd run my fingers through my hair and checked my tongue and teeth for mulled wine stains in the hall mirror, he was walking back from his van holding two flasks.

'One contains hot milk,' he explained. 'And the other is coffee – only instant, but I decided I was going to need lots of scalding coffee to get me through today.'

'Ditto,' I agreed, standing aside to let him in. 'Actually, you're not alone with the overindulgence. I had too much red wine last night too although mine was hot and with added Christmas chemicals. Never again.'

'Not the dreaded mulled wine?' He pretended to shudder. 'Why anyone would want to ruin a good bottle of red with cinnamon, sugar and slices of orange, I do not know.'

'Totally agree,' I said smiling before turning to shut the door behind him.

When I looked back at him, a grin was hovering on his lips. 'I've just realised. We've met before, haven't we? I recognise that smile.'

I nodded. 'At Nell's Nuts. You bought Brazils nuts and got accosted by my friend's dog.'

'How could I forget little Otto. Or that free sample of wasabi peas.' He pulled a face. 'Or as I now call them, devil's food.'

I laughed. 'They are a bit of a Marmite thing. I take it you won't be coming back to place another order?'

He grimaced. 'Unlikely. I used to bite my nails as a kid and my mum painted some revolting stuff on them. But having tasted wasabi, I think she'd have been better off using that.'

He stood on the hall rug and water squelched beneath his feet. 'Normally I'd take my boots off, but would you mind if I kept them on?'

'Why, do you have ugly feet?' I asked, deadpan.

'I have lovely feet, just ask the farrier who normally trims my toenails.'

'I'll take your word for it,' I said. 'The kitchen is this way.'

I was enjoying this conversation, I thought, leading the way to the back of the house. My life might be lying around me in a squidgy smelly mess, but I liked a man who could take a joke.

'Thanks.' He set the flasks on the kitchen table and looked around him.

'Shall I pour the coffee while you assess the damage?' I suggested.

'Yes please.' He shrugged his arms out of his coat and hung it on the back of one of the chairs. I intended to keep mine on; I could feel the cold rising from the wet tiled floor and now I'd moved from the fire I was beginning to shiver again.

'I almost didn't recognise you without your eye-catching yellow coat,' I said, pouring milk and coffee into two mugs. Just the sight of the steam made me feel a bit cosier.

'Do I detect a note of sarcasm?' He gave me a lopsided smile and picked up one of the mugs. 'You wouldn't be the first detractor I've had of that coat. My daughter always used to run up to the lollipop man at the school crossing shouting *Daddy, Daddy*. Used to drive my wife bananas.'

A sudden wave of exhaustion hit me; I rubbed a hand across my face and was surprised to find it was shaking. My shoulders sagged a little; it was only just beginning to hit me what a mess I was in and what a lot of work there'd be just to get the cottage back to how it was yesterday. At least that was what I thought had caused my drop in mood. The fact that he was married with children had nothing to do with it.

He looked at me carefully, as if sensing my sudden deflation. 'Are you OK? Stupid question, sorry. Of course you're not – you've got a hangover and a flooded house and a strange man poking around. Here, sit down.'

He took my shoulders and was about to sit me down at the kitchen table but changed his mind. Instead he led me into the living room. I sank onto the sofa gratefully while he fetched our mugs and slipped his boots off, leaving them in the hall.

'I'm Cole, by the way.' He extended a hand which I shook. 'In case you'd forgotten, and from memory, you are Merry, is that right?'

'Correct,' I replied with a weary sigh.

He coughed into his elbow, although I had a sneaking suspicion that he was hiding a smile at the fact that I couldn't have looked less merry if I tried. He handed me my coffee; I hugged it to me, relishing the warmth while he stoked the fire Daniel had started. The coffee was so hot that it brought tears to my eyes. I blinked them back but they kept on coming.

'There we go, at least the fire still works, and I'll drop round with some more wood, next time I'm—' He noticed my tears and his voice faded.

'I'm fine,' I insisted, brushing at my eyes. 'Honestly. It's just, you know, everything.'

He sat on the sofa, keeping a respectful distance.

'Merry, I'm not going to poke my nose in where it's not wanted, but in my experience the people who say *I'm fine* are usually the ones who definitely aren't,' he said staring down at his socks.

I stared at them too. They were black with coloured toes and the days of the week written on them. According to his left foot it was Wednesday, whereas his right declared it to be Friday.

He caught me looking. 'Now that might look like an accident to you, but in fact, I've got one foot in tomorrow and the other still stuck in the past, so it's actually quite an accurate representation of my life.'

'I'm just glad you're wearing socks,' I said. 'In case you're overdue a visit to the farrier.'

He laughed softly. 'So? Are you really fine?'

I shook my head. 'Not really. I'd only just started to make the cottage feel like mine. And home, well, it's very important to me.'

Cole nodded. 'I do know what you mean. And I'm very sorry about all this.'

'This couldn't have come at a worse time,' I continued. 'I've got bills coming in and I need to work to pay them. I work from home and I can't do that until the house is dry. And I've got the bloody Christmas Eve celebrations to organise too. If it was left up to me, Christmas would be cancelled this year.'

'I hear you.' He raised an amused eyebrow. 'But as a concept, I don't think it'll catch on.'

'I suppose you're right.' I felt my eyelids growing heavy with the heat from the fire. I couldn't remember the last time I felt this relaxed with someone I didn't know. 'I can't imagine you'd be very popular with your children if you told them you were cancelling Christmas.'

Cole drained his coffee and got to his feet. 'OK. Time to get cracking.'

'Bloody idiot builders,' I said, getting cross again. 'Did you know it's their fault the cottage is flooded because they've dumped debris in the river? It's an absolute disgrace. I was planning on heading round to the site and kicking up a fuss until someone came and admitted liability. I might even call the press and tell them what's happened once I know the name of the company.'

'Robinson Developments,' Cole supplied, grimly.

'Thanks. Well, Robinson Developments are going to feel the full force of my wrath.' I stood up and marched back through to the kitchen. 'And presumably the landlord will want compensation from them.'

Cole slipped his feet back into his boots and followed me. 'Merry, this is awkward. I'm Cole Robinson of Robinson Developments.'

'You're . . .?' My eyes widened. 'All this time I've been sitting here pouring my heart out and you're the man responsible for this fiasco.'

'Well, I wouldn't put it quite like that.' He raked a hand through his hair again. This time I had no desire to smooth his tufty bits.

'I think you should leave.' I folded my arms. 'You have entered my home under false pretences, which if not illegal is certainly . . . immoral.'

'I don't think I did; I came in to assess the damage,' he said, looking uncomfortable.

'I thought you were the landlord or the maintenance man or something,' I said crossly.

'I am.'

'What?' I glared at him. 'Stop talking in riddles, I'm not in the mood.'

'I am the builder,' he explained lifting up his hands in defence. 'But I'm also the owner of this house, or rather my kids are, it's in a trust for them. So, I'm on both sides of the fence in this situation.'

I pressed my hands to my face. 'Look, I'm too tired for this. I need . . . I need . . .'

The lump in my throat prevented me from finishing my sentence. I felt Cole's hands, one on each of my shoulders.

'I think,' he said quietly, 'that you need a hug. But as your landlord and the man behind your current situation, I'm sure I wouldn't be your first choice to provide it. So, I'm going to leave my hands here for a bit of support in case it helps.'

'It does help.' I made a half-sob, half-laugh noise. He towered above me and now we were close I could smell his cologne. I felt a stirring in my stomach and wished I was brave enough to say that actually a hug would be lovely.

'Apart from this, what can I do for you right now to make life a little better?'

Cole with the nice brown eyes and broad shoulders was both the builder and my landlord. So even if he was to blame for the flood, equally he was responsible for providing me with somewhere dry to live and he'd want the damage sorting out properly. And somehow, just knowing that he was here and helping already made life feel a little better.

I swallowed. 'I need somewhere to work. Somewhere dry and warm with power and light. The cosier the better.'

'Cosy, eh? I like a challenge.' He grinned. 'I'll do my best. I can arrange that. And what about sleeping arrangements until I can get the electrics checked out – do you want me to arrange alternative accommodation? You're entitled to it.'

'I can sort that myself,' I replied. I was sure Nell would put me up for a few days if necessary. 'Oh, the washing machine broke yesterday, I didn't get around to telling anyone.'

'Jeez,' he teased, 'you have been busy wrecking the joint. Anything else? What state is the bathroom in?'

I shrugged. 'It's OK if you wear flipflops. It's more of a wet room at the moment.'

'A wet room?' He raised an eyebrow. 'Very upmarket. I might have to put the rent up.'

'Too soon for jokes,' I said sternly.

'Sorry.'

But we both smiled anyway. He still had his hands gently on my arms and neither of us were moving. Inside my chest, I could feel the beat of my heart, steadier now than it had been. Then I had the oddest sensation, a sort of internal warm feeling that all of this flooding and emotional upheaval and mess and negative stuff had in fact all been serendipity, leading to this moment and it felt . . . OK.

A split second later, his phone started ringing, as did a bell in my head to remind me that he was somebody else's husband and wasn't mine to feel serendipitous about.

'Excuse me,' he said, pulling his phone from the pocket of his jeans. He read the screen. 'It's Castle and Court, the lettings agency . . . Cole Robinson speaking.'

I knew what the call was about, but to be polite, I looked inside the remaining soggy boxes sitting on the kitchen floor. Some were packed with the soy pellets I used for my candles. Safely bagged in plastic, so they'd be fine to use. A couple of others contained glass jars. I'd have to reorder packaging and labels, but at least I'd be able to crack on with pouring the candles, which was the time-consuming bit. Cole confirmed to the person on the end of the line that he'd be looking after the tenant at Holly Cottage himself and promised to keep them posted.

'Right.' Cole ended the call, shoved his phone away and clapped his hands together decisively. 'Let's get Operation Cosy underway, shall we?'

'Yes, let's,' I laughed, loving that he'd embraced my precise requirements. Thank goodness I hadn't stormed round to the building site and shouted my mouth off; this conversation would have been very different.

'I'm going to nip off and get some industrial dryers organised today so we can start drying the floors. In the meantime, you pack up what you need for your job and give me a couple of hours – I think I may have somewhere you can work for the time being.'

'Thank you, that would be great,' I said, showing him out.

'I'll get this sorted, Merry.' He gave me a reassuring smile. 'Trust me.'

'I'll try,' I replied.

I almost gave him a hug as he left but thought better of it and waved instead. I closed the door and sighed with relief. Experience had taught me to be wary of everyone until they proved themselves worthy of being trusted. I didn't know him very well, if at all really, but unusually for me, I'd felt comfortable with him. He'd said he'd get this sorted and strange as it seemed, I actually believed he would.

Chapter 14

Cole

Operation Cosy? Cole groaned as he left World's End Lane and turned onto the main road out of Wetherley. And then his departing 'trust me' line at the end. Where the hell had that come from? It was probably the cheesiest line he'd ever used.

Merry was no doubt on her phone now, calling that friend of hers, Nell from the nut stall. Both of them laughing at how he'd swooped in there acting like a superhero.

He dismissed the thought; perhaps he was doing her a disservice. She'd seemed genuinely relieved that he'd promised to get straight on with drying the place out and sorting the electrics. Was that a boyfriend leaving as Cole had arrived, he wondered? They seemed comfortable with each other, although if Merry was his girlfriend, he wouldn't have left her on her own to deal with a flooded house.

He wondered what would have happened if he'd gone straight to the site as he'd originally planned and Merry had turned up to confront him. He smiled; she'd looked like a lost puppy when he'd arrived: pale face and big green eyes, and she'd been understandably livid about the flood.

But when he'd persuaded her to go inside and have a hot drink it seemed more like she was in shock. She hadn't even seemed to notice that she was trembling from head to foot. Poor lass. And being in that cold house wouldn't have helped.

She'd done a great job with Holly Cottage in only a few weeks; it had been transformed since the last time he'd seen it. The kitchen and hall didn't smell great, obviously, after half the contents of the garden had washed through it, but the living room had smelled amazing, like really expensive perfume. He liked what she'd done décor-wise too. He'd left the bits of furniture, but she'd added to them to make it homely. There were little touches everywhere: vases and plants and rugs. Hopefully those rugs would dry out for her, bless her. Every time she'd looked up at him with those huge green eyes, his heart had turned over. Why did crap things happen to nice people?

He'd struck lucky having Merry as a tenant; she was being very reasonable to deal with, even after she'd found out that his building works was the root cause of the flood. Lots of people would have demanded to be moved into a hotel at great expense, compensation for lost wages while they sorted themselves out, etc etc. All she'd asked for was to be cosy.

He felt a wave of sympathy as he pictured her, admitting she wasn't fine. He hadn't spotted much of any great value, no pricey TV or gadgets, but the concept of home seemed to be what was important to her. That was what she had lost for the time being: a place to feel at home and cosy.

But what did cosy even mean? Was it just warm and dry or did she mean cushions and candles? He'd call Hester quickly hands-free and see what she suggested.

She picked up the phone on the first ring. 'Hey, make it quick, I'm having my make-up done and then I'm on.'

He was used to her in work-mode and got straight to the point. 'What does cosy mean to you?'

'Cuddling up with Paul in front of the fire, a mug of frothy hot chocolate or depending on the time of day, a glass of Baileys; a blanket, slippers, low lighting, candles maybe. Does that help?'

'Hmm. Not really.' That all sounded more like a romantic night in than a cosy space to work. 'What about flowers and cushions?'

She snorted. 'I guess so. You are so weird. Oh, I get it!' she gasped. 'You've had some interest from the app. This is excellent.'

'Which app?' Cole frowned and then it came flooding back to him. Hester had suggested he sign up for a dating app on his phone last night and had written a profile for him. 'Oh, no. This is nothing to do with that.'

'Not sure I believe you, but I've got to go. I'm selling anti-wrinkle cream today. Want me to get you some? Those frown lines are getting out of control and you'll have to start making an effort now you're back in the saddle. Got to go, big kisses, tell me everything tonight.'

She hung up before he could tell her to get lost. He pulled down the visor mirror and examined his forehead, lifting his eyebrows up and then scrunching them down. *Wrinkles*, he tutted to himself, amused rather than insulted; this face told a story, that was all. He flipped the visor back up and returned to considering Merry's needs.

First and foremost, she needed somewhere to work. Why hadn't he asked what she did for a living? Did she need a desk? Would she have customers or clients visiting her? There'd been nothing to give him any clues in the house, other than that it had been a bit of a mess. But then he'd excuse her that for the moment. Oh well, he'd just go with the basics and assume that if she needed anything special, she'd already have it.

He hadn't owned Holly Cottage long. It had been empty for a while; the previous occupant had passed away, and the family had apparently been unable to agree what to do with it. It wasn't his type of property, but it was characterful and quirky, features which always held their value. Although he'd kept that nugget of wisdom to himself when he'd negotiated a very favourable price on it.

Sorting out his tenant was adding to his workload at a time when he could do without it, but at least according to Josh, Holly Cottage was the only property to be affected. The cost wouldn't be beyond him and anyway, he reckoned he could get the landscaping contractor who'd created the problem to foot the bill. Cole would also demand that they clear out the river and dispose of the logs and branches before word got around. Otherwise, he'd have environmentalists and journalists breathing down his neck before anyone could say Greta Thunberg. He'd call the contractor next.

Holly Cottage would eventually belong to Harley and Freya. He'd set up a trust for them when he'd bought it. There was a mortgage on it but renting it out meant that it paid for itself. He'd taken them to see it before they'd gone to Canada. Harley had strutted around it, pointing out strengths and weakness of the location and the building itself. Freya had been enchanted with its woodland setting and vowed that when she grew up she was going to live there for ever and keep rabbits and fawns in the garden.

His precious little Freya; he felt a flicker of worry for his daughter after a conversation with Lydia earlier in the week. Lydia had gone into her bedroom in the middle of the night after hearing her cry out. Freya had wet the bed, something she hadn't done for years. Lydia had changed the sheets and reassured their daughter that it was nothing to worry about, but Freya had sobbed and confided that she'd been the only girl in their class not invited to some other kid's birthday party and that she really missed Daisy, her best friend from home. Cole was grateful that Lydia had told him; she could easily have kept it to herself. Since then, he'd made sure he'd spoken to his daughter every day and had sent Daisy's dad a text, asking if the girls could FaceTime each other next weekend. He couldn't do much from so far away, but he was doing his best.

And by investing in Holly Cottage for them, he thought, he was doing his best for the kids' future too. Who knew what the pair of them would eventually do with it, but in the meantime, he had a feeling that the cottage was in very good hands.

Within minutes he'd pulled up at Orchard Gardens. He walked around the site, had a word with his team and then after a tense conversation with the landscaping contractor, unplugged the mini fridge he kept there for keeping the milk cool in summer and slid it into the back of the van.

Stage one of Operation Cosy was complete, he thought and then laughed to himself as he got back behind the wheel. As cheesy as it was, he had a feeling that his tenant would appreciate what he'd done. Normally he hated shopping with a passion and avoided shops like the plague. But this wasn't about him, it was about making Merry happy. It was a while since he'd felt needed, he realised, and it felt good, he felt purposeful again.

He'd missed this feeling, especially now he didn't even have his kids close enough to need him on a practical level. Maybe, he thought tentatively, he was fed up with being on his own; perhaps signing up to that dating app had been a good move on his sister's part. Maybe he was ready to care for someone again, to have someone who knew how he took his coffee, someone to remind him where he'd put his keys. Someone who cared. It was something to consider, he thought, humming to himself, because he was beginning to think that living alone was overrated.

Chapter 15

Merry

The following morning, I was woken up by Nell snapping on the bedside lamp, its bright red Liverpool Football Club shade glowing like a warning light.

'Wakey, wakey,' she sang softly. She was holding two mugs.

'If I must.' I yawned and stretched. I was in Olek's son's room. It was only a single bed and my bottom had poked out of the duvet several times during the night. But the room was cosy and warm and had the added benefit of a wake-up call from my best friend.

'I brought you coffee. Strong *and* milky. Just the way you like it. Hutch up.'

'Now this is already a much better start to the day than yesterday.' I sat up and moved across towards the wall before accepting the mug from her. I inhaled the smell of fresh coffee and sighed with pleasure. 'It's still pitch black outside. Are you sure it's time to be getting up?'

'The early bird gets the best nuts.' Nell climbed into bed beside me and pulled the duvet up. 'I'll drink this and get ready for work.'

I winced as her feet touched my warm legs. 'Your feet are like ice blocks.'

'It's my superpower,' she said. 'If I ever want to get my own way, I threaten Olek with them. Anyway, stop complaining. I earned these sub-arctic trotters by making your morning coffee.'

'I'm very grateful,' I replied meekly. 'For everything. Feel free to warm them up all you like.'

'Glad to help. Sorry about this bedroom and its Liverpool FC theme; if I'd had more notice I could have cleared the spare room and made up the sofa bed.'

'I'm quite happy sleeping in red and white sheets. And the matching curtains are very bright and cheery.'

Nell had scooped me up yesterday, insisting that I come and stay in Max's room for as long as necessary. Although I wasn't sure Max would be quite so enamoured with the arrangement; he generally stayed with Nell and Olek every second weekend. Olek had been called out on a job last night, so the two of us had had a chance to talk about my heart-to-heart with Daniel. I'd told her how I no longer felt to blame for our break-up and that it would have happened sooner or later, even if my proposal hadn't been the catalyst.

'So now we can be just friends,' I'd said. 'I can be happy for him and not try and read meanings into his every communication with me.'

'That's a relief,' she'd replied. 'I was worried that you were counting on getting back together when I could see he wasn't the one for you.'

I'd nodded. 'I've realised that I'd been missing being in a relationship, more than Daniel himself.'

'We'll have you fixed up in no time,' she'd said loyally. 'There's someone out there looking for the same things as you, I promise.'

I'd gone to bed early, exhausted from the events of the day and very grateful to have my best friend in the room next door.

'Max isn't going to be here this weekend,' said Nell now. 'And if you still need to be here in a week's time, we can move you.'

'Cole says he's going to leave the dryers on for a week and then test the moisture levels, so fingers crossed I'll be out of your way by then.'

True to his word, my landlord had leapt into action and cracked straight on with sorting out Holly Cottage. He and his site foreman, Josh, had returned at lunchtime, set up two dryers and removed both of my sopping wet rugs to have professionally cleaned. I didn't like to tell them that I'd bought both of them from charity shops and that it would cost more to clean them than replace. There had also been a digger working by the riverbank removing the debris when I left. So hopefully, the flooding was only going to be a one-off.

My phone pinged with a text and Nell picked it up off the bedside table.

'It's Cole.' She made a moue with her lips. 'Obviously.'

'Will you stop, this is my married landlord we're talking about,' I said, grabbing the phone off her before she sent back an incriminating reply on my behalf.

'It's not me who put a kiss on the end of my message to him last night.'

'Oh God, don't remind me. That was mortifying.'

'Don't worry about it,' she said, tongue firmly between her teeth. 'I bet everyone talks like that to each other in the building trade. *Hi, can I get this skip collected please Gary, kiss kiss. Nipping out for some bricks, back in five, miss you already xoxo.*'

'Very funny.' I opened his text, deliberately holding the screen away from her so she couldn't see it.

'Meanie,' she muttered, taking a sip of her coffee.

Cole and I had been in touch with each other several times over the last twenty-four hours. Last night after dinner (which was Olek's grandmother's recipe for a delicious stew called *bigos* and made me almost glad I'd had to evacuate my own house), Cole had sent me a text to check I was OK and to reassure me he'd be back with news about a work space as soon as he could. It had been a thoughtful gesture and I'd responded immediately, telling him as much and without thinking, signed off with two kisses.

I read Cole's message but before I could relay it to Nell, there was a knock at the door.

'Come in,' Nell yelled. 'We're decent.'

Olek's round face appeared in the doorway, his cropped hair hidden this morning under a beanie and his ice-blue eyes crinkled with humour as usual; he laughed when he saw us both squashed into his son's bed.

'You two look like you're plotting something.'

'Merry's texting her hot builder-slash-landlord, and won't show me what she's written,' Nell answered. 'If that counts?'

'*Merry* was fast asleep two minutes ago,' I corrected her. 'My eyes haven't focused enough to type yet.'

'Sorry about that,' Olek said. 'I told her not to wake you but she's like a kid on Christmas morning and couldn't wait.'

'I needed to get up early, anyway,' I said, dismissing his apology. 'Lots to do.'

'Messages from her kissable landlord to reply to,' Nell piped up.

'Her landlord who dropped the fact that he has a wife and daughter into the conversation,' I reminded her.

Nell pulled a face. 'Shame, he seemed really perfect for you. Never mind, there are plenty more pebbles on the beach. We'll find you someone – I'll make it my mission.'

'Please don't.' I exchanged resigned looks with Olek, who shrugged helplessly. 'Thanks again,' I said to him. 'For letting me stay in Max's room. I appreciate it.'

'You are very welcome in my house, Merry.' He gave his wife a pointed look. 'Everybody is welcome here.'

'Come here and kiss me goodbye.' She hooked a finger at him. 'Before you go and set the world free from behind their jammed locks and snapped-off keys.'

He kissed Nell on the lips, which felt a bit intimate as I was close enough to feel the warmth of his breath. He patted my head with a grin before leaving the room.

'My hero,' she said with a dreamy sigh after he'd gone. 'Literally not a bad bone in his body.'

'He is lovely,' I agreed, simultaneously wondering if Cole's wife was kissing him goodbye this morning and thinking the same thing. I hoped so. I also hoped there was someone out there somewhere waiting to be my hero. If there was, I wished we'd hurry up and cross paths. 'What did he mean about everyone being welcome?'

She wrinkled her nose. 'Mum and Dad invited us to their house for Christmas. Their cruise has been cancelled and they don't want to spend it alone. But we've already promised Max and Olek's parents that we're spending it here, so we can't go to them. Olek wants me to invite my parents here instead.'

'Ah.'

'Exactly,' Nell said heavily. 'I mean I love them, but you know what they're like.'

I nodded. Nell couldn't relax when her parents were here. She felt like she had to be on her best behaviour all the time and whenever they did come and visit, she'd spend weeks spring cleaning and in some instances even redecorating just to impress them. It all stemmed from their initial disappointment with her choice of partner; she'd never stopped trying to prove to them that she hadn't lowered her standards by choosing Olek. I did understand how she felt but I still thought she was lucky. I'd lost my mum, and there was an empty space on my birth certificate where my father's name should have been. I'd choose difficult-to-please parents over no parents at all.

She pasted on a smile. 'Anyway, what does the message from the big bad builder say?'

'It says *Morning Merry, I've been thinking about you all night, are you free this morning for brunch?*'

Nell nearly choked on her coffee. 'No way!' she spluttered.

I laughed. 'Correct, no way at all. But he did ask if I could meet him at the market at ten a.m. because he's got something to show me. Do you think he's got somewhere for me to work in the centre of town? I hope so; that would be great, we could have lunch breaks together.'

She smirked. 'Perhaps he's rented that vacant stall for you. Can you even make candles *al fresco*?'

One of the market traders close to Nell had given up their stall recently. A man called Twiggy had been selling fake Bonsai trees and had been reported to the trading standards agency.

I shook my head. 'It's not a theory I want to put to the test. I asked him for somewhere warm and dry.'

'Does he know what your work entails?' Nell asked, easing her legs back out of bed and taking my empty mug from me.

I cast my mind back through our various conversations. 'I didn't specify, but there was a windowsill full of candles, jars of essential oils and my various bits of kit, so there were plenty of clues.'

'I can't speak for all men, obviously.' She examined her face in the mirror and poked at a spot. 'But Olek would need a lot more to go on than that. Besides, Cole would probably have been too busy gazing into your sad puppy eyes.'

'Looking at the ruined skirting boards, more like.' I climbed out of bed and opened the curtains; the red Liverpool FC curtains, obviously. 'Do you want to have the first shower? I'll go after you, I need to wash my hair.'

'For your date at the market?'

'For *myself*. I would never ever flirt with a man who I knew wasn't single,' I said, rummaging in my holdall for the jumper which brought out the colour in my eyes and whenever I wore it, people said how well I looked.

'I know,' Nell replied contritely. 'I'll stop teasing. And you don't have to take Cole up on his offer, whatever it might be. You can stay here, you know, take over the dining room with your candles. We don't use the room much anyway except for high days and holidays.'

'Like Christmas Day with *all* the family?' I said.

'Hmm.' She frowned. 'I love Christmas but stressing over Mum and Dad will squeeze the joy out of the day. Anyway, the offer is there if you need it.'

I shook my head. 'It's very kind. But I need a lot of space, now more than ever. Did I tell you Sally called me yesterday about the Christmas school fair?'

I held up my turquoise jumper and shook it to get the creases out.

'Tell her you can't do it, change of circumstances. She'll understand,' Nell said. 'I like you in that one.'

Astrid always said the same. The colour made my green eyes pop. And if you knew you looked nice, it helped you feel more confident in meetings. Absolutely nothing to do with the fact that the meeting was with Cole.

'Do you? Thanks,' I said innocently. 'I've already said yes to Sally. Mind you, I did nearly drop the phone when she told me that the person they had selling candles last year sold almost one thousand units.'

Nell widened her eyes. 'That works out at over three hundred sales of scented candles an hour. Not to be sniffed at. *Sniffed*?'

'Very good,' I grinned. 'I can't turn down that sort of money. I'm going to get in, sell my stuff and get out as quickly as possible and laugh all the way to the bank.'

'Good to know that your Christmas spirit is still alive and well,' she said, with a snort.

'So, in the run-up to that, I'm going to go up a gear production-wise,' I continued, ignoring her jibe. 'I'd employ someone if I had the money but as it is, I'm just going to have to put in longer hours, and don't warn me not to burn the candle at both ends because that joke has been done.'

I zipped past her into the bathroom.

'Oi!' She knocked on the door. 'I thought I was going first. You're getting on my wick.'

'You snooze, you lose,' I called back gleefully. 'Mine's toast with peanut butter, please!'

Chapter 16

Merry

I arrived at the market with fifteen minutes to spare and used the time to wander around with my Christmas Project hat on. The storm two days ago had washed the sky clean, and it was that beautiful crystal blue unique to winter. The sun was out, dazzlingly low and the overnight frost was still lingering, sparkling on pavements and rooftops as if they were sprinkled with glitter. There was a sharp nip in the air and I was glad I was wearing a scarf and gloves.

With just under six weeks to go to Christmas Day, Wetherley was already starting to prepare. The local council had already strung up the lights, which criss-crossed the two main streets leading to the centre and around the market square, from lamp post to lamp post.

Despite my misgivings about Christmas this year, I couldn't deny that I was looking forward to seeing Wetherley in all its festive finery.

The tree hadn't been delivered yet. It was always situated at the edge of the marketplace, directly opposite the old bank where it would be plugged in until early January. Now that I knew Cole was in charge of that building project too, I'd have a word with him, maybe see if the scaffolding could come down in time for the Christmas lights switch-on. There was a lot to be done, and not a lot of time to do it, and I was working hard to ignore the panicky feeling in my chest. I might be leading the Christmas activities, I reminded myself, but it was a town effort; I'd just have to plan it carefully and learn to delegate.

Cole was waiting for me when I got back to Nell's stall. I was intrigued about what he had got to show me. I'd sent him a text back saying that I was free at ten and asked if he could give me any more details in the meantime. He'd simply replied with a thumbs-up emoji.

His face lit up with a smile when he saw me. Nell was serving a customer but still managed to waggle her eyebrows at Cole's back suggestively.

'Hi,' I said. 'Sorry for keeping you waiting. I was just working out how to arrange all the Christmas trees around the marketplace next month.'

'There'll be more than one?' he asked, bemused.

'A lot more,' I replied. 'You should come to the Christmas Project meetings and you'd know what we're planning.'

'Ah, yes.' He nodded. 'The Benny Dunford tribute. I did mean to come to that, but I was busy and then . . . If I'm honest I'm not feeling Christmas this year, so I'm keeping a low profile on that score.'

'Same here,' I said, 'but somehow I just get sucked into these things.'

'I can imagine.' He laughed at my mystified expression. 'Thanks for meeting me and sorry to be vague and not give you any more details but I was worried you'd have preconceptions about what I'm about to show you, and it would put you off.'

'OK,' I said warily. 'I'll try and keep an open mind. But you're not selling it.'

'Have a little faith,' he grinned. 'I know you didn't have too many specific requirements, but this solution is a bit unconventional.'

My eyes slid to the empty stall next to Nell's where Twiggy's Bonsai trees used to be. 'As long as it's warm enough to work in.'

He nodded. 'Cosy, I think you asked for.'

I smiled. 'I did. I think if you have to spend all day working, you might as well be comfortable.'

'Don't ever think about becoming a builder,' he said wryly.

'Or a market trader. Here, on the house.' Nell handed him a brown paper bag, twisted over at the ends. 'For being such a sweetie to my best friend. She deserves a bit of looking after.'

'Oh.' Cole looked touched. 'That's very kind of you.'

I felt colour rise to my cheeks. 'Cole is being a responsible landlord, that's all. I don't need looking after, I'm not a delicate houseplant.'

'More like a cactus,' Nell muttered, just loud enough to make Cole laugh.

'Merry is right,' said Cole, 'it's in our contract to provide alternative accommodation if necessary. Anyone would do the same.'

Did he have to make it sound like such an onerous duty, I thought, trying not to look too deflated.

'You'd be surprised,' said Nell. 'Merry and I shared a flat once and the owner put it up for sale without telling us. We came home one day and found an estate agent in the bathroom demonstrating the thermostatic valve on the shower to three men from Barnsley.'

'He was clothed,' I pointed out.

Cole laughed and peered in the bag. 'It's not more wasabi, is it? Because my sinuses are still recovering from the last lot.'

'Pine nuts,' said Nell. 'Used for centuries by Native Americans for—'

'Making pesto,' I jumped in quickly before she could finish the sentence.

'Great,' he said, looking baffled at my sudden interruption, but tucked the bag in his pocket. 'Very useful.'

I gave Nell a long-suffering look and she grinned, lifting one shoulder insouciantly. I'd heard her tell customers before that pine nuts were the original Viagra. That was not something either Cole or I needed to hear right now.

'Shall we get going?' I suggested. 'I'm sure you're a very busy man.'

He gave a wry smile. 'I am. Even more so than usual thanks to my landscaping contractor, who, by the way will be financing the repairs to Holly Cottage.'

He gave Nell and me a potted explanation of what had caused the flood and then the two of us set off.

'It's not far,' said Cole, leading the way.

He wasn't joking. We stopped seconds later outside the old bank. I supposed it was obvious now I thought about it; Nell and I had seen him going in there, so he clearly had something to do with it and how many other spaces was he likely to have free for me to use without much notice?

'Is this yours?' I asked, 'or are you in charge of renovating it?'

'I bought it earlier this year along with other members of my family; well, with them and a hefty loan,' he said getting a bunch of keys out of his pocket. 'It's still in a bit of a state I'm afraid, but there's plenty of space to do whatever it is you do. It's got running water and electricity.'

'It's huge,' I said with a gasp as I stepped inside after him. I looked at the beams and the windows and the old wooden floor. It looked quite small from the outside. 'And beautiful.'

It was also completely empty and our voices echoed off the walls. There was no form of heating in this downstairs room and our breath formed clouds in front of our faces as we talked. I made a mental note to get myself an electric heater. At the times I'd be melting wax, I'd be warm enough, but it would quickly get cold in here when I was packing or labelling or doing the sales invoices.

'It will be,' he said, following my gaze. 'It's a work in progress, but with one thing or another, I haven't managed to make much progress at all. But that's going to change. By spring, this place will be unrecognisable. And in the meantime, it's yours for as long as you need it.'

'I'm very grateful,' I said. 'But I might need you to help me bring the kitchen table from the cottage to work at.'

'I'm hoping what I'd arranged is better than that.' He looked pleased with himself. 'It's entirely up to you, but I thought you might feel a bit on show downstairs, especially when the lights are on here and everyone can see in through with the windows from the pavement. I've made a workspace for you upstairs on the first floor instead. Come and take a look.'

'Listen, Cole,' I shook my head in amazement. 'I haven't even seen it yet, but I'm already flattered that you've gone to all this trouble.'

'Well,' he said, 'it took me all night, but it's amazing what you can do with some old pallets and a few camping chairs.'

That didn't sound particularly comfortable, but ten out of ten for effort.

'Oh, I see.' I tried to arrange my features into an encouraging smile. 'Lovely.'

'Follow me.' Cole made an odd noise as he walked off and I couldn't work out whether he was coughing or laughing.

He pushed open another door and with a chivalrous gesture, invited me to go first. We were in a corridor with a door out to the back of the building and he pointed out the small car-park space I could use. I was familiar with the layout because it was the same as Daniel's shop and I'd been in and out of there many times.

As we climbed the stairs the air became warmer, which was a blessing. At the top of the first flight of stairs was a landing with three closed doors off it. The staircase continued up again to another floor. Cole pushed open one of the doors to reveal a large room with a kitchen sink and small adjoining worktop and a small fridge. A selection of mugs, a posh coffee machine, a kettle and several canisters were arranged on the worktop. A small round table and four chairs had been set on a rug by the window, looking a bit lost in such a big space. It was absolutely ideal for Merry and Bright. I couldn't believe my luck.

'The facilities are a bit basic,' he admitted. 'I'm going to be putting in a brand-new kitchen over Christmas. But in the meantime, at least you can make yourself a drink. There's fresh milk in the fridge. The sink works and there is power in here and I've turned the hot water on. There are no radiators but I've had a couple of fan heaters going all day to take the chill off.'

I nodded. 'This is a great space, thank you. Even more room to work than the cottage.'

I had a couple of hotplates which I'd used for melting wax when I'd been briefly based in Daniel's shed; they'd be perfect.

We moved along the corridor to the second door. Cole put his shoulder to it and pushed hard until the door opened.

'In here is the bathroom . . . well, toilet and hand basin. The door sticks and the lock is dodgy, so whatever you do, don't lock the door. Taking the locking mechanism out and trying to fix it is on the list of immediate jobs.'

'So I can't lock the door when I go to the loo?'

He wrinkled his nose. 'I know, I'm sorry, I'd go as far as to say don't even properly shut it for now.'

I blinked at him, chewing my lip. I didn't fancy getting stuck in the loo, but I didn't want someone coming up the stairs and finding me sitting on the throne either.

'OK, understood,' I said, not liking the idea of getting stuck in the smallest room.

Cole must have read my expression. 'Only two people have keys to the building.' He fished in his pocket for a smaller bunch of keys and held it out to me. 'Me and now you, and I promise I'll get the lock sorted as soon as I can.'

'Thank you, I'd appreciate that.' I leaned into the bathroom and flicked the light switch and the bulb flickered into life, so at least that worked.

We headed to the final door: Cole opened it and then stepped aside to let me go ahead of him.

I walked in slowly, taking it all in. 'It's . . . wow, I'm lost for words. I wasn't expecting this, any of this. It's lovely!'

He grinned. 'Glad you like it. Go in, look around.'

The large rectangular room was filled with natural light thanks to a row of mullioned windows at the far end. A small leather sofa was scattered with velvet cushions in shades of green and blue and the floorboards were covered with several colourful rugs to match. A desk and chair had been placed under one of the windows. On the desk was a lamp in the shape of a dachshund with a colourful shade. A trio of candles decorated one side table and on another, a huge bouquet of lilies, stocks and roses still in its cellophane wrapping sat in a water jug; the perfume was incredible. The room had an eclectic and welcoming feel to it and, despite its size, felt very cosy.

'Will this do?' he said, joining me by the window where I was admiring the outlook over the market.

'*Will it do?*' I repeated incredulously. 'It's amazing, I love it.'

'I'm sorry the view is a bit spoiled by the scaffolding,' he said. 'It was ready to come down, but now I've got a roofer coming next week. The tiles are ancient and I want to check for damage following that wind. Then it can be removed.'

'In plenty of time for Christmas,' I said. 'I'll be able to look out at the top of the tree!'

'Um.' Cole turned away from the window and straightened the corner of a cushion and gave a self-conscious cough. 'The flowers are to say thank you for your understanding and for being so easy to deal with. And the candles, well, they're not scented or anything, but I thought it made the room—'

'Cosy,' I finished for him. 'It really does. I'm going to enjoy working here.'

'Thank heavens for that.' He wiped his forehead, pretending to be relieved. 'I think that means Operation Cosy is mission accomplished. So, what is it you actually do?'

'I run a small business—'

I was interrupted by *The Flintstones* theme tune ringing out from Cole's phone.

'Sorry about that.' He noticed my amusement and grinned. 'That's the ringtone I keep just for my dad, whose name is Fred. I'd better take this.' He strode towards the door as he answered. 'Hi Dad, you OK? Oh, hello, yes, this is Cole.'

My ears pricked up at the change in his voice; it sounded as if someone else other than Mr Robinson senior was on the other end.

'Oh dear. Thank you very much for letting me know, and thank you for looking after him. I'll be there as soon as I can. And who am I talking to? Thank you.' He ended the call, frowning.

'Is there a problem?' I asked.

Cole gave me a thin smile. 'He's had a fall, not too serious, but I think it's shaken him up. He lives the other side of the square in the retirement complex.'

'Oh dear, your poor dad. I have a friend who lives there too: Astrid, you met her and her dog, Otto.'

He nodded. 'It was Astrid who called me, I thought I recognised the voice. She's looking after my dad until I get there. So, is there anything else you need or . . .'

'Absolutely nothing at all, you go and see him. I'll lock up here and get Nell to help me move in later,' I said and blew out the candles, which had a soft vanilla fragrance. 'Never leave a naked flame unattended, that's my motto.'

'Very wise,' said Cole with a twinkle in his eye. 'You've already flooded one of my properties, I'd rather you didn't burn down a second.'

'Me!' I gasped with mock indignation as he headed for the stairs. 'You can go off people, you know.'

Although it was unlikely in this case, I thought, because Cole Robinson was growing on me each time we met.

Chapter 17

Cole

Cole was standing outside the old bank trying to get through to Merry, but her phone was engaged. He knew she was there because the lights were on. This wasn't a scheduled call but he had been on his way to visit his dad when the roofer phoned to confirm he'd be doing the job at the old bank tomorrow. He could send her a text, he supposed, but he felt it would be more professional to pass on the news personally. He grinned to himself; who was he kidding? He was here because he liked her. Plain and simple.

He'd passed by the old bank several times since he'd given her a set of keys, and every time the lights in the first-floor windows had been on. He'd intended to come back the following day and mend the lock on the bathroom door, but things had gone a bit manic, and he'd just not had the chance.

The flood had really messed things up for him. The sisters had immediately pulled out of purchasing two of the houses. They didn't want to risk living on a flood plain. No matter how hard he'd tried to explain that the river had never and would never naturally flood the land

171

where Orchard Gardens was being built and that the fault lay entirely with the landscaping contractor, they said they couldn't risk it. He'd been counting on the money from their deposits to pay the next tranche of bills; he was feeling the pressure to find another buyer to ease his cashflow.

And then there was his dad to worry about. Physically, Fred was fine after his fall last week, he was only in his early seventies and he'd always been fit and active, well until he'd moved to Rosebridge last year, that was. It had been Fred's pride that had suffered most, due to having tripped up right in front of Astrid and then having to be dependent on her to help him back home. Ever since then, he'd been very subdued and Cole and Hester were concerned about him. Until he perked up again, they were taking it in turns to pop in as often as they could.

Cole tried Merry's number once more and this time she picked up.

'Hi Merry, it's Cole Robinson, I'm outside, is it OK to drop in?' Cole realised he was holding his breath and hoping the answer would be yes.

'Er, OK, yes, sure. Come on up. The door's locked but the keys are up here with me.'

It wasn't the most enthusiastic welcome, but then she was probably as busy as he was.

Cole unlocked the front door and let himself in. A smile crept across his face as he walked through the bank towards the staircase; he was looking forward to seeing her, he realised.

He'd found himself thinking about Merry a lot recently. She was good fun, and although it wasn't the most important thing, she was gorgeous. He liked her company, and he enjoyed the way conversation sparked backwards and forwards between them. Her friend Nell had said she was newly-single, but there had been that guy at the cottage when Cole had arrived on the morning of the flood, so maybe she was newly-taken again?

The dating app that Hester had signed him up for was one where men had to wait for the women to make the first move, which was fine by him. It had been so long since he'd asked a woman out, he wasn't sure what you were and weren't allowed to say or do anymore. He'd gone along with Hester at the time, mainly because they'd both had a couple of glasses of wine, and it had been a bit of a laugh. But he'd put it out of his mind soon after, until Hester had asked him how he was getting on and insisted on checking his notifications.

'Twenty-five!' she'd squealed. 'I knew that bio would work!'

He'd cringed, regretting ever letting his sister talk him into signing up. And he certainly shouldn't have let her write his bio. According to her, he was a rufty-tufty builder with a heart of gold and a good sense of fun, whose likes included red wine, log fires and big scruffy dogs.

'I know you don't have a dog,' she'd said, justifying her white lie. 'But that's the sort of dog you would have, and there's no point me setting you up with a chihuahua owner because you call them rats.'

Which he'd had to admit was true. But twenty-five women all sending him messages? He'd been exhausted just reading them. Not to mention a bit scared. And as for what they were looking for in a date, that had been even more exhausting. He'd been all for deleting the app from his phone, but Hester had persuaded him to at least reply to the ones he thought sounded nice. In the end he'd agreed, but on the condition that she didn't get to see which ones he'd chosen or to read his replies. He'd only replied to one woman. Her name was Evelyn; her profile had made him laugh and she'd got more clothes on than the rest of them. They'd sent a few messages backwards and forwards but then she'd asked to see a bit more of him. It took him a while to realise she meant naked photos. What sort of woman wanted to see his personal credentials before they'd even met in real life? It had put him right off her. Maybe that was how it worked these days, but it didn't work for him and he didn't return her messages after that. The whole thing felt sleazy.

Merry was waiting for him at the top of the stairs as he came up, still holding her phone. She was wearing a long apron over a flowery dress. Her feet were in thick sheepskin boots, her cheeks were flushed and ringlets of damp hair had escaped from a bun and framed her face. His heart fluttered unexpectedly; she looked adorable. Wholesome, but in a totally hot way. Plus she was real and not just a bio on an app. Cole made an instant decision: when it came to dating, he was going to stick to the old-fashioned way.

'Hi,' he said, suddenly feeling tongue-tied. *Come on Cole, get a grip.* He could organise teams of labourers, manage multiple property projects and talk banks into lending him thousands; surely he could chat to a woman?

'Please say you've come to mend the lock on the loo?' Merry said, pushing the hair off her face with her forearm.

'Damn,' he muttered, annoyed with himself. 'I'm sorry. I haven't got my toolbox with me. Tomorrow. Definitely.'

She looked down at her phone screen and back at him and sighed. 'No worries.'

As Cole reached the top of the stairs, a pungent aroma hit the back of his throat and made him cough. Either she had gone overboard with the air freshener or she was making something weird. Although she couldn't be baking because there wasn't an oven.

'What's that smell?' Cole sniffed the air. 'Is something burning?'

She shook her head. 'It's essential oils. It's meant to be a relaxing aroma.'

Merry opened the kitchen and an even stronger smell wafted out.

'Wow, what are you doing up here?' he grinned, pretending to be horrified. 'Running a massage parlour?'

'Oops. Is that a problem?' She looked at Cole's stunned expression and let out a peal of warm laughter. 'Don't worry, it's all above board. I make candles. Come on in, I'll show you.'

Cole followed her into the kitchen and was amazed at what he saw. The derelict room had been transformed into a mini factory: there were two long tables, one covered in small empty glass jars and the other in boxes. The kitchen worktop had two hotplates on it, with pans of water on them. The rest of the surface was covered in more glass jars which had been filled with wax.

'Welcome to my scented world.' She waved an arm around the room. 'These are soy wax candles, small batch, hand-poured and made with love and the very best quality organic oils. And today I've been working on a new scent for a client.'

Cole picked up a very professional-looking box and read the logo. 'Merry and Bright. I've seen this brand before.'

'At the moment I sell on Etsy and on Nell's Nuts – you might have seen them there.'

Cole had never been on Etsy so assumed it must have been on the nut stall. 'Do you know what, you're a life-saver. I need Christmas presents for all my suppliers – a handmade candle would be just the job.'

His main priority was getting stuff for the kids; Harley had given him some ideas, but Freya was still working on her letter to Santa and he didn't like to point out that Santa needed a longer lead time this year. Lydia had already suggested that she buy them a big present each from both of them, which would help, but he still wanted to choose things especially for them.

'You buy gifts for your suppliers?' she asked, looking surprised. 'Shouldn't it be the other way around?'

'Tactics,' he said, putting on a sly expression. 'I butter them up at Christmas so that I'm their favourite customer, then when I need a favour, like for example an emergency requirement for dryers in Holly Cottage, they come up trumps for me.'

She looked impressed. 'It's a good strategy; perhaps I should buy my landlord a present so he hurries up and finishes my house.'

'Quality workmanship can't be rushed,' he said, pretending to be insulted. 'But if you can't stay at your friend's any longer, I'll happily pay for a hotel.'

'I'm teasing,' she said, her green eyes sparkling up at him. 'Nell's happy for me to be there and I'm loving working here. I make the candles in this room, and then do my admin in the front to make the most of the view.'

He pressed a hand to his forehead and groaned. 'I've just realised I put candles in the living room for you. And they weren't small poured, scented whatevers, they were just bog-standard supermarket ones. They must seem really cheap and nasty to you.'

'No, no, not at all!' she insisted. 'It was a lovely gesture. Besides, you can never have too many candles in your life; it's like having too many books: completely impossible. And to be honest, I rarely get to keep them for myself anymore, I'm too busy trying to fulfil the orders I've got.'

Cole nodded. 'Same here. I'm so busy building houses for other people that I don't have time to build one for myself.'

'You don't have a house at all?' Her lovely face fell. 'Now I feel bad for complaining.'

'Don't worry, the situation is only temporary.' He hoped, anyway. 'Now what sort of candles should I buy?'

As Merry listed her range of scented candles, he started to regret his decision: raspberry, lemon, vanilla. Most of his suppliers were men; they'd probably prefer the bottle of booze he usually got them.

Cole scratched his head. 'Do you have anything a bit more . . . manly?'

'I've never really thought of my candles as having a gender bias.' She gave him a bemused look. 'OK, how about lemon? Rosemary?'

'Can you make them gin-scented?' he suggested, thinking that this might be a compromise.

She thought for a moment. 'I can try. And actually, that might be a nice one for the school Christmas Fair.'

'Great, I'll have twenty-seven large ones please. Gift wrapped if possible, in a manly way.' He grinned, feeling very pleased with himself. That was most of his Christmas shopping done in one fell swoop. 'Actually, make it twenty-nine, I'll get my sister and my dad the same.'

'Wow,' she beamed at him. 'Thank you so much! This is turning out to be a great day. How about adding an extra one for yourself and making it a round thirty?'

'OK, why not.' He chuckled. 'Are you always this enthusiastic when you get an order?'

She blushed. 'I suppose I am a bit. This time last year, candle-making was only a hobby; I wasn't sure I'd ever be able to make enough money from it to do it full-time.

But to be honest, I've got orders coming in thick and fast. I'm working all the hours just to keep up, not that I'm moaning.'

'It's a good problem to have,' he said, nodding sympathetically. 'Can you employ someone to help for a few hours?'

'Not right now; I lost quite a bit of money when the cottage flooded.' She winced. 'I hadn't got around to sorting out my contents insurance.'

'Oh, God, I'm sorry.' Now he felt even worse. It was on a different scale of course, but there was no way he could operate his business without having insurance.

She shrugged, looking sheepish. 'My own fault. I'm trying to be more organised, but it doesn't come naturally.'

What did come naturally was her lovely smile, her obvious joy in what she did and her ability to brighten his day by just being herself. He gave himself a shake, realising he was gazing at her. 'So how much do I owe you?'

'Um,' she rubbed a hand over her face. 'Quite a lot I'm afraid. They're ten pounds each so that's three hundred pounds.'

'Ten pounds? Is that all?' He was shocked. 'Hand-produced, organic oils, gift wrapping . . . that's not enough.'

She chewed her lip thoughtfully and then gave a decisive nod.

'You're right. OK . . .' She tilted her chin up and Cole had to fight an urge to touch her face; there was a naivety about her that he found so refreshing. 'Thirteen pounds fifty and that's my final offer.'

He laughed out loud and stuck his hand out for her to shake. 'Then it's a deal.'

'Phew,' she said, her eyes sparkling as she took his hand. 'I hate negotiating. I'd have been happy with twelve.'

Her fingers felt soft and warm in his hand and he felt a flicker of heat in his belly. This was what he was missing: being touched, the twinkle of an eye, the flush on her cheeks as he looked at her.

He held onto her hand for as long as he could. 'And I'd have happily paid fifteen.'

'No way!' she gasped. 'Then I guess we're both winners.'

'I guess we are,' he agreed. 'So are you finished for the day now?'

He cast his eye over the tables and at the piles of boxes and labels. It was difficult to see how far she'd got with production; it all looked a bit haphazard to him.

'Yes and no,' she sighed. 'Do you want coffee? I'm having one; I need caffeine to keep me going.'

Without waiting for a reply, she filled the water tank up on Cole's machine and pressed the button. He took his phone out of his pocket and glanced at the time discreetly. His dad would be expecting him so he couldn't be long. He smiled to himself, remembering that he was thirty-eight, not eight. His dad wouldn't mind.

'I'd love one, thanks.' He sat down at the table by the window while he waited.

It was nice spending time with a woman other than his sister. He wouldn't want to swap his job for the world, but ninety-nine per cent of the time he was with other men. He hadn't been totally celibate since he and Lydia split. There had been one particularly fun night at a hotel in Manchester with a woman he'd met while on a rare lads' night out; they'd agreed it was just a one-off. She admitted that she didn't want a man in her life permanently. He'd pretended he felt the same, but he wanted the complete opposite. He wanted to be part of a couple; he missed having someone who knew how he took his coffee, someone to care for, who cared about him. He knew he'd made mistakes with Lydia; he wanted to get it right next time.

Merry set down a mug in front of him. 'Sorry I haven't used hot milk, but I hope you like it.'

'Thanks,' he said, pleased she'd remembered.

She sat down next to him with a sigh and lifted her own mug to her lips, blowing away the steam.

'Are you OK?' he asked. 'That's about your tenth sigh.'

'Sorry, you must think I'm really rude.' She pulled an apologetic face. 'It's the Christmas Project. I hadn't realised how hard it would be to find someone to be our special guest for the Christmas lights switch-on. I hoped Benny's widow Pam would do it, but she said no. I've tried the local radio, I've even asked the vicar and still no joy. Now it's less than two weeks and I haven't got anyone to do the honours. There's a progress meeting tomorrow night at which everyone is expecting me to come up with a name. And I've got nothing. Absolutely nothing.'

'Oh dear.' He winced. 'That is tricky.'

'Yep.' She sighed again. 'Don't suppose you know any celebs, do you?'

'Um . . .' His sister would kill him, but Merry looked so overwhelmed and he'd love to be the one to come to her rescue. 'As it happens I do.'

He took out his phone, opened his sister's Instagram page and clicked on her profile picture. 'This is my sister.'

He handed the phone to Merry, feeling a little bit smug that he was about to make her day but as he did so, it pinged. His stomach dropped like a stone. That ping meant a new notification from the dating app. Before he could grab the phone back off Merry, she swiped the screen, clearly thinking that it would get rid of the message, but instead it opened it.

She frowned. '*Hey Rufty-Tufty. I've shown you mine, now you know what to do.* Ugh!' She thrust the phone back at him. 'Nope, definitely don't recognise her.'

'Shit, sorry,' said Cole, forcing himself to look. It was Evelyn. Topless. 'That was not who I was trying to show you. That is not my sister.'

'Good to know,' she said archly. 'I take it it's not your wife either.'

'I don't have a wife,' he said, wiping the phone on his sleeve to polish it. 'I'm divorced.'

Merry pressed a hand to her chest. 'Thank goodness for that. Because if you were married and you were getting notifications for a dating app, then you wouldn't be the person I thought you were.'

'I'm single, I promise.' Despite his total embarrassment, he did take some comfort from her words. 'If you don't mind me asking, are you single?'

'I am.' She sighed and then laughed at herself. 'Sorry, another sigh.'

'I hear you,' said Cole, shifting in his seat. 'My mates think I should be having a great time now I'm a bachelor again. But I look at their wives and I'm envious.'

She cocked an eyebrow. 'And how do your mates feel about you staring at their wives?'

'No, no,' he groaned. 'That came out wrong, what I meant was—'

'I know what you meant,' she said. 'I'm teasing. I thought I was with "the one" until recently. So much so that I proposed to him. But heyho, it wasn't to be.'

He blinked. 'You asked him to marry you?'

'Yep.'

'And *he turned you down*?' He shook his head in disbelief.

Merry's cheeks flushed. 'I know. How rude! You've met him actually . . . Daniel. He was leaving the cottage on the morning of the flood when you arrived.'

'Ah yes, I remember.' Cole nodded; that explained why they'd seemed close. And it also explained why he hadn't stopped to help her out when her home was flooded. The man was clearly an idiot. Anyway, none of his business, the main thing was that Merry was definitely single.

'So, after that slight detour into my disastrous love life, back to you.' Merry propped her elbows on the table and leaned closer. 'If that wasn't your wife or sister, who is she?'

'*She* is history,' he said, pressing on the app and deleting it permanently. He was never, never going to dabble in internet dating again.

She giggled. 'Well, that's a relief. Because if she was your suggestion for a celebrity to switch on the Christmas lights, it wouldn't make for a very family-friendly show.'

Cole laughed softly, grateful that she seemed to have a good sense of humour. 'But thankfully my sister is. Have you heard of *The Retail Therapy Show* on the shopping channel?'

This time he made sure that he found Hester's Instagram profile before he handed his phone back to Merry.

'No way.' She gasped. 'Hester Smart is your sister?'

Cole nodded proudly.

'I absolutely *have* heard of that show. Nell and I watched it last week. Nell bought some wrinkle cream for her mum for Christmas.'

'Will she do as your celebrity?' Cole asked. 'I mean I know she's not exactly A-list but—'

'Are you kidding me?' Merry nodded excitedly. 'This is amazing, Cole, you've made my night, my day, my week! Will she really do it?'

Cole swallowed and mentally crossed his fingers. 'She really will.'

'My absolute hero.' Merry leaned forward and kissed his cheek. 'Thank you.'

Cole's heart felt like it was too big for his chest all of a sudden. Whatever it took to get Hester to agree to it, he'd do it. There was no way he wanted to let this woman down.

Chapter 18

Merry

Following Cole's visit yesterday I was feeling a lot more perky this morning. Today was the day I was going to get really organised. I'd spent the first hour of the morning jotting down a list of things which needed to be done as soon as possible. There were a lot of them, but if Cole could really get his sister to do our official lights switch-on, it would solve the biggest of my problems and, I had to admit, it would be a bit of a coup for me too. I hoped I heard from him soon; there was another meeting tonight and I wanted to tell everyone the good news. Talking of which, I should probably see if I could buy a clipboard from the market, it would help me to look efficient at the meeting.

I had already got a brand spanking new whiteboard, which I'd ordered last week and I couldn't wait to get it up on the wall so I could start using it. This was going to be my new way of keeping track of my to-do list, and the sooner I got it hung up, the better. I'd more or less given up on my diary. I'd tried to keep it up to date, but there was only one small box for each day and when I ran out of room there, I'd been turning to any old empty page and continuing my notes there. Now I couldn't find anything, and I'd started to get muddled.

I chose my spot, set the whiteboard down, found the tacks I'd also had delivered and slipped my boot off. I was about to bash the tacks in when my phone rang. It was Astrid, who was outside the bank with Otto. I let her in, pleased to see her.

'*Guten Morgen, mein liebes Mädchen.*' Astrid kissed me and held out a tin. 'I bring you my first-ever mince pies to try.'

'Yum,' I said, mildly disappointed that the tin didn't contain her special German cookies. 'Can't wait.'

'You look different,' I said, once she and Otto had had a look round my new workspace and given it the seal of approval. 'Gorgeous as ever, obviously, but definitely different. You've changed your style.'

'Have I?' she replied innocently, as she unwrapped a pale pink wool scarf.

'Yes,' I said, wondering why she was denying it. 'And you've made mince pies – have I finally turned you into a Brit?'

She was normally a 'more is more' sort of dresser: layers of colours, textures and patterns. Today's outfit was much more understated: soft pink jumper and jeans, like something Mary Berry might wear.

'Let's see what they taste like before you adopt me on behalf of your country. Tea or coffee?' she asked.

I left her in charge of making us both tea and returned to the hanging of my whiteboard.

'Are you allowed to hang things on the wall?' Astrid asked dubiously, looking up from the kettle. 'I'd have thought there were rules about an historic building like this.'

I paused. I really wanted to just get on with it, but I supposed she might have a point. Besides, there would be an advantage to checking first . . .

'You're right, I'll phone the landlord,' I said, putting

my boot back on with a sigh. 'Are you staying a while? I could do with some help.'

Astrid said she was happy to stay and I set her the task of gift-wrapping and packing up some samples of a new rose and frankincense fragrance that a client had asked for, while I tried to contact Cole.

He didn't pick up for ages and I was about to hang up when he came on the line.

'Merry?' He had to yell down the phone to make himself heard over the background noise. It sounded like the clunking of diggers and somewhere there was a vehicle making a reversing beep signal. 'Everything OK?'

'Yes,' I bellowed back. 'Just need to ask you something.'

'Hold on, let me go inside where I can hear you.' The noise died down and I heard a door shut. 'OK, fire away. I'm afraid I haven't seen my sister to ask her yet, in case you were wondering. I'm meeting her at my dad's later.'

'Great, thanks. The committee meeting is at seven o' clock; if you find out by then, would you let me know straight away?' I asked.

'I promise, don't worry.' I could hear the smile in his voice. 'Was that all you wanted?'

'No, actually, I was just checking it's OK to hang something on the wall in the kitchen. A whiteboard.'

'I don't see why not. Do you have your own tools with you?' Cole sounded impressed. 'What are you using to hang this board?'

'Some pin things and the heel of my boot. It'll be fine,' I promised. 'My boot is indestructible.'

There was a moment's stunned silence down the phone. Behind me Astrid gave a chuckle.

'Categorically no,' came the stern reply. 'I'll do it when I come and fix the lock.'

'Fine, I'll leave it on the floor for now,' I said, insulted by the implication that my handiwork wasn't up to scratch, 'but don't worry about the lock, it's already mended.'

'Don't tell me,' he said amused, 'you walloped that with your boot too.'

'Of course not,' I replied haughtily. Which wasn't strictly true, I had hit it a few times but to no avail. 'I poured some eucalyptus oil inside the mechanism and wiggled the handle. Works a treat and smells lovely. There you go, saved you a job.'

'Thanks,' he said, laughing. 'I'll be taking you on as an apprentice soon. Anything else I should know about?'

'Just one thing. I could do with borrowing a ladder; a couple of the bulbs are flickering and I want to change them before they stop working. I tried stacking two chairs on top of one another, but I'm still not tall enough.'

There was a gale of laughter from Astrid.

'You did what? Merry, have you got a death wish?' said Cole in disbelief. 'I will bring a ladder when I come and do that whiteboard. In the meantime, promise me you won't clamber up any chair towers or hit things with your shoes.'

'It's a deal.' I was smiling as I ended the call.

Astrid raised an eyebrow. 'It is good that you get on with your landlord so well.'

'It is. I'm very lucky. So far he has proven very useful indeed.'

'*Useful*?' she pulled a face. 'That is not a word to set the heart racing.'

I felt my face grow warm under her scrutiny. My heart *did* race even at the thought of phoning him. There had been a moment yesterday when he'd asked if I was single when I thought he might be going to ask me out, but the moment had passed. I wasn't going to admit my feelings for someone new to Astrid unless I had concrete proof that they were reciprocated. I might be back on an even footing with Daniel, but the fear of rejection was real.

I helped myself to a still-warm mince pie and changed the subject. 'Oh my word, Astrid, this is heavenly!'

'Really?' She beamed. 'I'm so pleased. I've made a new friend at Rosebridge and he told me that since his wife died, one of the things he misses the most was the smell of her baking.'

'Oh, that's sad,' I replied. 'The power of our sense of smell is very underrated. An aroma can transport us back in time so vividly it can trigger memories we thought we'd forgotten.'

Mum and I had never made mince pies, but we had made jam tarts. Just the smell of Astrid's was enough to remind me of the fun we'd had and the sticky mess I'd created when I'd dropped a jammy spoon onto the floor. What I wouldn't give for one more day with her, the questions I'd ask her: *who were you, Mum?* Where was your family, *my* family? You made sure I was safe, but what about you? Why didn't you seek help when things became unbearable?

'Mince pies were his wife's speciality. I thought I'd surprise him with these. Mine won't be as good, but at least I've made the effort,' said Astrid.

'He'll love them,' I said, 'and if he doesn't, you can always bring them round to me.'

For the next hour or so, Astrid gave me a helping hand while Otto slept peacefully under the table. There was plenty to do and it made a lovely change to have a colleague to chat to. She prepared the wicks and jars for twenty-five of my peony and sandalwood candles and I melted the wax and added the fragrance oils.

We had to leave the wax to cool down before pouring, so after I'd thrown a toy for Otto for a few minutes, until he flopped down again, I propped the whiteboard up on a chair and picked up a marker pen.

'Here are my three main jobs,' I said, drawing three cloud shapes on it and labelling them. 'The Wetherley Christmas festivities culminating on Christmas Eve, the Christmas Fair at school, and Merry and Bright direct orders.'

Astrid smiled proudly. 'When I think back to that little teenager who thought she'd never amount to anything.'

I nodded, remembering my early teenage years. I'd had little confidence in myself and I used to wonder what was wrong with me that no one wanted me to be their child. How I'd yearned to be adopted, to have adults who loved me. It was only years later, in adulthood, that I'd learned how few teenagers were successfully placed in permanent homes. It wasn't about me, it was about would-be parents preferring younger children.

'You told me I could be anyone I wanted to be,' I replied, squeezing her hand. 'For a long time, I didn't believe you because I didn't believe in myself. But now I feel like I'm finally becoming the person I want to be.'

'Oh, Merry.' She put her head on one side. 'You were already that person, you don't need to change. The people who really love you, love you just as you are.'

'That is probably the nicest thing anyone has ever said to me,' I smiled, genuinely touched. But the fear of rejection was so deep-rooted in me that I couldn't quite believe it was true.

Daniel's rejection had been the latest in a long line. Even though he'd said lovely things about me and assured me that this was about him and not me, the end result was the same. I was still alone. The only way I could be part of a family was to create one of my own. And if that meant packing away the more chaotic and spontaneous aspects of my personality, then that was what I would do.

'The Christmas Fair is going to test me,' I said, bringing my focus back to the whiteboard. 'I'll have to squeeze production in around my other orders.'

'My tip for selling at school events is low prices,' said Astrid.

A warm feeling swirled in my stomach, remembering the banter Cole and I had had yesterday as we'd negotiated the price of his candles.

'Children like to buy presents for their parents and grandparents at these things, so make sure you carry some stock for them.'

'I will,' I said softly, 'that's a lovely idea.'

I remembered the year I'd had two pounds to spend on a present for Mum. There'd been a special children's stall at the Christmas Fair for exactly that purpose. I'd chosen a little bottle of perfume for her because she didn't have any of her own. I'd wrapped it up for her and kept it under my pillow until Christmas morning. She'd cried when she opened it and said it was the best present she'd ever had. I'd forgotten what it was called but occasionally I caught a whiff of it when I was in a crowded place and it always took me right back to that happy Christmas Day.

'And what about Merry and Bright orders?' Astrid asked, pulling me back to the present. 'How are they?'

'I deal with those as they come in.' I pulled a face, 'Usually. I'm a bit behind at the moment but now I've got this huge space, it will make it easier to scale up.'

Astrid shook her head sternly and tutted. 'Merry and Bright is your brand, your reputation rides on not just excellent candles but excellent customer service too. This should be your priority until you are big enough to employ a team to help you.'

'I hear you, but right now this Christmas Project is my priority,' I said, tapping the bottom of the pen against my cheek. 'I'm determined for this to be the best one Wetherley has ever seen. All I have to do is promote it so that community groups sign up for a tree, order and pay for the trees, fill in all the right forms with the council, liaise with Tasha at school about the children's choir and . . . what are you chuckling at?'

'*All I have to do,*' Astrid mimicked me. 'You have a lot on your plate, I'd say the first job is to delegate.'

I scratched my head. 'I know you're right, but I've never delegated before; I don't really know how to go about it.'

'Telling people what you need help with is a skill.' Otto stood up just then and nudged Astrid's leg with his nose. The two women laughed. Astrid scratched his head fondly. 'As you can see it's something he has mastered easily.'

She dropped a few crumbs of mince pie, Otto hoovered them up and flopped back down again. 'The important thing is confidence. You go into the committee meeting tonight prepared with a list of tasks you need volunteers for. You start by reminding everyone why you are all there.'

'To make sure Wetherley's festivities are the best ever in memory of Benny Dunford.' I definitely needed to get hold of a clipboard before then.

'Good,' she nodded. 'And then you go through your list of jobs and ask for volunteers to fulfil each one, and don't move on to the next one until you can put a name next to a job.'

'What about if no one volunteers?'

Astrid gave a half-laugh. 'That will definitely happen. In my experience, during the many years I spent on the board of school governors, most people were there simply to be seen to be doing good. If this happens, say something like "Daniel, I notice you don't have a job yet, would you like to be in charge of . . ." etcetera, etcetera.'

'Brilliant,' I said, beaming at her. 'I should be able to manage that.'

I stood up to check the temperature of the cooling wax. One hundred and sixty degrees; ready for the next stage. I picked up the metal jug and began slowly pouring the hot wax into the waiting glass jars.

'What about the Christmas lights switch-on?' Astrid asked when I paused for a rest.

'Fingers crossed, I might have that sorted,' I said. 'Almost. Cole's sister is hopefully going to be our celebrity; the council will organise the main tree and the big button for her to press and all the shops are staying open until seven p.m.'

'I'm looking forward to meeting Hester,' said Astrid, 'Fred has told me all about her.'

I looked at her in surprise. 'I didn't realise you knew him well?'

'Not well.' She went pink. 'He is a lovely man and lonely I think. Since he moved into Rosebridge, he has spent a lot of time on his own. I'm trying to encourage him out of his flat.'

This was the first time I had ever seen Astrid blush.

'Does he like mince pies by any chance?'

My phone rang before I could get anything else out of her.

'Hold that thought,' I said, reaching for the phone on the table, 'I need to know all about you and Fred.'

'Hey, I thought we had a lunch date?' said Nell when I answered her call.

'Sorry!' I said, noticing the time. 'I've been so busy.'

'No worries,' said Nell, 'shall I grab us soup and rolls from the market and bring them up?'

'Sounds good. Astrid is here too. Astrid, do you want soup?'

She shook her head. 'I'm having cottage pie for lunch.'

The thought struck me that that was a very un-Astrid thing to eat but I relayed my soup order to Nell and five minutes later, she arrived with tubs of creamy leek and potato soup and freshy crusty rolls.

'Wowsers.' Nell stared at the whiteboard and the tables covered in candles in various stages of production. 'It's like a military operation in here. Who are you and what have you done with my freewheeling friend?'

'The devil's in the detail,' I said, tapping my nose. 'I'm not leaving anything to chance. But I must admit my brain has started to hurt.'

'Then sit and eat,' said Astrid. 'I have been here for two hours and you are busy all the time. You're working at a hundred miles an hour. Come.' She pulled out the chair next to her and Nell and I sat down to tuck into our soup.

'I wasn't going to eat carbs today,' said Nell, ripping her bread. 'But then I had a call from my mother wanting to know about our Christmas plans, and so now I need the comfort.'

Astrid shook her head and laughed. 'Considering it is the most wonderful time of the year, Christmas certainly brings with it its fair share of stress.'

'Is she still hoping you'll visit her?' I asked, sprinkling a sachet of black pepper onto my soup.

'She is. And she's ordered Christmas in a box from a very well-known London food emporium to lure us over.'

'But you are not tempted?' Astrid asked.

Nell pulled a face while she chewed and swallowed her bread. 'The food would be amazing and everything would be beautiful. But in our house I can relax. At theirs, no sooner do you put your empty mug down – on a coaster, naturally – than Dad has whisked it away to stack in the dishwasher. Mum has even extended the invitation to Olek's parents and Max, which is a sure sign that they're getting desperate.'

I did feel some sympathy for Mr and Mrs Thornberry; they might be a bit overbearing and difficult to relax around, but Nell was their only daughter and they weren't getting any younger.

'Is that not a good compromise?' I said, 'all of you going to them, so you can still be together?'

'Not really, because my mother-in-law likes to be in charge of dinner on Christmas Eve. She makes the most amazing food; you've tasted her *pierogi*.'

I nodded. They were out of this world; I'd had all sorts of savoury ones filled with potato, cheese and cabbage, but my favourites were blueberry dusted with icing sugar.

'And unfortunately,' Nell continued, 'there's no way on earth my mother could share her kitchen.'

'What a blessing,' said Astrid wistfully, 'to have such a large family to argue with.'

'I suppose so,' Nell said, chastened.

Astrid was an only child born to older parents who had now passed away, and like me she had no family. It was another reason why she had felt drawn to me when she'd been my art teacher.

'I think you should consider Olek's suggestion and invite everyone to you,' I said.

'And tell them not to cancel the Christmas in a box, they can bring it with them,' Astrid added.

'But our house is tiny. My parents are used to a bathroom each. And at Christmas I like wearing pyjamas all day and drinking Prosecco and not washing up for hours.'

'Then do that,' I said simply.

She shook her head. 'If Mum comes it'll be all meals at the table and dressing for dinner. I'll be on edge the whole time.'

'Your house, your rules,' I said.

'If your parents love you,' said Astrid kindly, 'they will accept you as you are. They will be happy just being with you.'

'You haven't met them.' Nell let out a long breath. 'But I'll sleep on it. Thanks, ladies.'

'Before you arrived, I was hearing about Fred,' I said, understanding she was ready to change the topic. 'Astrid has a new male friend who just happens to be Cole's father.'

'Ooh!' Nell's eyes twinkled. 'Is he as handsome as his son?'

'You are making mountains from molehills,' Astrid said, rearranging the mince pies on the tin quite unnecessarily. 'I saw him reading the poster for my art classes, that's all. He told me that he was interested in birds and asked whether if he came could he paint them. I said that it was a good idea and I invited him to come for a walk with Otto and me.'

'Was that when he had his fall?' I asked.

'Very unfortunate.' Astrid winced. 'He tripped over a tree root. Although at least it meant I was able to see inside his flat. He has been very private until now.'

'What's it like?' I asked.

She frowned. 'It is neat and clean. He has lots of books and he says he likes watching films. He keeps a bird table on his balcony and he is experimenting with different seeds to see which birds he can attract.'

'I'm hearing a *but*,' said Nell, dunking bread into her soup. Otto inched closer in anticipation of crumbs.

'There is no sense of his previous life,' Astrid said. 'Who was Fred Robinson before he moved to Rosebridge?'

'Not even any photographs?' I asked.

She gave a little sigh. 'There are lots of photographs of his wife, a nice neat-looking woman, and a couple of the family, but not much else. Even the furniture looks new. I cannot imagine parting with all the mementos I've collected of my life. But never mind, we are all different.' She dismissed her comments with a wave of her hand. 'It was nice to meet Cole after hearing so much about him.'

'Cute, isn't he,' Nell put in with a cheeky wink. 'And even cuter now we know he isn't married anymore.'

My heart gave an unexpected squeeze and I realised how much I wanted Astrid to like him. 'What did you think? He's been very good to me and obviously cares about his family too. He said his sister's fence blew down and he went round to mend it and he dropped everything when Fred had his fall.'

She smiled. 'I think he too might be lonely. Like his father.'

'Interesting.' Nell jerked her head to me. 'He definitely likes you, Merry – invite him for a walk and hold his hand in case he trips.'

I shook my head. No way; my mouth went dry at the thought of it. 'I can't do that. Firstly, I'm far too busy at the moment and secondly, if he said no, I'd be mortified.'

'Why would he say no?' Nell gave an exasperated huff.

I shrugged. 'Why would he say yes?'

Astrid and Nell groaned and immediately launched into the many reasons he'd want to go on a date with me.

I held my hands up in protest. 'Daniel and I might be over, but my heart is still bruised from being knocked back; I'm not sure I'm ready for any more rejection.'

'You can't rule someone out just in case it doesn't work out,' Astrid said. 'I'm assuming we're having this conversation because you do like him?'

I nodded sheepishly. 'But Cole is so different to me: he's organised and professional and methodical. Even the way I knock nails in horrifies him. Why would a man like that be attracted to a woman like me? I'm attempting to change my ways but it doesn't come naturally.'

Nell frowned. 'Why not be yourself? We shouldn't have to change our behaviour to make someone love us.'

I gave her a knowing look. 'Isn't that what you do when your parents come to visit?'

She went very quiet.

'*Mein Gott*,' said Astrid, touching her fingers to her lips. 'I am guilty of doing that also.'

'With Fred?' I guessed, thinking of the mince pies and the cottage pie and the Mary Berry outfit.

She nodded. 'I thought that my hippy dresses would put him off, especially after seeing the picture of his late wife.'

'I'm just as bad.' Nell shuddered. 'I'm thirty-five but I still conform to my parents' way of thinking when I'm in their company.'

'So what do we do?' I said, automatically turning to Astrid for her wisdom.

She reached for my hand and squeezed it. 'It is like I said earlier: the people who really love you, love you just the way you are. I think we all need to remember that, yes?'

'Yes,' Nell and I agreed.

From nowhere my eyes filled with tears and it hit me that maybe it was time to think about what I really wanted from a partner. Giving and accepting love required honesty and openness. If I was to find the stability my heart demanded, it was only going to happen within a relationship built on truth and trust. Was I ready for that so soon after Daniel and I had broken up? Maybe I was being too intense, but I wasn't interested in a no-strings fling, I wanted the real thing: hearts, flowers, commitment, a future together. Was Cole interested in the same thing, I wondered? Was he ready to move on after his divorce? The app on his phone would suggest he was ready to date again. Perhaps that was all he wanted for now. He seemed very committed to his children, but did that leave room for a relationship, for me? I took a deep breath, my mind whirring. As much as I'd enjoyed having Astrid and Nell here, now I was ready for them to leave. I wanted time to think: what was it I really wanted; or should that be, who?

'Time to get back to my stall,' said Nell, as if reading my mind. She stood and cleared our lunch things away.

'I'd better be going too,' said Astrid, 'poor Otto will be crossing his legs before long.' She stood up and slipped her arms into her coat, wrapping her scarf around her neck.

'Astrid, I notice you haven't got a job for Christmas Eve and I'm sure you'd want to help,' I said breezily. 'Shall I put you down for making mince pies?'

She opened her mouth to argue but I held her gaze until she caved in.

'OK, OK, I will do that,' she laughed and patted my cheek. 'And now my work here is done, *Liebling. Bis bald.*'

I crossed 'mince pies' from the list. One down, approximately ninety-nine to go. If Cole's sister could be so easily persuaded, it just might make the Christmas Project that little bit more merry. My fingers were well and truly crossed.

Chapter 19

Cole

'Thanks, but no thanks!' Hester yelled from the kitchen, where she was making her brother and father tea. 'Not if you paid me. *Were* they planning on paying me?'

Cole had just sprung his favour on his sister; her reaction was exactly what he'd expected. He didn't have a clue about the money side of it; he hadn't thought to ask. But he suspected the budget would be somewhere around zero. 'Think of it as an investment in your profile. You'll be in all the local press, not to mention being the talk of the town.'

He winked at Fred, who chuckled, used to hearing his two children bickering.

It was early evening; he and Hester normally came separately to see their dad so he'd have more visits, but he'd been very quiet when Cole had called in yesterday, so they'd agreed to come together to cheer him up. He'd been hoping to pop in with the stepladders to change the bulbs in the old bank before coming over to see his dad, but he'd run out of time and had had to come straight here. He felt bad about letting Merry down but if he could persuade his sister to help her out, then he was pretty sure it would make up for not having hung the new white-board for her.

'My profile? The Wetherley Christmas lights switch-on?' Hester scoffed, carrying through a tray with three mugs on it. 'It's hardly the Rockefeller Center.'

'Then think of it as doing your bit for the community,' he tried. 'Please. Hester, do this for me.'

'I'm supposed to be on a girls' night out on the first of December,' she grumbled, handing Fred tea in his own special mug.

'The more the merrier,' Cole replied, undaunted, 'bring them along.'

'Ask my friends to stand around in the freezing cold, sipping lukewarm mulled wine while I flick a switch?' She gave him a dubious look.

'And you say I've got no Christmas spirit,' Cole said drily.

'My daughter,' Fred marvelled, pausing to take an enthu-siastic sip of tea, 'doing the Christmas lights. Wait until I tell the others at Rosebridge. They'll all be wanting to meet you. Your mother would be so proud.'

Cole's ears pricked up: *the others*. Was Dad finally venturing out and making friends? This was real progress.

Hester's face softened. 'Oh, Dad, thank you.'

Cole held his breath; there was no way she could say no to his request now, could she? Not when it would mean so much to Fred. He couldn't wait to tell Merry; he sneakily glanced at his watch and wondered how soon he could leave. He'd love to see her face when she got the news. He couldn't wait to tell Freya and Harley either; they both loved Christmas. He suppressed a sigh, thinking how much more he'd be looking forward to Christmas if he was spending it with them.

'Fine, I'll do it, but only if you're there too.' She flopped down on the sofa beside him and shot him a dirty look. 'I'm sure I can rearrange my night out.'

'Have I told you lately that you're my favourite sister?' He couldn't help but laugh; she'd been pulling that face since they were kids.

'Oh, shut up,' she said, unable to stop her lips twitching into a smile. 'You'll come, I hope, Dad?'

'Wouldn't miss it for the world,' said Fred, after slurping his tea.

'How did you get roped into this anyway?' Hester asked, tucking her feet under her and making herself comfortable.

'The Holly Cottage tenant is in charge of the project and was really struggling to find a suitable celebrity; she asked me if I knew anyone famous.' Cole gave his sister his most winning smile. 'And luckily for me, I do.'

She raised an amused eyebrow. 'Ah, now I get it, is she the one you kitted the old bank out for, with all the little romantic touches? You should have said, I'd have agreed straight away. I'm looking forward to meeting the woman who's managed to get my brother buying flowers and candles.'

'Oh, shut up,' he replied, mirroring her reply.

'Is that the lass organising the Christmas Project in the market square?' Fred asked.

'Merry.' Cole felt a buzz of energy running through him at the chance to talk about her. 'Yes, have you met her?'

'No, my friend told me about her.' Fred gave a self-conscious cough. 'My friend Astrid.'

'A Christmas Project,' said Hester slyly. 'And I thought you were cancelling Christmas this year.'

'I am. Christmas without my kids isn't Christmas at all,' said Cole gruffly. 'I'm just going to crack on at the old bank. Get the kitchen in.'

'I know this year will be different,' said Hester not unsympathetically. 'But you've been working flat out. You are entitled to a break now and then.'

'She's right, Son,' Fred said wisely. 'Besides, if you're not there there'll be no chance of decent roast parsnip for Christmas dinner.'

'Rude,' said Hester, 'but true.'

Cole laughed; he did a mean honey-roast parsnip, if he did say so himself. 'It's good to know I have my uses, but you should be glad I'm a hard worker. It's your investment too. The sooner we get it finished, the quicker we can turn a profit on it.'

'Except for the fact you've put your new friend in there.'

'*Tenant*,' he corrected. 'And not for long. Holly Cottage will ready for her to go back to by early December.'

He hadn't anticipated that the repairs would take this long, but once they'd stripped back the kickboards under the kitchen units, they'd found that the water had risen up the back of the cupboards and swelled the wood. The kitchen had seen better days anyway, he told himself. He was making a good job of it because it made business sense, that was all, nothing to do with being fond of his tenant.

'You're a model landlord, I must say.' Hester looked at him knowingly, an amused smile playing on her lips. 'I take it she's single?'

Cole ignored her. 'Have you been taking it easy since your fall, Dad?'

Fred scowled. 'I wish everyone would stop saying a fall. I fell. There's a difference.'

'Correct,' said Hester promptly. 'When you fall, you get up again, brush yourself down and carry on. When you have *a fall*, a friend helps you home and calls your next of kin and you sit around for the next week with a hot water bottle on your privates.'

'Oi,' said Fred, 'you might be thirty-something but I'm still your father, so less of your lip.'

'We just care, Dad,' said Cole. 'My heart did stutter a bit when I got that call from your friend.'

'Groin strain for pity's sake. Pass me that pouffe,' Fred grumbled, lifting his feet up so Cole could slide it under his legs. 'The indignity of it. On one hand it was a good job that Astrid was there but, by Jiminy, I've never been so embarrassed in my life. How did I get so unfit? Get me a mince pie from that tin on the dining table will you, Son?'

Hester gave a snort.

'I can't imagine,' said Cole, fetching the tin and squeezing his sister's shoulder as he passed her.

The tin wasn't one he'd seen before. It looked a bit battered and well loved and had a picture of the snowy Alps on it. He took the lid off and the smell of alcohol hit him; they were chunky and a bit misshapen but nonetheless looked delicious. He was transported straight back to his mum's kitchen. It had been one of the family's traditions; she used to bake non-stop as Christmas approached: cakes, pies, sausage rolls. He wanted to do that, he realised: instil some traditions of his own. Maybe the kids would like to join in? Next Christmas would be different, he promised himself.

Fred bit into a mince pie, chewed for a moment and set it on the coffee table beside him.

'Actually, who am I kidding?' he said, sounding subdued. 'I'm unfit because I've been sitting on my backside for the last year. Losing your mum messed me up, kids. A lot more than I realised.'

Cole exchanged looks with his sister; Fred had been a closed book since his wife had died. Perhaps he was about to start opening up?

'That's natural, Dad.' Hester moved up the sofa until she was within touching distance and covered Fred's hand with hers. 'You were grieving.'

'I'm sure you still are,' Cole added. 'We probably all are.'

Fred dipped his chin to his chest and nodded. 'The long and short of it is that I felt guilty still being alive when your mum wasn't. It felt wrong sleeping in our bed, with that lovely quilt she made over me, enjoying the garden she'd planted, digging out pies she'd put in the freezer. It didn't seem fair. That's why I had to move house.'

Fred paused to swipe at the tears which had appeared in his eyes.

'I wish you'd told us how you felt at the time.' Cole shook his head sadly. 'We would have listened.'

Fred shrugged. 'I couldn't. I didn't want to talk about it; besides, I knew you'd try and talk me out of selling the house. And at the time I was so sure it was the right thing to do.'

Cole felt awful; he remembered how cut up he'd been himself after his mum died, how he'd wanted to spend time in the family home, surrounded by her things, her scent, her stamp on every room in the house – a lifetime of his memories. He'd already lost the home he'd shared with Lydia and the children, losing this one too had been a terrible blow. When Fred had announced he was selling the house, Cole had thought him heartless; now he realised he was anything but.

'Mum wouldn't have wanted you to feel guilty,' said Hester softly.

'I would have thought it would have given her comfort, to know you were in the home you both made together,' agreed Cole.

'I've realised that now,' Fred said resignedly. 'At the time I felt as if I should stop everything. I tried to turn my back on my old life, not just the house, but all the things I used to do: the DIY, the gardening, the walking. I didn't just stop being active, I stopped living. I've lost a lot more than muscle tone, I've lost all the things I loved the most. Except you two of course, I've still got you, and the grandchildren.'

That reminded him, Harley had sent Cole a photo of him on his snowboard yesterday, dazzling snow, bright blue endless sky and Harley's obvious happiness; it had lifted and broken his heart in equal measure. His boy was loving life, but it was a life without him. He took his phone out and showed them both.

'Wow, look at my handsome nephew,' Hester gasped, pressing a hand to her chest.

There was a recent one of Freya too in her school uniform. How he missed kissing her soft cheek at night and tucking her in.

After everyone had finished looking at the pictures, Cole spoke again. 'Dad, I don't think you've really left your old life. You've moved house, admittedly, but looking on the bright side, you've got that out of the way. Most people downsize sooner or later and those who don't usually regret it. Eventually that house would have been too much and the thought of moving would have been overwhelming.'

Fred nodded thoughtfully. 'Good way of looking at it.'

Hester leaned forward and kissed her dad's cheek. 'You're still in there, Dad, you haven't changed. Mum wouldn't want you to be a different person just because she's not around anymore.'

'That's the conclusion I've come to,' Fred agreed. 'So I'm letting the real Fred Robinson back in. Since I've been here I've held back from getting involved with things. Again, because I felt guilty doing something that your mum couldn't join in with. But I'm going to start getting out again, and joining in more.'

'That's great,' said Cole, with a grin. 'I hope the Rosebridge residents know what they're in for.'

'Well for starters, my friend, Astrid,' he said, smoothing his thick white hair and looking a little flushed, 'has suggested that we at Rosebridge put our names down for a tree as part of that Christmas Eve event. We're brain-storming a theme tomorrow in the lounge. I've already got an idea for it.'

'I'm feeling out of the loop here,' said Hester. 'I'm the only one who hasn't met this Astrid.'

'She's German and lives on the floor above me,' Fred chuckled. 'Always at the centre of things, quite . . . I won't say bossy, but definitely knows her own mind. Oh, and as you've tasted, she makes a pretty decent mince pie. Not as good as your mother's,' he added hastily. 'But different, which isn't a bad thing, is it?'

'No, Dad,' Cole smiled.

'Age? Appearance? Come on, I need details,' Hester demanded.

Fred gave a dramatic sigh, pretending to be reluctant to talk about her, but anyone could see that there was a new lightness to his eyes.

'She used to be an art teacher and you can tell, she looks like an exotic bird, wears colourful clothing, a touch bohemian. Most of the time . . .' He frowned and then shook away whatever he was thinking. 'I've been spending quite a bit of time with her lately. Just as friends, all above board.'

'She sounds great, Dad,' said Cole, his heart clenching for his dad and understanding how it felt to yearn for company. 'I'm pleased you've made a friend.'

'I've been lonely. I *am* lonely,' Fred admitted.

'And now you've got Astrid,' Hester sighed, clasping her hands together.

Fred cleared his throat. 'I thought I might ask her out to dinner, would that be all right with you both?'

'Oh Dad.' Hester dabbed her eyes. 'We love you. You don't need our permission.'

'You don't mind?' His shoulders sagged with relief.

'No.' He and Hester spoke at the same time.

'And I'm sure Mum wouldn't either,' Cole added.

'Thank you.' Fred chewed his lip. 'Probably won't come to anything. She might say no, why would she want to spend time with a lonely old codger like me?'

'You won't know until you ask. Which will just leave Cole on the shelf,' said Hester, her eyes twinkling. 'Looks like it's you we've got to fix up next, then.'

'Oh no, you don't,' said Cole firmly, checking his watch; Merry's committee meeting was about to start. 'Your internet dating suggestion was enough help for a lifetime, thank you. Now can I definitely tell Merry that you'll do the lights switch-on? If I leave now, I can get there in time.'

'Hmm,' Hester tapped her forefinger on the tip of her nose as if she'd just solved a mystery. 'I notice the first thing you think of when I mention dating is your tenant. Interesting.'

'Will you stop meddling?' he said, not wanting to start a Spanish inquisition.

'Do you have to go?' Fred's face dropped. 'I've got us some nice prawns from the fishmonger.'

'And fresh bread?' Hester perked up as Fred nodded.

It was tempting. Cole was taken right back to the occasional special teatime at the Robinsons' when they were kids. Fred didn't cook much but he did do a mean prawn sandwich: fat fresh prawns smothered in mayonnaise, a squeeze of lemon and a generous grind of black pepper, sandwiched between two thick slices of soft fresh bread. His mum had always declared it to be her favourite meal ever.

His dad was looking at him hopefully and Cole felt a pang of guilt. Fred had literally just admitted that he was lonely; he couldn't possibly leave now.

'Course I'll stay, Dad,' he said. 'Prawn sandwiches sound lovely. As long as you're making them.'

Fred pushed himself up to standing immediately and shuffled towards the kitchen. Hester and Cole high-fived each other; it looked like they were getting their old dad back.

Cole sat back and finished his tea, he wouldn't make it to the meeting but he'd send Merry a quick text instead to let her know Hester was up for it and that he needed all the details. That would give him the perfect excuse to call in on her tomorrow. And with that pleasant thought, he pinched his dad's footstool and put his feet up.

Chapter 20

Merry

My new clipboard and I had arrived at the Buttermarket early. I wanted to be the first one there to welcome others as they arrived as I thought that would help me to feel more in control of the agenda. I took a seat at the front where I could keep an eye on the door. For the next ten minutes, nobody joined me and I started catastrophising that no one was going to turn up. That there'd be no one to hear my plans and no one to put their names against the list of jobs I'd written, and I'd have to do everything myself.

On the other hand, it was quite nice to have a moment to myself in the old building and just sit and breathe. I'd rushed around all day. Since the conversation with Astrid and Nell at lunchtime I'd barely had a chance to sit down, let alone think about the things we'd discussed.

Once I'd packaged up the day's orders and had handed them to the courier, I made a trial batch of cinnamon, tangerine and clove-scented candles for the Christmas Fair. They smelled heavenly and by the time I left them cooling, the old bank was filled with the aroma of Christmas cake. I locked up and made a trip over to Holly Cottage. I needed to pack some more clothes to keep at Nell's and I looked for my bottle of juniper oil while I was there. Cole had asked if I'd mind staying away for another week or so while he had a new kitchen fitted. I hadn't minded at all, working in the old bank was far easier than at home: more space, no TV to distract me when I should have been working. But there was something else, too. As much as I loved living at Holly Cottage, working in the heart of the town suited me. I felt part of the community in a way I never had before. In fact, I liked it so much that if this meeting finished at a reasonable time, I might even get back to work and experiment with the juniper oil. It wouldn't work on its own, it needed other oils to balance it. Rosemary and lemon maybe, would that be 'manly' enough for my discerning customer, I wondered?

On the subject of Cole, I checked my phone again hoping for a message from him. Nothing. I was sure he wouldn't let me down; he knew I was hoping to hear from him so I could report back to the meeting this evening. My finger hovered over his name. Should I text and ask him, or was that being too pushy? Either he hadn't had an answer from Hester yet or he had asked her, and she'd said no and he hadn't had the heart to tell me. The third option, I thought with a flutter, was that Hester had said yes and Cole was planning on turning up tonight to deliver the good news.

A fraction of a second later my heart leapt as the door handle creaked. I held my breath, hoping I was right. It wasn't Cole but instead, in walked someone who I was delighted to see.

'Tom!' I jumped up from my seat and flung my arms out wide at the sight of Daniel's younger brother. 'I haven't seen you for ages!'

He plonked a noisy kiss on my cheek. 'Not since dinner at yours — I mean Daniel's — in September. You look great, Merry.' He pulled back to study me. 'Really great. I'm so pleased.'

'I feel great,' I replied.

And I did, I realised with surprise.

The night Tom had come round for dinner I'd been feeling at my lowest ebb, living with a man who undoubtedly loved me in his way, but who I knew would never make me truly happy. Since then, I'd taken myself out of an unhappy situation and moved on. And now, I thought, glancing back at the door, perhaps I was ready to move forward again. With someone new.

Tom's path and mine hadn't crossed since Daniel and I had split up. He preferred to live a few miles out of town for some peace and quiet. 'Otherwise you get kids popping up saying *Hello, Mr Hughes* when you least want to be noticed,' he'd told me once. 'Like when you're buying twenty-four rolls of toilet paper, or after a few too many red wines on a sunny day in a pub garden.'

'It was a shame that you two split up.' He pulled a sad face. 'I've missed you.'

'Thanks, you too.' I felt a tug at my heart. That was one of the worst things about a break-up for me: the inevitable loss of the family I'd become a part of. And as nice as the Hughes family was, it wouldn't be right for me to try and keep the same relationship I'd had with them while I was Daniel's girlfriend.

At thirty-two, Tom was the baby of the family and it showed. He was still a big kid at heart and I could imagine that the children in his class adored him. He was smaller than Daniel and fine-featured, with sparkling grey eyes and an enduring love for Kylie Minogue.

'I didn't have you down as a likely volunteer for the Christmas Project,' I said, looping my arm through his and taking him to the front row where I'd been sitting.

'I'm deputising for my boss,' he said, lowering himself neatly into the chair beside me. 'Tasha has got some reports to write and can't make it tonight.'

'We're all busy,' I said, with an edge to my voice that I wasn't proud of, a hangover from my jealousy during the early days of mine and Daniel's break-up. I didn't want to be that person, I realised. Tasha had been perfectly nice to me on every occasion. I glanced at Tom but he hadn't picked up my tone.

'Ain't that the truth,' he grinned, rolling his eyes. 'Especially as some bright spark has decided to set the nativity in outer space this year because Year Five have been doing a project about the International Space Station. But I don't mind doing this for Tasha tonight. I'd do anything for her, all the school staff would. She's a breath of fresh air after the last head we had. That one used to flinch when the children tried to hug her and she would wrap an antibacterial wipe around door handles before she touched them. Tasha is warm and approachable and thinks nothing of getting down on the carpet to play with the kids.'

'Even in those heels she wears?' I said doubtfully.

He shook his head, laughing. 'She only wears heels for meetings, the rest of the time she's in trainers. In fact, she's relaxed the dress code for all of us, which is much more sensible. The amount of suits I've ruined with bleach after clearing up children's vomit, you wouldn't believe.'

'Thanks for that image.'

'Seriously though,' Tom said, 'I know you and Daniel thought I should have applied for the promotion but I'm so glad I didn't. I'm happy standing in for her now and again but being the boss isn't me. And having her in school is like having Glinda the Good Witch floating around the building.'

'Wow, you really *do* like her,' I laughed, pushing his arm playfully. Tom was obsessed with *The Wizard of Oz*. He'd even used the film as the theme for his thirtieth birthday party; he'd dressed as Dorothy and his partner Chris had dressed up as Toto. I hadn't known Daniel then, but the party had gone done in the annals of Hughes family history.

The door opened again and a few more people arrived and sat down. I automatically scanned every face for Cole, but he hadn't come. It occurred to me that since Pam and Jim Dunford weren't going to be here this week, I would have to decide when to kick the meeting off, but Nell hadn't arrived yet, so I could safely carry on talking to Tom for a few minutes yet.

He looked at his watch and then around the room.

'It's not going to take long, is it?' he whispered. 'I want to get a second coat of paint on my space-age stable before I go to bed.'

'Not if I can help it,' I whispered. 'I'm hoping to work later too; I've got candles coming out of my ears at the moment.'

'That sounds painful,' he winked. 'Unless you mean Hopi candles?'

'No,' I sniggered. 'Frankincense and myrrh.'

'I'll have a couple of those for nativity, we can burn them when the wise men walk in. Maybe you should do some special nativity-themed candles for the Christmas Fair?'

'Which scent would you like, madam,' I said tongue in cheek, 'little donkey or three wise men?'

We both laughed.

'Fair enough,' he said. 'I think I'll stick to set design, leave the candles to you. Daniel told me how well you were doing, I'm pleased for you.'

'Is Daniel coming tonight?' I asked, glancing at the door again.

Tom shrugged. 'No idea. You probably see him more than I do.'

'You'd think so,' I said, 'considering we work next door to each other, but I rarely bump into him.'

'It's good that you've stayed friends. It hasn't always been the case with his break-ups. He went out with a girl called Stella once. She did not take it well when he called off their engagement,' he said and winced.

My eyebrows shot up; Daniel had been engaged?

'Oh dear,' I managed to say. 'That is awkward. What happened?'

He pursed his lips and leaned in. 'Well, she started stalking us all, not just Daniel. Mum got freaked out once when she found Stella asleep in the car outside their house; she'd been there all night because she thought that Daniel was inside. Of all Daniel's girlfriends, you took it the best.'

'I'm not sure what you mean,' I said, baffled. 'Took what?'

'He's always been the same,' Tom continued. 'He gets so far and then seems to suffer from cold feet. I don't know what his problem is. But the family did think you'd be the one to break down his commitment barriers. He seemed happier with you than he'd been with anyone else.'

Except along came Tasha, I thought, wondering if Daniel had told his family about her yet. It didn't sound as if Tom knew.

'He's a lovely man,' I said diplomatically. 'Perhaps he's just waiting for the right woman.'

'You are sweet,' said Tom, giving me a twinkly smile. 'As I say, I'm glad we can still be friends.'

The door banged and Astrid and Nell marched in followed by Nigel, Audrey from the china stall and Sadie from the pub.

'Sorry I am so late!' said Astrid, unbuttoning a long blue velvet coat with contrasting buttons. 'I was waiting for the icing to cool on my biscuits.'

'German biscuits?' I asked hopefully, noting the return of her usual style.

'Of course,' she said, with a knowing smile. 'I have been making these biscuits all my life, it wouldn't be Christmas without them.'

'I'm late because I couldn't decide what to wear,' Nell added, giving us a twirl in her emerald green poncho.

I beamed at them both and sent up a silent prayer hoping that the two of them never changed.

'And I've brought some mulled wine for us to try,' said Sadie, placing a stainless steel urn down on one of the tables.

'Fabulous!' declared Tom, clapping his hands. 'Shall I be mother?'

I glanced at the door one more time, willing it to open for one last arrival but it remained resolutely shut. Which left me with a dilemma: did I mention the possibility of Hester's appearance, or would I have to tell everyone that the search for a celebrity continued?

Just then my phone buzzed with a text, startling me out of my daydream. My legs went to jelly with relief when I saw Cole's name appear:

DRUMROLL . . .! Hester says yes! Actually she said she hated me and that she would make me pay for the rest of my life too, but we'll cross that bridge when we come to it. So you have your celebrity. Cole x

This was fantastic! A warm fuzzy feeling spread through me; not only had he come to my rescue but he'd signed off with a kiss. A kiss! That had to mean he regarded me as more than just a tenant, didn't it?

I replied straight away:

Thank you, I owe you one.

And after a moment's hesitation, I added a kiss of my own. I pressed send and my face softened into a smile as a thought which had been hovering timidly in my head gained sudden clarity.

I'd asked myself earlier today what, or rather who I wanted. And now I thought I might have my answer. The fluttering of anticipation in my chest every time the door had opened to reveal new arrivals, the disappointment which replaced it when I realised that it wasn't him. It was Cole who was setting my heart racing; Cole's face my imagination conjured up whenever I allowed my mind to wander.

Nell was convinced he liked me. I'd denied it at the time but if I was really honest with myself, I thought she might be right; I had felt a frisson between us.

Excitement fizzed through me. The tingling feeling of new beginnings, of possibilities, of the delicious moments I'd spend thinking about him, wondering whether he was thinking about me, talking about him to Nell, catching a glimpse of him across a crowded room. Yes, I thought with a rush of pleasure; I did have my answer. I wanted Cole.

With that momentous revelation sorted, I got to my feet clutching the clipboard.

'Right everyone,' I said, positioning myself front and centre. 'Let's get this party started, because I have had some very good news. Who's heard of *The Retail Therapy Show*?'

An hour and a half later, the meeting had come to a close and people were drifting off and out into the night. The refreshments had gone down well, although Nell and I had both given the mulled wine a wide berth after our last encounter with it. Even though everyone who'd come to the meeting were adults, excitement for Christmas was growing. People speculated about the main Christmas tree, which was due to arrive soon, about when everyone would be putting up their decorations at home, who had done their Christmas shopping already and who hadn't so much as written a card (unsurprisingly, that was me). We talked about the roast chestnut and hot chocolate vendors we'd be bringing in for the lights switch-on, and everyone started recounting details of their best-ever Christmas. And I had been caught up in the magic of it all. I'd closed my mind to Christmas this year because I wouldn't be spending it with Daniel. But maybe this year I'd start making my own Christmas traditions to build on so that when I did have a family of my own I could pass them on . . .

'Considering that was the first meeting you've ever chaired,' said Nell, sidling up to me, 'you did very well. I think you're a born leader.'

'It did go well, didn't it,' I said, yawning. It had been a long day and it wasn't over yet. 'I've allocated almost all of the jobs. I can do the rest myself.'

'Most excellently delegated,' said Astrid with a wink. 'Almost too good; I seem to also be making *Pfefferkuchen* on top of the mince pies. And I'd already suggested I'd be in charge of organising a tree for Rosebridge. Have you got us down, Nell?'

'I have,' Nell assured her, liberating the last of Astrid's delicious ginger biscuits from the tin. I'd designated her to be the keeper of the Christmas tree list after she'd failed to offer to do any of the jobs. 'Along with the market traders, the Bristly Badger, the hair salon, the Women's Institute, the men's choir and Wetherley under-sixteens football team; ooh and Tom's children's tree. The list will be going up first thing tomorrow in the market square and will remain there for two weeks.'

'It's going to look amazing,' said Tom, giving me a hug. 'Thanks for agreeing to my idea for the Santa trail. I know Tasha wanted to have a Santa's grotto where all the children get a present, but I think this will be fun and easier to organise.'

Tom's idea was that there would be a series of hidden letters around the market square which spelled out Merry Christmas. Once the children had found all the letters, they could come and write their Christmas wish on a star and hang it on a tree.

'Christmas shouldn't be just about gifts,' I agreed. 'This will be much more interactive.'

'And cheap,' said Sadie. 'I'm going to get our regulars to make decorations out of beer mats. Ooh and do you think I'll be able to get fairy lights that will flash when it's last orders?'

'I'm sure there will be someone who could rig that up for you,' I said, thinking of Cole who seemed to be able to turn his hand to anything.

Nigel rubbed a hand over his bald head. 'I'm trying to decide whether to do a tree with my dogging mates, or the bowls team. I can't decide.'

'Gosh,' said Tom, stifling a laugh as he buttoned up his duffle coat. 'What a dilemma. And on that note, I shall bid you good night.'

'I think you mean your dog-walking mates,' said Nell, 'and as a favour to the rest of us, please choose the group least likely to decorate the tree with inflatables pulling moonies.'

Nigel scratched his beard. 'That might be a tough call.'

'It's the celebrity guest I'm most excited about,' said Sadie, twisting the lid back onto her mulled wine urn. 'I'm addicted to that show; I've lost count of the number of gadgets that Hester Smart has managed to sell me.'

'I'm excited to meet her too,' I admitted, although in my case I was more interested in the fact that she was Cole's sister than a TV presenter. I wished I knew what the protocol was for these things. Did I need to present her with a bouquet, or a gift of some kind, and what about a microphone – would she want to make a speech? I added a note to research celebrity appearances to my list and sighed.

Nell hooked her arm through mine as we headed to the door. 'You look shattered. Fancy calling in at the pub before we go home?'

'Is everybody out?' Nigel yelled into the empty hall before switching the lights off. Determining that everyone was, he locked up and handed me the key.

'I'd better not,' I said to Nell reluctantly, although the thought of a lemonade and a bag of crisps in front of the real fire in the Bristly Badger sounded heavenly. 'I've got thirty gin and tonic candles to make.'

'Ooh.' Sadie pricked up her ears. 'Can you make alcohol-scented candles?'

I nodded. 'I can make pretty much anything if there's a fragrance oil for it.'

'Stick me down for ten G and Ts and half a dozen mulled wines,' she said.

'Small or large?' I asked.

'Need you ask?' She hooted with laughter. 'I'm a land-lady; my order is always a large.'

'Consider it done, and as you're donating mulled wine on Christmas Eve, I'll throw in gift wrapping too,' I said, smothering another yawn. And added her request to my ever-increasing list.

Chapter 21

Cole

It was far later than Cole had planned to leave his dad's flat, but Fred had asked them to stay for a game of Scrabble. One game had turned into the best of three and by the time Hester had conceded that Fred was still the better player, it was after ten o'clock.

Fred showed them to the door, walking even more stiffly after being seated for so long.

'Thanks for our prawn sandwiches,' Hester said, kissing Fred's cheek. 'And for trouncing me at Scrabble – you've still got the knack.'

Fred chuckled. 'Not lost my marbles yet.'

'And thanks for talking to us,' said Cole, giving him a hug, 'you know, about Mum and how you felt.'

The old man stroked his chin. 'Doesn't feel right admitting to your kids that you've been a silly old fool, but if I can stop you making the same mistakes I have then it'll be worth it, eh, Son?'

'We'll always miss Mum,' said Hester. 'But she'll be with us in our hearts for ever. Life changes, for better or worse, but we still have to carry on.'

'You're right, love,' said Fred, but his eyes were fixed on Cole. 'When your mother was alive, I always looked forward to tomorrow. It's taken me a while to understand that I need to find new reasons to keep getting up in the morning. But I'm getting there now. Life's too short to be lonely.'

Cole felt a lump in his throat; how lucky his parents had been to have a love like that. And his dad's message wasn't lost on him; he'd forged ahead with business since he and Lydia had split, but his personal life left a lot to be desired. He wondered if subconsciously this was why he hadn't put down permanent roots – because he didn't want to do it alone?

A nudge from his sister dragged him from his thoughts.

'Do you hear that, big brother? What have I been telling you?'

'Yeah, yeah,' he said good-naturedly, putting an arm around his sister's shoulders. 'Goodnight, Dad.'

Fred waved them off and the two of them headed down the stairs and through the communal hallway. Cole thought about Merry and how pleased she'd been to get his text about Hester being available to switch on the Christmas lights. He was already looking forward to calling in to see her tomorrow to talk about it. And he'd make sure he had his tools with him this time. That bathroom door lock was going to need proper adjustment, no matter how confident Merry was that she'd mended it. Hitting it with her boot and pouring oil in it . . . he laughed under his breath.

'What are you grinning at?' Hester asked as they stepped out into the dark together and walked towards her car. She pulled her scarf tighter around her neck.

'Nothing really,' he began and then let out a breath. Why not be honest for a change, take a leaf out of his dad's book. 'OK, I'll tell you, but don't make a massive deal out of it.'

'You've met someone?' Her eyes were like saucers, shining in the light of the lamp post.

'We-ll.' He waggled his head from side to side. 'Sort of.'

His sister squealed and jumped up and down. 'I knew it! It's that tenant, isn't it?'

'Merry.' He shot a sideways look at his sister and nodded. 'Yeah. I really like her.'

Hester looped her arm through his. 'I can't wait to meet her, what's she like?'

'Single, which is a good start. Pretty. She makes me laugh. Today she asked me if she could hang a white-board up on the kitchen. Her tool kit comprises the heel of her boot and some pins.' He shook his head and laughed.

Hester's brows wrinkled. 'What's wrong with that?'

He rolled his eyes. 'Women.'

'Don't be sexist. So?' she prompted. 'What are you going to do about it? Come on, even Dad has managed to make the first move with his lady friend. Groin strain notwithstanding.'

Cole shrugged. 'I haven't got a clue. It's a bit weird with me being her landlord.'

'Only if you make it weird,' Hester replied. 'Ask her out for a coffee or something.'

He wrinkled his nose. 'The last time I chatted a woman up I was twenty-two. I don't even know what to say.'

'That bit I can help you with,' she said, getting out her phone. 'I read an article the other day and I was going to send it to you to help you with your online dating chat, but then you gave up.'

She sent it to him, and he read the title of it: *Questions to ask on a first date*. 'Thanks, now all I have to do is get her to say yes to a date at all.'

Hester hugged him. 'Easy! Anyway, she owes you one for getting me to turn on the Christmas lights for her. Good luck!'

He waited until she was in the car, waved her goodbye and then set off towards his own van. The night air was bitterly cold, and he shoved his hands into his coat pockets. He was almost back at his van when he realised that drinking all that tea at his dad's had taken its toll and now he was desperate for the loo.

He sighed and his breath swirled in a cloud in front of his face. He could go back to Rosebridge but he didn't want to disturb his dad again or get embroiled in another long conversation. Alternatively, he wasn't far from the old bank. He would nip in, run upstairs, do his business and leave. Merry would be long gone by now.

Decision made, he changed direction and headed to the market square.

Cole glanced up at the first-floor windows to be on the safe side, but the place was in darkness. His key slid into the door smoothly; he smiled to himself, wondering if Merry had put some oil on that as well. He didn't bother locking the door behind him, he was going to be in and out in five minutes and it would only slow him down. It wasn't as if Wetherley was a hotbed of crime. He walked through the ground-floor rooms, trying to imagine what sort of business would do well here. If he got on with it, he could have the space ready to rent in a couple of months. The plan had been to rent it commercially down-stairs and have a residential tenant upstairs. At one point he'd considered living here himself; it would make a great bachelor pad. He frowned at the thought – that wouldn't do. Regardless of his status, he'd never think of himself as a bachelor; he was going to have to put down roots again for the kids when they came home. *If they came home*, said a little voice inside his head. He ignored it.

Taking the steps two at a time he ran upstairs, his big boots thundering on the old wooden treads, echoing through the dark, empty building.

There was a sudden clattering noise from above him, followed by a muffled scream. Cole's heart thumped with shock and he stood still, his breathing coarse from climbing the stairs. Someone was here; it wouldn't be Merry, so who? He slid a hand into his pockets and took out his phone and keys, the only things he had which were vaguely weapon-like. He was almost at the top now and he began to move slowly, soundlessly, towards the light switch. The kitchen door flew open and Merry burst out.

'Jesus Christ!' Cole gasped, his heart pounding.

Screaming, she launched herself into the bathroom and slammed the door.

Her sudden movements startled him so much that he almost lost his footing and fell backwards down the stairs. He leapt up the last couple of steps and snapped on the light but nothing happened. The bulb must have gone. He pushed open the kitchen door so that the light illuminated the corridor.

'Merry?' he called, trying to catch his breath. 'It's only me – Cole.'

'What the hell?' she yelled. 'You frightened me to death. My heart is going like the clappers. Oh shit! The light bulb in here doesn't work, I broke it trying to remove it this morning. And I hate the dark. More than anything.'

From the other side of the door, he heard her try the the door handle.

'I'm so sorry, I would have called if I'd thought for a second you'd still be here at this hour,' he said. Poor lass, she must have been petrified. He could kick himself.

'Well, I am,' she cried. There was a note of desperation in her voice. 'I've been making your gin and tonic scented candles and—' She paused. 'Oh, I must have fallen asleep.'

'Come out, Merry, please,' he said.

'I'm trying!' she said in a wavering voice, 'but it's stuck. And it's as black as coal in here. Can you try, Cole? Two coals.' She made a noise which sounded like a cross between a sob and a laugh.

'I'll twist the handle and put my shoulder to it.'

He pulled out his phone and swiped the torch function on to examine the handle. 'It's all oily, I can't get a grip.'

'Yeah, that was me, remember,' she said, sniffing. 'Eucalyptus oil.'

He propped his phone on the floor and wiped his hands on his jeans.

'I can see light!' she said with a gasp, 'just a little strip of light under the door.'

'It's the torch on my phone.'

'Keep it there, please.'

'I will.' His heart went out to her. 'Try not to worry, we'll soon get you out of there.'

'I hope so,' she said in a small voice. 'But telling me not to worry is like telling someone who hates spiders that the one under their bed won't bother them in the night.'

'Right, I'm going to push the door as hard as I can. Stand back.' This time he grabbed the door handle with both hands and put all his weight behind it. He pushed and pushed, grunting with exertion but the door didn't budge.

He let go to give himself a break and leaned against the wall, panting. 'It's well and truly stuck.'

'Just try again, please.'

He did as she asked but he knew it was no good. The door needed taking off its hinges and planing and he was pretty sure that something inside the lock mechanism had snapped. 'Sorry,' he said, rubbing his shoulder. 'It won't budge.'

'What are we going to do?' Her plaintive voice was coming from low down behind the door and he had an image of her crouched down, staying close to the light.

He rubbed a weary hand through his hair, trying to think what was the best thing to do. 'I'll go out to the van and fetch my tools. I'll smash the door down if I have to.'

Which would also give him a chance to find a quiet alley and have a wee. Not that he would normally condone such vulgar behaviour but he was practically bouncing on the spot with desperation.

'No!' she yelped. 'Don't leave me in the dark. Please.'

'OK, OK, I won't.' He strained to listen; he was fairly sure he could hear the sound of faint crying. It was on the tip of his tongue to tell her not to cry but he almost felt like crying himself so he didn't blame her. 'Merry, I feel terrible.'

'This is literally my worst nightmare: being locked in a dark room.'

'Then why did you run in there?' he asked softly.

'Don't turn this around to being my fault,' she snapped. 'You promised to mend this lock ages ago, remember?'

He raked a hand through his hair. 'Sorry, it's not your fault. It's totally mine.'

'How was I supposed to know that you weren't an intruder?' she continued. 'I panicked. I thought locking myself in the bathroom would be the safest thing to do.'

'Well, you're certainly safe now,' he said ruefully.

'We'll have to call Olek,' she said with a sniff. 'The locksmith. His number is on my phone in the kitchen.'

'On it.' He smiled faintly to himself as he went to find her phone; he wasn't at all surprised that she had a locksmith in her contacts. She struck him as someone who got herself into scrapes on a regular basis.

The kitchen was warm and inviting and really did smell strongly of gin and tonic. On the kitchen worktop were two electric hotplates glowing red and rows of still-warm candles. He switched off the hotplates and then for some reason dotted his fingertip on the wax of one of the candles. He winced as his finger came away coated in wax; he'd ruined it.

'It's on the table somewhere,' she shouted. 'Please hurry up, I prefer it when I know you're on the other side of the door.'

'Give me a second.'

He turned back to the table and knocked over a whiteboard which had been leaning against the leg of a chair. The whiteboard that he needed to hang for her, he presumed. At the top was the word *schedule*, which she'd underlined. Then there were three cloud shapes full of illegible scribble. He thought of his schedule of works on a spreadsheet on his laptop and suppressed a smile. Hers was very . . . Merry.

He found her phone on the table, under a pile of handwritten thank-you cards which looked like they accompanied her orders. The phone screen had a crack in it and was covered with notifications and messages. None from men, he noticed, but a couple of them were from Nell. He felt a bit guilty for prying but justified it by telling himself that he was only checking that the way was clear before he asked her out for that coffee. Although he'd have to pick his moment carefully before he did that; tonight was definitely not that moment.

Cole went back to the bathroom door; he could hear her singing 'The Sun Will Come Out Tomorrow' under her breath and his heart flipped.

'Merry?' he said softly, 'you're going to have to give me your passcode.'

She blew her nose. 'One–two–three–four.'

He shook his head. That had to be the worst passcode ever; this woman was unbelievable. Adorable, but totally crazy.

'I'll have to change it now, which is a shame.'

'Yeah, might be an idea,' he said, trying not to smile. 'What did you say the locksmith was called?'

'Olek Dowmunt. Pronounced Doffmunt. He's Polish.'

Cole scrolled through the numbers but couldn't see anything vaguely like Olek.

'He's under N for Nell,' she added after a few seconds. 'Hurry up.'

Cole was confused but found Olek's number under N and called it. The phone was answered immediately.

'Thank the Lord!' Cole recognised Nell's voice from the market. 'Are you OK? Why are you calling Olek, not me?'

Cole switched it quickly to speaker phone. 'Nell, this is Cole,' he explained. 'I'm calling Olek because we need an emergency locksmith.'

'COLE?' she screeched. 'Why have you got her phone? Is Merry there? Is she OK?'

'Nell!' Merry yelled from the other side of the door. 'Send Olek immediately, please! I'm locked in the loo in the dark on my own and I'm literally wetting myself.'

That made two of them, thought Cole.

'And I'm in the corridor outside the bathroom,' he added.

'What a nightmare!' Nell gasped. 'That's awful. Hold on, I'll shout him.'

She moved the phone from her mouth and her voice was muffled but still very loud as she yelled. 'OLEK? Get dressed again, Merry needs unlocking.' She lowered her voice. 'He's just had a bath but he says he'll get dressed and be with you asap.'

'Thank you,' said Merry with a sniff.

'Listen, Cole,' said Nell, 'this is very important. Merry gets anxious in the dark, please look after her, stay with her.'

'Sure,' he replied. 'I'm not going anywhere. And please tell Olek that the front door is open, he can come straight up, he'll find us on the first floor. Oh, and the light's not working outside the bathroom either, tell him he'll need to bring a torch.'

With reassurances from Nell that Olek was already pulling on his jeans, Cole hung up.

'So Nell's partner is Olek the locksmith,' he said, checking he'd got his facts right.

'Yeah, they're probably worried,' she replied in a small voice. 'I said I'd be back by ten o'clock.'

'It's ten-thirty now,' he said. A full thirty minutes since he'd realised he needed the loo. He tried not to think about it. 'How long will it take him to get here?'

'Twenty minutes. Oh God,' she sobbed. 'I have to get out of here.'

There was a sudden scrabbling noise followed by the door handle rattling again.

'Merry!' he called over the racket. 'Take some deep breaths and focus on the light on the floor from my phone. I'm right here with you, you're not on your own.'

He heard her breathing shakily, in and out, in and out and matched his breath to hers. He slid to the floor, with his back against the bathroom door, taking care not to disturb the beam of light from his phone. Ironic really, he'd been looking for an opportunity to spend some time with her, to get to know her, but Merry having a panic attack on the other side of a locked door had not been on his wish list. On the up-side it would certainly be a memorable night for them both.

'Arrrggghhh!' She gave the door another thump.

Cole grimaced; it sounded as if she was getting angry. Was anger better than fear? He wasn't sure, but he did know that he ought to try and take her mind off things. He wondered what had triggered this phobia of the dark; it was obviously bad because even Nell had brought it up. He suddenly remembered that article his sister had sent him, the one about questions to ask on a first date. Maybe he should read it for inspiration, have a look at that and see if he could keep her talking by going through them.

'Hey, Merry?' He turned the torch on her phone on, shone the light under the door and picked up his own, quickly finding the article. 'Let's talk, it'll make the time go quicker.'

She sighed heavily. 'What do you want to talk about?'

'Um,' he scrolled down the article, rejecting rubbish ones like: *are you a picky eater?* and *are you reading anything good right now?* 'If you could time travel to any moment in history what would it be?'

'Half an hour from after I've been let out of this bloody room,' she shot back immediately.

'Fair enough.' Cole pressed his lips together hard to stop a laugh from escaping; he couldn't help it, he just loved how sparky she was.

He checked the time again; only another eighteen minutes to go. *Put your foot down, Olek . . .*

Chapter 22

Merry

I sent a silent plea to Olek to hurry up. I was exhausted and shaky and wanted to get out of this bathroom more than life itself. I pressed my ear closer to the door but I couldn't hear anything; Cole had better not be laughing at me.

My eyes had become accustomed to the dark a bit now and I could make out the shapes of the toilet and wash basin, but still panic washed over me in waves. It felt as if there was a tight band across my chest constricting my lungs and making it hard to breathe, and there was a solid blockage in my throat at the little dip between my collar bone. My heart was racing and when I put my fingers in my ears I could hear the blood rushing through my veins. My body was in full-on fight or flight mode but it couldn't do either. It was hard to explain how terrifying it was for me to be in the dark, *locked* in the dark in this case, which turned the fear factor up by a hundred per cent. I shook off the memory of where this phobia started, not wanting to give it headspace.

The small bathroom was draughty and smelled of lemon-scented bleach with a faint undertone of eucalyptus around the door lock, thanks to my repair which I'd been so proud of. I was sitting on the floor leaning against the wall, with my legs bent and my hoodie pulled over my knees for warmth. The cold had seeped into my bones and my bum was already beginning to go numb. Talk about a rude awakening. I'd been taking a break between pouring one lot of candles and melting the next lot of wax and hadn't noticed that I was drifting off to sleep. The next thing I knew heavy footsteps were pounding up the bare wooden stairs. I was only half awake when I ran and locked myself in the bathroom; I'd thought it would be the safest place. I'd got that right; so safe that no one could get in or out . . .

At Holly Cottage I kept a light on somewhere at all times. I was ultra-conscientious about checking lightbulbs and replacing them as soon as they went out. It was just my thing. I was kicking myself for what I'd done; normally I left the door ajar when I went to the loo. And I'd known that this bulb wasn't working; I'd twisted it half out of the socket before nearly falling off the chair I'd been standing on. I'd given myself such a fright that I'd abandoned the job.

But if I had to be locked in at all, I was glad it was Cole who was waiting it out with me. Arguably, if he hadn't come, I wouldn't be in this mess at all, but even so, his presence was reassuring. Whenever he moved, he cast shadows on the ribbon of light beneath the door and I put my hand on the floor to connect us.

At least Olek was on his way; never had I been more grateful that Nell had married a locksmith. I was sure Cole could do it with the right tools, but there was no way I was letting him leave me here while he went back to his van to collect them. What if he had an accident and I was stranded here all night?

It struck me then how odd it was that he was here at all. I swallowed and tried not to sound wobbly. 'Cole?'

'Yes?'

'What are you doing here?'

'You mean what am I doing in the old bank late at night?'

'Yes. You didn't bring tools, so you weren't planning on doing any jobs and you didn't think I'd be here, so . . .?'

He coughed. 'Well, it's a bit awkward. Obviously I thought the place was empty.'

'Checking I hadn't left any naked flames?'

'No, no, nothing like that. I er . . .' he exhaled. 'I er . . . I came to use the bathroom. I've been at my dad's and must have drunk three mugs of tea and after I left his flat and went out into the cold, well, I needed to go.'

'I see.' Poor, poor man. Nothing worse than being really desperate. Except perhaps being locked in the dark. 'Do you still need to go?'

'Well, yes,' he replied brusquely. 'I do.'

Before I could stop it, a noise escaped, half sob, half laugh. 'Oh dear,' I said squeakily.

'I'm glad you find it funny.'

'I can't help it,' I said, holding my stomach, unable to control my laughter. 'It's just all so ridiculous: me desperate to get out and you desperate to get in.'

He gave a low rumble of laughter and then groaned. 'Don't make me laugh, I'm in agony here.'

'Sorry,' I said in a strangled voice, trying to pull myself together. 'Will asking me another question help take your mind off it?'

'Maybe.'

I heard him making umming and ahhing noises until finally he said, 'OK, tell me something about yourself that not many other people know.'

I touched my fingers to the torchlight on the floor and tilted my head back. There were so many things which fell into that category.

'Where to start,' I said. 'We could be here all night.'

'Let's hope not, eh?' He gave a half-laugh. 'I'll tell you something about me if you like.'

'Go on then.'

'My mum had a vegetable patch in the garden. Quite big, there was more veg patch than actual usable garden by the end. Anyway, one year when I was about eight, she managed to grow cucumbers for the first time. She was so proud of them.'

Already I was interested. A vegetable patch, a garden and a mum who could grow cucumbers; a childhood a million miles away from mine.

'I had a thing at the time about having midnight feasts. I used to stash food away in my bottom drawer and then wake myself up late at night and eat it by torchlight.'

'That's so sweet.' I gave an inaudible sigh, imagining Cole as a little boy in shorts with grazes on his knees and his hair cut like Christopher Robin, he'd have been so cute.

'Hmm, not sure about that. Anyway, for some reason known only to eight-year-old Cole, I decided to pick all of Mum's cucumbers and hide them in my drawer ready for the next midnight feast.'

'That sounds like a healthy feast,' I commented. My diet in my early years had consisted mostly of things from tins.

'That night I crept out of bed really late and took a bite out of the end of one of them. The taste was horrible, all bitter and hard, it can't have been ripe. I spat out my mouthful and shut the drawer and forgot all about them. When my mum noticed that her cucumbers had all disappeared, she was devastated. They weren't even ripe, she told us all. She was convinced we'd been burgled. I denied all knowledge and then didn't dare move them in case I got found out. I forgot about them until everyone started to complain about the bad smell upstairs. Eventually my dad narrowed the pong down to my room and discovered my crime. I'll never forget the disappointment on my mum's face. Not only had I picked them, but I'd lied about it.' He laughed softly. 'I don't think I ever told her another lie after that. There you go, that's my story: the case of the missing cucumbers.'

'I lied to my mum too once,' I said.

'Phew,' he said jokily. 'I'm not the only criminal then. What did you lie about?'

I closed my eyes as the memories came raining down on me like icy hailstones. I could do what I usually did and make something up, or I could tell him. *Honesty and openness*, I reminded myself, thinking about my earlier musings, *truth and trust*. I took a steadying breath and began.

'My mum was only seventeen when she had me. She'd been living rough when she got pregnant. We had what they called a studio flat, which was a posh way of saying bedsit. I have memories of her dancing around, so proud of her home. She said she felt like a queen in her castle and I was the princess. There was only one bed and we both slept in it. She'd be up later than me and she kept a lamp on so she could read; to begin with she'd read stories to me and then afterwards her own book. All I'd ever known was falling asleep with the light on.'

'She sounds like a fun mum.'

'Sometimes she was, and at other times she'd be ill and couldn't look after me. She was ill quite a lot. And then I'd be taken away from her and put into care. Looking back, she was obviously suffering with her mental health, but I didn't understand that at the time.'

'Bloody hell, Merry, I'm sorry. That doesn't sound like fun at all.'

'I stayed with quite a few foster parents. Most were OK, but one lot said I was too old to have a nightlight on and made me sleep in the dark. I lay there petrified, worried that there might be a monster under the bed and I wouldn't be able to see it. I was still awake hours later when the door opened and a stripe of light from the landing hit the floor and lit up the room and I was so happy. It was the man, Michael. He came in and closed the door behind him and I was in the dark again. He sat down on the bed, telling me to shush.'

My mouth had gone dry and I paused to swallow hard. I was right back in that small damp room with cork tiles on the wall and condensation running down the windows and heavy woollen blankets on the bed which smelled musty. The fear that had stolen my voice, rendering me silent, threatened to grab me again.

'Merry?' Cole's voice startled me; I was so wrapped up in the story that it felt as if I was back there in that house. 'If this is too painful, you don't have to tell me. I suggested it to pass the time, not make you feel uncomfortable.'

His voice was kind and full of concern, and tears pricked my eyes. I'd never told anyone this story, even Nell didn't know why I had such a phobia of the dark; she simply accepted that I had and that I didn't want to talk about it.

'Would you prefer it if I didn't?' I asked, realising that I was oversharing in a mammoth way. I didn't even know Cole that well, but sitting here in the silence, with a door separating us, felt right somehow.

Cole exhaled. 'I'd prefer it if this door was open and I could give you a big hug.'

'Me too,' I said, brushing away a tear from my cheek.

'But carry on if you'd like to, I'm listening.'

I nodded into the darkness. 'As soon as he sat down, I could smell him. His clothes smelled of cigarettes and his breath was sour. He started to stroke my hair and tell me I was a good girl. I lay there, my heart thudding and wishing with all my heart that my mum would be better tomorrow so that I could go home. And then the door crashed open and it was Maureen, Michael's wife. She lunged at Michael and they had a bit of a fight and then they both left. I wet the bed but didn't dare tell anyone; I just pulled the sheet off and got back into bed. Nobody said a word about it the next day.'

'How old were you?' Cole asked in a heavy voice.

'Seven? Eight maybe?'

'You said you'd lied to your mum. So far in this story I'm hearing lots of wrong-doing, but you were the innocent in all of this.'

'I'm coming to that. I was allowed to go home a few days later and Mum asked me if I'd had a nice time. I lied. I told her I'd had a lovely time and that I really liked the foster parents. I thought that would be what she wanted to hear, but she cried and cried and said that I'd be better off with other people who could look after me better than she could. It was the worst thing I could possibly have said.'

I heard Cole swear softly under his breath. 'You were trying to protect your mum, which was incredibly mature of you.'

'After that I went to foster carers every few months to give Mum a break. Never back to Michael and Maureen, luckily. Then one year, when I was twelve, I went into a children's home, I think it was around November time. Mum said that she'd definitely be better before Christmas and that I'd be home to spend it with her. But by then she had . . .' I shuddered as the memory came whooshing back. The day I was called into the head teacher's office at school to find the manager of the children's home waiting solemnly to break the news to me. 'I didn't go home again because she took her own life. My beautiful mum, Sammy, aged twenty-nine. Gone for ever.'

There was a long silence on the other side of the door. A pulse beat in my temple. Had this been too much truth? I swallowed, willing him to speak.

'Jeez, Merry,' Cole said with a groan. 'When I think that all I had to worry about was cucumbers . . . You were so little to be worrying about that sort of thing. I have a daughter, Freya, who's eight and if I ever thought . . . I can't begin to imagine. I'm so sorry you had to go through that.'

A wave of relief rolled over me; I felt strangely lighter after telling him. Although the same could possibly not be said for poor Cole. He'd probably got a good deal more than he bargained for this evening.

'So now you know why I don't like the dark,' I said. 'And why I've got a complicated relationship with Christmas as well.'

'Not surprised. You poor kid.'

'I turned out all right in the end though,' I said. 'So don't feel too sorry for me.'

'Sorry for *you*?' he grumbled. 'I'm the one locked out here with a full bladder.'

I erupted into laughter and the tension which had held my whole body in its grip eased away. I laughed and I laughed until my sad tears mingled with happy tears and on the other side of the door, Cole laughed too, simultaneously moaning that he was in pain and that he was dangerously close to having an accident.

'OK, let's take your mind off your bladder,' I said, pulling myself together. 'You've told me snippets about your kids, tell me more.'

And for the next few minutes I listened, rapt, while Cole talked about Harley and Freya. About the summer they'd spent together going camping and swimming and building dens in the garden of Holly Cottage while Cole was getting it ready to rent out. How they were living in Canada for a year with their mum and loving their new life. He told me proudly how bright they were and that despite only having been in their new schools for a few months, they'd adapted to the new education system easily. His voice was full of love and tinged with regret and it was evident how much he was missing them.

'They are why I work so hard, why I get up in the morning,' he said. 'When the sale of the houses at Orchard Gardens go through I'll be able to buy us a proper home, so that they enjoy coming to visit.'

'You sound like a great dad,' I said softly, privately thinking that Freya and Harley would probably love visiting him even if he lived in a cardboard box. 'I didn't have one at all. There's a blank space on my birth certificate where his name should be. I remember asking her who my dad was. She never told me his name but said things like he was her best friend, a lovely kind man, but he hadn't been able to stay with us. By the time I was old enough to demand more information, Mum had died.'

'You've made me realise how lucky I am; I can't imagine not having my parents in my life.'

I shrugged even though he couldn't see me. 'I do miss Mum. I sometimes wonder about my dad. Where he is. Who he is. Is he still alive? But what you've never had you can't miss.' I'd been trotting out that cliché all my adult life. It was complete rubbish. I'd only had to look around me to see what I'd been missing and what I still missed: a family to belong to.

'I do worry that my kids will forget me,' he said, 'that they'll get so used to living with Lydia that they won't want to stay with me when they come back.'

My heart melted for him. 'I somehow doubt that will happen. When will you next see them?'

'Not soon enough,' he began and then paused. 'Hey, did you hear that?'

I strained to listen. 'No?'

And then suddenly I heard Cole scramble to his feet.

'Hello? Olek?' he shouted. 'Is that you?'

'Yes, I am here,' Olek replied.

I let out a breath of relief at the approach of his heavy footsteps.

It took Olek several minutes to dismantle the lock and break into the bathroom while I sat on the toilet out of the way. Finally, the door swung open and I blinked at the sudden bright light from Olek's torch.

'You all right?' Olek asked gently.

'Yes, thank you,' I said, relief flooding through me, but my eyes slid past him to Cole who was standing behind him, his brown eyes intense and a look of concern on his face.

Had he meant it when he said he wanted to give me a hug? Because right now that was what I needed more than anything.

'Merry?' Cole opened his arms wide and without a second thought I hurled myself from the bathroom and straight into them. His embrace tightened and I leaned into him, burying my face into his chest, my cheek resting on his jumper. I caught the faint smell of his aftershave and I realised how much I'd missed this, being held, being cared about, by a man. He rested his chin lightly on my head and rubbed my back. 'You're OK now. I've got you.'

I nodded. I was safe. Cole had me, and I was safe.

Chapter 23

Cole

Cole fixed the forklift attachment onto his dumper truck and drove it to the corner of the site where thousands of bricks were sitting on wooden pallets waiting to be used. His team were getting through them fast today; the cold weather made everyone want to keep moving to stay warm. He lifted a pallet-load and delivered it to plot number four where Josh and one of the lads were installing layers of mineral wool insulation between the inner and outer walls.

They were feeling the pressure now; the man who'd called in on spec last week had been back with his girl-friend on Saturday and they had decided to go ahead and buy. It was to be their first home together and Cole had really got a kick out of seeing how happy they were about their future. Now, he had just two left: the ones which the sisters had originally shown an interest in. He'd splashed out on some advertising in the local property press and was confident that this would generate some interest. He only needed to sell one; whichever one was left he'd keep for himself. Providing the costs didn't escalate any higher, that was. The flooding had unnerved almost all of his buyers and rather than continue to insist that the risk was minimal, Cole had suggested installing additional drainage channels. It had pacified his purchasers but had taken a big chunk out of his contingency fund.

He jumped down from the truck, noticing how solid the ground felt; the sun wasn't out today, which meant that the frost hadn't thawed all morning.

'This cold weather is a bit of a pain,' he said, as Josh came to join him.

Josh took off his hard hat and scratched his head. 'I know, but I'd rather not pull the lads off the job if I can help it.'

The temperature had plummeted this week, dropping to minus figures at night. At the moment it was only five degrees above freezing. If the temperature dropped much further the mortar wouldn't set properly, which would be a disaster for the integrity of the build. Cole bent down to inspect the brickwork and nudged the edge of a brick with the end of a trowel, setting it straight.

'I'm selling these houses as high spec,' Cole reminded him. 'We can't take any risks with the quality of the brickwork. I think we have to err on the side of caution.'

'Understood, but two of the houses are almost there,' said Josh. 'One final push and we'll be at roof height.'

The roof trusses had already been delivered; Cole had the bill for them on his desk. With a bit of luck a couple of the houses might have their roofs on before Christmas.

Cole pulled on his gloves. 'Let's get cracking then. Let's see who can lay the most in an hour.'

Josh grinned. 'You're on.'

Cole once spent a summer working as a brickie for a house builder on the Costa Blanca. Cheap beer, brilliant social life and the deepest suntan of his life. Cole didn't do much bricklaying these days, no point when the lads he employed were so much better and faster than him. But he was happy to muck in when he had to.

The lads whistled when they found out Cole was lending a hand.

'Watch you don't break a nail, boss,' one of them shouted, resulting in raucous laughter from everyone else.

'Yeah, yeah, very funny.' Cole grinned and climbed the scaffolding to begin work.

He and Josh settled into a pattern: Cole laying the bricks while Josh worked from the inside of the building, laying the internal block work. It was skilled work and required his full concentration but that didn't stop his mind wandering to Merry and that hour they'd spent together waiting for the locksmith to arrive. That had been over a week ago, but if he was honest with himself, Merry hadn't been far from his thoughts ever since.

What a woman. And what a start in life she'd had. And he bet she'd barely scratched the surface. He'd been thinking about how it would have been for a kid on her own like that being part of the care system, without anyone to call family, to call 'hers', to feel as if she belonged. And that bloke who came and sat on Merry's bed in the darkness, that had sounded horrific. No wonder she had a phobia of being in the dark. He'd been back there the following day, changed the bathroom lock and changed every bulb in the place so that he knew none of them would blow for the rest of her time in the building.

He might be separated from his kids, but they knew he loved them; he told them every time they spoke, even though he knew it made Harley cringe. He listened to their stories, he made sure he knew the names of their new friends, of their teachers, of the places they liked best in Whistler.

'All right, boss?' Josh asked, looking amused. 'You've got a right face on you. Not enjoying being at the sharp end, after all? Have you gone a bit rusty?'

'Hey, watch it,' Cole grinned, not stopping from scooping up mortar and slapping it onto the bricks. 'Remember who pays your wages.'

'Good point,' Josh said with a laugh.

Cole focused on lining up the next brick. 'I'll tell you what is rusty: my dating skills. I've met someone and I'm not sure whether to make a move.'

He groaned inwardly; he sounded like a predator. He couldn't even master the language of dating, let alone the actions.

He'd always been fairly extroverted, never had a problem approaching girls and chatting them up. But that was a long time ago and before he'd messed up his marriage. Somewhere along the line he'd lost his confidence. Merry was . . . well, she was special, he might only get one chance to ask her out and he didn't want to risk stuffing it up. Without wanting to be big-headed, he did think she liked him. She was always fun and friendly, and they had made each other laugh. But did she like him romantically? He was too out of practice to tell. She had stepped into his arms and she hadn't pulled away from him for ages, but that could just have been a reaction to being set free. Although she had kissed his cheek. Perhaps if Olek hadn't been there, making the next move might have happened naturally.

Josh's ears pricked up. 'Have you got a picture of her?'

'Um,' he frowned, 'I don't think so. Why?'

'I want to see if she's worth the hassle before we go any further.'

Cole shook his head, laughing. 'Is that how brutal it is these days?'

246

Josh shrugged. 'Works both ways; she'll be showing pictures of you around for a second opinion.'

'Only if she's interested in me. You've met her,' Cole continued. 'She's the tenant at Holly Cottage.'

Josh tipped his head to one side, considering. 'She's nice. Good choice.'

'So what do I do?'

'Ask her for a drink,' he said with a shrug. 'The worst she can say is no.'

Cole felt nervous at the thought of it; the last girl he'd asked out on a date was Lydia over thirteen years ago. He lifted another brick from the pile, placed it on top of the fresh mortar and tapped it into place. 'Where did you take Vicky on your first date?'

'To a gig. And we had backstage passes.'

'Was she impressed?'

'Oh yes.' Josh pulled a smug face and they both laughed.

'And now look at you,' said Cole. 'Living together and with a baby of your own.'

'I know. It's mad.' He shook his head as if he couldn't believe it. 'Vicky's going to visit a nursery later this afternoon, she's going back to work after Christmas.'

'Aren't you going with her?'

Josh tapped the block into place with the end of his trowel. 'Nah, the only appointment they had was at three and I'll still be at work.'

Cole was reminded of himself at the same age; he'd thought exactly the same. If Lydia specifically asked him to be there, he'd do his best, but to his shame, he'd rarely offered.

'Your call, but if you want my advice, be involved,' Cole said. 'Vicky will appreciate your input, I promise. Joint parenting means just that. I know Vicky is not at work just now and it makes sense for her to do all the appointments, but I wish I'd done my fair share of the crap jobs, not just turned up to play with them at bath time. Know Alice's shoe size, go to the doctors and dentist, the hairdressers, all of that.'

Josh smirked. 'She doesn't have any teeth or wear shoes and she's got a massive bald patch at the moment which Vicky frets about, but point taken, I hear what you're saying. And I do my bit when I'm at home.'

'Could you buy nappies without Vicky telling you what to get?' Cole asked, pretty sure he knew what the answer would be. Because when his kids had been in nappies, he hadn't had a clue. Next time around, he'd make sure . . . The thought stopped him in his tracks. It had never crossed his mind before, but now it had. He probed the notion a bit more. The thought of having more children one day made his heart beat faster. Yep, definitely; Cole wanted a second chance at fatherhood.

Josh was looking at him as if he was mad. 'No way. Have you seen the nappy section of the supermarket recently? I have to get her to write it down.'

'And who writes it down for *her*?' Cole chided. 'No one. Trust me. There's a lot more to being a dad than watching Vicky be a good mum.'

Josh rubbed his nose with the back of his hand and studied the length of blockwork still to be completed. 'I hate asking for time off.'

'I know you're a hard worker,' Cole laughed. 'But you're a family man now, which is just as tough. Your days of backstage passes are behind you, you've got to impress her with your nappy knowledge.'

'So, can I knock off at two today?'

'Thought you'd never ask,' Cole replied with a wink.

Once Josh had gone, Cole decided to call the brickwork to a halt; at this stage of the build there was plenty to be getting on with. He handed new jobs out and went back to his site office to book the crane they'd need to lift the roof trusses into place.

No sooner had he made himself a mug of tea when Lydia rang. His heart skipped a beat, immediately worried something had happened.

'Lydia?' He calculated the time in Whistler to be just after seven in the morning.

'Hey, sorry to bother you when you're at work.' She sounded flustered.

'No worries. What's happened, are the kids OK?' He sat down, gripping his phone to his ear.

'They're both fine.' She hesitated. 'Harley's fine. But I'm a bit worried about Freya. She's wet the bed every night this week. Something's obviously bothering her, but whenever I ask her if she's unhappy at school or if there's someone upsetting her, she insists that nothing is the matter and that she's happy.'

'Poor kid,' Cole muttered, his heart aching for his daughter.

'I didn't want to tell you because you'll probably think it's my fault. I dragged our kids halfway across the world, so it's my problem to solve.' There was a crack in Lydia's voice and Cole felt awful for her. 'But then I thought if you find out from the kids about the bed-wetting that you'd think I was keeping things from you.'

'Hey,' he said softly, picturing her hunched over her phone, her voice low so that the kids didn't hear her. 'I'm glad you told me. We're both her parents; that means we both have to sort out any problems. And as for it being your fault, I gave you my blessing to go to Canada. I'm not going to start pointing the finger as soon as things get tough.'

'Thank you,' said Lydia, sounding dangerously close to tears. 'You don't know how much it means to hear that.'

'Would it help if I flew over?' he suggested. He could if he had to; work would have to wait.

'You are a good dad,' she said.

'I'm trying,' he replied.

Lydia sighed. 'I'm meeting up with another ex-pat woman later, she and her husband are out here with their children – let me see if she's got any advice before we do anything drastic.'

'Sure,' he said. 'But the offer is there, just say the word.'

The story Merry had told him about lying to her mum came back to him then, about her misguided efforts to make her happy by pretending she'd had a good time with her foster parents. Maybe that was what Freya was doing: protecting Lydia's feelings?

'Perhaps you could talk to her about how you feel,' Cole suggested. 'Maybe she needs to hear that it's OK to feel sad, or angry, or . . . I don't know, homesick even, and that there are things you can do to make those feelings better.'

'You know, I was wondering if being homesick might be behind this,' she said, 'although she is adamant that she loves school and our apartment. But the bed-wetting has certainly been worse since she had a video call with her old classmates.'

'She can love being in Canada and still feel homesick,' he said. 'The two aren't mutually exclusive.'

'Tell me about it,' Lydia said drily. 'What I wouldn't give sometimes for fish and chips and a mooch around some decent shops.'

He shook his head, laughing softly at the memory of many a Saturday afternoon spent following her round the shopping centre, followed by a fish and chip supper at home. 'I think maybe Freya needs to hear that too.'

'You're right. Thanks for listening.' He could hear the smile in her voice now. 'And thanks for giving such great advice. By the way, you haven't forgotten the cut-off date to send parcels to Canada in time for Christmas?'

'Me miss a deadline?'

'Good point.'

They both laughed.

The cut-off date was two weeks away, but he wasn't going to leave it to the last minute; it wasn't Cole's way. Give him a deadline and he liked to smash it. He'd bought almost everything: for Freya, art stuff and a portable karaoke machine which Lydia hadn't been over the moon about; joggers, jeans and pyjamas for his son who'd apparently shot up since September. He still wanted to get little stocking fillers, things to make them smile on Christmas morning. But that wouldn't take him long.

'Will you be OK on your own this Christmas?' Lydia asked out of the blue.

There was a note of guilt in her voice, he noticed. She felt bad for depriving him of time with his kids over the festive period. She still cared about him in a way, and he cared about her. He was glad they'd overcome the initial stiffness in their relationship which had followed their break-up. Now they could focus on what was important: doing the best for their kids.

'I'll be fine,' he told her. 'I've got lots to keep me occupied.'

And besides, if he ever managed to pluck up the courage to ask Merry out, maybe he wouldn't be on his own after all.

Chapter 24

Merry

It was Friday afternoon, two days before the school Christmas Fair and the town lights switch-on and I was working in the kitchen in the old bank, humming to myself as I experimented with my new essential oils.

I was attempting to create an aroma which had been haunting me for the last week. It was a scent which had the power to lift my mood, set my pulse racing and induce a feeling of calm all at once. It was woody, fresh and peppery but with hints of sweetness to lighten it. It would appeal to men and I had a feeling that women would adore it too and when I finally got it right, it was going to make the most amazing candle.

This was my third batch, and I was getting closer to my goal with each one. Lime had been the wrong addition to batch two, so this time I was trying lemon with sandalwood, pink peppercorns, and the merest hint of vanilla. Satisfied that it was thoroughly combined, I poured the concoction of oils into the waiting hot wax and stirred rigorously. Then I jotted down the proportions of oils in this batch before I forgot them and finally, I poured the wax into two plain glass jars.

This was the part of making candles I loved the most: mixing, blending, adjusting, more of this oil, less of another. It was fun and creative and challenged my olfactory organs to be ultra-responsive, to detect the minute differences each oil made to the finished candle. I was like a kid playing with a chemistry set and it didn't feel like work at all. I was overdue some play-time, I thought, reaching for the kettle to make another pot of coffee. I'd never been so busy in my entire life. Not that I was complaining, I loved every minute of it. I made candles all day long and went to bed dreaming of candles, well mostly; there was one other subject which had infiltrated my dreams lately.

Scented candles, it seemed, were on everyone's list this Christmas. I was waking up every morning to a fresh flurry of orders from Etsy, and Nell seemed to get through as many as I could make. January could be a completely different ball game, but I'd worry about that when it happened; for now, I was making hay while the sun shone, or should that be making candles while the days barely got light before they started getting dark all over again?

But at least it wasn't dark in the old bank anymore. Every light burned brightly, Cole had made sure of that; he'd been and put new bulbs in every light fitting, even the ones which hadn't needed it. It had been no bother, he'd assured me, and he felt happier knowing I wouldn't be plunged into darkness again for a while.

Warmth bloomed somewhere deep inside me as I conjured him up. Again. Cole Robinson featured as frequently in my thoughts and dreams as my candles. There was something about him which made my heart tingle. He was good-looking, obviously, but it was more than that. He had a good heart too; I could tell from the way he talked about his dad and his sister, and his kids especially. And he had been so good to me that night when I'd been locked in the dark. He hadn't mocked me for being scared or told me I was overreacting. Instead, he'd done everything in his power to put me at ease. He'd listened to me, and when he *had* spoken, he'd somehow known exactly the right words to calm me down. The moment Olek set me free and the door had opened and I'd seen Cole waiting for me was a moment that kept playing on a loop in my head. It had been the most natural thing in the world to be in his arms. If Olek hadn't been there, would he have kissed me, would I have been bold enough to give him more than a peck on the cheek? I felt a bit breathless at the thought.

Since that night our paths hadn't crossed. We'd sent each other text messages and he'd left me various notes about things he'd fixed after he'd been here once or twice late at night. A part of me was worried that I'd put him off with my oversharing. But what was done was done, I told myself, as I tipped cold coffee from the coffee press down the sink and gave it a wash.

Cole probably didn't realise how privileged he was that I'd confided in him; I didn't talk about my early years much to anyone. It was hard for people to hear about a child being placed regularly in the care of foster parents, and even harder to learn of an orphan, completely without family, growing up in a children's home. I wasn't ashamed of my background, but I knew from experience that some people found it impossible not to have preconceptions about a child who'd gone through the care system. That needed to change. The more I opened up, the more I'd challenge those preconceptions. And didn't those special to me deserve to know as much about me as I'd want to know about them? And Cole was someone I counted among the special ones.

My mum was still special to me too. Our life together had been painfully short and hadn't fitted the mould of a traditional family unit, but it had been the only family I'd known, and I'd never stopped wanting it back. A family to call my own, big or small, was my one true goal in life, not money, or nice cars, or big houses, just a place to call home and people I belonged to.

And I had a feeling from what Cole had said that the concept of home was important to him too. Ridiculous as it sounded, I missed him and had started a new habit of checking my phone every five minutes to see if he'd sent me a message, and then jumping every time my phone rang, hoping that it would be him. Nell said I ought to deliberately spring a leak somewhere as an excuse to get him to visit, but as tempting as it was, I couldn't do that – I knew how busy he was.

Besides, Hester Smart would be attending our lights switch-on event and Cole had promised to chaperone her, so I only had another two days to wait. Hester and I had had several conversations about Sunday's proceedings; she sounded lovely and down to earth and very chatty, but surprisingly she was almost more interested in asking about me than the event itself. Was that because Cole had talked about me? Or was it the opposite and he hadn't mentioned me at all? Either way, I was looking forward to meeting her.

As I was pouring boiling water on fresh coffee grounds, my phone rang. I gave a yelp and almost dropped the kettle in my haste to answer it.

It rang a lot at the moment, either with an order enquiry or one of my fellow committee members on the Christmas Project keeping me updated.

Only a few minutes ago I'd been on the phone to the Christmas tree farm. After our initial worries that we wouldn't be able to accommodate everyone, we'd only had forty-seven requests for Christmas trees, which was just right. The closer we got to Christmas, the more I was beginning to realise what a big logistical job it was going to be to coordinate the allocation and decoration of an entire forest's worth of fir trees in and around a busy market.

This time the call was from Nigel. 'Merry!' he boomed. 'Seasons greetings! You haven't got a snow machine I could borrow, have you?'

'Sorry, no,' I replied, laughing. 'I don't have much need for one.'

'Pity,' said Nigel. 'I'm just walking around the market-place and thought we could take the Narnia theme one step further and spray everywhere white.'

'We'll have to hope for real snow instead.' I had to hand it to Nigel, I might not always agree with his ideas, but at least he had plenty of them.

'It's cold enough, so you never know. Oh, by the way,' he added. 'Just been talking to the Christmas tree man, he wants to give you a present for all the extra business you've sent his way. OK if I give him your address?'

'That's so kind,' I said, flattered. 'How about he delivers it to the old bank for ease? I'm using it as a work studio at the moment.'

'Nice. You ought to open a shop in there,' said Nigel, 'it would do well, I reckon. And it's been empty for too long. The more the merrier, I say. Get it? Merry? Anyway, got to get back to my own shop, got a delivery of neon reindeer due in this afternoon.'

'Thanks, Nigel, see you Sunday.' I stifled a giggle, imagining Nell's face when she found out; at least they weren't inflatable.

The scent of coffee pulled me back to the moment. I poured myself a cup and took it through to the front room and looked down at the marketplace. It was always busy on Friday afternoons with people stocking up on fresh produce for the weekend, but even so I could pick out Nigel in his Christmas pudding bobble hat waving a sprig of mistletoe at Audrey on the china stall.

I turned my gaze to the newly installed Christmas tree which sat only a few metres away from the entrance to the old bank. It was a gorgeous tree; even Astrid had commented on what perfect proportions it had. Its regal green branches were hung top to bottom with giant shiny baubles in jewelled colours of emerald, ruby, sapphire and topaz and topped with an oversized gold star which would be lit from within from Sunday. It reminded me a bit of Astrid, who after a brief foray into the world of muted dress, I was glad to say, had reverted to full-on technicolour.

Strings and strings of multi-coloured lights zig-zagged its branches, and garlands of matching lights encircled the marketplace too. There was a rope cordon around the tree to keep little fingers away from the electrics, and yesterday the other committee members and I had been given a demonstration of how to orchestrate the official lights switch-on. Daniel was going to be in charge of the PA system so that Hester could do a countdown over the microphone before pressing a big fake button, and Nigel was going to flip the actual switch. It was all beginning to feel very real and the responsibility of getting it right regularly set my stomach to 'fast spin' whenever I thought too deeply about it.

My phone rang again, sending my heart into a flap for a second time in as many minutes. It was Nell.

'I can see you skiving at the window. Wave,' she said. In the background I could hear music from another stall and someone shouting the price of tangerines and mandarins.

I spotted her waving her arm high in the air, her copper curls squashed under a cream woolly hat and I waved back.

'I'm not skiving,' I said, holding up my mug. 'Coffee break.'

'All right for some. Hey, guess who was just here at my stall buying nuts?' Nell said, her voice bouncing with glee. 'Cole!'

'Really?' I said casually, immediately scanning the market for him. 'Did he mention me? What did he say, what did he buy?'

'Not that you're at all interested,' Nell sniggered.

'Nell, tell me!' He must still be down there. I could get my coat and go for a wander and pretend to bump into him.

'Ten minutes ago, caramelised almonds, and he didn't really get a chance to talk about having the hots for you, even though he probably wanted to, because I had a queue of customers at the time. Honestly, Merry, I always forget how busy it gets in the run-up to Christmas. And this year, people can't get enough Brazil nuts all because there's a trend on Instagram for nut-based—'

'What was he wearing?' I interrupted impatiently. 'His yellow coat, or his black ski jacket?'

Why couldn't I see him, I thought irritably. It should be easy. Perhaps he'd gone and I'd missed him. I hoped not.

Nell laughed. 'Yellow coat.'

'Can you see him from where you are?' I demanded. 'Keep looking.'

'You've really got it bad, haven't you?'

'No,' I said. A blatant lie. 'It's just that I haven't seen him since that night and I feel like we won't be able to move past it until we've met in person again. He was so kind to me, you know.'

'He put his arms round you, and he said you were safe and you almost cried with relief,' Nell recited. 'Yes, you've mentioned that. Once or twice. And stop stressing, Merry. He likes you.'

Did he? I wondered, or did he simply feel protective towards his anxiety-ridden tenant?

I let out a breath. 'I'm overthinking it. It'll be fine.'

'So how are your Cole-scented candles doing?' she said. 'Have you managed to capture the essence of builder yet?'

'Almost,' I said absently. 'I've just made some more – I might have cracked it this time.'

'Try adding brick dust and stewed tea,' she said with a snort.

'You may scoff,' I said, refusing to be drawn, 'but if I can make a candle that smells as good as Cole, I'll be a millionaire this time next year.'

'Of course you could always text him. *Dear Cole, what aftershave do you wear because I can't stop thinking of the smell of your skin and I kept that jumper on in bed so I could sniff you all night.*'

I bit my lip, worriedly; did I really talk about him all the time, as Nell was implying? Perhaps she was right; maybe I did have it bad. 'Shut up. I only did that once.'

'Oh, I can see him again!' Nell squeaked. 'Heading towards the Buttermarket.'

I caught sight of his yellow coat next to the flower stall.

'Got him,' I said, straining to see what he was buying.

'Perhaps he's buying flowers for his special tenant?' Nell said in a singsong voice.

'Haven't you got customers to serve?' I said. 'I thought you were busy.'

I watched as Cole tucked some flowers in the top of one of his bags and then took out his phone.

'I'm closing early,' Nell replied. 'I'm virtually nutless.'

Just then my phone beeped with a text. A thrill shot through me. It was Cole.

'He's just texted me,' I gasped.

Nell squealed in my ear. 'And? What does it say?'

My mouth had gone dry. 'It says *can I pop up and see you?*'

I typed back my reply:

Yes of course, let yourself in.

Great, see you in five.

'He's on his way,' I said, my throat suddenly tight.

'Then get off the phone, put some lippy on and for God's sake brush your hair.'

'No way!' I said, full of indignation. 'He can take me as he finds me.'

'Yeah, right,' Nell snorted.

I ended the call and scrambled to make myself presentable. I checked under my eyes for smudged mascara and scraped my hair up into a bun to hide the fact that it was overdue a wash. By the time I heard his footsteps on the stairs, I'd arranged myself artfully at the table in the front room with a paintbrush in one hand and a stack of the hand-painted gift cards in front of me which I'd made this morning in between candle batches.

'Merry?' Cole called from the staircase.

'In the front,' I shouted, wincing from the pain of my too-tight bun. I loosened it quickly, freeing some strands and hoped the effect would be Boho chic rather than dragged-through-hedge casual.

'Hey,' he said from the doorway.

My insides melted as he walked in, bringing the wintry air with him. His cheeks were pink from the cold and his eyes were bright, one hand full of shopping bags. It was so good to see him. He was so handsome, and I loved the rich caramel colour of his hair, somewhere between red and brown. Pecan pie. That was it. That might make a nice candle too. Perhaps I could make an entire range based on Cole's best bits. I stifled a giggle, aware that my mind had gone skittish at the sight of him.

He strode across to me and produced a bunch of flowers from behind his back. 'For you.'

My spirits soared. He'd filled the living room with flowers for me when I'd first seen the room, but I'd assumed that was just a one-off, to make the space feel more comfortable. This felt different, more intimate.

'Me? Thank you.' I looked at his face and felt a flicker of doubt; despite his confident stride he looked uneasy, as if he had something on his mind. 'Any particular reason, or am I just a lucky girl?'

'Um, I just wondered, I just wanted . . .' his voice trailed away and he looked down at the floor. 'To say sorry for you getting locked in the bathroom.'

I smiled at him, half disappointed that there wasn't a more personal reason for the gesture, but glad it wasn't to soften bad news. I buried my nose in the bouquet. The delicate scent of stocks, roses and freesias was soft and feminine; a complete contrast to the manly scent of the candles I'd been working on. 'Thank you! They are gorgeous but you needn't have and you don't need to apologise.'

He shrugged. 'Maybe, but I can't stop thinking about it.'

My heart squeezed. 'It wasn't your average evening, was it? And I must say, it's better to see you in person and not be sitting on the other side of a door trapped in the dark.'

'It's good to see you too.' He lowered his bags to the floor.

My smile was so wide that my cheeks were beginning to ache. I'd been so worried about this first conversation following that night and I needn't have been. We were good; I felt the tension ease from my shoulders.

'And now I know that all I need to do to distract myself from having a panic attack is to pour out all the secrets of my sordid past to a stranger,' I said, pulling a comical face.

Cole sat down on the edge of the sofa and stretched out his long legs. 'It wasn't sordid. And we're not strangers anymore, are we?' he smiled, a question in his lovely eyes. 'We're friends.'

Friends. I felt a wave of disappointment. Had I been friend-zoned? I hoped not. The hug I'd had from him that night had taken my breath away; I didn't want it to end there. I wanted more. I wanted to feel his mouth against mine. I wanted to taste . . .

'Merry?' Cole laughed uneasily, 'are you OK? Are we not friends?'

'Yes, yes of course we are,' I confirmed briskly. I jumped to my feet. 'Coffee?'

He hesitated. 'Oh, go on then, you've twisted my arm, but I can't stop long, I've got Christmas wrapping to do.' He nodded to his bags; there were two rolls of paper poking out of one of them.

'I'll help if you like,' I offered. 'I'm good at wrapping.'

'That's an offer I can't refuse,' he grinned. 'I'm all fingers and thumbs where sticky tape is concerned.'

Five minutes later, I'd made us both drinks, put the flowers in water and the two of us were sitting on the sofa with Cole's Christmas shopping on the floor in front of us divided into two piles.

'Is this one for your daughter?' I pointed to the pile on the right where a small pair of slippers decorated with rainbows sat on top of a long packet of pastel highlighter pens and a toy vet's kit.

He laughed. 'How did you guess? Freya is still into toys. Harley is only interested in snow sports or bits for his laptop or phone.'

I found us both a pair of scissors and some sticky tape and we set to work, me on Freya's toys and Cole wrapping things for his son. It was a lovely way to spend time, I thought, as together we ploughed through the pile of chocolate, books, pyjamas, card games and colouring sets.

'You're very organised,' I said, wrapping three pairs of fluffy socks in a square sheet of paper, 'getting all your Christmas shopping done so early.'

I hid a smile, watching as he struggled to find the end of the sellotape.

'Not all of it,' he replied. 'So far, I've only bought stuff for my special people.'

His kids. He seemed to be such a dedicated dad. I could almost feel my ovaries pinging to attention. Although of course, he might feel he'd already done his bit for the future of the species. Which would be no good to me; I hadn't even started. I gave myself a shake, imagining if Nell could hear my inner monologue. He had literally just pronounced us friends and here I was, sizing him up as a potential Baby Daddy.

'I've only got one special person to buy for,' I said, pulling myself together. 'And it's something I can order online. No Christmas magic required.'

By special, I meant children. Nell's stepson Max. He'd even supplied me with a link to make sure I didn't get the wrong thing. As far as everyone else went, I didn't have a clue what I was going to buy or when. But it would get done eventually, it always did.

Cole didn't reply for a moment, concentrating on cutting the paper in a straight line.

'But you have got a special person, which is great,' he said finally. 'And if you've bought them the gift they wanted, I'm sure they'll love you for it.'

I shrugged. 'You can't go wrong with an Xbox game.'

'I suppose not.' He blinked at me. 'I have to admit, I wasn't looking forward to shopping, I've always seen it as a necessary evil. But as I was choosing things, I was imagining their happy faces on Christmas morning and I got quite a kick out of it. And the fact I can mark something as done on my spreadsheet is even better.'

I raised an eyebrow. 'You enter Christmas shopping onto a spreadsheet?' I set the socks to one side for Cole to add a gift tag to it and picked up the vet's set.

He nodded. 'I enter *everything* onto a spreadsheet, whether it's for work or pleasure, otherwise it doesn't get done. I work best when I've got a structure to stick to. I colour code everything by priority.'

Everything? A wicked thought crossed my mind. What colour did he use for sex? I stifled a giggle. Cole looked at me and smiled.

'You're thinking what a geek I am, aren't you?' he said with a grin. He picked up some sort of gadget for Harley and peeled the price sticker off the back of it. I stared at his large strong hands, the callouses on his palms and wondered if they'd be rough against my skin.

'No!' I felt myself blushing, glad he couldn't tell what I

was really thinking. 'I'm seriously impressed. I remember doing spreadsheets at school.' I shuddered. 'The stuff of nightmares.'

He laughed softly. 'We're all different. What sort of scheduling system do you use for your business?'

I smiled to myself, thinking of the scribbled reminders on my whiteboard; he'd be horrified.

'I just make a massive list and try and get as much ticked off by the end of the day as I can. Anything left over gets put on the list for tomorrow. Simple.'

'Oh, Merry, no,' Cole stared at me incredulously. 'Now *that's* the stuff of nightmares.'

We both laughed and for the next few minutes continued our Christmas wrapping in companiable silence until we both reached for the scissors at the same time. Heat flooded my body as his fingers touched mine. I kept perfectly still, hoping he'd take my hand, bring it to his lips.

'Whoops, sorry.' He pulled his hand away. 'Ladies first.'

'Thanks,' I mumbled, feeling a whoosh of disappointment.

'Nice jumper by the way. I thought you didn't like Christmas?' He gestured at my jumper, which featured a line of reindeer pulling a sleigh.

'Actually, Christmas is growing on me,' I said, realising that that was true. I'd been hung up on spending this Christmas as one half of a couple, but now I was actually looking forward to being able to do as I pleased. 'But this jumper belongs to Nell; I've run out of clean things and I've been too busy to do any washing.' No need to mention that I didn't want to wash my favourite jumper yet, not while the scent of him still lingered on it.

'In that case I have good news,' Cole said, pausing from wrapping to sip his coffee. 'Holly Cottage is ready for you to move back into. You've even got a new washing machine.'

'Oh wow, thank you!' I clapped my hands together. 'I hope you got that reckless landscaping contractor to foot the bill?'

He grinned at my feisty tone. 'Some of it. The company is usually very good and I didn't want to sever all ties with them; the guy who owns the business is pretty decent. He sacked the person responsible for dumping the debris in the river and has more than made up for the damage caused on site. He's even agreed to provide apple and pear trees for each of my houses. Which will tie in nicely with the name of the development – Orchard Gardens.'

'So all's well that ends well,' I said, impressed with Cole's way of dealing with someone who'd let him down. I couldn't wait to wake up in my own cosy cottage again and I was sure Nell and Olek would be grateful to have the house to themselves. Although the extra workspace at the old bank had been a boon.

'Could I carry on working here for a bit longer, would you mind?' I asked. 'Just until we're past the Christmas rush. The thought of transporting all my stuff back to the cottage right now does not fill me with joy.'

'I don't see why not.' Cole sorted through the offcuts of paper for a piece to fit a deck of magic cards. 'I did notice a lot of boxes in the corridor.'

I held up my crossed fingers. 'Most of those are my stock to sell on Sunday at the school Christmas Fair before the lights switch-on. I've been roped in to having a stall.'

'I miss all that stuff, the Christmas parties, the nativity plays, the carol concerts with my kids,' Cole said wistfully. 'It was great being part of their world.'

'Why don't you join me?' I said, thinking how much more fun it would be if Cole came along. I had Astrid lined up to assist me, but she wouldn't mind taking a rain check. 'I could do with the help, although maybe leave the gift-wrapping to me.'

We both looked at the length of mangled sellotape in his hand and laughed.

'I would have loved that,' he said, looking genuinely touched. 'But I'm having a Sunday lunch with my family before we come over to Wetherley for the event; I don't want to let them down. Considering I live with my sister and her husband, I hardly see them, we've all been so busy.'

'Me too. I've barely had time to draw breath. All work and no play, as they say.'

Cole scribbled a message on a gift tag to Harley and peeled the self-adhesive sticker off the back.

'So, when do you think you will have time to, you know, *play*?'

'Play?' I blinked at him, unsure of his meaning. Was he leading up to asking me out? If he did, I'd say yes; in fact, my yes was so ready to come out that I thought I might burst.

He cleared his throat. 'You know, the opposite of work, time to go out and have fun.'

Cole was a confident, straightforward sort of guy. I was sure if he wanted to ask me out, he'd just do it, he wouldn't beat about the bush. Besides, he'd implied often enough that his children were his priority. All of which led me to the conclusion that this conversation was not leading up to a date.

'I'm busy right up until the end of Christmas Eve,' I said with a sigh. 'But on Christmas Day I shall wake up late, eat chocolates in bed for breakfast and watch my favourite Christmas film with a glass of champagne.'

Cole nodded his approval.

'Sounds like a plan, I wouldn't mind doing that too.' He raised a hand to his mouth. 'Sorry, that sounded like I was inviting myself into your bed. Please forget I said that. I've made myself blush. I never blush. You were saying? About a film?'

My heart pounded against my ribs. Forget he said it? Like that was going to happen. The thought of waking up to find Cole Robinson in my bed on Christmas morning was awakening delicious sensations I hadn't felt for a long, long time.

'*Home Alone 2.*' My face felt like a furnace; now we were both blushing. *Christmas morning, Cole, champagne . . .*

Cole swallowed. 'Wasn't expecting that.'

Chocolates for breakfast. With Cole. Neither was I. I couldn't get the image out of my head. I looked around for something else to wrap but we appeared to be finished.

'You should try it. It has much to recommend it . . .' My voice trailed away.

'I can imagine,' said Cole, who was starting to smile again.

I'd lost track of what I was actually referring to now: the lovely scene when Kevin's mum finds him by the tree in the Rockefeller Center, or watching it from beneath the covers. With a friend.

I couldn't wait to relate this conversation to Nell; she was going to die of laughter.

Together we gathered up all our parcels and repacked them into Cole's bags.

'And have you got plans to spend the day with your special person?' he asked once we'd finished.

I shook my head. 'No, but you never know, maybe if I hang around under the mistletoe, I might bump into "the one". They say anything can happen at Christmas.'

I groaned inwardly. Had I really just said I was going to stand under the mistletoe and pounce on some poor unsuspecting bloke? *Why yes, Merry, yes you did.*

'Well,' Cole said slowly, eyes pinned to the floor. 'Let's hope so. But I meant the special person whose present you've already bought?'

'Oh, that special person!' I cringed, hiding my face behind my hands to hide my flaming cheeks. 'Why is it that whenever I'm with you, I have a terrible habit of oversharing? The present I bought is for Max, Olek's teenage son. The locksmith?'

'I see. I think.' Cole grinned.

'And I'm not sure about Christmas Day. I've had offers, but I'm quite tempted to spend the day in peace. Alone.'

Nell had begged me to go to hers so that I could drink Prosecco with her in the kitchen while she hid from her mother. She had bitten the bullet and invited her parents, who had accepted immediately. Ever since then, she'd been veering from spring cleaning her house from top to bottom, to declaring that they'd have to take them as they found them or bugger off home. So far I hadn't committed myself either way.

He held my gaze for a long moment, and I watched as about ten different expressions flickered over his face.

'Home alone. That does sound tempting,' he said gruffly.

I nodded, not sure how to respond. I was so confused by this man; one minute it felt as if he was flirting and the next he was backing off.

His watch started to beep, startling us both. He switched it off and let out a sharp breath.

'That's my alarm to remind me that the kids are phoning in thirty minutes. Thanks for all your help but I'd better go.' He got to his feet and I noticed him shake his head

269

as if frustrated about something. 'It's been illuminating as ever, Merry. Take care. I'll see you on Sunday. And in the meantime, good luck under the mistletoe.'

He bent and kissed my cheek, his lips as light as a feather against my skin.

Wow. I touched my fingers to my face, watching as he walked away, already missing him, his delicious smell once again taking my breath away.

It was him, I realised, my heart trembling with a rush of emotion – Cole. There was no need to hang around, waiting to bump into the one. Because I was almost sure I'd already met him.

I pressed a hand to my chest, aware of the thudding of my heart. So that was my Christmas wish list sorted. Now all I had to do was hope that I featured on his.

Chapter 25

Merry

'Can you think what your mummy's favourite smell is?' I asked.

The small girl in front of my candle stall nodded. 'Our kitten's paws.'

Her face had been painted to look like a glittery snow-flake and she was holding a skewer of marshmallows dripping with melted chocolate, much of which was down the front of her pale blue princess dress. In her other hand she clutched a sticky purse. I couldn't recall the smell of kittens' paws, in fact I wasn't sure if I'd ever had the pleasure of smelling them. But I had a feeling that it might not work in candle form.

'That is a nice smell,' I agreed, discreetly wiping the chocolate from the edge of my table. 'I don't think I have a candle that smells of kittens. Maybe she might like this one.' I held out my specially produced *Winter Forest* candle for her to sniff.

Her eyes widened. 'It smells of Christmas trees.'

'Would she like that one, do you think?'

The little girl nodded and without warning thrust her skewer at me to hold for her while she checked the contents of her purse. I held my breath while she counted out the coins, hoping that she had enough money. She did, well, thereabouts anyway, so while she chose a gift card to give to her mum, I pocketed the coins, wrapped the candle and sent her on her sticky way.

After she'd gone I leaned back on the tiny chair which must have come from one of the children's classrooms and sipped the coffee which Tom, or Mr Hughes as he was known around here, had brought me. He'd been around all the stallholders earlier, taking their refreshments order, dressed in his Christmas jumper and Santa hat, followed by an adoring gang of little helpers who foisted mince pies on us all.

There was no mistaking that Christmas had well and truly arrived in Wetherley. The main hall, where my stall was, was a cross between Santa's workshop and a German Christmas market. The air was warm and cinnamon-scented, Christmas music was being piped through enormous speakers mounted just below the ceiling and there had been two queues which hadn't died off all afternoon: one for Santa and one for the ladies' loos. Rows of small stalls selling everything from Christmas cake to Christmas stockings lined the room and in the centre were all sorts of fundraising activities from the bottle stall (over 18s only) to pin the nose on Rudolph. If you were so inclined, you could design a Christmas card, make a stained-glass window from cellophane or decorate a biscuit. Hordes of children, fuelled by the chocolate fountain and wall-to-wall Christmassy-ness, ran around at high speed, while the large group of mums in charge of the mulled wine stall had got pinker and louder as the afternoon had worn on.

It was peak Christmas chaos and I was having the best time. In the run-up to today, I'd focused on making enough

Christmas-themed candles for this event while simultaneously fulfilling my other orders, and, of course, preparing for the Christmas lights switch-on later this evening. The Christmas Fair had simply been another chore on my calendar. What I hadn't predicted was how much I was going to love spending time in the company of small people for whom the wonder of Christmas was too great for their little bodies to contain. Their excitement was contagious and I'd found myself singing along gustily to the Christmas songs. And when the children had gathered around the big Christmas tree in the school reception area to sing 'Silent Night', I'd had a lump in my throat the size of a tennis ball.

If I'd needed confirmation that I wanted children, then spending the afternoon at Wetherley Primary School had provided it in spades. When my offspring eventually appeared, I'd definitely send them here. It had a cosy community feel to it, and although the Victorian building was small and old-fashioned, there was no shortage of gadgetry and technology, from the security entrance system to the laptops in the computer suite. But perhaps more importantly, the children seemed genuinely fond of their teachers and it was impossible not to be impressed by staff who'd fully embraced the Christmas spirit, with their festive knitwear and unadulterated enthusiasm.

I'd bucked the trend by not wearing a Christmas jumper, on the basis that Tom had warned me how quickly the hall became overheated. But I was wearing bauble earrings handmade by Astrid and I'd been asked about them so many times that I fully expected Astrid to have her own stall here next year selling them.

Astrid was in her element. She'd spent the first twenty minutes with me, gift-wrapping candles for customers. But after Tom had confided in us that the face painter had cancelled at the last minute, she had immediately offered to fill in. So for the last two hours she'd been sitting on a velvet chair with children at her knee while she created the most exquisite Christmas-themed art on their faces. I wasn't sure who was enjoying it more: Astrid or her little customers.

There were two women heading my way, one holding the hand of a little boy and the other wearing a papoose, a pale yellow hat just visible over the top of it. I set down my coffee out of harm's way and smiled welcomingly at them.

'These are lovely. Look Cesca!' said the one carrying the baby.

'Oh yes, Mum would love one.' Her friend picked one up and sniffed it, and then held it out so that her little boy could smell it too. 'How much are they?'

'Uh–uh, I'm getting one for Mum, I saw them first!'

'I'm guessing you're sisters?' I grinned at them as they pulled faces at each other.

'Fliss has literally been moaning that she saw it first my entire life.' The two of them laughed.

I handed them a price list. 'And it's one pound extra for gift wrapping.'

'Is that all?' Cesca gasped. 'Where do you live? I'm tempted to drive round to give you the rest of my wrapping at that price.'

I told them it was a Christmas Fair offer only and between them they bought eight candles, all gift-wrapped.

'Are you local?' Fliss asked. 'I promise I won't bring you presents to wrap, but I would like to buy from you again.'

I nodded. 'Yes, all handmade from my cottage in World's End Lane.'

Not strictly true at the moment but I had moved my things back in and had spent my first night there last night.

Fliss's eyes widened. 'Did you hear that, Cesca? This lady lives in World's End Lane.'

Cesca, who had been rifling through a large, quilted bag looked up. 'Really?'

The two women looked at each other and then back at me with renewed interest.

'Doesn't it worry you, being so near the river?' Fliss asked.

'Not at all,' I replied. 'It's really peaceful and I love being surrounded by the trees. I'm actually the cottage right at the end, so I can hear the river flowing on a calm day.'

This morning I'd woken to such a thick frost that at first I thought it had snowed. You could keep your Saks and your Selfridges window displays; as far as I was concerned, Mother Nature did hands-down the best Christmas decorations in the world and all for free.

Cesca produced a cloth from her bag and wiped the baby's face. 'But the floods—'

Fliss nodded vehemently. 'Did you flood very badly recently?'

'Um . . .' I looked from one to the other, wondering why they seemed so bothered on my behalf. 'A bit.'

'Sorry, we're interrogating you,' said Cesca. 'It's just that my sister and I, we were going to buy houses next door to each other on Orchard Gardens and then the flood put us off and we pulled out of the sale.'

Cole's houses. It sounded like he'd been more affected by the damage than he'd let on. But it hadn't prevented him from getting straight on with the remedial work on Holly Cottage. I made a mental note to thank him for all his efforts; the cottage was even nicer now than when I'd moved in and the new kitchen was absolutely gorgeous. Christening the shiny new hob this morning with a double fried egg sandwich had been a very special moment.

'Oh, you'd love it there! There are going to be fruit trees planted in every garden, so it'll be like a real orchard. The children would especially,' I said and turned to the little boy, 'I had two rabbits and a real deer in my garden this morning, can you believe it!'

'A big one?' The little boy's eyes were like saucers. 'Did it have a red nose?'

'It was little and cute and its nose was sort of red,' I said, massaging the truth a little. The little muntjac deer had been nibbling on foliage at the end of the garden and had skittered off through the trees when I got close to the window. But for one happy moment I'd felt like Snow White; all that had been missing was a handsome prince to share the sight with.

'The woodland setting was what drew us,' Fliss admitted.

'We did really like the houses,' Cesca added. 'But I'm quite risk-averse.'

'I totally get that,' I replied. 'But according to my landlord, that was the first time in Holly Cottage's five-hundred-year history that there's been a flood. So I'm not worried.'

The sisters looked at each other again.

'Your call, obviously,' I said, aware that their hearts were pulling them in one direction and their heads another. 'But it was a one-off thing. A contractor who should have known better dumped a load of tree trunks in the river which made a dam. It would be a shame if that meant you didn't get your dream homes together.'

'Perhaps we should reconsider,' Fliss murmured to her sister. 'We haven't found anything else as nice.'

Cesca stroked the baby's head absent-mindedly. 'It wouldn't hurt to take another look.'

'Just think,' I said brightly, 'next summer you could be sitting in your garden looking out at the rabbits and deer like me.'

'Thanks,' said Fliss, tucking her purse back in her bag. 'I'm so glad we bumped into you.'

As the women walked away clutching gift-wrapped candles and chatting excitedly, I felt a rush of pride that I might just have sold two houses for Cole. I picked up my phone and turned it over in my hands, wondering if it was a legitimate reason to send him a text. Before I'd come to a conclusion, Daniel arrived with a book of raffle tickets and shook a biscuit tin full of money at me.

He was wearing the most enormous hat, a knitted Christmas tree complete with pompom decorations and a knitted gold star perched on the top.

'I like your hat,' I teased.

'So did I at first, but I'm ready to self-combust under here,' he said, sitting down heavily on my spare chair. 'Tasha made me wear it, seeing as I hadn't dressed up in Christmas attire.' He glanced at my outfit. 'How come you got away with it?'

'Baubles,' I replied, pointing to my earrings.

'Smart move. Oh well, it's all for a good cause I suppose.' He pulled off the hat and ruffled his hair. 'Glad you came?'

'Definitely,' I said. 'I've sold loads and I've really enjoyed being with the children.'

'It's great isn't it?' He cast his eyes around the room, his gaze soft. 'I'd forgotten how exciting it is for kids. I remember being just like them, being so enthralled with the magic of it all. Makes you realise, doesn't it; how precious it is to have children around. It's what Christmas is about.'

I stared at him in complete disbelief. 'I thought you were anti-children?'

He grinned at the look on my face. 'I'm quite surprised myself. Tasha said that just because someone didn't want children of their own, it didn't mean they wouldn't enjoy spending time with them, and she was right.'

I smiled at him. 'I'm pleased you're not a child-hater. Because being here has definitely made me broody and if we're going to stay friends . . .'

His bright blue eyes twinkled at me. 'Don't you worry. When you have kids, I'll be the uncle who turns up just before bedtime causing mayhem with bags of sweets and plastic trumpets.'

'You'd do that?' My jaw dropped as he nodded.

I rubbed my arms. 'Daniel, that's given me goosebumps.'

'Sorry.' He raised his hands. 'OK, fair enough, maybe not the trumpets.'

'No, I mean you wanting to be their uncle.' I started to laugh. 'I realise we're discussing hypothetical children here, so I won't hold you to anything. But, seriously, you'd do that even though we're not family?'

'Of course, if you'll let me.' He shrugged. 'Everyone has those family friends who you call auntie and uncle even though they're not relatives. I'm sure Nell will be Auntie Nell.'

'I'd love that,' I said simply. I hadn't had those sort of family friends growing up, but he was right about Nell. She would insist on being called their auntie as well as being godmother to all of my children.

He beamed. 'Me too.'

I looked across at Astrid who was kneeling next to the nativity scene, deep in conversation with two little boys who were intent on feeding the hay to the rag-taggle collection of stuffed animals in the stable. She would make a wonderful grandmother; she'd be called Oma, the German word for granny. I sat back in my seat, suddenly overcome with emotion. I'd always thought of myself as being alone in the world because I didn't have any blood relatives, but it wasn't true; I had people who cared, who'd be there for me, and what more could you ask from your family than that?

'Thanks, Daniel,' I said, feeling a bit tearful.

He must have sensed my mood because he slipped an arm around my shoulders and gave me a squeeze. 'Hey. That's what friends are for.'

I wondered why we'd never had a discussion as open and honest with each other like this when we were together. Perhaps neither of us had dared. Perhaps on a subliminal level we'd both known it would lead to conflict. Now more than ever, I was so glad we were just friends and nothing more. This felt right.

I swallowed the lump in my throat and smiled at Daniel. 'So how's it going with you and Tasha?'

'Good,' he said, flushing slightly. He fiddled with the star on the top of his hat. 'Really good. She's buying me an iron for my fortieth and taking me away for the weekend to a golf resort in Marbella.'

'You've already got an iron.' The memory of the creases in Daniel's pyjama bottoms made the corners of my mouth twitch. I bet Cole didn't iron his. If he even wore them. I had a sudden delicious vision of him naked in bed.

'A different sort of iron. Are you all right?' he said, narrowing his eyes with concern. 'Your face has turned really red.'

'I'm fine,' I said, fanning myself. 'Anyway, so has yours.'

He grinned boyishly. 'It still feels odd to talk about her. We haven't told many people yet. But I will before my birthday.'

'Merry Shaw?' A vaguely familiar voice broke into our conversation. 'It is you! Fancy seeing you here!'

It took me a moment to place the woman in front of my stall with short burgundy-red hair and a chunky baby in an elf onesie in her arms. And then it came to me: Trisha, last seen crying in the ladies' loos at Tractor World at the prospect of imminent redundancy. Standing beside her was a younger woman who, apart from the obvious pregnancy bump, was the spitting image of her mother.

'Fancy seeing you here!' I said, standing up to give her a hug.

'This school is where my little grandson will be going when he's older. We thought we'd come and check it out.' Trisha patted the head of the little elf.

'Good thinking,' said Daniel. 'Never too early to get organised.'

'This is my daughter, Stacy,' Trisha continued, pointing to the younger woman. 'Stacy, this is my ex-colleague from Tractor World, the one who offered to take voluntary redundancy so that none of the rest of us would get the chop.'

Ah. I felt Daniel's eyes bore into the side of my head. I daren't even look at him. Instead I gave a high-pitched laugh. 'That's me,' I said with false jollity. 'Nice to meet you, Stacy. How is everyone at Tractor World?'

'No idea!' Trisha replied with a giggle. 'I got offered a much better job just after you left. I'm a Sales Office Manager at Rotary Mowers now. A promotion.'

'You left?' I felt my mouth gape and forced it shut. I'd sacrificed my job for hers and she left? I couldn't believe it.

Trisha nodded. 'I did. And I don't regret it for a moment. Looks like it worked out all right for you too, running your own business. What are you selling, then? Ooh, candles. Go on then, I'll take two small ones.'

Daniel didn't speak until after Trisha and her family had left.

'So,' he turned to me, bemused. 'I'm sure you said you'd been made redundant.'

I tucked my hair behind my ears and licked my dry lips, wondering how to spin this one. 'Ah, well. The thing is, she was really upset and worried and so I . . .'

I didn't go any further because I realised that Daniel's shoulders were shaking with laughter.

'Oh, Merry,' he shook his head, a wide smile on his face. 'That is just the sort of thing you'd do.'

I exhaled with relief. 'You aren't cross?'

'Of course not,' he assured me. 'You did a kind thing, and it all worked out for the best in the end, didn't it?'

We held each other's gaze for a second, and a feeling of contentment washed over me.

'It did,' I said softly.

'There you are!' came a tinkling voice from across the hall.

Both of us looked up to see Tasha making her way towards us. She looked absolutely gorgeous in a tightly belted red wool Mrs Christmas outfit edged with white fur around the hem, cuffs and hood. I'd have looked like a comedy mailwoman in that, but she looked like a Rockette straight off the set of New York's *Christmas Spectacular*.

Apart from when we'd been setting up, I'd hardly seen her. She'd been stationed at Santa's grotto all afternoon, organising the queue of eager children. According to Tom, ten men had offered to be Father Christmas this year after Tasha had announced her intention to dress up as Mrs Christmas. Last year apparently only Brian the caretaker had volunteered and the children had struggled to understand him due to his lack of teeth.

'Hey, Merry!' Tasha stood, hands on hips, surveying my stall. 'Looks like you've sold loads!'

'I have,' I said. 'Thanks for suggesting I take a stall, it's been really enjoyable. And the children are a credit to you.'

'They're adorable, aren't they?' She pressed a hand to her chest and sighed. 'How are the raffle tickets doing, Danny?'

Danny? I almost choked. He normally hated it when anyone shortened his name.

Daniel went a bit pink. 'I've been round everybody at least twice; I think I've fleeced people as much as I can.'

'I'll buy some,' I said and pulled a handful of coins out of my cash tin to pay for them.

Daniel tore some tickets off for me and I tucked them into my bra so I didn't lose them.

'You've done so well with your candle business,' said Tasha, looking genuinely impressed. 'Daniel told me how you started up after being made redundant. You're a real inspiration.'

'Agreed,' said Daniel, sliding a sideways glance at me. 'It was quite a shock at the time, wasn't it?'

'It was always a hobby I loved,' I said, ignoring his jibe. 'I'm lucky I had the chance to turn a passion into a job.'

'We have a gifted and talented art club at school,' Tasha continued. 'Perhaps you could come and visit them one day, run a workshop? You might even sell more candles if we give the parents some notice.'

'I'd really like that,' I said, genuinely touched.

Tasha put a hand on Daniel's arm. 'The staff are flagging; I think it's time to do the raffle – will you help me? Five minutes?'

'Sure,' he said, covering her hand with his for a second.

We both watched her walk away, stopping almost every few steps to speak to a child or greet an adult. She had star quality, no doubt about it; no wonder Tom had said the staff all loved her. And maybe, I thought, watching his lovestruck expression, Daniel did too.

'I'd better go and do as I'm told.' He stood up and then hesitated. 'Merry, I meant what I said about being an inspiration. One day, you'll make a great mum too.'

'One day,' I echoed, holding up my crossed fingers as I watched him walk away.

I hoped he was right, and I hoped I got the chance to find out. There was just the small matter of getting the man of my dreams to agree.

Chapter 26

Merry

At twenty past six I walked from my parked car at the back of the bank to the market square.

I was running late. Not unusual for me, but this time it wasn't really my fault. The Christmas Fair had overrun by half an hour because there were still so many people milling about and by the time Astrid and I packed up to leave I'd sold all but two candles, which I gave to her as a thank-you for coming with me. Then, once back at Holly Cottage, I'd run a bath, intending to have a quick reviving dip but I must have been more tired than I'd realised because I'd dropped off, only to wake when my head had slipped underwater and I spluttered back to consciousness. But there was still forty minutes to the lights switch-on, and another ten before I'd arranged to meet Cole and Hester. My stomach fizzed with a mix of anticipation and nerves at the thought of seeing him again, and meeting Hester of course.

Night had fallen, the air was as clear as crystal and a slender crescent moon hung delicately in a star-studded sky. The temperature hadn't lifted much above freezing all day and tiny ice particles on window ledges and pavements made the whole town sparkle. As my breath formed clouds of air in front of my face, I congratulated myself on remembering to put thick socks on inside my boots and I shoved my gloved hands into my pockets for extra warmth.

I rounded the corner into the marketplace and gasped with surprise. The residents of Wetherley had come out in force; there were people everywhere. I'd never seen the square so packed. Wetherley, it seemed, was ready to get Christmas underway.

There at the centre of the action stood our enormous Christmas tree. Even without its lights on, it shimmered majestically in the glow of the streetlamps. A stage had been set up close to the base of the tree behind the cordon. Huge speakers stood like bookends at either end of it, and Christmas music blasted out across the square. As I got closer I could see Nigel on stage behind a set of decks, one hand clamped to his headphones and the other raised, pointing a finger as if he was setting Ibiza's dancefloors alight instead of cranking up Slade's golden oldie from the seventies. Front and centre on the stage was a table on which sat a tinsel-covered plunger device that Hester Smart would be using to turn on the lights.

I stepped over the cables which had been taped neatly across the cobbles leading to the door of the old bank; I'd lent my keys to Nigel this morning who'd supervised the electricians in their preparations. It struck me as quite odd that the tree lights were plugged in inside the old bank. I knew it had always been the case, ever since Benny had been the bank manager. But what was to stop someone inadvertently turning the lights off and plunging the tree into darkness? I pushed the thought aside; it wasn't my problem, all I had to do tonight was to make sure our celebrity was looked after. I was sure the event would go smoothly. It all looked very professional and I felt a dart of pride for what the committee and I had managed to organise.

'MERRY! Cooeee!'

At the sound of my name, I searched the crowd and spotted Nell waving at me. Olek was beside her, buying a bag of roast chestnuts. I waved back and went to join them. There were a number of stalls which had opened up around the edge of the market especially for the lights switch-on, mostly selling refreshments and toys, and I made a mental note that if we were going to repeat this next year, we ought to make more of the shopping opportunity and perhaps run a one-off night-time market to accompany the event. I'd met plenty of stallholders at the school fair today who might be interested.

'Where have all these people come from?' Nell cried, looping her arm through mine. 'Last year's crowd mainly consisted of all the old ladies who had a crush on Benny Dunford.'

'No idea, I've never been before, I assumed it was something aimed at kids,' I said, pulling up the collar of my coat to keep out the cold. I'd forgotten my scarf in my haste and could feel a draught around my neck.

'It is,' said Nell, nodding at her husband wearing a Santa hat. 'But some kids are bigger than others.'

Olek offered round a bag of piping hot roast chestnuts. 'It is sad that a TV personality has a bigger fan base even than Mr Dunford, God bless him. He was the best of men. The Dowmunt family owe him a lot. You know when my father came over from Warsaw, he went to several banks but Mr Dunford was the only one who would listen to him about his plans and lent him money to start his business.'

Nell took one and blew it before peeling. 'True.'

'I've never met a celebrity before,' I admitted, taking a chestnut and peeling it. I bit into it and instantly regretted it. It was dry and crumbly and seemed to remove any trace of moisture from my mouth. 'I'm quite nervous.'

'I have,' Olek said. 'An actor. He lost the keys to his holiday cottage while walking up Wysedale Peak. I had to let him back in. He paid me one hundred pounds in cash on top of my fee to keep quiet.'

Nell gasped. 'You never told me that before. Who was it?'

Olek grinned and shook his head. 'I am a man who keeps his word.'

'Sometimes I hate that you're so honourable,' she grumbled.

'Why did he want to keep it secret?' I asked.

Olek shrugged. 'Usual reason. I think the lady with him was not his wife.'

'That story just goes to prove that nothing good ever happens on Wysedale Peak,' I said darkly, remembering the scene of my disastrous marriage proposal.

'Oh, I don't know,' mumbled Nell, burning her mouth and dropping the hot kernel back into her hand. Olek handed her a bottle of water. 'I think these things happen for a reason.'

I thought about it for a moment and realised that she did have a point. The relationship Daniel and I had now felt right. Plus, if I'd still been with him I might never have got to know Cole. And that would have been a shame.

'Do you know what?' I said, still trying to swallow the crumbs of chestnut, 'I think you've hit the nail on the head. And now my children will have a lovely Uncle Daniel, so all's well that ends well.'

Nell choked on her water. 'Children, an uncle? Have I missed something?'

I laughed and was about to explain but Olek let out a low whistle.

'Wow.' He stared over our shoulders, his mouth open. 'I think I understand the number of fans now.'

Nell and I turned in unison and my heart did a little skip.

Striding towards the stage, and us, was Cole. He was easy to spot because he was a head taller than most people. He looked snug in a down jacket and woolly hat and he had his hand protectively on the shoulder of a slim woman in the most amazing red cape and long strawberry blonde hair. Her resemblance to Cole was unmistakable; Hester was every bit as striking as her brother.

'Stunning!' Nell gasped. She tugged Olek's arm. 'I know I said I didn't want anything for Christmas but that cape is to die for. Merry, find out where she got it.'

The crowd parted for Hester like the zip on my jeans after one too many slices of Astrid's *Stollen*. Progress was slow; Hester greeted everyone with a wave or a smile, signed one or two autographs and posed for selfies here and there.

'Merry!' Nell gave me a shove. 'Stop fangirling and go and do your thing!'

'What? Yes. Right.' I snapped back to attention and took a swig of Nell's water to wet my whistle. 'See you later, wish me luck.'

'Yeah, good luck,' Nell held up her crossed fingers and added in a lower voice, 'under the mistletoe with her big brother.'

'Thanks.' A shiver of apprehension ran through me as I dashed forward to the stage to meet them.

Cole's face lit up when he spotted me at the steps to the stage. He bent to Hester's ear and whispered something and then guided her towards me. As she got closer I could see the rest of her outfit: tight-fitting leather trousers and spiky-heeled boots. She looked warm *and* oozed glamour; I'd managed the warm bit but my look was more Paddington Bear.

'Hey,' I said, unable to hide my pleasure at seeing him. *Them*, obviously. 'You made it.'

'We did,' he said, his smile mirroring mine. 'Merry, I'd like you to meet my sister, Hester,' he said proudly. 'And Dad's around here somewhere too. Hester, this is Merry, who—'

'I know who Merry is, you goon, you've been going on about her for weeks,' his sister teased, punching his arm. 'Hello, Merry.'

My heart twanged as I listened to their banter; it was so natural and playful and made me miss the siblings I had never had. I thought briefly of the two sisters I'd met today and wondered whether I should mention anything to Cole. No, I decided, I didn't want to get his hopes up, and if they did decide to buy, he'd know soon enough.

'I wouldn't put it quite like that,' Cole gave a long-suffering sigh and then addressed me. 'Hester knows that Holly Cottage was unfortunately flooded and that you've been working in the old bank for the last few weeks.'

I nodded. 'It's been quite an adventure.'

'Yeah, so I've heard.' She raised a knowing eyebrow and I felt heat rise to my face, wondering how much Cole had told her.

'Hester,' Cole warned. 'Behave.'

'Don't worry, Mr Grinch.' She winked at me. 'So, Merry, I know that you make candles and that you don't like the dark or Christmas or mulled wine but that you're exceptionally good at wrapping presents.'

'Sounds like he's been giving away all my secrets.' I twinkled my eyes at Cole.

'I should have warned you what a terrible gossip my sister is,' he said, with a bark of laughter. 'You can see why she's the perfect host for live TV – she leaves no conversational stone unturned.'

'At least one of us doesn't get struck dumb under pressure,' she said, raising her neat eyebrows at her brother.

'I haven't said how grateful we are that you can spare us the time, Hester,' I said. 'So thank you.'

'Oh goodness, don't mention it!' Hester pulled me close to her and kissed both my cheeks. 'I'm glad to. I mean, obviously I feel as if I know you already,' her eyes slid to her brother. 'But it's lovely to finally put a face to a name.'

My cheeks burned as I tried to interpret her coded comments. Was it too much to hope that Cole had really been talking about me that much, or was she referring to the phone conversations she had had with me over the last weeks?

'Likewise,' I said. 'Although in your case I've seen your face on TV, but it's not the same, is it, until you meet someone in the flesh? And in real life you're even prettier than on screen. Much prettier. I love your cape by the way and so does my friend, Nell.'

That speech had all come out in a rush and I realised I was a bit starstruck. But Hester didn't appear to notice.

She leaned forward and whispered in my ear. 'Bought it in a thrift store in New York for twenty-five dollars and had it jazzed up with some faux fur around the hem. Don't tell anyone.'

'My lips are sealed,' I said, and then for added effect I mimed zipping them, feeling disloyal to Nell because I couldn't possibly spill the beans after promising not to.

'I like her,' Hester said to her brother, flashing her teeth at him in a wide smile. 'Well done.'

'I thought you might,' Cole replied quietly in a tone which sent warmth flooding through me.

Hester clapped her hands together. 'Now, Merry, what's the score then, what's the plan?'

'Um, well, there's the stage, and we've got a microphone,' I said, pointing out the obvious. 'The man who always used to turn the lights on passed away this year, but his widow, Pam will be here. No one knows if she's planning on saying anything because she only got back from her holiday a few days ago, so we're playing that one by ear. Then after that if you don't mind saying a few words and we'll do a countdown from ten to one then you press the plunger and um, that's pretty much it.'

'Cool,' said Hester.

I shivered again as another draught managed to slither down the back of my coat. 'Very cool,' I agreed.

'She's chilly, Cole,' Hester nudged her brother. 'Offer her your scarf.'

'Of course.' Cole instantly started to unravel the charcoal-grey scarf from around his neck.

'There's no need, really,' I protested.

'He insists,' Hester replied on his behalf.

'He does.' Cole gave me a long-suffering look and we all laughed.

He stepped closer and looped the scarf around my neck.

'Thank you,' I murmured, feeling my breath catch in my throat. I lifted my hair free of it and he tied the ends in a loose knot.

'You're welcome,' he said gruffly, letting the scarf trail slowly through his fingers.

All at once I was enveloped with his cologne. He smelled so good. I closed my eyes and pressed the soft wool to my face, inhaling those delicious aromas. Definitely sandalwood and vanilla, and certainly citrus, but the lemon I'd used hadn't hit the mark . . .

Hester coughed and my eyes flew open and Cole took a step back.

'I don't know about you,' said Hester with a smirk, 'but I think it's hotting up already.'

Luckily, at that moment Daniel, Audrey, Nigel and Tasha appeared and the next couple of minutes were filled with introductions and thank-yous. Tasha pulled me to one side and gave me a huge wintry bouquet to present to Hester on behalf of Wetherley.

'I didn't think you'd get time to organise one,' she whispered.

It was such a lovely gesture and I was genuinely touched; not least because she was easily as busy as I was, if not more so. Hester managed to get us corralled into a group with her at the centre and took some selfies for her Instagram.

'We've got another fifteen minutes until I need you on stage,' Daniel told Hester.

'Would you like a drink?' Audrey asked. 'There's a hot chocolate stall or tea and coffee and . . .' She pulled a hip flask out of her pocket with a flourish. 'I can add a little extra rum to spice it up a bit?'

Hester laughed. 'You're all lovely. But if it's OK with Merry, I'd really like to see her candle workshop?'

'What, *now*?' I said, trying to remember what sort of state I'd left the kitchen in when I'd loaded up the car with candles for the fair this morning. 'It's hardly a workshop. It's more of a table and two electric hotplates.'

'And after all that effort I made to make it cosy,' said Cole, mock offended.

'It is cosy,' I said hastily. 'Hester, we don't have much time, but of course you're welcome to see it.'

'We've got bags of time,' said Hester airily. 'Besides, I'm a co-owner of the old bank and I haven't been inside for ages. Look, here's Dad.' She waved a hand and a dapper-looking gentleman in a navy wool coat and tweed trilby raised a hand in return. 'Just in time, Dad, we're going to see Merry's candle workshop.'

'Pleased to meet you, Mr Robinson,' I said, extending a hand.

'Call me Fred, dear.' He took my hand between both of his. 'Merry. A beautiful name for a beautiful young lady and so apt for the town's Christmas planner.'

'I'd hardly call myself that,' I laughed. 'It's a team effort and between you and me, I'm rather a novice at planning.'

'Guys,' Cole tapped his watch. 'The clock's ticking. Dad, stop flirting please. Merry, I apologise, my father had a sherry before lunch and a Baileys afterwards.'

'No apology necessary. Shall we?' I offered Fred my arm and the four of us crossed the marketplace to the old bank.

Lots of pairs of eyes followed us, or at least, they followed Hester. I'll say something for the Robinson family – they were an attractive bunch. Mr Robinson senior would have been a looker in his day; he was still quite a charmer, I could see why Astrid was attracted to him.

I did a double take when we reached the door. It was adorned with a beautiful fresh Christmas wreath bursting with fragrant foliage, cinnamon sticks and pine cones and finished off with stripy pheasant tail feathers. And the wreath wasn't the only new addition to the doorway; a huge bouquet of mistletoe had appeared too, fixed under the porch.

'This is gorgeous!' Hester exclaimed, running her fingertips over the feathers. 'Where did you get it?'

'It just appeared!' I said incredulously.

'And I thought you weren't a big fan of Christmas,' Hester teased. 'Doesn't look that way to me.'

'Oh, I think it must be gift from the Christmas tree man,' I said, remembering Nigel's words the other day about him wanting to give me a present. 'It brightens up the doorway nicely.'

'Watch him under that mistletoe, Merry,' Cole warned, nodding his head to his father. 'No woman is safe.'

'You're not too old for a clip round the ear, young man,' Fred retorted.

To Fred's surprise, I leaned over and pressed a kiss to his cheek. 'Merry Christmas, Fred.'

'And to you, love,' he mumbled, his eyes shining behind his glasses.

'Go Dad!' Hester laughed and then nudged Cole who looked down at his shoes and said nothing.

I would very much have liked to kiss Fred's son under that mistletoe too, but perhaps not with the rest of his family as an audience. Was he thinking the same? Hester seemed to be dropping a lot of hints, but I was sure I remembered something about her being the one who set him up with a dating app, so maybe she was like this with every single woman he encountered. It was so difficult to tell. I gave myself a shake, conscious of the need to get the Robinson family back to the stage in a matter of minutes.

Once we were inside, Cole snapped all the lights on and we headed upstairs.

'I'm using the kitchen mostly,' I explained, pushing open the door and sending up a silent prayer that it didn't look too awful. 'I make all the candles in here.'

Fred rubbed his hands together. 'It's like a little chemistry lab.'

294

'Dad used to be an industrial chemist,' Cole explained. 'He'll be in his element.'

'It smells divine.' Hester inhaled deeply and narrowed her eyes in thought. 'This aroma reminds me of something.'

'Me too,' Cole said, sniffing the air.

'Smells of aftershave to me,' said Fred, picking up one of my cotton wicks and twirling it in his fingers.

'It'll be the oils I've been experimenting with this week,' I said, pointing out the last batch I'd made on Friday. I pulled Cole's scarf up to my nose again and inhaled. My candle version was almost there; I'd try one more version on Monday if I got time.

Hester picked up a candle and sniffed it. 'I know what it reminds me of!' she exclaimed, her eyes bright. 'Sauvage by Dior.'

I almost gasped aloud. So that was what it was! Now that I knew what it was called, I could look up the ingredients and perfect my blend. Not that I'd ever try and plagiarise another brand, but a bit of inspiration wouldn't hurt anyone.

Silently, Cole picked up a candle and inhaled the aroma, his eyes flickering with curiosity. 'That's what I wear.'

'What a coincidence,' I said weakly. I cleared my throat. 'Anyway, as I say it was just an experiment and it made a change from the frankincense, myrrh and cinnamon oils I've been mixing for the last month.'

Hester laughed. 'OK, your dislike of Christmas is getting ever more unbelievable.'

'Seriously,' I said. 'I've had enough of the smell of cinnamon to last me a lifetime.'

'I can sympathise,' Hester winced. 'We did a slot selling mince pies last week which involved me tasting them repeatedly throughout the day. I'm done now till next year. Give me a plate of sprouts any day.'

'Same here!' I agreed. 'The only good thing about Christmas is the certainty that sprouts will be on the menu.'

'Ooh,' she closed her eyes. 'Shredded and sautéd with bacon and garlic.'

'Or roasted with butter, honey and black pepper,' I added.

'Or banned from the dinner table altogether,' said Cole.

We all laughed.

'What will you be making this week?' Fred asked, moving towards the worktop and looked at all my candle-making equipment.

'Candle-making is very seasonal,' I replied, 'so I'll still be doing my wintry ones for a while. My products for the New Year will be very different. Calming, clean, fresh, relaxing. If Marie Kondo did candles, that sort of thing.'

'Ooh, sounds interesting.' Hester picked up a finished candle. 'Can I put a picture of these on my Instagram stories?'

'Sure.'

She took out her phone and arranged some candles for her photo.

'How was the Christmas Fair?' Cole asked.

'Hectic,' I said. 'But also profitable. And the children loved my little painted gift cards. Which reminds me. Wait there.'

I fetched a cardboard folder from the front room and came straight back with it, handing it to him. He opened it to reveal two watercolour Christmas cards: one of an angel on top of a Christmas tree with Merry Christmas to Freya on it; the other, which was to Harley, featuring a boy on a snowboard heading downhill towards a snowman.

Cole's face was a picture. 'These are awesome.' He looked up at me, shaking his head in disbelief. 'Seriously,

I can't thank you enough, they are going to love them.'

'You're welcome,' I said, glowing with pleasure.

He showed Fred, who agreed both his grandchildren would be impressed.

'Well, that's just raised the bar for next year's Christmas cards,' Hester teased. 'How are you going to top that?'

'I'm sure I can come up with something for next Christmas,' I said.

'I look forward to seeing it,' said Cole in a low voice.

The intensity of his gaze sent shivers of longing through me and for a second I forgot there was anybody else in the room.

Fred picked up bottles of oils and sniffed them. 'I'd love to have a go at making candles.'

'Then you shall,' I said, dragging myself away from Cole's burning glances. 'Pick a day next week.'

'Tomorrow?' His face lit up. 'Might as well strike while the iron's hot.'

Talking of irons made me think of my conversation with Daniel earlier, which in turn made me think of Cole naked.

Fred was waiting for an answer. 'Or if Monday's no good . . .?' he prompted.

'No, no, that would be lovely,' I said, trying to get my breathing under control. 'It's a date.'

Hester nudged her brother. 'See. Easy.'

'I am going to kill you,' he muttered.

Outside the bells on the church tower began to chime the hour.

'Oh no!' I gasped with panic. 'We're late! Come on everyone!'

Chapter 27

Cole

1 DECEMBER

'Good evening, Wetherley!' Hester yelled into the microphone which had just been handed to her by Daniel. 'And thank you for inviting me to join in your Christmas celebrations!'

Rapturous applause, hooting and whistling rippled around the market square and Hester held out the edge of her red cape and curtsied.

Cole grinned at his sister, remembering her initial reluctance to attend tonight's event. Who had she been kidding, she loved this stuff. It was a shame Paul hadn't been able to make it due to some work thing; he was as proud of his wife as Cole. He'd take plenty of pictures to show him, and Hester had asked him to take some for her Instagram too.

His eyes moved along the rest of the group and he spotted Daniel stepping down from the stage. Merry had introduced the men to each other moments ago. Daniel, she said, was an old friend. Cole, she introduced as her landlord and then had laughed shyly and said that he was a *new* friend and that he had been very good to her. Which had pleased Cole no end and had made Daniel pump his hand firmly and pat his shoulder like an approving brother.

Daniel seemed pleasant enough but as Cole knew, he'd let the glorious Merry slip through his fingers. It had been brave of her to propose to him; he knew from experience what a nerve-wracking thing it was to ask someone if they'd like to spend the rest of their life with you. He imagined Merry's pretty face crumpling in disappointment when he said that no, he didn't want to marry her. Daniel was a fool.

His gaze reverted to Merry and he felt his heart skip. She was simply standing there, a big smile on her lovely face and Cole couldn't take his eyes off her.

He'd been kicking himself since Friday. How difficult was it to ask a woman out on a date? If he ran his business in the pathetic way he ran his love life, he'd have been bankrupt years ago.

'Look at her up there,' Fred whistled under his breath. 'What a girl.'

'I know,' Cole replied. 'Bloody gorgeous.'

Fred laughed and Cole realised he'd been talking about Hester.

'Sorry, Dad.' He put a hand on Fred's arm. 'I'm miles away.'

Fred's eyes twinkled. 'About bloody time.'

Cole and Fred were at the front of the crowd. Next to Fred was Astrid, who'd met them outside the old bank. Cole couldn't be sure, but he had a sneaking suspicion that their meeting wasn't an accident. Crafty old sod, he thought, smiling to himself. He was genuinely happy for his dad that he had a lady friend and when Astrid had remarked on the icy pavements, Fred had offered her his arm and the two of them had proceeded arm in arm to the stage.

'She is a very special girl,' said Astrid, 'we are lucky to have her.'

Her remark could have been referring to either of the women, had it not been for the sideways look Astrid had given him as she said it.

He shook his head, laughing to himself. Was it that obvious? It was just a shame that he didn't seem capable of making his feelings apparent to Merry. But for some reason, he seemed to go to jelly when he was with her. Take Friday for instance. He'd psyched himself up to ask her out on a date, he'd even bought her a bunch of flowers. He'd been fine all the way up to that moment when he'd presented them to her and then . . . boom. He'd taken one look at her lovely face and bottled it.

It wasn't that he hadn't wanted to ask her out, far from it, but he'd had a sudden attack of cold feet.

The thing was, he realised, that he liked her too much to risk it going wrong. What if she'd said no, where would he have gone from there? The way he felt about her was too important to risk blowing it. So, he'd bottled out.

But looking on the bright side, she had admitted that she was ready to meet someone, how did she put it . . . she was going to hang around under the mistletoe and wait for *the one*. So that was encouraging, maybe that was his answer: maybe he should do something daft like pin a spring of mistletoe to the front of his woolly hat and see what her reaction was.

Cole tuned back into Hester's speech about how she'd always loved decorating the tree when she was a little girl and how that marked the start of Christmas for her; and that it was such an honour to be asked to switch on the lights in Wetherley. Her words were being met with great applause, thank goodness. She was a tough cookie, she understood that being in the public eye left her exposed to comments from strangers about everything from her hairstyle to her weight. She'd even had angry emails from a viewer once criticizing her terrible French accent after introducing a range of French hair products. Despite her breezily happy-go-lucky exterior, Cole knew that unwarranted criticism cut her to the quick. But tonight's event was going well, she'd leave Wetherley with a smile on her face, happy that her appearance had been well received.

Standing next to Hester was Mrs Dunford, Benny's widow, who'd made a short and teary speech about her husband and his well-known love for Wetherley and his lesser-known love for Hester's TV show, which had delighted Hester and had gone down very well with the audience.

He looked at Merry again, her face just visible between a woollen hat and his scarf, cheeks pink, nose too, her hands, in ridiculous stripy gloves, clapping as Hester waved to the assembled crowd. Then she pulled the scarf over her nose as if she was smelling it. Was it too much to hope that it reminded her of him? The thought gave him courage and he felt a smile tug at his lips.

He couldn't look at Merry without smiling, he couldn't even *think* about her without smiling. She was quite simply and unexpectedly the one thing which had brought him joy this winter. Every minute he spent in her company left him wanting more. Every smile she gave him made him want to make her smile again just to see her happy. The story she had told him about her childhood churned like acid in his stomach. He was in awe of her resilience and positivity. She deserved to be happy. Maybe it was a bit macho of him, but he had a burning desire to protect her, to make up for all the things that had happened to her in the past. Prove to her that not all men were unreliable, that *he* could be trusted.

Also, he thought, feeling a low tremble in the pit of his stomach, she was as hot as hell. Earlier, when they'd reached the old bank and she'd noticed the mistletoe under the porch, he'd wanted so much to pull her into his arms and give her a kiss that would take her breath away. But there was no way on earth he could have done that with his sister and father looking on. Then she'd kissed his dad! Which he loved her for. Not loved, too strong, he corrected himself swiftly, but anyway, the look on old Fred's face had more than made up for the fact that Merry was kissing the wrong man under the mistletoe. And then to add insult to miserable injury, she and his dad had managed to make a date for candle-making on Monday. Just like that. She'd even said, *it's a date*!

Her next free day was Christmas Day. Other than fitting the kitchen in the old bank, he didn't have any plans that day either. Could that be the day of their first date, he mused. As far as he knew she was going to be at home watching her favourite film, and he'd never seen the sequel to *Home Alone* . . .

'OK, Wetherley,' Hester said, 'the moment you've all been waiting for. Shall we light up this Christmas tree?' She cupped her hand to her ear and the night air rang out with cheers and shouts of *YES*.

Just in time Cole remembered that he'd promised to take photos for Hester, and video it to show Freya and Harley their aunt doing her celebrity thing. He pulled his phone out and snapped a few pictures and then set it to record.

'Ten, nine, eight . . .' Hester chanted, and the crowd chanted along with her. 'Seven, six . . .'

Cole panned around the marketplace to capture the atmosphere. Couples of every generation stood hand in hand, parents jiggled babies on their hips, children bounced up and down on the spot in their excitement and the older ones hung about in groups, doing their best not to look interested, but secretly sparkly-eyed with joy.

Freya and Harley would have loved this.

As he held up his phone, Cole felt a pang of longing for his children so sharp that it brought tears to his eyes. It was made worse by the fact that Lydia had confirmed that Freya was suffering from homesickness and was missing him. Harley too had become moody, and Lydia was worried that he wasn't getting on as well at school as she'd initially thought.

Those kids were his world and without them, his life had an emptiness which no amount of overtime could fill. What he wouldn't give to have them both here now, Freya's small hand in his, and Harley, too grown up to hold hands, but lurking nearby.

He heaved a sigh. His fractured family, his kids thousands of miles away, his daughter putting the angel on top of a Christmas tree that he'd never see, his son getting so tall that he'd be able to hang the decorations on the top branches for Lydia; their Christmas plans that didn't include him, their father who loved them more than he loved himself. He swallowed hard and forced himself to smile as Hester shouted, 'Merry Christmas, everyone!'

She pressed down on the plunger and as the Christmas tree lit up with thousands of tiny lights, cheers and whoops and whistles of delight rang around the marketplace. The music started up again and Elton John started singing about stepping into Christmas and all Cole could think about was stepping on a plane and feeling his children in his arms again. He zoomed in for a shot of Hester dancing and then stopped the video and shoved his phone away.

He mumbled something to his dad about needing to make a phone call and walked away from the stage before anyone noticed that his eyes were full of tears.

Chapter 28

Merry

1 DECEMBER

Hester pressed down on the plunger and with incredible precision, Nigel pressed down on the real electricity supply in perfect synchronisation. The crowd cheered as our Christmas tree came alive with thousands of jewel-coloured lights. As the applause and cheering continued to echo around the marketplace, I exhaled the breath I'd probably been holding for weeks. We'd done it! For days I'd been reading disaster stories of trees which didn't light up, or lit up five seconds *before* the official switch-on, but here in Wetherley our Christmas Project team had smashed it and the relief was immense.

I looked down from my position on the edge of the stage into the happy faces below and a feeling of euphoria rippled through me. This event and the school Christmas Fair earlier had kicked off the Christmas season for so many people, and I had played a part in both. I'd achieved quite a lot in the last few months since that first committee meeting: grown my business, moved on from my sadness over Daniel and turned our relationship into a real friendship. I smiled, remembering how he'd eyed up Cole, assessing him as boyfriend material, just like a big brother would, and how he'd secretly winked and given me a thumbs up when Cole wasn't looking. Yes, I thought, I had every right to feel proud.

I spotted Nell in the crowd and waved; she blew me a series of big kisses and I smiled back, feeling a wave of love for my oldest friend. Next I searched for Cole's handsome face, but couldn't see him in the throng. I'd seen him only moments ago standing by Fred and Astrid. He'd been holding his phone in the air videoing his sister, which I'd thought was so sweet.

Where had he gone? I felt a tingle of disappointment, a longing for our eyes to meet, a chance to share a celebratory smile with him. I frowned, my eyes roaming the various stalls, trying to spot his broad silhouette, but to no avail. Love was a stealthy emotion, I mused; it had a way of creeping up on you so gently that you barely noticed. It was a bit like watching the sun rise: one minute it was barely there, just a possibility, a shimmer on the horizon, and the next it was so big and bright you couldn't fail to be caught up in its dazzling light.

The feelings I had for Cole had been there from the first moment I'd seen him shopping at Nell's Nuts. I'd been attracted to his eyes, his laugh, his sense of humour. Now, whenever I thought about him, a fierce flame warmed me from within. Maybe I was thinking about love too soon, but I didn't care. I'd had enough of squashing down my emotions and being worried about other people's opinions about me. If I'd learned anything about my break-up with Daniel, it was that the truth will out eventually, so why not sooner rather than later?

The applause was gradually dying down now and Daniel stepped forward to relieve Hester of the microphone. She held onto it for a few more moments, thanking everyone for being such a lovely crowd and then Nigel got back into his stride as Wetherley's resident DJ and the crowd started to disperse.

I took a step towards Hester to lead her down from the stage but Pam Dunford pounced on her first, looping an arm through hers and regaling her with tales of Benny's online shopping adventures after watching Hester's show, recounting a miscalculation of knitting yarn which had turned up on their doorstep.

My phone buzzed again for the fifth time in as many minutes and I took it out of my coat pocket to look at the screen. More Etsy orders and a screenful of notifications to say I had new Instagram followers. I'd hoped for a quiet day tomorrow, showing Fred how candles were made, but it seemed I'd be busy after all. I often got a handful of enquiries over the weekend, but it was most unusual to get a cluster of them like this. How bizarre.

Over Pam's head I noticed Hester signalling with her eyebrows to be rescued.

'He thought he'd ordered forty-eight balls, but he'd clicked on forty-eight cartons! We declared it a right balls-up,' Pam chuckled, shaking her head fondly. 'I knitted enough baby bonnets to last the neo-natal unit for a decade.'

'Easily done,' said Hester kindly. 'I've done the same with crates of wine. At least that's what I tell my husband.'

Pam giggled and asked Hester if she could have her autograph, which of course, Hester supplied.

'Talking of drinks,' I said, seizing my opportunity to butt in, 'can I get you anything, Hester?'

She shook her head. 'Thanks, I've got a bottle of water in my bag. But could you find Cole for me? If you don't need me for anything else, I'd like to go home – I've got an early start in the morning.'

'Of course, and thanks again, you've been a big hit with Wetherley, thanks so much for doing this.' I was about to head off the stage when I felt my phone vibrate with an Instagram message. I looked at the screen and suddenly realised what was happening. 'Hester, how many followers do you have on Instagram?'

'Twenty thousand.' A knowing smile spread across her face. 'Why do you ask?'

'It might be a coincidence . . .' I shook my head, unsure whether I was being foolish in my assumptions. 'I've had loads of new followers and a flurry of Etsy orders since you posted that picture of my candles.'

'Yes!' Hester punched the air and then pulled me into a tight hug. 'I'm so pleased for you. Most of my followers count shopping as their number one hobby. Whenever I post something I love, there's usually an uplift in sales. This was precisely what I hoped would happen.'

'So this is the Hester Smart effect!' I stared at her, my stomach fizzing with delight.

'Nonsense.' She waved a hand modestly. 'I'm no Kylie Jenner, but if I can help a friend out, I will.'

I was touched that she counted me as a friend. 'Well, thanks again, I really appreciate it. I might even get Fred to help me make them when he comes in tomorrow.'

'Thanks so much for sorting that out,' she said, eyes twinkling. 'You're quite a big hit with the Robinsons. Senior *and* junior.'

'No trouble,' I said, wondering if she was referring to herself or Cole as the junior Robinson. 'The feeling is entirely mutual. Now let me go and find your brother and you can be on your way.'

I left the stage and set off down the steps. In the distance I spotted Nell and Olek in the middle of a group of people cooing over a new baby and I saw Audrey tipping her hip flask into Nigel's hot chocolate.

Astrid and Fred were waiting at the bottom of the steps, looking every inch as if they'd been a couple for ever.

'Well done, *mein Schatz*.' Astrid kissed both of my cheeks. 'I am so proud of you.'

'You did good, lass,' Fred agreed, taking my hands in his. 'I'm so glad I came tonight, this has set me right up for Christmas. Astrid and I are going to get the Rosebridge lot whipped up into action ready for Christmas Eve, aren't we love?'

'We are. Our *Weihnachtsbaum* will be the envy of the town.' Astrid tucked her arm through his as they swapped fond looks and I don't think I could have been more delighted for her.

'I'm looking forward to it. Have you seen Cole?' I asked.

Fred shook his head. 'No, but when you find him can you tell him that we're leaving now.'

Fred and Astrid spoke at the same time.

'We're off for a nightcap.'

'I need to let Otto out.'

The two of them laughed at Astrid's little white lie.

'I'll tell him,' I said. 'But don't be too late going to bed, Fred, I'm expecting you on candle duty tomorrow.'

As I began to move away, Fred caught hold of my hand. 'I think Cole needed a moment alone; I could tell he was feeling a bit low.'

'Oh dear. Has something happened?' I asked.

'He misses his kids, that's all. It must be hard for him, being surrounded by families and not having his own with him.'

My heart ached for him. 'Should I leave him in peace?'

Fred shook his head. 'No love, I think you might be exactly what he needs.'

I hoped so, I thought as I bid them both goodnight.

As my eyes continued to scout for Cole, I noticed a light burning from inside the old bank. We must have left one on when we were in there. I decided to head that way and quickly nip in and turn it off. I speeded up, not wanting to keep Hester waiting any longer than necessary and hopped into the road which separated the market from the rows of shops which surrounded it.

As I rounded the cordon behind the Christmas tree, I noticed Daniel and Tasha slipping off, hand in hand. I paused to watch them for a second and felt a brief pang of nostalgia for what Daniel and I had had. But I quickly brushed it away. I was genuinely happy for them; they were a perfect match.

I turned away with a sigh, only to come to an abrupt halt as I collided with a solid wall of man. I'd found Cole.

'Merry!'

'Oh, hello!' My face was suddenly wreathed in smiles.

I felt his arms go around me and he pressed me tightly to him, squeezing the air from my lungs.

'I'm sorry you had to see them together,' he murmured, lowering his cheek to the top of my head. 'It must have come as a shock, I'm sorry.'

I knew I should have told him straight away that Daniel and Tasha weren't news to me and that I really didn't mind, but I was enjoying the sensation of being wrapped in his embrace way too much, so for a moment I allowed myself to lean against him, absorbing his warmth.

Finally, he pulled away and looked at me, his gaze intense. 'Merry, are you OK?'

I bit my lip, trying to hide a guilty smile. 'Absolutely fine. A bit odd to see him with someone new, but he and I weren't right for each other.'

He laughed in surprise. 'Am I comforting you under false pretences?'

I laughed. 'Definitely not. No hug is ever wasted.'

'That sounds like a motivational quote,' he said with a grin.

His hands had slid from my shoulders to my arms and I could feel the cold air between us.

'Tell me to mind my own business, but your dad thought you might be missing the children – are *you* OK?'

His body seemed to sag a little. 'I haven't seen them since August. Most of the time I'm fine, but Christmas is such a special time with kids and I'm missing them more than ever.'

'I can imagine. Would another hug help?'

He attempted a smile. 'Let's try it.'

I stepped forward and reached around his neck to pull him close, burying my face in the front of his jacket. His arms tightened around my waist and I squeezed my eyes shut, drinking in his closeness. 'Better?' I asked.

'Much,' came his reply, his warm breath tickling my cheek.

'Hester!' I gasped suddenly, jerking away from him. 'I completely forgot, she's ready to go home and she asked me to find you.'

'And I thought you'd come to check if I was OK,' he laughed. 'Hester will be fine for a minute or two, I just want to pop into the old bank before I go back; we must have left a light on earlier. Will you come with me?'

'Sure. I was heading there too.'

He took my hand as if it was the most natural thing in the world and we crossed the cobbles towards the old bank.

'Merry?' His hand gently squeezed mine and when I met his eyes, there was a look of vulnerability about him that made my heart turn over. 'Those candles you were making?'

'Yes?' At once I knew where this conversation was heading.

'The ones that reminded Hester of Sauvage by Dior.'

'I know the ones.' I swallowed.

We reached the door and Cole released my hand to dig in his pocket for his keys.

'Was it a coincidence that that's what I usually wear or . . .' He let the question dangle in the air between us.

My heart thudded and I looked away to compose myself. This was it. The moment I'd find out whether my feelings for him were reciprocated or not. But when I looked back at him, all my doubts flew away. It was there in his gaze, in his hopeful smile. Slowly I shook my head.

'Not a coincidence.'

'You made a candle that smelled like me?' His voice was filled with wonder.

All at once, I wanted him to understand what he meant to me. Honesty and openness, right from the start. I took a step towards him and he did the same, until our bodies were pressed together and I could feel the heat radiating from him.

'That first time you took me in your arms and held me close, your scent lingered on my skin for hours afterwards and it made me feel . . . safe.' I ran my hands slowly up his chest and tipped my chin up to his so that our faces were almost touching. 'I wanted to feel like that again, so I thought if I could recreate the aroma and make a candle from it, you'd be there with me whenever I wanted.'

'Oh, Merry.' Cole's voice was gruff as he lowered his head to mine. 'I'll be right here for you, whenever you want.'

Then his mouth met mine and the taste of him on my lips sent shockwaves through me. I'd dreamed about this moment so many times, but the reality of his kiss was far, far better than anything my imagination could have conjured up. I pulled him closer and felt him sigh with pleasure as

311

his hands cupped my face, deepening the kiss. Then we pulled apart, laughing and breathless with delight. He was leaning on the door and flapped a hand to brush away the feather which was tickling his cheek and then I remembered.

I lifted my eyes upwards to where a hanging bouquet of green stems studded with white berries formed a festive canopy above our heads.

Cole looked up and then looked at me and waggled his eyebrows suggestively. 'It would be rude not to.'

'And maybe if I hang around *here*, I might bump into "the one",' I said, pulling his face towards me again.

He gave a low sexy laugh which made my every nerve-ending tingle. 'They say anything can happen at Christmas.'

This time our kiss was slower, more tender and I felt myself melt into him as our bodies pressed together. The world around us faded away, the sound of the Christmas music in the marketplace a faint melody in my ears until there was just us and the moonlight and a huge bunch of mistletoe.

'Wow,' I said, when the kiss ended. 'That mistletoe is magical.'

'You are magical,' he said, tracing a finger tantalisingly slowly along my cheek. 'Same time tomorrow?'

'It's a date,' I said, and we stared at each other, completely and utterly mesmerised by what had just happened.

'Uh-oh, here comes trouble,' said Cole, straightening up, as behind me I heard the sound of laughter. I turned around to see Hester, grinning from ear to ear.

'Finally!' she said, her voice warm with amusement. 'Now please may we go home?'

Chapter 29

Merry

'I'm dreaming of a white Christmas,' Fred crooned from his seat at the little table beside me. He was carefully sticking Merry and Bright labels to glass jars. He was making an exceptionally good job if it; he'd invented a template so that the labels went on perfectly straight, first time.

'I think you might be right.' I leaned on the window frame as I sipped my coffee and gazed up at the putty-coloured sky. 'If I were a betting person, I'd put money on it.'

'Me too,' said Fred. 'But if the snow could just hold fire until tomorrow night after I've gone to bed, I'd be very grateful. Once Christmas Day comes and I can admire it from the comfort of Hester and Paul's living room, it can snow all it likes.'

'It would be very beautiful though,' I said dreamily. 'Imagine walking through all those Christmas trees tomorrow evening with snowflakes kissing our faces.'

'And slipping on my backside in the slush and spending Christmas in Accident and Emergency?' Fred chuntered. 'No thanks.'

I laughed and turned back to my job of packaging up the orders which would be sent out tonight. The last ones I'd send until after the Christmas break.

It was Christmas Eve Eve. Only twenty-four hours to go until I could wave goodbye to the Christmas Project for good. Plans had continued apace for the last three weeks and although I'd been swept along with festive cheer, I was looking forward to a well-earned break after Christmas Eve.

Fred and I had taken to working in the front room whenever possible to take advantage of the perfect view of the marketplace. The lights on the Christmas tree twinkled brightly all day long and the canopies of the market stalls were all decked with lights and tinsel too. The market traders themselves had entered into the spirit of things and were warmly dressed in Christmas hats, scarves and sweaters and so too were a good proportion of their customers. Wetherley, it seemed, was a town which fully embraced the magic of Christmas.

And tomorrow we were stepping it up a gear. Fifty spruce trees had been delivered and were waiting, wrapped in netting, to be handed over to all the community groups after lunch. I felt a frisson of excitement, longing to see how the area would look when they were all in place and decorated. It might have seemed odd, leaving it so late to add such a major installation to the town's festivities. But the aim of the Christmas Project was to honour Benny Dunford, who'd always organised Wetherley's Christmas Eve gathering. And as Nell pointed out, the trees would remain in place until Twelfth Night, for people to enjoy once Christmas Day was over.

The weeks since the Christmas lights switch-on had flown by in a whirl. Thanks to Hester and her loyal Instagram followers, my own Etsy shop and Instagram profile had had more new hits since the first of December than they'd had since I'd set it up. Every man and his dog, or at least that was how it felt to me, wanted one of my candles to add a little bit of perfumed ambience to their Christmas at the moment. On top of that, word had spread as more and more people discovered us.

I mean, Yankée Candle wouldn't be getting worried any time soon, but by my normal standards, orders were pouring in. Quite frankly I'd have been in a bit of a pickle but as luck would have it, I had a new assistant, or technically, a new volunteer as he refused to take any money for the many hours he'd been putting in since that first Monday.

'Twenty-four more Mistletoe Kisses ready for boxing up,' said Fred, standing up and stretching his shoulders. 'Plus, a batch of Midnight Forest samples making two hundred and fifty in total.'

'Right you are,' I replied, making room for them on the table.

We'd started making sample-sized candles – Fred's idea – mini candles in tiny containers the size of shot glasses. They'd be perfect for lighting at any future fairs to demonstrate the range and for the moment I was giving one away free with every order. Maybe I would charge for them one day. But I felt as if I'd had plenty of good fortune where the business was concerned, and decided to pay it forward by rewarding all my customers with a free candle. It was paying off; we were getting as much social media coverage for the samples as for the actual products. After all, who didn't love a freebie?

'Right then, boss, I've got half an hour before I need to go and get my dancing shoes on ready for the Christmas party.' He grabbed my hand and twirled me around on the spot.

'Fred, you do know the party starts one hour from now?' I laughed, trying to hang onto my coffee as he tried to get me to dance. Astrid, I happened to know, had been getting ready since first thing this morning, having booked herself in for a hair appointment, followed by a facial and manicure courtesy of the mobile beautician who looked after all the residents at Rosebridge.

'I do,' he said solemnly, not picking up on my point. 'So is there anything special you'd like me to do, or shall I wash up the used pouring pitchers?' he asked, knowing that given half a chance I'd leave them to be scrubbed in the morning. Cleaning solidified wax off our equipment was almost the worst job.

'I'd rather you updated the spreadsheet with today's orders.' I gave him a beseeching look. 'Pretty please?'

Any job to do with the spreadsheet was far, far worse than cleaning. Cole and Fred had spent an afternoon creating a spreadsheet which they alleged would make my life a breeze. I showed willing, but try as I might, I couldn't get to grips with putting all the information into tiny squares on a computer. Where was the space for me to scribble notes about how nice the customers were? And it was all very well knowing that a particular day should be spent on making two hundred Midnight Forest candles, but what if I'd woken up with an idea for an exciting new scent and couldn't wait to experiment with fragrance oils?

'You're supposed to be improving your spreadsheet skills,' Fred said, narrowing his eyes. 'For when I'm not here to do it.'

'Don't talk like that,' I said, shuddering, patting his hand. 'You'll be around for ages.'

It wasn't until Fred had begun turning up every day to help me with Merry and Bright that I became aware that there'd been a dearth of older men in my life. Not only had I never had a father, but I hadn't had a father figure either. Fred had filled a vacancy not only in my business

316

but in my heart. Cole had found a spare set of keys for him so now it wasn't unusual to find Fred here when I arrived, with a pot of tea brewed and the orders which had come in overnight already printed out. We'd become fond of each other and I was already worried about what would happen after Christmas, when I relocated the business back to Holly Cottage and his new workplace was no longer a quick stroll across town for him.

'I'm not planning on turning up my toes just yet,' he said with a chuckle. He cleared his throat. 'But I might consider a trip to Germany in the New Year. I've heard wonderful things about cruising down the Rhine. What do you think?'

He meant what did I think of him taking a holiday with Astrid. He was probably testing the water to gauge my reaction before broaching it with his children. But he needn't worry on that score; both Hester and Cole had confided in me that they hoped that the relationship between my two dear older friends would develop into something more.

'It's a lovely idea,' I said, giving the old man a hug. 'A holiday I can deal with, as long as you come back. You're my favourite member of staff.'

'What a coincidence,' he said with a twinkly smile, sliding the laptop onto his knee. 'Because you're my favourite boss.'

We both laughed and settled into a companiable semi-silence for the next few minutes. Not complete silence because Fred made all manner of noises when he worked, exclaiming, tutting or whistling as the moment necessitated. But it was quiet enough for us both to jump when my phone rang.

'My son and heir by any chance?' Fred teased, no doubt noticing the smile on my face.

'Hey, you!' I answered while nodding to Fred. 'That's great, see you in two.'

Cole was downstairs. The heavy fire door at the back of the building opened and clanged shut again. My heart began to race. We hadn't seen each other for a few days. In fact, since the first of December, we'd hardly managed to get together alone at all, apart from some snatched moments here and there.

Cole was working crazy hours on site at Orchard Gardens, pushing his team to make as much progress before the Christmas break as possible since his buyers were pushing for moving-in dates. I was rushed off my feet not only with Merry and Bright orders but with the final preparations for the Christmas Project. I'd managed to take half a day off to go Christmas shopping with Nell. I missed her now I wasn't living with them, and of course, she wanted to know every detail of my new romance with Cole.

There wasn't much to report on that score at the moment. Cole and I were mostly communicating through text messages through the day and talking on the phone, usually late-night conversations, quite often in bed. We chatted about anything and everything, slowly revealing ourselves to each other, piece by piece like a long-distance jigsaw puzzle, and although I was dying to carry on where we'd left off after the lights switch-on, there was something deliciously exciting about the wait. I carried these new feelings around with me, like an extra layer, keeping me warm. I felt energised and alive and full of hope. Anticipation was building for Christmas Day when we could finally spend the entire day wrapped up in each other.

I met him at the top of the staircase, and he pulled me into a bear hug.

'This is a lovely surprise,' I said, relishing the solid feel of his chest beneath his jacket. He'd brought the cold air in with him and looking at his boots, he'd come straight from the building site. He kissed me and I shut my eyes. He smelled of fresh air and frost and something undeniably sexy which was doing all sorts of things to my insides.

He leaned back to look at me. 'I needed to see a friendly face. Have you got a minute?'

'Of course. Come into the packing room and you'll see a second friendly face.'

Cole sniffed the air as he entered the room. 'Smells good in here.'

'Winter Wonderland,' Fred said. 'One of our newest. Pine, eucalyptus and sage. If you close your eyes you could almost be in Lapland.'

One of the most surprising things to come out of Fred's arrival in the business was the discovery that he had an incredible nose for perfume. He had a talent for finding exactly the right quantity of fragrance oils to mix to find the perfect scent. It had been he who'd finally blended the scent I'd been trying to capture for so long, the one which reminded me of Cole. He'd swapped bergamot in for the citrus fruits I'd experimented with and now Mistletoe Kiss, as we'd named it, was going down a storm on Instagram.

Cole took a seat, resting his elbows on his knees, his body rigid with tension.

I sat on the arm of his chair and placed a hand on his neck. 'What's up? Are the children OK?'

He blew out a breath. 'According to Lydia, Harley's refusing to go back to school in January.'

I felt for Cole, he was caught between wanting to present a united front with Lydia and doing his best for his kids. 'It's natural for him to have a wobble, especially at Christmas.'

He smiled up at me and squeezed my hand. 'I sent the kids that video of Hester switching on the lights and I think that might have been the catalyst.'

'Don't start blaming yourself, son,' Fred said. 'He's been through a lot. Don't you remember how you were whenever you were away from home for any length of time?'

Cole sat down wearily. 'This is a bit different, though.'

Fred winked at me. 'Cole went on a trip with the boy scouts and got homesick.'

'Dad,' Cole warned, but he was already starting to smile.

'His mother had to fetch him because he'd threatened to go on hunger strike if they didn't let him go home.'

'You poor thing.' I ruffled the hair at the back of his neck, imagining a little russet-haired boy, brown eyes pooling with tears. 'How long had you been away?'

'Ooh.' Fred scratched his head pretending to think. 'All morning.'

'I see,' I said gravely.

Cole shrugged sheepishly. 'What can I say, I'm a home-loving kid.'

'Why don't you book your flights for February?' I suggested. 'At least they'll be able to count down the days until you arrive; it'll give them something to look forward to.'

'Good idea,' said Fred, standing up and putting on his coat and hat. 'And not just for the kiddies either; getting away in the New Year is good for the soul, whatever your age.'

I flashed him a smile discreetly; seed nicely planted, Fred.

'I think I will,' said Cole. 'And in the meantime, they're off to that fancy house tomorrow with the outdoor hot tub, so hopefully it'll take their minds off England.'

Fred chuckled. 'When I was growing up, we had a toilet at the bottom of the garden and a tin bath in front of the fire on Sundays. We dreamed of having an indoor bathroom; now if you're rich enough, you get one built outside!' He shook his head in disbelief. 'Right, folks, I'm off to trip the light fantastic at the Rosebridge Christmas Party.'

'Have fun, Fred,' I said. 'And watch out for the punch. I seem to remember Astrid overdoing it and having a hangover for days after last year's party.'

'Now that I have to see,' Fred chuckled. He tipped his hat to us. 'Bye, kids.'

'Bye, Dad,' Cole replied, 'see you tomorrow.'

After Fred had gone, Cole pulled me onto his lap and kissed me.

'I could get used to this,' I said, curling my arms around his neck. 'Maybe you should call in every afternoon.'

He grinned. 'Maybe I will. Today, however, I'm after more than just a kiss.'

I flashed my eyes at him. 'Tell me more.'

He rubbed a hand over his jaw. 'I've got a dilemma. I've had offers for my last two houses.'

'That's fantastic!' I searched his face and realised he was frowning. 'Isn't it?'

'I'd always had in the back of my mind that I'd keep the last house for myself and the kids.'

'Can't you accept one offer and not the other?'

He shook his head. 'They're all one big family who want to live side by side.'

'Fliss and Cesca!' I exclaimed. 'They came back to you after all!

Cole looked bemused. 'Have you got something to do with this?'

I nodded guiltily. 'I met them at the school fair. I did paint a rather lovely rural picture.'

'Is that why one of the children kept asking to see the reindeer?' He shook his head and laughed. 'You should be on commission.'

'But I've done the wrong thing?' I asked worriedly.

He tucked a strand of my hair behind my ear and kissed me softly.

'Not at all, it's just that the kids will be home for Easter and I'd hoped to be settled into a home of my own by then. I'd never be able to afford something as large as an Orchard Gardens house if I had to pay full price.'

I cupped his face in my hands. 'Cole, the children will be looking forward to spending time with you, they won't care if you're all stuffed in one room, believe me. Being together is all that matters.'

We shared a knowing look; he understood how much I'd wanted to be with my mum, regardless of how little space we had.

He let out a breath. 'I want to have a home that they love coming back to.'

'It's you they'll love coming back to,' I promised him. 'You represent home.'

His gaze softened. 'How do you always know what to say to make me feel better?'

I glowed with pride that I was capable of making this man happy. 'I'm just telling the truth.'

He smiled. 'Deep down, I know you're right. It's head over heart. It makes financial sense to let the property go, but my heart was set on it.'

'Your heart will love the thought of those two families growing up together,' I told him. 'Besides, if you haven't found somewhere to move into by next spring,

I'll move out of Holly Cottage and you can bring the kids there.'

Cole shook his head in wonder. 'Looks like you've covered all the bases. OK, Fliss and Cesca get the houses. So that's that sorted.'

'Anything else I can help you with? I pressed a line of kisses along his jaw, breathing him in.

He groaned. 'There is one other problem, but I'm going to need Santa Claus to fix this one.'

I raised an eyebrow. 'What's up?'

'All those presents you helped me wrap? It appears the delivery company has lost them. I've tried putting in the tracking details on their website, but it tells me the number isn't recognised. In the absence of a Christmas miracle, the kids aren't going to get any of the presents I sent them.'

'Oh, Cole.' He didn't have to tell me how disappointed he was, I could read it in his body language. I really felt for him; he'd tried so hard to be the best dad. It just wasn't fair.

He shook his head, looking defeated. 'And I'd made sure they were sent plenty early enough. Best-laid plans and all that.'

'OK,' I said, determined to shine a positive light on the situation. 'The presents might still turn up, but let's make a contingency plan. Once my courier has been to collect today's orders, I'm all yours. I can go shopping for you, we can wrap them tonight, and send in the morning. They won't arrive in time for Christmas, but at least you'll know they're on their way and I'm sure we can make up a story about Santa getting muddled up for Freya's benefit.'

Cole grinned. 'That's really good of you, but I can't ask you to do that, they're my kids.'

'Well, you're my . . . I faltered, daring myself to say the word. I met his gaze. 'Boyfriend?'

He nodded gently, a lazy smile spreading over his face. 'Does that mean we're official?'

'Yes.' My heart leapt as his mouth covered mine.

'Have I told you recently that you're amazing,' he whispered softly against my lips.

'Tell me again.'

We remained in each other's arms until the courier arrived. Between us we carried the parcels downstairs and then Cole said he had to go and kissed me goodbye.

'Oh, by the way,' he turned back, frowning. 'I had the energy bill for this place this morning. Something weird has happened with the electricity supplier. The consumption has quadrupled in the last few weeks. Any ideas why?'

'None at all,' I said, perplexed. And then I remembered. 'Yes! The Christmas tree.'

He looked perplexed. 'But you haven't got a Christmas tree.'

'I haven't, but Wetherley has.' I pointed out of the window where the twinkly lights on the enormous tree could be seen.

Cole's jaw dropped open. 'What the hell?'

'I thought you'd know.' I winced. 'It was a gentlemen's agreement struck up years ago between Benny Dunford and the town council. The old bank supplies power to the Christmas tree.'

'You are kidding me.' He squeezed his eyes shut and massaged his brow with his fingertips and for a moment my heart thudded with worry, wondering what his reaction would be. But when he opened his eyes they were dancing with amusement. 'This Christmas just gets better and better.'

I knew he was joking, but I couldn't help thinking that he might just be right.

Chapter 30

Merry

At two o'clock on Christmas Eve, as the market traders packed away their wares for the last time before Christmas, the snow arrived in the form of big graceful floating flakes. And because the last few days had been cold and dry, within minutes Wetherley was transformed into a scene straight out of a Dickens novel. It was, I thought, as I picked my way carefully to the Buttermarket to meet the other team members, the perfect backdrop to my winter wonderland project. It was exactly how I hoped it would be when I dreamed up the idea in October.

'Here she is! The woman of the hour,' Nell cried as I stood at the door, stamping my feet to get rid of the snow.

The assembled group gave me a round of applause. Daniel was still in the shop and Tasha had flown to Mauritius at the end of term to spend Christmas with her parents, but Tom and Sally, the school secretary, had come to support us and Mrs Flowers, the music teacher, would be here later on to look after the school choir. And sitting in the corner looking very sorry for themselves were Fred and Astrid, who had Otto on her lap.

'It's a team effort, remember,' I was quick to point out. 'And sorry I'm late, I had a cryptic message from Hester and when I called her back she didn't pick up.'

Her message had told me to expect a nice surprise. Maybe she'd sent me a gift, which would be wonderful but also a bit awkward because I hadn't got her anything. I'd phoned her back to pump her for more information but had only reached her voicemail.

'She's on air from two until five,' said Fred weakly, resting his head in his hands. 'Try after that.'

'Are you two OK?' I asked, concerned about the state of them; they seemed barely able to keep themselves upright.

Astrid's eyes were hidden behind dark glasses, but she nodded. 'I underestimated how potent the Christmas punch would be. Again.'

'And I'm never touching flaming Sambucca again in my life,' added Fred.

'Good party then?' I giggled, relieved that they were only hungover.

'The best,' Fred chuckled, 'but I'm glad I've got a year to recover until the next one.'

'So.' I picked up my clipboard. 'Let's run through the itinerary, shall we? People will be arriving from two-thirty to collect their tree for their community groups. I've drawn a rough plan of where all the trees can be placed in a circle around the main tree and there's a copy for everyone.' I passed them around. 'Nell and Audrey, please can you be in charge of the list of groups and allocation of spaces. The trees are only five feet tall so they shouldn't be too cumbersome, but Tom and Nigel, I'm hoping you can lend a bit of muscle if anyone can't carry their tree.'

'I've never been referred to as a bit of muscle,' said Tom, flexing his biceps.

'I have,' said Nigel, stroking his beard mysteriously. 'In my younger days.'

'Are you sure they didn't mean gristle?' Sadie marched in carrying two large flasks, her glasses steaming up as she stepped out of the cold. 'Coffee with and coffee without to keep you going,' she said, holding up first one flask, and then the other.

'Without *sugar*?' Tom asked.

'Without whisky.' Sadie took off her glasses and wiped them on her Santa jumper. 'It'll put hairs on your chest in this cold weather.'

Astrid looked a bit green and Fred made an odd gulping noise. Otto wisely jumped down off Astrid's lap and hid under her chair.

'I've got to dash back to the pub,' said Sadie, 'we've got a full house. What time do you want me back with the mulled wine?'

'The school choir are on at five o'clock,' I said. 'So, shall we say four-thirty? Then everyone can have a drink before we start.'

'Roger that. See you later.' She put her glasses back on and dashed back outside.

'Let's aim to get everyone finished with their tree-dressing and lights switched on by four o'clock. The weather forecast says that the snow should have stopped by then,' I said. 'Which means we'll have the perfect snowy scene by five o'clock, ready for our singers to process around the marketplace singing their first song before climbing up onto the stage. Someone can say a few words . . .'

'That would be you,' Nell piped up.

'OK,' I groaned. 'And then the choir can lead everyone in a singalong.'

'Mrs Flowers will take over from there,' said Tom. 'Sally and I have got song sheets to pass around for anyone unsure of the words of "Away In a Manger" and "Silent Night".'

'It'll be so moving,' said Sally, who looked as if she was already welling up.

Just then the door banged open again and a man in a full-length waterproof coat and wellies scurried in.

'Hi folks!' He stepped forward, hand outstretched and seeing my clipboard, jabbed it in my direction. 'I'm Will, head of external comms for the council.'

'What's that when it's at home?' said Nigel, removing what looked like a leaf from his beard.

'Communications,' Will explained. 'Anyway, fab news. The *Derbyshire Bugle* want to cover your Christmas Project. They're sending someone along with a camera.'

Nell laughed. 'I'm so glad my mother doesn't know the paparazzi are coming. She'd be turning up in her tiara.'

Nell's parents had arrived yesterday afternoon, their Range Rover stuffed to the hilt with Christmas offerings. Nell had called me with an update last night.

'She's even bought her own bloody tree,' she had whispered down the phone from the sanctuary of her bedroom. 'And she wanted me to take ours down and replace it with hers. But I refused. So our cheapo one stayed put and Olek stuck hers in the front garden.'

I told her I was proud of her for being herself, and even more so for drawing up a cooking rota so that both her mother and mother-in-law could have a turn at being Masterchef over the Christmas period, but with strict boundaries in place so that when it wasn't their turn, they weren't allowed to interfere.

'This is exactly the sort of feel-good story we need right now.' Will clapped his hands together. 'So if someone could look after the photographer and make sure they capture all the key moments, that would be super. Well done everyone, don't let me stop you. If you don't mind me saying, it isn't looking very much like a winter wonderland at the moment.'

'Stay and help if you like,' I offered hopefully. 'The more the merrier.'

'I'd love to.' Will made a moue with his lips. 'But sadly, I've got to get to a champagne reception at County Hall, you know what it's like.'

'Not really,' said Nigel. 'But can you tell them my auntie's bin hasn't been emptied for a month, if they're not too busy drinking at the taxpayers' expense.'

'I'll see what I can do,' Will laughed and made his way to the door. 'Good luck, see you in the newspaper!'

I checked the time myself after Will had disappeared and my stomach did a loop.

'It's almost half past two,' I said. 'The Christmas Project is officially live. Let's get to work.' I paused. 'And thanks everyone, I didn't really have the experience to manage this project but you've made it so easy for me and I appreciate it.'

I got another round of applause for that and so it was with rosy cheeks that I led my little band of helpers back out into the market square. With the exception of Astrid and Fred, who paused to help themselves to coffee with whisky.

'Hair of the dog,' Fred muttered sheepishly.

Outside, the snow was coming down even thicker than before. There was a lovely satisfying crunch to my footsteps and although visibility wasn't great, the festive mood among the various community groups was plain to see.

The traffic had thinned out and the sound of the remaining cars was being muffled by the snow and everywhere felt other-worldly. Although we were in the centre of town, the snowy silence lent a sprinkle of Narnia to the scene. Children raced around catching snowflakes on their tongues and flinging themselves onto the ground to make snow angels. Otto was in his element, snapping at the snowflakes and chasing his tail whenever one landed on it. A queue had already gathered for the trees but like a well-oiled machine, we all knew what our jobs were and before long, Christmas trees were popping up all around the marketplace.

'When do we crack open Hester's mince pies?' Nigel asked as he brushed past me with a sturdy little tree for the Girl Guides.

'And Astrid's delicious German cookies,' Fred added, earning himself a peck on the cheek from Astrid.

After learning that one of Benny's traditions was to supply mulled wine and mince pies on Christmas Eve, Hester had rounded up several cases of unsold gourmet mince pies from the studio and sent them our way. We'd be doing them a favour, she'd promised me, confiding that her three mince pies a day habit had got to stop.

'Not until all the trees are in place,' I said sternly. 'And don't forget the rule: FHB.'

'I don't know this rule?' Astrid frowned. At least I think she frowned; it was hard to tell behind the dark shades.

'Family hold back,' said Fred. 'I haven't heard that for a while.'

'I haven't used it for a while,' I said with half a smile.

I'd learned it at my favourite foster home. My foster mum used to say it. There had been eight of us children at one point and whenever there was a party of any sort, she'd always remind us about it so that our visitors wouldn't go without. I'd always liked the saying because of the implication that I was part of something.

Just like now.

Fred squeezed my hand. 'That's the nicest thing anyone's said to me for a long time. Feeling as if you're among family is the biggest compliment you can pay someone.'

'Thanks, Fred.' I leaned against him. 'I agree; it's the best feeling in the world.'

'Merry?' a man shouted in the distance.

I looked up straight away, hoping it was Cole. But it was a man from the rambling club who needed help with his fairy lights. For the next hour or so, the snow continued to fall, and I continued to watch out for Cole as I oversaw the progress of our project. I bumped into people who'd become customers and friends over the last few months and seeing how much they were enjoying decorating their trees warmed my heart.

The Women's Institute had done a lovely job on their tree. It featured exquisite felt figures which one of the ladies kindly explained to me were of historical women who'd changed the world over the last five hundred years.

Astrid was directing proceedings at the Rosebridge retirement village tree. The decorations appeared to be a combination of paintings and handmade garlands.

'What do you think?' she said, slipping her arm casually through Fred's as if it were the most natural thing in the world. Both of them seemed to have a bit more colour in their cheeks; I suspected Sadie's whisky might have had something to do with it.

'Have you painted all these?' I said, examining the decorations.

'We all did one during Astrid's art class,' Fred nodded proudly. 'Then someone's grandson came in with his machine and laminated them all.'

'That way, they'll stay waterproof,' Astrid explained.

'The garlands were my idea,' Fred put in. 'Everything we used is edible for birds, they'll be glad of it if this snow holds up.'

I smiled at them both fondly, delighted that they'd found each other and that they'd found a way to showcase their interests and talents on a Christmas tree.

Olek arrived with a crowd of family: his son Max, his parents, Mr and Mrs Dowmunt; and his in-laws the Thornberrys, who were dressed head to toe in expensive-looking ski-wear.

Nell had divided the tree into sections so that everyone could decorate part of it in their own way. Max, who must have had a growth spurt since I last saw him because he towered over Nell, had a can of spray snow and was taking great delight in spraying snow graffiti on the back of people's coats. Olek was hanging sparkly gold keys around the top branches. Mr and Mrs Dowmunt senior had a small hessian sack from which they produced some beautiful handmade baubles, which they hung reverently on their section of the tree. Mr Thornberry was doing exactly what his wife told him and Nell was threading baubles made from nuts onto ribbon.

'Your tree is looking very . . .' I fumbled for the right word. 'Eclectic.'

Nell laughed. 'Sounds about right. Mum brought along a load of decorations from Harvey Nics. I think she thinks it's a competition. I keep telling her that throwing money at something doesn't make it better. And the tree should symbolise what's important to us.'

Nell's mum approached at that moment with something under her coat as if she was hiding stolen goods. 'Hello, Merry dear. Can we stick this thing at the back, darling?' Mrs Thornberry opened up her coat to reveal Max's Liverpool FC bauble. 'The red does rather clash with the rest.'

'No, Mum,' Nell said firmly, 'this tree represents everyone in the family and we're all just as important as each other. In fact, let's put that red one right at the front, Max will love it.'

'I don't mind,' Max said good-naturedly. 'Gran can put her glittery one at the front if she wants.' He looked hesitant. 'Can I call you Gran?'

Mrs Thornberry's face lit up. 'Yes, dear, I'd like that. Actually, I think there's room for both at the front, what do you think, Max?

Behind her mum's back Nell and Olek high-fived each other, and smiling, I left them to it.

For the next hour I didn't get a moment to myself. There was so much to do, so many small details to iron out, but gradually my vision of a winter wonderland came together and by four o'clock every tree was lit and the various stepladders and boxes and crates that people had brought along containing their decorations had been stashed away. It hadn't really got light this afternoon, but now the sky was properly black and as the snow clouds moved away, a clear starry sky was revealed and the temperature had dropped to zero. I'd been too busy to feel the cold, but now as I climbed up on the stage and looked around at the scene we'd created, I realised that my face and fingers had gone numb and I couldn't feel my toes anymore. But inside my chest, my heart glowed with warm pride.

My breath caught as I gazed around. Somehow, I, a person who'd always shied away from the fuss and furore of Christmas, had brought people together on Christmas Eve to create something magical. A well of unexpected emotion rushed through me. I looked out across the twinkling lights and breathed in the evocative smell of pine trees and listened to the happy shrieks of the children who'd already built an army of little snowmen in the deserted street and hundreds of tiny memories flashed through my head. Of sipping hot chocolate in bed on Christmas Eve while Mum made up stories about Santa and the naughty reindeer. Of opening the presents in my stocking which had miraculously appeared during the night. And of my first Christmas without her, which had coloured every Christmas since.

Christmas meant so many things to so many people and for me it had always been a reminder of what I didn't have. But now, looking around me, I felt an enormous sense of gratitude for what I did have: a home, a blossoming business, my friends who had become as dear to me as family. And, although it was early days, a new love too . . .

Chapter 31

Merry

As I climbed down from the stage, a sixth sense made me turn around and my heart leapt as I saw Cole striding through the snow towards the old bank. He was holding his phone out in front of him, talking into it.

I waved and trudged over to him, blinking away the soft snowflakes as they landed on my eyelashes. We met by the front door. He mouthed an apology for being on the phone and wrapped an arm around my waist. I snuggled into him while I waited for him to end the call, glad of his warmth.

'A gentleman's agreement which has stood for thirty years is possibly even more outdated than the electricity supply in the building,' Cole said, laughing softly. 'I think it's time for Wetherley Town Council to fund the electricity for its own tree.'

He paused while the person on the other end spoke.

'I'm pleased to hear you think the same. The only trouble is that I was planning on rewiring the kitchen tomorrow, which will mean disconnecting the power,' he said with a wince. 'I don't want to be responsible for extinguishing the tree lights and ruining everyone's Christmas.'

He listened again and then nodded, looking pleased. 'Within the hour? That's great, thank you! And a Merry Christmas to you too.' Cole ended the call and blew out a satisfied breath. 'There's a team of engineers in the area. They're going to drop by and divert the power supply from the old bank.'

'It won't interfere with our Christmas trees in the market square will it?' I asked nervously.

He shook his head. 'The council had already laid a network of cables for those, don't worry.'

'You're very impressive when you're in work-mode,' I said, with a frisson of longing.

'Why thank you.' He looked at me properly then and smiled, his brown eyes crinkling at the corners. 'And so are you. My dad doesn't stop singing your praises and my sister is your new biggest fan; she's convinced your brand is going to go stratospheric, as she put it, next year.'

My heart soared; I felt like the luckiest woman in the world to have found myself pulled into the embrace of the Robinson family.

'And what about you?'

He answered me with a kiss, pulling me tightly against him until I was breathless in his arms.

'I'm sorry I didn't make it back to you last night after you'd gone to the trouble of buying new gifts for the kids,' he said, trailing a warm finger down my cheek. 'Fliss and Cesca insisted on coming over to pay deposits on the two properties so that they knew the houses would definitely be theirs.'

I assured him that I hadn't minded. The presents were all wrapped and ready to send and we'd agreed that the postal service would probably be more reliable after Christmas anyway. And it was just as well he hadn't come over to the cottage after work because I'd been snoring in front of the fire by nine o'clock.

'By the way, Hester sent me a message earlier, something about a surprise, do you know what it is?'

He shook his head. 'No idea, read it out to me.'

I took off my gloves and dug my phone out of my pocket. On the screen was a notification of a voicemail message.

'Sorry,' I said. 'I should probably listen to this; it could be an order.'

I pressed play and held it out in front of me so we could both hear it.

'Hey, this is Conan O'Regan, the producer of *The Retail Therapy Show*. Hester has told me all about your candle company and the new range for the New Year. The line I think you used was something along the lines if Marie Kondo did candles?' He reeled off his number and requested a call back before ten p.m.

That must be Hester's surprise. I was stunned. I stared at Cole, hardly daring to believe what I just heard. 'Does that mean . . .?'

'It means you're going to be on TV! Congratulations!' With a whoop, he swept me up off my feet and swung me around in the air. 'This is brilliant news, Merry! You're going to go national, maybe even global!'

Merry and Bright candles on TV. I could hardly breathe or think or speak. This was beyond my wildest dreams! I couldn't wait to tell Nell. My insides were fizzing excitement as he lowered me back down. 'Wow.' I smiled at him; my eyes wide in disbelief. 'I don't know what to say.'

'You, lost for words!' Cole laughed. 'I'm going to have to take a picture of that. Come here.'

He pulled me in close and we pressed our faces together for a selfie. Our first photo together. I made him send the picture to me so I could look at it later. My heart was full to bursting with happiness and hope for the future.

'Come and see all the Christmas trees,' I said, conscious of the time. I took his hand and together we walked back towards the stage; it was almost four-thirty and the mulled wine would be arriving as well as the children's choir, and I really wanted to catch up with Pam Dunford to see what she thought of what we'd done.

We crossed the cobbled street and entered the market square. Even though I'd seen it already, the sight of all those trees lighting up the darkness took my breath away. It was the most beautiful thing I'd ever seen. Cole laughed under his breath.

'This is magical,' he breathed, gazing at our forest of Christmas trees. 'Even better than I imagined from your description.' He turned to me and shook his head in wonder. 'Merry, you should be really proud of this.'

The pride in his voice made my heart soar. 'I am,' I admitted. 'I resisted doing it at first because it was so far out of my comfort zone.'

'And now?' He brought my gloved hand to his lips and kissed it.

'I guess my comfort zone has grown. And in future I'll be less worried about doing things that scare me. In fact, bring it on.'

He grinned. 'In that case, are you up for spending Christmas Day knocking seven bells out of the kitchen in the old bank with me?'

It was the 'with me' that swung it, but I pretended to consider it.

'I suppose so, as long as you promise to watch *Home Alone 2* with me.' I smiled wickedly at him. 'But I have to warn you, I will be watching it in bed, it's tradition.'

338

He let out a warm laugh that set my heart aflutter and bent to kiss me but before his lips met mine, we were interrupted by Nigel tactfully coughing to attract my attention.

'Sorry to interrupt, chaps.' Nigel gave us a wink. 'The guy from the newspaper is here and wants a word with the boss. That's you.'

'And Mrs Flowers needs to know where you want the children to start their procession from,' Sally piped up. 'The singers are here, and she wants to get them in position now.'

Tom thrust a steaming cup into my face. 'Sadie's mulled wine – I got you some before it disappears.'

I pulled away from Cole and smiled regretfully. 'Sorry.'

'I'll leave you to it.' He pressed a quick kiss to my cheek. 'A council van has just gone past; I'll go and see if it's the electricians. See you in a while.'

For the next twenty minutes I scarcely had time to catch my breath: I briefed the journalist, Robin Barker, sorted a few last-minute problems and walked around the Christmas forest with Pam and Jim Dunford, who both agreed that Benny would have absolutely loved what we'd created in his honour. Then at five minutes to five I took my place on the stage beside the other members of my team.

'This is amazing,' Nell whispered in my ear.

'It really is.' I squeezed her arm, desperate to tell her about the TV show, but knowing I didn't have time.

'Remember, I'm expecting you for lunch tomorrow, Cole too, if he'd like to come.'

'Thanks.' I felt a rush of warmth knowing that I had a plus one and not just any plus-one, but someone who made me feel like the very best version of myself.

I took a moment to gather my thoughts and gazed out at the wintry scene around me: the velvet indigo sky, the snow-laden roofs, twinkling lights and the circle of beautiful Christmas trees which flashed and twinkled and sparkled, each one beautiful in their own right, but collectively they created a Christmas magic like I'd never experienced before.

So, this was what Christmas was really about, I thought, with a shaky breath. Christmas was on all the faces now turned towards the stage. In the smiles and laughter, in the hands being held and in the families, hugging each other for warmth; it was in the sharing of food and drinks and squeals of joy from the little ones.

And then as a microphone was thrust into my hand, Cole was there below the stage, blowing me kisses and wishing me good luck.

'Go Merry,' whispered Nell.

I cleared my throat and took a small step forward, waiting as the crowd stilled. 'Welcome everyone and Merry Christmas to you all. Tonight, by taking part in our Christmas Project, we are carrying on the tradition started by Benny Dunford, a man who was the beating heart of Wetherley and whose selflessness and kindness touched us all. Benny loved any opportunity for us to come together and unite as a community and none more so than at Christmas. Many of you will know that gathering together with friends and family on Christmas Eve was the highlight of his year and we hope he'd approve of what we've done to celebrate Christmas this year. The first without him.

'There are fifty trees here this year, as different as they are beautiful, representing who we are and what we stand for, but wherever we come from and whatever we believe in, there's something that unites us all and that is love. From all of us here on the Christmas Project, we wish you a happy and joyful Christmas.'

340

I lowered the microphone for a second as people clapped and cheered.

'And now,' I began again, 'if we all listen carefully, we'll be able to hear "Jingle Bells" as we welcome the Wetherley Primary School Choir.'

A few metres away, Mrs Flowers quickly shuffled her choristers into two rows. They were beginning and ending at the stage to take in a full lap of the square. At the front and back of the lines were several children holding a variety of percussion instruments, all of them wearing an assortment of Victorian outfits. She waved her arms and beckoned the children forward.

Jingle bells, jingle bells,' the children sang at the tops of their voices as they processed through the trees and performed their lap of Christmas honour.

Everyone joined in with the singing, apart from those whose voices were too cracked with emotion – Nell was literally mopping her tears. Parents took photos and videos and Robin Barker leapt from place to place to get the shots he needed for the *Derbyshire Bugle*.

Bubbling over with excitement and stage fright, the children filed onto the stage to begin the main part of their performance. Tom and Sally quickly handed out the song sheets and I, along with the others, descended the steps from the stage to let Mrs Flowers take over and rearrange her choir into height order with the little ones at the front.

I crunched through the snow to Cole's side and hooked my arm through his.

'Great speech.' He pulled me close. 'Even I had a tear in my eye.'

'Shush,' I giggled, slipping my hand into his pocket. I'd left my gloves on the stage after taking them off to hold the microphone and was already regretting it. My fingers were starting to freeze.

'And now,' announced Mrs Flowers, standing a little too far away from the microphone. 'We're going to sing my personal favourite, "Silent Night".'

Against my hand, I felt his phone vibrate.

'You've got a call,' I said. Luckily it was on silent, but I took it out and handed it to him.

He frowned and showed me the screen. It was Lydia. Together we wove our way to the edge of the crowd where he could answer it without disturbing anyone.

'Lydia?' His voice was full of concern. 'Is everything OK?'

He held the phone out in front of him on hands-free.

'I'm on my way to the hospital.' Her voice was shaky as if she was trying to stop herself from crying.

Cole froze. 'What?'

'Harley was out playing on the slopes with his friends and came off his board. Roman, one of the boys' fathers, scooped him up and took him straight to the hospital.'

'Oh my God, Harley.' Colour drained from Cole's face. 'Where is he hurt? Did he hit his head?'

'Roman thinks it's a broken ankle. Maybe concussion.'

'Lydia, phone me as soon as you get to the——' Cole looked at me in shock. 'The line went dead.'

He tried to call her back but couldn't get a signal and in the next fraction of a second the world went black. The streetlights, the tree lights . . . every single lamp in every single window, all out, plunging us into complete darkness. A wave of terror ran through me and I felt my legs go weak.

I clung to his arm, paralysed by fear and my breathing started to quicken.

'Power cut, that's all we need,' Cole groaned. He looked at me as my grip tightened. 'You OK?'

I nodded. 'Don't let me go.' Then I gasped, remembering the choir. 'Cole! The children on stage. They'll be scared to death.'

Hand in hand, we dashed back into the square. It was chaos. After an initial second or two of shocked silence, people were shouting to each other, kids shrieked or cried, dogs barked, parents were flocking to the stage to retrieve frightened children and Mrs Flowers, Tom and Sally were desperately trying to keep tabs on who exactly was removing which child.

Cole let go of my hand and tried his phone again and I could feel myself trembling.

'Excuse me?' The photographer from the newspaper shone his phone torch in my face. 'Merry Shaw, isn't it? The one in charge?'

'Yes? How can I help?' I forced myself to concentrate on him.

'I've got some shots of all the trees, but I really need to take a picture of your kids' choir on stage before I go.'

'I'm sorry about this,' I said, taking a deep breath. 'I'm sure the electricity will be back on soon. Cole, how long do you think . . .?' I turned to him to ask if he had any bright ideas, but he wasn't there. 'Cole?'

I whirled around, searching for him, but he seemed to have vanished.

Suddenly a huge flashlight lit up the stage and shone onto the face of a man in a hard hat and fluorescent coat.

'Really sorry folks,' he yelled at the top of his voice. 'Wetherley Town Council engineer here. We've cut through a cable. We'll have the power on as quick as we can.'

'How quick is quick?' someone shouted.

The man shrugged. 'Hard to tell, an hour? Two?'

'But we can't wait around in the cold!' shouted a diminutive old lady with a surprisingly booming voice. 'Some of the elderly ones will catch their death.'

I bit back a sob. This was turning into a disaster. And where was Cole? I could have done with his comforting presence right now.

Tom touched my arm. 'Merry? Shall I tell the music teacher to let the kids go home? They can't wait for an hour.'

'No, not yet!' I cried, feeling tears sting my eyes. 'This is what we've been planning for months. Let's hang on a bit longer, I can't admit defeat. I don't want to be a failure.'

'You're not a failure, Merry,' Tom said, giving me a cuddle. 'None of this is your fault. It's the contractors who've cocked it up.'

A crowd of people had gathered around me looking for answers and I wanted the ground to swallow me up.

Behind me someone cleared their throat to get my attention. I looked around to see the photographer putting the cap on his lens.

'I think I'll head off. There's a Santa sack race in an hour in Bakewell, I've got to be there at the finish line.' He stuck his hand out for me to shake. I took it briefly, wondering how he'd managed to stay so warm; my teeth were starting to chatter.

'Of course, I understand,' I said glumly.

'Sorry,' he said, taking pity on me. 'Shame those kids haven't got Victorian lanterns to go with their outfits.'

'Oh!' A picture popped into my head of the two hundred and fifty samples of Midnight Forest I'd got sitting upstairs in the workshop. I couldn't conjure up lanterns, but I could lay my hands on a large number of candles. 'You've just given me an idea. Please don't go. This is going to make a lovely photo. Give me five minutes.'

He sucked in air. 'Go on then, as it's Christmas.'

I started to feel a bit brighter, and my eyes were getting accustomed to the darkness too. If only I knew where Cole was. I was worried about him. And Harley, poor kid.

Nell, hand in hand with Olek, appeared by my side. 'Do you know what's happening?'

'Yes I do and you're just the people I need to help me.' I grabbed hold of them and began dragging them to the old bank. 'We're going to do this by candlelight. I've got enough candles to give one to almost every adult.'

'*Give*?' Nell squawked. 'You're giving all your candles away for free?'

'Yep.' Using the light from my phone, I unlocked the door and we all raced up the stairs. I loaded cartons of candles into Olek's arms and tucked several boxes of safety matches into his pockets. Then Max appeared wanting to know what was going on, so I gave him a box to carry down too.

'Cool,' he said, nodding. 'Can my friends have one?'

'Sure,' said Olek. 'But be sensible.'

'Unlike Merry,' Nell muttered. 'This will cost you a fortune. Of all the spontaneous things you've ever done, this takes the crown.'

The thought made me smile. It seemed I hadn't changed at all. I still acted on the spur of the moment without stopping to consider the consequences.

'Thanks,' I grinned. 'I'll take that as a compliment.'

She sighed. 'I thought you might.'

The four of us ran back to the market square as fast as we could and began dishing out candles, instructing people not to light them until I gave the word. I bumped into Astrid and Fred, who'd seen us run off.

'Hand these around,' I said to them, passing Fred a box.

He looked at the candles and then up at me. 'But we need these.'

'Wetherley needs them more,' I argued swiftly. 'This is no time to worry about money. I promised I'd produce a fitting tribute to Benny and that's what I intend to do.'

'Yes, boss,' said Fred.

'You are an angel,' declared Astrid.

'Where's Otto?' I asked, noticing he was missing.

'Home warming his paws,' she chuckled, 'he was getting frostbite.'

'Where's Cole?' Fred asked, looking over my shoulder.

'I wish I knew,' I said, debating whether to tell him about his grandson. I decided against it. I wasn't sure what the rules were in this situation and anyway it would be better coming from Cole. When he reappeared.

Robin, the journalist, was tapping his watch and so I sent them on their way and within less than two minutes, everyone who could be trusted had been given a candle. I even slipped one into Robin's pocket so he could relive the story when he got home.

'Merry?' Tom called, his arm around a shaken Mrs Flowers. 'Shall we get the children back up on stage?'

'Yes, please.'

I bolted up the steps and picked up the microphone, which thankfully was battery-operated.

'Ladies and gentlemen, I would like to invite you all to light your candles.'

Murmurs and exclamations and a few muffled expletives followed as people began to light their candles. I breathed a sigh of delighted relief as tiny flames began to glow, dissipating the darkness, and gradually the faces of Wetherley began to reappear again. For an emergency solution, I thought with a rush of pride, it was incredibly effective.

'And now, please give a big cheer as we welcome back to the stage, the wonderful Wetherley Primary School Choir singing "Silent Night" by candlelight. Thank you.'

The children, hand in hand, filed back onto the stage and I quickly laid down a line of candles at the edge of the stage and lit them.

'Are we ready, children?' Mrs Flowers whispered. 'Big bright smiles, everyone. One, two, three . . .'

'Silent night, holy night,' chimed the children in harmony, *'all is calm, all is bright.'*

The pure joy of those little voices brought a rush of goosebumps to my skin as I moved off to the edge of the stage. I paused at the top of the steps to cast my eye out across our Christmas-tree-filled space. My Merry and Bright candles had illuminated the town and the effect was magical. The scent of fresh pine, eucalyptus and mint filled my nostrils and for a second or two, I allowed myself to simply breathe it in and enjoy the moment.

A few feet away, I saw Tom again, this time with his arm around Sally who was sobbing with emotion. He caught my eye and grinned.

'Amazing work, Merry,' said a familiar voice close to my ear as Daniel placed his hand on my shoulder.

'Thanks,' I managed to croak, feeling overwhelmed with emotion.

'By the way, if you'd like to come to join us on Boxing Day for a buffet, you're very welcome,' he said kissing my cheek. 'You can bring your new friend too.'

It was such a lovely gesture that it brought fresh tears to my eyes.

'Thank you, I'd like that.' I leaned my head briefly on his shoulder and then I slipped away to find Fred.

'Any sign of Cole?' I whispered.

Fred shrugged and squeezed my hand. 'He finds this sort of thing difficult when his own kiddies aren't here.'

I nodded, trying to quell my worries; what if something serious had happened to Harley?

'And now to finish,' Mrs Flowers announced, '"We Wish You A Merry Christmas".'

But before she could count the children in again, the noise of a diesel engine pulling up behind the stage drowned out the sound of her microphone. I looked across to see Cole's van with a trailer attached to the back of it. I ran to the front of the stage.

'Give me a few seconds, Mrs Flowers!' I called and she gave me the thumbs-up.

Cole had come back. I didn't know what he was up to, but I didn't care. He'd come back and that was all that mattered. I ran through the snow to get to him. Olek was already there, helping him unload stuff off the trailer.

'What are you doing?' I shouted up to Cole over the noise of a clattering engine.

'Setting up some lights,' he shouted back, 'which I'm going to run from this generator. Grab this and put it over there as close to the stage as you can get.'

My chest felt tight as I realised what he was doing. He handed me a tall lamp on a tripod stand. It was heavy and cumbersome, and I panted with effort to do as he asked. Cole and Olek did the same a little further along. Once all three were in place, Cole plugged them into the generator.

'OK, fingers crossed this works,' he shouted.

I held my breath as Cole flicked the switch and immediately the stage was flooded with light. Everyone cheered and clapped, and seizing the moment before anything else happened, Mrs Flowers waved her arms and the children launched into a rather fast version of 'We Wish You A Merry Christmas', and this time absolutely every member of the audience joined in.

'Sorry I was gone so long,' Cole murmured in my ear, his breath warm on my cheek. 'I knew I had to act fast if I was going to get those lights set up in time and there was no way I could call you without a signal.'

'When I couldn't find you, I thought you'd left.' I could feel a lump forming in my throat. I was so full of emotion that I couldn't work out if I was happy or hurt or relieved. Maybe I was all of them.

He put his arm around me. 'I shouldn't have disappeared without telling you, especially leaving you in the dark.'

'I coped all right in the end,' I said, realising that somewhere along the line I'd stopped being scared.

The song ended and the applause went on for ages and Mrs Flowers and her choir took several bows before leaving the stage. It was over.

'Bravo!' shouted someone who sounded very like Astrid. *'Sehr gut gesungen!'* Definitely Astrid.

'Bravo,' I whispered to Cole. I pulled his face towards me until his lips grazed mine. 'My hero.'

A camera flashed somewhere, but I didn't look up.

'Did I just save Christmas?' he murmured, his breath hot against my mouth.

'Technically, I saved it first with my candles, but I suppose I could share the limelight.'

'What a team,' he said, stepping closer until I could feel the warmth of him through our layers.

'Have you heard how Harley is?'

He nodded. 'I managed to get a signal from the van. I've spoken to Lydia and to Harley. He has broken his ankle. He's had a cast put on it and he's on painkillers for now. They're keeping him in overnight to check for concussion, although he sounded OK to me. Apart from being really fed up because they can't go to that mansion anymore and they're stuck in their apartment for Christmas.'

'Poor Lydia,' I said, feeling desperately sad for all of them. 'And the kids. How miserable for them.'

'Yep, all their plans ruined.'

'Hmm.' I had just had a thought.

'Still, nothing we can do about it.' He held out his hand. 'Fancy a drink at the pub? You look like you need thawing out.'

I took his hand but didn't budge when he started walking. 'There might be something you can do about it.'

He grinned at me. 'Thawing you out? Yes I suppose . . .'

'No, you idiot!' I laughed. 'About saving their Christmas, Harley and Freya.'

He looked confused. 'Help me out here. I'm lost.'

I tugged him towards me by his lapels and tutted. 'Go,' I said, planting a kiss on his lips. 'Book a flight and go. I bet you can still reach them on Christmas Day if you try.'

His eyes widened and he laughed. 'It's a lovely thought but I can't just fly to Vancouver.'

I challenged him with my stare. 'Why not?'

'Because . . . because I've got plans to go in February. And we've got plans tomorrow, remember? And I'm a man who sticks to a plan, always have been.'

I rolled my eyes. 'And my life is chaotic and messy and always has been. However much I try and stick to a spreadsheet. We are who we are and that's fine, but both of us need to listen to the other now and again to hear a different perspective.'

His eyes twinkled. 'OK, I'm listening.'

'Good,' I said, breathing a sigh of relief. 'What's the most important thing here: seeing Harley and Freya at Christmas or sticking to a spurious plan like a stubborn goat?'

'A *goat*?' he said, insulted, but his lips were curved in a smile.

'Some of the best things in life happen when you go off-plan.'

'I'm not sure about that.' He looked unconvinced.

'It's true!' I declared. 'I planned and planned today to the nth degree, but then we had a power cut and we ended up singing carols by candlelight and it was amazing.' I waved my arm across the marketplace to prove it. Many of the candles were still lit – as they should have been; I'd designed them to burn for four hours. 'And look at us. You didn't plan to flood my cottage but I'm glad you did because it brought you into my life and my life is a hundred times better for it.'

Cole cupped my face between his hands. 'Say that again.'

I shook my head laughing. 'No, not until you change your plan.'

He looked at me thoughtfully. 'Are you serious? Do you really think I should go to Canada, now, tonight?'

'Yes!' I cried, elated that he seemed to be warming to the idea.

'But what about us? Our plans?'

Admittedly that was the downside of my idea; I was going to miss him. But this was more important. There'd be plenty of time for us to be together. Cole needed to see his kids; he'd feel so much better after having checked up on Harley himself. I pasted on a smile.

'We were fitting a kitchen,' I reminded him. 'Nothing bad is going to happen if we delay that.'

'And you'll be OK on your own?'

'I won't be on my own, I have plenty of offers.'

He scratched his head and thought about it. 'But I couldn't just turn up out of the blue without warning Lydia, could I?'

It was on the tip of my tongue to say yes, but then I caught myself. There was a time and a place to be spontaneous and turning up unannounced on your ex-wife's doorstep on Christmas Day on the other side of the world might not be it.

'Call her,' I said firmly. 'Now. While I search for flights to Vancouver.'

His face split into a grin and he gave a bark of laughter. 'I might actually be able to see my kids for Christmas.'

'Call her!' I laughed, shaking him by the front of his jacket. 'Now!'

'In a minute,' he said, 'just let me do this one thing.'

He kissed me, gently at first and then with more heat until I thought I might burst into flames.

'Just so you don't forget about me.' His eyes looked deep into mine.

'As if.'

'Merry Christmas, Merry Shaw.'

Chapter 32

Cole

The following few hours flew by in a whirl. Never had Cole stepped so firmly out of his comfort zone as new plans and arrangements were made too quickly for him to worry about schedules or spreadsheets.

While Merry went back to Holly Cottage to grab some things, he drove home, phoning Hester on the way to let her know his plans. As soon as he pulled into their drive, Hester ran out, squealing for more details and then ran back in again to tidy up when she heard Merry was on her way. Cole slipped away and called Lydia, telling her what he proposed and asking her permission to visit them on Christmas Day – tomorrow. To his surprise she'd burst into tears, declaring that she couldn't think of a more perfect way to spend the day. By the time he'd shoved some things in a bag and found his passport, Merry had arrived and Paul was helping Fred out of his car along with Astrid and Otto, who had accepted a last-minute invitation.

Hester had prepared supper for everyone: an array of tapas and canapés, dips and nibbles, which along with the bottle of champagne she'd insisted on opening, added an extra celebratory air to a night which was already buzzing.

353

Merry, who was driving, only allowed herself half a glass and by nine o'clock they were on the road bound for the airport.

'You're driving quite fast,' Cole pointed out once they'd reached the motorway. He smiled at the gorgeous woman beside him, unable to believe his luck that she was his. 'Can't you wait to get rid of me?'

She glanced sideways at him and laughed. 'I can't wait to get to the hotel so we can be alone.'

'We're alone now.'

'We are,' she agreed, drumming her thumbs on the steering wheel. 'But what I want to do takes both hands.'

He gave a laugh of surprise. 'Wow, in that case put your foot down.'

'I can't believe I just said that.' She blushed and he thought his heart would burst with joy.

Moments later she pulled off at the next motorway services. Ahead of them, the main restaurant building had been decked out with the kitschiest Christmas decorations he'd ever seen: red and green lights were strung around every lamp post, a whole herd of inflatable reindeer covered the roof and a family of giant snowmen standing in a fake snowdrift guarded the entrance.

He glanced at her. 'Do you need to stop?'

'Just for a moment.'

Her jaw was tense as she pulled into a parking space and stopped the car.

'Cole, there's something I need to tell you before we go any further.' She looked at him, her big green eyes sparkling in the shimmer of the overhead lights.

His breath caught in his chest. Had she changed her mind? Was she ill? Was all of this: her, them, too good to be true? 'OK, I'm listening.'

She straightened her spine as if to draw courage and turned to looked directly at him.

'You and me. I know we're only just starting out and this is ridiculously premature, but I don't want a casual thing, I want the *real* thing. I really like you. But I need to tell you that I want children. I want to be a mum, have a family.'

He let out the tense breath he'd been holding and reached for her hand; he gazed at her beautiful face and thought that this was probably the happiest he'd felt since he'd waved his children goodbye at the airport in the summer. 'Well,' he began.

She dipped her head, interrupting him. 'And you've already got children, so I understand that having more might not be on your agenda, but it is on mine, so I know I'm being incredibly forward and it's a bit intense to be springing this on you while you're trapped in a car with me, but . . .'

He silenced her with a kiss before she ran out of oxygen and then whispered in her ear, 'I'd like more children.'

'That's all right then.' She heaved a sigh and started the engine again.

And then without another word, she steered them back onto the motorway and put her foot on the accelerator to get them to the hotel as quickly as possible.

Cole leaned back on the headrest and smiled to himself. This woman was incredible, and he had a feeling this was going to be one hell of a ride.

Chapter 33

Merry

CHRISTMAS DAY

It felt like the middle of the night when the alarm went off next morning. I turned it off and reached for Cole under the covers. My fingers connected with his and with one swift move he pulled me towards him.

I quivered with pleasure at the feel of his skin against mine.

'Merry Christmas,' he murmured.

'Merry Christmas,' I replied. 'I haven't bought you a present.'

'Oh, I don't know about that,' he said huskily, running his hand down the contours of my body. 'I'm pretty sure you gave me one last night.'

I rolled onto my side to look at him and trailed a hand down the line of fine chest hair. 'You did mean it about having more children?'

'I did.'

'I might be pregnant already,' I said, testing the waters. 'What would you say if I was?'

He tucked his hands behind his head and gave a satisfied sigh. 'I'd say I was a superstud.'

I let out a snort and pushed his arm playfully. 'Be serious.'

'OK.' With his fingertip he stroked my bare shoulder, my breast, my stomach. 'Then I'd say that next Christmas is going to be a lot of fun.'

I held his gaze then, although I could barely focus, thanks to the tears of joy blurring my eyes. 'That's a lovely thing to say.'

'I'm a lovely guy.'

'In that case, do you want to make the coffee or put the film on?' I prised him off me, tempting as it was to let his hand continue its journey. Cole's flight left in four hours and we just about had time to watch *Home Alone 2* before I had to drop him at departures.

He laughed gruffly, his voice still thick with sleep. 'You're really going to make me do this, aren't you?'

'Of course,' I said, sitting up and tucking the sheet primly across my chest. 'It's tradition. And if we don't start now, we won't have time to watch the whole thing.'

'At least I don't have to go far.' He sighed dramatically and got out of bed. I didn't even pretend not to watch his lean muscular body cross the bedroom and fill the tiny kettle. He rattled cups and tore open sachets of coffee and pots of milk. While the kettle boiled, he pulled open the curtains.

'Wow!' He turned back to look at me. 'I hadn't realised this hotel was quite so close to the runway.'

'Me neither.' I got out of bed to join him at the window. We watched as a plane taxied along the runway in the dark and out of sight.

I hadn't had much sleep last night and not only because Cole had kept me from my slumber. I was so excited for the future, with Cole and also with Merry and Bright. I'd phoned Hester's producer, Conan, last night while I was packing my overnight bag and he was going to be in touch formally after Christmas with more details. Hester said I should expect to sell up to two thousand candles in one

357

slot. I'd been so taken aback that if I hadn't been driving, I'd have probably asked for a brandy for the shock.

The kettle finished boiling, but Cole didn't move towards it. Instead, he slid his hands down my back, making me weak-kneed with longing.

'I really appreciate this, you know,' he said, stepping closer. 'Especially setting off in the dark and in the snow last night and waking up in a soulless hotel room, instead of at home on Christmas Day.'

'But I did,' I replied, folding myself into him, loving the feel of his broad chest against my skin.

He raised an eyebrow. 'You're going to have to explain that one to me.'

'I have woken up at home.' I smiled up at him. 'Home doesn't have to be a place or a house. It's a feeling. Being home is about being happy in your own skin, knowing who you are and saying, *this is me. Take it or leave it.*'

He kissed me with infinite tenderness, his lips at once gentle and full of passion.

'I take it,' he said.

'Take what?'

'If this is you, then count me in,' he said, holding my gaze with such an intensity that I could scarcely breathe. His arms tightened around me. 'I'm at home right here.'

'Then so am I.'

As our lips met again, I felt heady with love for the man who'd finally given my heart a home. It was the perfect Christmas gift and one I intended to hang onto for ever.

The Thank Yous

THANK YOU, dear readers, for reading my first ever Christmas novel! I'm very grateful that of all the books you could have chosen, you chose *The Merry Christmas Project*. I do hope you enjoyed it and that it has put you in the Christmas spirit.

THANK YOU to some special people who helped me to get the details right in the story, particularly Tara Mallinson, Emma Ward and Mark Townsend. Thanks goes to Lesley and David Purveur for the anecdote many years ago about plugging the lights for the village Christmas tree into their electricity supply for the season – I still laugh about that. I never base a character on a real person, but in this book, I've made an exception. Otto is based on a gorgeous *real* dog owned by my good friend Dr Lisa Cove. He's a Cavapoochon and looks like a little teddy bear and melts my heart.

HUGE thanks to my publishing team at Orion who have worked so hard over the past year on my publishing. I couldn't wish for a more dedicated bunch, you're all amazing and I'm so proud of what we've achieved together. Special thanks to my agent Hannah Ferguson and editor Harriet Bourton, both of whom had to cheer me on when I broke my arm (shudder!) on New Year's Day and had a mini meltdown. A grateful round of applause to Sally Partington, my talented copy editor, who always adds a sheen of magic to the final manuscript and sorts out my dubious grammar. Thanks, Sally.

A MILLION THANK-YOUS to the BookCamp crew for all your kindness, support, and friendship. You are such an amazingly talented group of women and I'm grateful to have you on my side. Thanks to Cesca Major for masterminding BookCamp and making it possible, what a woman.

THANK YOU to my lovely Bramley family for all your support and encouragement; I couldn't write my books without you. Phoebe and Isabel, you make me proud every day and I love your input into my writing. Thanks to Henry for lending your colouring to Cole and thanks to Conan for the ten words you gave me – probably the best line in the book, and you even got a name check. Thank you, Chickens.

Finally, a massive THANK YOU to the booksellers, who have kept us all in reading material during a difficult year, with a special shout out to my local bookshop, The Bookcase in Lowdham, who post signed copies of all my books all over the world for my readers. What a service!

The Merry Christmas Project is dedicated to the lovely Milly Johnson because, not only is she a champion of the women's fiction genre, a tireless fundraiser for her charities, a straight-talking, leading light in publishing and a gifted writer, she has shown me such kindness and friendship during difficult times and no matter how busy she is, always makes time to check in with me. I'm honoured to call you my friend, Milly.

Much love,
Cathy xxx

Credits

Cathy Bramley and Orion Fiction would like to thank everyone at Orion who worked on the publication of *The Merry Christmas Project* in the UK.

Editorial
Harriet Bourton
Lucy Brem

Copy editor
Sally Partington

Proofreader
Clare Wallis

Audio
Paul Stark
Amber Bates

Contracts
Anne Goddard
Humayra Ahmed
Ellie Bowker
Jake Alderson

Design
Rachael Lancaster
Joanna Ridley
Nick May

Editorial Management
Charlie Panayiotou
Jane Hughes
Bartley Shaw

Finance
Jasdip Nandra
Afeera Ahmed
Elizabeth Beaumont
Sue Baker

Production
Ruth Sharvell

Marketing
Katie Moss
Brittany Sankey

Publicity
Alainna Hadjigeorgiou

Sales
Jen Wilson
Esther Waters

Victoria Laws
Rachael Hum
Ellie Kyrke-Smith
Frances Doyle
Georgina Cutler

Operations
Jo Jacobs
Sharon Willis

Three women. Three secrets.
One unforgettable summer.

The sparkling seaside village of Merle Bay, with its beautiful beach scattered with seaglass, is a place where anyone can have a fresh start.

For Katie, it is the perfect hideout after a childhood trauma left her feeling exposed. For Robyn, the fresh sea air is helping to heal her scars, but maybe not her marriage. For Grace, a new start could help her move on from a heartbreaking loss. When they meet on Seaglass Beach one day, they form an instant bond and soon they're sharing prosecco, laughter - and even their biggest secrets...

Together, the women feel stronger than ever before. So can their friendship help them face old fears and find happy endings - as well as new beginnings?

Praise for Cathy Bramley:

'Filled with warmth and laughter'

Carole Matthews

It started with a wish list.
Now can she make it happen?

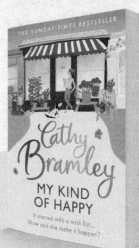

'Flowers are sunshine for the soul.'

Flowers have always made Fearne smile. She treasures the memories of her beloved grandmother's floristry and helping her to arrange beautiful blooms that brought such joy to their recipients.

But ever since a family tragedy a year ago, Fearne has been searching for her own contentment. When Fearne makes a chance discovery she decides to start a happiness wish list, and an exciting new seed of hope is planted...

As Fearne steps out of her comfort zone and into the unknown, she starts to remember that happiness is a life lived in full bloom. Because isn't there always a chance your wishes might come true?

Praise for Cathy Bramley:
'A warm hug of a book'
Phillipa Ashley

Can she find her perfect fit?

Gina Moss is single and proud. She's focused on her thriving childminding business, which she runs from her cottage at the edge of The Evergreens: a charming Victorian home to three elderly residents who adore playing with the kids Gina minds. To Gina, they all feel like family. Then a run-in (literally) with a tall, handsome American stranger gives her the tummy-flutters...

Before a tragedy puts her older friends at risk of eviction — and Gina in charge of the battle to save them. The house sale brings her closer to Dexter, one of the owners — and the stranger who set her heart alight. As the sparks fly between them, Gina carries on fighting for her friends, her home and her business.

But can she fight for her chance at love — and win it all, too?

'A book full of warmth and kindness'
Sarah Morgan

Wickham Hall

Holly Swift has landed her dream job: events co-ordinator at Wickham Hall. She gets to organize for a living, and it helps distract from her problems at home. But life isn't quite as easily organized as a Wickham Hall event. Can Holly learn to let go and live in the moment?

The Plumberry School Of Comfort Food

Verity Bloom hasn't been interested in cooking ever since she lost her best friend and baking companion two years ago. But when tragedy strikes at her friend's cookery school, can Verity find the magic ingredient to help, while still writing her own recipe for happiness?

White Lies And Wishes

When unlikely trio Jo, Sarah and Carrie meet by chance, they embark on a mission to make their wishes come true. But with hidden issues, hidden talents, and hidden demons, the new friends must admit what they really want if they are ever to get their happy endings...

The Lemon Tree Café

Finding herself unexpectedly jobless, Rosie Featherstone begins helping her beloved grandmother at the Lemon Tree Café. But when disaster looms for the café's fortunes, can Rosie find a way to save the Lemon Tree Café and help both herself and Nonna achieve the happy ending they deserve?

Hetty's Farmhouse Bakery

Hetty Greengrass holds her family together, but lately she's full of self-doubt. Taking part in a competition to find the very best produce might be just the thing she needs. But with cracks appearing and shocking secrets coming to light, Hetty must decide where her priorities really lie...

A Match Made In Devon

Nina has always dreamed of being a star, but after a series of very public blunders, she's forced to lay low in Devon. But soon Nina learns that even more drama can be found in a small village, and when a gorgeous man catches her eye, will Nina still want to return to the bright lights?

A Vintage Summer

Fed up with London, Lottie Allbright takes up the offer of a live-in job managing a local vineyard, Butterworth Wines, where a tragic death has left everyone at a loss. Lottie's determined to save the vineyard, but then she discovers something that will turn her summer – and her world – upside down...

Loved reading *The Merry Christmas Project*?
Make sure you don't miss out on the
heartwarming sequel *Merrily Ever After*!

**Two strangers. One big secret.
And a Christmas to remember . . .**

Merry has always wanted a family to spend Christmas
with, and this year her dream comes true as she says
'I do' to father-of-two Cole. But as she juggles her
rapidly-growing business, wedding planning and the two
new children in her life, her dream begins to unravel.

Emily is desperately waiting for the New Year to begin,
so she can finally have a fresh start. She has always put
her family first, leaving little time for happiness and love.
When her beloved father Ray moves into a residential
home, she discovers a photograph in his belongings that
has the potential to change everything.

As past secrets come to light, will this be a magical
Christmas for Emily and Merry to remember?

Coming Autumn 2022

Pre-order your copy now

Read on for an exclusive chapter

Chapter One

Merry

There was no mistaking that autumn was making way for winter, I thought, as Cole and I, plus his children, set off for a walk after our Sunday lunch. Mornings were frosty, sometimes even inside the old-fashioned window frames in Holly Cottage, our double bed was piled high with cosy blankets, and hot chocolate with whipped cream had become my daily winter warmer after work – a treat which Harley and Freya had particularly enjoyed this week while they'd been staying with us during the school holidays.

Outside, most of the trees were bare now, except the holly bush in the front garden, which was rosy with berries, and like ours, the other homes along World's End Lane had daily twists of smoke spiralling from their chimneys. In the small Derbyshire town of Wetherley, where we lived, the council had erected the lights which would be officially switched on next week and this morning I'd heard my first Christmas song on the radio, Michael Bublé's velvety voice singing about a white Christmas.

It was a bit early to be thinking of Christmas, even for me, an avid festive fan. But the temperature was hovering above freezing and only thick layers were preventing *me* from hovering just above freezing too.

I shivered and Cole squeezed my gloved hand.

'Chilly,' he asked, and then added with a grin, 'or was that a shiver of relief that the kids are going back to Lydia's tonight?'

Cole and I had only been living together since September, and this was the longest time they'd spent with us at the cottage. Yesterday, we'd carved pumpkins and then taken Freya trick or treating, while Harley met up with his friends. It was all very new to me, and I was loving every minute.

'Absolutely not!' I retorted. 'It has been great fun and I've enjoyed spending time with them. It has felt like . . .' I faltered, not sure whether to say what was on my mind.

'Go on,' he said, his eyes bright with encouragement.

'Like we're a family,' I admitted. 'It has been really fun.'

'Good.' He brought my hand to his lips and kissed it, smiling to himself. 'That's great.'

After leaving home via the gate Cole had installed in the back fence, we'd tramped through the woods separating Holly Cottage from the new houses he had finished building in the spring. They were all occupied now and looking more lived-in as each season passed by.

Now, we'd emerged from the trees and the four of us were following the footpath along the river into town: nine-year-old Freya was skipping ahead, in a world of her own, and Harley was behind her, his gaze fixed on his phone. At thirteen, he was almost as tall as me; he'd had a growth spurt since the summer, when he'd relocated back to the UK from Canada with his mum and sister.

The plan for the afternoon was to burn off some energy and make room for a slice of freshly baked *apfel strudel*, which, according to my friend Astrid, would be out of the oven and cooling by the time we arrived at her flat in the Rosebridge retirement village.

Astrid was my old art teacher from school, she had always been like family to me, but now our bond was even stronger because she and Cole's dad, Fred, were 'courting', as Fred put it. He lived at Rosebridge too, but although they spent most of their time together, each had their own flats for a bit of space now and then.

'Merry?' Freya stopped in her tracks and whirled around, causing Harley to tut and elbow past her. Her cheeks were pink with cold, and the ends of her plaits were sticking out from under her woolly hat. She couldn't have looked more adorable if she tried.

'Yes, sweetheart?' I said, catching hold of her hand.

'Did you have a pet when you were growing up?' she asked.

I shook my head. 'My mum and I didn't have room because we lived in a very small flat.'

'Astrid lives in a flat,' Freya replied, 'and she has Otto the dog.'

'She does, but it's bigger than our flat was,' I said, not adding that, regardless of space, my mum didn't have the spare money to spend on a pet. 'Mind you, there was a snake at one of my foster homes,' I added, pulling a face at the memory. 'They used to feed it whole frozen chicks and mice.'

'Cool.' Harley looked at me over his shoulder. 'Maybe I'll ask for a snake. The boys at school would like that.'

'I don't think your mother would,' said Cole dryly.

I winced, imagining the look on Lydia's face when Harley suggested they got a snake, particularly when he told her where he'd got the idea from.

'They grow very big,' I said hurriedly. 'And live for years.'

'Even better,' replied Harley, nodding enthusiastically. He tapped his screen, mumbling under his breath as he typed, 'UK, pet snakes...'

'Daddy, did you have a pet?' Freya asked innocently.

Cole caught my eye before answering and we both suppressed a smile; this was well-trodden ground and all part of his daughter's campaign to get an animal of some description.

'I did,' he replied. 'Your granny had chickens, until the fox got them. And we had an old cat called Fergus, who only lost all his front fangs so we—'

'Changed his name to Fangless!' Freya finished for him. 'Poor Fergus. So could I . . .?'

'It's snowing!' Harley yelled suddenly. 'I just felt a snow-flake on my face. YES!'

I looked up to the sky. A few tiny specks floated in the air. It was certainly cold enough, but it was a bit early in the season for Derbyshire to get its first snowfall.

'Hello, snow, I've missed you!' Freya squealed, instantly forgetting about her mission to get a pet.

She stretched her arms out, attempting to catch the snowflakes on her tongue.

'Me too,' said Harley, heavily.

'Just sleet, I think,' Cole commented, examining the dots on the sleeve of his coat.

'Typical,' Harley muttered.

'You never know,' I said, noting how quickly Harley had slumped down. 'It might snow properly before the day is out.'

'I hope so, because then school will close, and I won't have to go. Not like in Whistler. The weather doesn't stop anything there,' Harley commented, his voice managing to combine hope with nostalgia.

I felt for him; whilst Freya had slipped seamlessly back into the life she'd had before their year in Canada, Harley was still missing what he'd left behind. It didn't sound as if he was too keen on school either.

I glanced at Cole to see if he'd picked up on his son's tone, but it didn't look like it. Instead, he scooped up his daughter and pretended to dance with her.

'Oh, the weather outside is frightful,' he started to croon. 'But Freya is so delightful.'

The little girl laughed and wriggled free. 'If it snows lots, I'm going to build a snowman. And sledging!' Her face lit up at the prospect. 'Can we go sledging?'

'But it won't snow lots, will it?' Harley said flatly. 'Because this is England. Anyway, we left our sledges in Whistler.'

I put a tentative arm around his shoulder. 'Then we should get new ones, so that when it does snow properly – which it will at some point – we'll be ready. You'll have to show me how it's done; I've never been on a sledge in my life.'

'No way!' Harley looked at me in disbelief and then grinned. 'It's easy, I can teach you.'

'You're on,' I said, pleased to have made him smile. I was still working on my role in their lives; as their dad's girlfriend, I wasn't always sure what I should or shouldn't say or do. This time, it looked as if I'd got it right. I felt something on my face and looked up. 'I think it might be snow, you know.'

Harley and Freya scampered ahead, chatting about where the best place to go sledging would be, and Cole wrapped his arm around my waist, drawing me close.

'Thank you,' he murmured, leaning in to kiss me.

'For what?' I asked, checking that the kids weren't looking.

I wasn't yet comfortable with public displays of affection with their father. My best friend Nell once told me that it had taken two years before she felt able to even hold hands with Olek in front of his son, Max. I'd scoffed at her at the time, but now I knew exactly how she'd felt.

'For being a wonderful woman.' He kissed me again. 'For being brilliant with my kids and making co-parenting so much more fun than when I was doing it alone.'

'You're welcome.' My voice was casual, but inside my heart soared. Sometimes I felt like pinching myself; I loved this man and I knew he loved me.

Ahead of us, the children were laughing as Freya got stuck climbing over the stile. Once on the other side, we'd almost be in town. Another five minutes or so and we'd be at Astrid's, where, no doubt, Fred would be waiting for his slice of *apfel strudel* too.

Cole and I picked up our pace and I snuggled against him. 'Is there anything more exciting than the first snow in winter?' I mused happily.

He pretended to think about it. 'Actually, yes, I think there is.'

He was very handsome, my man, I thought, taking in his rugged features, the healthy glow from a working life spent outdoors and deep brown eyes which were sparkling with mischief.

'It was a rhetorical question,' I said with a laugh. 'I'm sure if I really thought about it my brain would come up with something. But look how much fun your kids are having. And imagine if we were to get snowed in and had to spend the day cosied up in front of the fire or digging our way out of Holly Cottage to fetch supplies.'

'Hmm. True, but even more exciting than snow is waiting to get a word in edgeways, to ask a wonderful woman the most important question a man can ask.' He stopped walking and, taking hold of my scarf, tugged me gently towards him.

I raised an eyebrow, intrigued. 'Ask away.'

His eyes were on mine, my hands in his, and suddenly I realised what was happening. 'Merry, I'm in love with you, you make my every day magical. And I wondered . . . will you do me the honour of becoming my wife?'

My heart stuttered in my chest, and I stared at him, for once completely speechless. The rest of the world faded away until there was just him and me, snowflakes fluttering like confetti; a tiny perfect moment stretching between us, one I'd remember for the rest of my days.

Finally, I gasped, incredulous and elated. 'Cole, is this . . . Are you proposing?'

He nodded. 'If you'll have me. This year has been one of the best of my life and it's all because of you,' he said, his expression soft and earnest and full of love. 'You said yourself it feels like we are a family and seeing you with the kids this week has made me love you even more. The only way next year could top this one is if we were married. So, what do you say?'

A bubble of laughter escaped from me. 'I say yes!' I threw my arms around his neck and kissed him, for once not caring that the children might see. *Married.* I was going to be Mrs Cole Robinson. 'Absolutely! Thank you.'

Cole's face relaxed into a smile of relief. 'No, thank *you*, darling, you've made me a very happy man.'

'I love you,' I said, kissing him again. 'So much.'

'Dad? We're going on ahead,' Harley shouted, interrupting. 'See you at Astrid's.'

I stepped away from Cole automatically, but he held onto me.

'Wait there, please!' he called to them and then lowered his voice. 'I want to tell them now before we tell anyone else, is that OK with you?'

A wave of nerves wiped the smile from my face. 'Do you think they'll mind?'

'Not at all, they'll be pleased! They've had a great week staying with us and they'll be excited about the wedding.'

'Hurry up then!' Freya yelled.

My stomach lurched as we ran to catch up with them, wishing I could share his optimism. What if they were completely against the idea? I thought they liked me, but that was as their dad's girlfriend, maybe they didn't want a stepmum? What if Harley stormed off? What if Freya burst into tears?

'I'm thirteen,' Harley protested when we reached them. 'I walk home from school by myself, I don't need to walk with you.'

'I know, son,' said Cole, reaching for my hand. 'But that wasn't why we asked you to wait. We've got something to tell you. I've just asked Merry to marry me and she said yes.'

I held my breath as I watched the expressions on their faces, hoping that this would be good news.

'Oh right.' Harley frowned and shoved his hands in his pockets. He was impossible to read. Maybe he wasn't sure himself how he felt about it. After all, it had come as a surprise to me so it would certainly be a shock to the children. 'Erm, congratulations, I guess.'

'Thank you,' I murmured.

Cole ruffled his son's hair. 'Thanks, mate, I appreciate that.'

'When?' Freya asked. 'Because this tooth is wobbly and I don't want a gappy smile on the photographs.' She peeled off her glove and gave one of her top teeth a good wiggle to demonstrate.

'We haven't set a date yet,' I told her, taking heart from the fact that she saw our wedding as something to be happy about. 'But your smile will be beautiful no matter what. Would you like to be my bridesmaid?'

'Yes!' Freya launched herself at me, wrapping her arms around my hips. I hugged her back, grateful for her simple approval. 'Do I get a long dress and flowers, and can I wear make-up?'

'We can sort all that out,' said Cole, fondly. 'And you'll be an usher on the day, I hope, Harley?'

'If you like,' he replied with a shrug. 'Can we go to Astrid's now?'

Cole nodded. 'Make sure you hold hands across the road.'

'Can we tell Grandad and Astrid?' Freya demanded.

Cole looked at me for guidance and I nodded.

'Yes!' she jumped on the spot, punching the air with both fists. 'Come on, Harley, let's run.'

Once they'd gone, I sagged against Cole with relief. 'At least Freya is excited, although Harley didn't show much enthusiasm.'

Cole didn't seem perturbed. 'Don't worry about him, it's not cool to show your emotions at thirteen, that's all. Oh, by the way, I've got something for you.'

He pulled out a small blue velvet box from his jacket pocket and lifted the lid. Inside was a ring with a square-cut diamond in the centre, three smaller diamonds set at each side of it.

'Oh Cole, that's beautiful!' My eyes filled with tears, and I wiped them away, laughing. 'What I can see of it.'

My hand was shaking as he slid the ring onto my finger. 'There. Now we're officially engaged. Does it fit OK?'

'As if it was made to measure,' I said, holding up my hand and examining my finger.

He looked very pleased with himself. 'I measured your finger with a piece of cotton while you were asleep. I didn't want to waste any time getting it altered.'

I laughed. 'You think of everything, my clever husband-to-be.'

'I think of you,' he replied, drawing me in for another kiss. 'Almost all of the time.'

'Come on then,' I climbed up onto the stile, swung my leg over and jumped down. 'I can't wait to tell Nell, she'll be amazed, maybe I'll phone her from Astrid's or go round later tonight and flash my beautiful ring at her. Do you want to come, we could—'

'Just hold on a second,' Cole said, laughing as he hopped over the stile effortlessly and landed beside me. 'Before you get carried away with who you need to tell first, I have one more surprise, or rather a question.'

I stopped admiring my ring finger for a second to look at him. 'Ooh intriguing.'

'The thing is . . .' He paused and bit his lip sheepishly. 'I've already called the registry office to get a rough idea of when they'd be able to fit us in . . . And they'd had a cancellation on Christmas Eve. So we could actually be married by Christmas.'

I could see he was holding his breath, waiting for my reaction.

'*This* Christmas Eve?' We stared at each other, our breath forming icy clouds in front of our faces as my brain processed what he'd said. 'As in just a few weeks from now?'

Cole nodded. 'Seven weeks and five days to be exact.'

'Wow. But . . .' I blinked at him. 'That's not long to organise a wedding. You're a man who likes to plan everything properly.'

'And you're a woman who likes to fly by the seat of her pants. Pants that I very much approve of by the way.' He kissed my neck, making my legs go weak. 'Let's face it, if we had a year to plan a wedding, you'd leave most of it until the last minute and then race around like a whirlwind, with me tearing my hair out.'

I laughed. 'I love that you know me so well and despite that still want to marry me.'

'So, I thought if might be fun to compromise,' he continued. 'We organise a last-minute wedding. What do you think: crazy idea or brilliant plan?'

My mind whirred. There'd be a lot to do, decisions to make, things to organise, but . . . I could feel anticipation bubbling inside me.

'I'm up for it.' I smiled at him, my eyes sparkling with the prospect of the challenge. 'One hundred per cent. It's crazy *and* brilliant. I mean, what are we waiting for? Let's do it.'

'Thank goodness for that.' He pretended to wipe his brow. 'Because it's already booked.'

'I can't believe this is happening,' I said, laughing. 'You were right: getting married on Christmas Eve is far more exciting than the first snow in winter.'

And then I kissed my new fiancé with a passion that earned us a toot from the horn of a car.